# The Difference

## C. D'ANGELO

Jane, Thanks for the support!
C. D'Angelo

Printed in the United States of America
Cover design by JRC Designs/Jena R. Collins
Edited by Bambi Sommers
Proofread by FWS Media/Lynda Ryba
Internal formatting by Qamber Designs & Media

Print edition ISBN: 978-1-7372624-1-1
Digital edition ISBN: 978-1-7372624-0-4

www.CDAngeloAuthor.com

For my grandpa, Anthony, who will always be my hero.

# PART I

# *Chapter 1*

C alm down, calm down, calm down.

This mantra isn't working. No! It's having the opposite effect.

"Rachel?" Brian raises an eyebrow.

I should be used to that look, but this isn't normal from him. Other people, yes, Brian, nope. Help!

My fingers tremble and my legs go limp, all the way down to my toes. Maybe I should try some deep breathing. *Go.* I attempt to inhale, but my lungs reject the air.

"What's going on? You look strange." He reaches out and puts his hand on mine.

Oh no, I can't hear anything. What is he saying? What's happening to me?

"Are you okay? Rach?" Brian's lips move but there's no sound. He leans closer to me over the table, our faces almost touching, his eyes wide and alert. He grabs my shoulders and shakes me.

Everything around me slows then the room spins and the lights go out.

Let me get you up to speed. It's a doozy.

"Already?" I mumble, unable to open my eyes.

I reach toward my alarm and hit the snooze button again, not ready to wake up for today. Despite the beautiful New York City spring day that is surely waiting outside my door, I still feel the same dark cloud that covered me yesterday, the day before, and the day before that too.

The scent of coffee fills my nose, pulling me from under my cozy down comforter and toward the kitchen in my typical groggy morning state. I snatch the mug next to the coffee pot, fill it with heaven's nectar, and reach for the creamer in the fridge. The drop I add spreads in the cup, and I help it with a swirl, not with the effort of grabbing a spoon. My feet automatically drag me back to my bedroom and I drop down on the bench in front of the window.

Bright green leaves bring life back to the somber winter trees. Colorful flowers bloom in planters visible in all directions. People on the sidewalks seem to have a bounce in their step, happy to exchange their heavy winter coats for airy spring jackets. The city is waking up from its winter slumber, so why can't I?

I watch the people shuffle around on their way to wherever they're going this morning. Does that person have some high-powered executive job in Manhattan? Or do they work at a fancy department store on 5th Ave? Do they compare themselves to others like I do? Are their lives exciting and spontaneous or are they stuck on repeat like I am—work, home, work, home?

*Meow.*

Pulled from my ruminations, I look down to find my sweet friend, his little brown eyes sparkling in the bright morning sunlight. "Yes, Harrison, I know. It's time to get the day started."

Harrison meows again and rubs against my leg then leaps onto the bed, curling into an orange ball of fluff.

"Okay, okay. I know you want me out of your house. Thank you for reminding me."

I make my way over to the closet and stare at my clothes as I take another sip of coffee. Most days, I'm all about minimal effort—no makeup, hair pulled back, and a simple outfit. An olive-green cardigan catches my eyes. I've always been told that color makes my green eyes glow—and with my pale skin, unruly, curly red hair, and abundance of freckles on my nose, I'll take all the help I can get. Reaching for the sweater, I scan the row for a white shirt and my brown pair of pants to complete the look. Comfortable, yet still professional. I nod my head in emphasized satisfaction.

After throwing it on my body, I give Harrison a quick peck on the top of his head and walk to the kitchen to drop my mug in the sink. When I reach for the loaf of bread to make my toast, I notice something on the counter.

"Argh! How did I not see that earlier?" I shove the orange juice into the fridge as my heart beats faster and my cheeks grow warm. Every morning, my boyfriend, Brian, leaves the dumb container on the counter. And every morning, I have to put it away as I try to rush out the door. He's brilliant, but absent minded. Get over it, Rachel.

Looking at my watch, I realize I don't have time to eat, and especially don't have time for other nonsense. A snack will have to suffice. Popping a breakfast bar into my tote, I take a deep breath to insert some hope of energy into my body.

As I step out of our building onto the Chelsea sidewalk, I see an adorable little girl walking with her small hand engulfed by a man I assume is her grandfather. I do that a lot. Assume, that is. Anyway, she has the biggest smile a girl could fit on her small face. Memories of my own grandpa come flooding in like a tidal wave. That sweet child looks like I did when I was eight years old, awe and admiration all over her face as she gazes up at him, not a care or worry in the world.

My grandfather, good old Salvatore Granza, was the sweetest, kindest, most loving Italian grandpa anyone could ever have. Oh, how I miss our time together. As a kid, I was his shadow—in the house, in the garage while he tinkered on whatever project he had going, or in the backyard while he tended to the vegetables and herbs in his garden. I tried to dress like him too, with his newsboy caps and strange baggy plaid pants. He looked like a golfer but never golfed a day in his life.

I loved my grandma dearly, and the incredible Italian food she prepared with ingredients from Grandpa's garden, but I had no interest in cooking in the kitchen with her. I was hanging out with my hero. My grandpa.

There was always something extra special about my relationship with my grandpa. We had such a deep connection, and our personalities were interchangeable. Plus, we were the only two family members who were stick thin with pale skin and curly red hair. The family joke was that Grandpa and I were two peas in a pod. And since Grandpa liked gardening, it was the perfect metaphor.

I almost walk past where my office is while deep in my reminiscing. Heaving open the heavy old door, a blast of heat hits my face. It forces me to shift my thoughts to the full day ahead of me. I take a deep breath for motivation and climb the stairs.

You can do this, Rachel.

One big reason I love being a psychotherapist is that I don't have to think about my problems when I am trying to help others with theirs. I couldn't be selfish even if I wanted to. Since my clientele is strictly children who come in for mental health therapy, it's even more important that my focus remains on them and their heartbreaking issues. They need me. And I guess I need them too.

When I walk into the waiting room, I'm greeted by a mother and son who are awfully early for their 8 a.m. appointment. That always throws me off. I need time to ease into my office, check my email and voicemail, and wrap my mind around my schedule for the day. But it isn't like I can climb in through the window and avoid walking through the waiting room…could I? I wish.

I set those thoughts aside and paste on a smile. "Hello. You must be Ethan and Mrs. Hank. Just give me a few minutes to get settled and I'll come out to get you."

"Thank you." Mrs. Hank smiles and sinks into her chair. Her shaking leg lets me know she's more nervous than her face expresses.

Ethan sits on the edge of his seat and swings his feet back and forth, staring down at his hands and muttering.

I hurry into my office and shut the door behind me. Why would I have made a new client appointment first thing in the morning? I must have been feeling overly ambitious the day I scheduled it. I slide into my chair at my desk and turn on my computer to check email. One from Brian is at the top of the unread messages.

Thursday, March 15, 2012 7:11 a.m.

**Subject:** Hi

**From:** Brian.Holden@TurnerM.com

**To:** Rachel.Granza@myemail.com

Hey Rach. I thought I'd send a quick hello to you this morning to brighten your day. When I left you lying in bed, you looked so peaceful and beautiful. You must have been dreaming of me. :) Have a good one and see ya tonight.

Brian

I'm surprised he had the time to send an email. He's normally too busy to read my emails when he's at work, let alone send one on his own. Aww, he can be a sweetie when he wants to be. Maybe I should forget about the orange juice.

I scan the remaining emails for anything urgent, but no crises are present. After a quick review of my client's preliminary information, I bring Ethan and his mom into my office. Luckily, he has a straightforward case—an anxiety disorder. I know that well, let me tell you. So, we have a productive session and I send him home with a new coping strategy to try before our next visit.

The rest of my morning consists of a third-grade boy who can't seem to stay seated in class, a preschool-aged boy who hardly speaks but bites everyone in sight, and a high school girl who may have an eating disorder. By noon, I am ready for a break.

My head is in a different place today. This must be what it feels like for my kids with attention issues. Earth to Rachel. Ms. Granza…hello?

I forgot to pack a lunch this morning, so the decision to get takeout is easy. Tacos sound appetizing and there's a great food truck just around the corner from my office. Mmm, yes.

I love New York City. I can find any cuisine I feel like eating, any time of day. Oh, you'll see how much a certain lady loves to eat. But, it really is the city that never sleeps, perfect when I need a rainbow cookie fix at 3 a.m. Just kidding, I'd never be up at that time. But if I were, I could gobble it down with a side of cannoli.

My entire childhood was spent in the suburbs of Philadelphia, or just Philly to us locals. I always dreamt of living here, thankful we were close enough to come for special events or mother-daughter outings. I enjoyed the Broadway shows, the shopping—even if it was only window shopping—and the unique restaurants. Frozen hot cocoa? Yes, please! See, my love of food started young. Anyway, I loved the museums too. There are some noteworthy museums in Philly, but nothing compares to those in my new city, at least for me.

When I finally moved here for college, no other city made my heart soar like this one did. But something has changed. My flame died out long ago and I'm drifting, waiting for something to bring that spark back into my life.

The hour hand on the clock finally lands on the five and I pack up my belongings in record time. I turn off my office light, lock my door, and poke my head into Annabelle's office on the other side of my wall to let her know I'm leaving. Oh, she owns the practice with me.

She points at her phone and waves. She must be talking to her husband, from the smile on her face. They're disgustingly adorable.

Annabelle's the best office mate, though. With our similar work ethic and yin and yang personalities, we complement each other well. I work with kids and she only sees adults, so our separate businesses don't compete. To have someone to bounce ideas off of and share the expenses of an office within this city doesn't hurt either.

I mouth a goodbye and head for the front door of our waiting room. Rushing down the three flights of stairs, I exit the building and gulp the fresh air like my life depends on it. I always look forward to this moment, the time of no obligations for the rest of the day. Until tomorrow, you brick beauty.

As I walk home, I remember Brian has a work dinner tonight so I'm on my own until at least 9 p.m. While I love our evenings together, I'm looking forward to the glorious quiet waiting for me. I've got big plans to curl up with Harrison and the new book I've been obsessed with lately. The thought speeds up my gait.

Harrison's sitting next to his empty food bowl when I walk in my apartment. Throwing my keys on the counter and dropping my tote, I say, "It's coming, little guy." I refill his water bowl and dump a can of wet food into his other bowl then pet him. He closes his eyes at my touch and digs into his feast.

The light's blinking on the answering machine, so I click play. "Hey, girl. It's Maggie. I just wanted to see if you'd be up for being my wing-woman tonight at that new bar in Soho. Call me and let me know. I really don't want to go alone but need to leave here tonight. My roommate is driving me up the wall. Love ya. Bye!"

She knows I never want to go out, especially to a bar. I'd much rather stay in comfy clothes in my comfy apartment than dress up and be surrounded by uncomfy drunk strangers. I love my best friend,

Maggie, but she dates a lot of men. When she meets a new man, she nitpicks him for a week or two before finding the dealbreaker. Then she's on to the next one.

The last guy she dated didn't blink at the rate she thought was normal, so she felt like he was staring at her. The one before that cleared his throat too much and she couldn't stand it. She would always sing that old '90s song "Let Me Clear My Throat" as a joke when talking about him. It's humorous but gets old.

I drop onto the couch and wonder if Maggie is too picky. Or am I not picky enough? Brian certainly isn't the world's most perfect man, but we've been together for four years now and living together for two of those. I'm happy with him. I think. Marriage is the logical next step, right? Maybe it would fill the void in me that feels so out of reach as the years go on. And I want to be Mrs. Brian Holden. Rachel Holden sounds nice. Or Rachel Granza Holden. But why is he taking so long to propose? And why am I so afraid to talk to him about this? I do love him and I think he still feels the same. I should be able to talk to him about anything if he's the one, right?

My cell phone chimes, bringing me out of my thoughts. I look over and see a text from Maggie. Do I really have the energy to help her find another throw-away guy tonight? I let out a deep sigh and click the call button. She'll keep calling both phones and texting if I don't respond.

"Rachel, you gotta get me out of here." Mags usually doesn't waste any time with hellos.

"Why now?" I laugh as I speak.

"No, this is for real. SOS. I can't deal. Save me! Go out with me."

"I'd love to, but I have a date with a ginger tonight." I look over at Harrison, whose belly must be full since he's licking his paws.

"Don't you want to get out of that apartment and see the world? You know, there's more to life than books." She tsks to add a little umph. I know her moves by now.

"I do know that, ironically. But thanks for reminding me." I giggle. Her antics always lift my mood. Why doesn't it last more than a few seconds?

"Come ooooon. I know you want to."

Usually, her rebuttals are stronger. Hmm, she must be getting weak in our old age of thirty-two. My guilt won't win tonight, though. "I'm so sorry. I just sat down and I'm exhausted from today. You know sometimes I can't talk, listen, or even think after work. It's one of those days."

"It's been like that a lot lately…so I'm here to shake it up. Third time's the charm tonight?"

"Love ya, but nah. Rain check. I promise."

"All right." She takes a deep breath and exhales into her mouthpiece for dramatic effect. "I'll see who else wants to go. But you're always my number one. Don't you forget it."

"Thanks, Mags. And you are too."

"Later, Rach."

"Talk soon." I set my phone on silent and turn it face down on the couch as soon as we disconnect.

Harrison cuddles up next to me on the blanket as I open my book. My favorite throw is a ballet pink one that's as soft as a baby's blanket. I'm constantly running my fingers over it when I wind down on the couch. I have no idea what the fuzzy material is, but it's remarkable. It makes me feel safe. Can I be wrapped up in it forever?

I find myself thinking about my grandpa more every day so it's no surprise that the book I'm reading is set in Italy. My dream is to visit Genoa and walk the same streets he did before moving to the States. The book falls into my lap and I stare out the window, my mind drifting into a daydream about my grandfather. His Italian accent never left him and I can hear him calling my name right now in his sweet voice. What I wouldn't give for him to be alive, to embrace him in a hug, to tell him about my life, and to ask him the million questions that have arisen since his death fourteen years ago. I know I was lucky he lived until age ninety-six, but it wasn't long enough. It never would be. And, his lips were sealed about his immigrant past and how our family ended up in Philly. When he died, a part of me died with him, along with the chance to know anything about his youth. It bugs me more as the years go by.

Before I know it, Brian's walking through the front door.

"Hey, stranger." I push myself to get up and give him a hug, blinking to orient myself.

"Whatcha doing?"

"I'm reading that book I started last week." Or daydreaming and missing my grandpa. "How was your dinner?"

"It was okay. I don't know if we're any closer to closing the deal." Brian grabs a water bottle from the fridge and sits on a bar stool at the counter. "I just wish these guys would decide what direction they want us to go. They keep changing their minds so we have to redo the entire campaign every time. Either they don't understand that, or they don't care."

"I'm so sorry it was a rough day for you. I hope they get their acts together soon." I walk over and lean on the counter next to him.

He lets out a sigh. "Yeah, me too."

"Want to watch some TV before we head to bed?"

He stands up and gives me a kiss on the cheek. "No. I just need to go to sleep."

My shoulders fall and I step away. "Oh. Okay."

"Night." He walks into our bathroom and shuts the door behind him.

A new record has been set. Less than two minutes together. I don't think I can feel more alone than I do right now.

*Chapter 2*

"**G**ood morning, sleepy head. I left a little coffee in the pot for you." Brian, the king of pep, walks into the bedroom, fixing his tie.

I ease open my eyes while still buried in the comforter. My voice cracks out a noise meant to show my appreciation. I am *so* not a morning person.

"Hey, I was thinking that maybe we can go out for dinner tonight." Brian lifts his eyebrows as he waits for me to respond. After a few seconds, he exhales, as if he was holding his breath. "I feel like we haven't spent much time together recently. I shouldn't have to work late."

Did we just end up on the same page here or am I still asleep? "Um, sure. That would be great." I crawl deeper into the covers, thinking about his quick escape last night. "Call me later and we can figure out the details."

He kisses me goodbye in a solid lip lock and I feel a hint of hope rising inside of me, overtaking the dash of anxiety and sprinkle of confusion from a moment earlier. Maybe we still have something worth saving. Will an engagement be in my reality soon?

"Love you. Talk to you later."

"Love you too," he calls out right before the door shuts.

The alarm rings and I slap it. There's that horrid sound. Thank God today is Friday. I have been dragging all week and need a weekend at home to recuperate.

Harrison is snuggled against my blanket-covered feet but the smell of coffee wafting in from the kitchen makes it a little easier to crawl out of the warm bed.

One of the reasons we chose to live in our apartment was that it is ridiculously close to my practice, for New York standards. Brian usually takes the train to his office. Most days, I can't take the chaos of the subway. Stop touching me, strange man. Hello there, kid who doesn't notice me trying to get by because he's listening to music and looking at his phone. Argh! Even on the coldest of days, I'd much rather walk to get away from that mess.

When I enter the waiting room of our practice, I learn that Annabelle's first client didn't show up for her appointment, since her office door is wide open. Good, we have a few minutes to catch up.

I stop at her door before unlocking mine. "Hey there."

She looks up and smiles. "Well, hey there to you too." She pushes one of the stacks of files on her desk into another mountain so she can lean on her hand.

"I seriously do not understand how you stay organized." I shake my head.

She looks at the various piles and knick-knacks around her room. "It's a whole system. There's a method to my madness."

We both smile. Her neon orange dress glows amidst her whimsical furniture.

"I need to ask you about a new psychiatrist in Chelsea while you have a sec."

"Sure, shoot." She examines her hot pink nails then looks back at me.

"Have you referred anyone to Dr. Schmidt? I heard he works with kids who have substance concerns as well as adults."

"Nobody yet, but I can ask around if you want."

"Yeah, thanks. I have someone who needs to transfer to a doctor who's a better fit for their needs. Let me know."

I'm glad to have a quick conversation. It's few and far between for us some weeks. Connection with anyone right now is welcomed, yet difficult. Ugh. I lean on the door frame and loosen my arm so my tote reaches the floor and lessens the weight on me.

"Did you see that Bradley Cooper movie? I saw it last night," she says.

I wonder if she's trying to churn up some energy for me by changing the subject to a mutual celeb crush. "Nope. Not yet of course. That would require me leaving my apartment."

"And being up to date on the pop culture scene." Annabelle sometimes snorts when she laughs and this is one of those times.

I shake my head again. "Oh, Annabelle. Catch me about five years after something is cool. That's my sweet spot."

"Don't I know it. So, what's your day look like?" She glances at her computer.

"From what I remember, it seems pretty easy today."

"Never say that!" She waves her finger as she turns to face me. "You know as soon as you say that, you'll be stuck here until seven dealing with an involuntary hospitalization or something."

I chuckle and hold my hands up. "Okay, I won't say that again. Let me rephrase. I have some cases that don't appear as intense as usual, which is perfect for a Friday. Is that acceptable?"

"Better. Do you have any plans for the weekend?" She smiles and adjusts her sparkly silver headband.

"Brian wants to go out for dinner tonight. What about you? Any married people things you are doing?" I giggle, while motioning for her to come with me to unlock my office. I have to turn away or she'll see my eyes give more away than I'd like. I'm not being genuine in laughing; I'm dying inside. What I wouldn't give to look as Barbie-like as her and have the most fabulous relationship ever.

We enter my room and she makes herself comfortable on my couch as I drop my tote and lunch on my organized desk. Annabelle answers, "Peter and I will be going to Connecticut for the weekend. Another couple rented a house with us on the beach."

"That sounds like fun. It must be beautiful." I hear her continue, but also can't fight my mind wandering to my relationship because of her storybook married weekend. They sound so happy, so in sync. How I would love to have that kind of relationship with Brian. Will I ever?

Before I dive deeper into my comparisons or miss anything she's saying, my office phone rings. Saved by the bell. Annabelle looks at me with eyes questioning if I'll answer. "I think I will let it go to voicemail. It's a horrible practice of mine, I know, but I can't deal with any issues this early in the morning. I like to be prepared and not be taken off guard by a random complex issue by phone."

"Yes, that's my girl. Listen to the message and think of all possible responses."

"Ha, yeah pretty much. Sorry, Ann, I should get started." I give an exaggerated frown. "Let's talk later. Maybe we can grab a coffee this afternoon?"

She gets up and puts her hand on my shoulder. "Love it. Have fun with analyzing that message."

I half smile. Looking back at my computer, I take a deep breath and try to gain energy for the day.

Today ran like clockwork. Everyone was on time, parents were calm, and progress was made with every client. I imagine giving myself a pat on the back. But the triumph fades instantly when I reflect on the suggestions I made to clients today. They impacted me more than usual. I have been encouraging them to try to have difficult conversations with their families, yet I haven't been practicing what I preach. I'm expecting this major change from kids when I'm an adult who doesn't do it? What kind of a therapist am I if I can't live the same way I try to help others live?

As I amble home, I think that I need to somehow get up the courage to talk about the distance between Brian and me. It's time. I have been thinking about it more often, but don't want to face the conversation. I can't keep doing the usual Rachel protocol with waiting for a miraculous change to happen to put passion back in our relationship. It didn't work with past relationships and it won't work now. I hate to ruin an enjoyable evening out tonight, but there is never a good time. It's now or never.

When we spoke on the phone, Brian said he would come home so we could go together to a surprise restaurant. Nice. So now I have no idea what to wear and he won't give any hints. Gazing at my dressy options in my closet, I choose a little black dress with ample room for comfort. Throwing it on, I feel fancy, despite this mop of hair on my head. My standard black flats will match, so I retrieve them from the front door and slide them on my feet.

A hint of nausea washes over me as I attempt to mentally prepare myself to talk to Brian about our relationship and the future. I pull my hair back into a low ponytail to air my neck and fan it with my hand. Maybe I should make a quick list to refer to if I forget certain points. I spot my trusty pad and paper for these occasions on the counter, scoop them up, and start brainstorming.

Hmm. I bite the end of the pen. Once I start writing, the words flow.

1. You are working too much.
2. We used to be more affectionate.
3. You used to say I look pretty more often and you haven't said it much lately.
4. Why don't we go out together much anymore?
5. Dating for 4 years so what about marriage? Do you ever even think about it?

I cross off the last one. I don't think I can ask that question. It's not my goal, really. I want a solid relationship and if marriage happens, it happens. But still, what if? It would be nice.

Maybe I will just keep the other points and let that huge question sit on my mind a while longer. It is a little too overwhelming. I don't know.

As I rip the paper from the notepad and slip the list into my purse, Brian walks through the door. Phew, good timing.

"Hey, pretty lady."

"Hey." My voice is an octave higher than usual.

He walks to the kitchen and gives a peck on my lips. "I just need five minutes to get ready."

I stare at him as he walks to our bedroom. Speak, Rachel. Respond. But before I can open my mouth, he looks back with a raised eyebrow, which kicks me into gear. "Yeah. That sounds good. I'm ready." I manage a smile.

I grab my list and review it again. I can do this, right? Right. I can.

True to his word, Brian is ready in just a few minutes. Tonight, he's wearing a blue and yellow plaid button down shirt. I bought it for him a few Christmas' ago and it's my favorite. The blue in the shirt is a perfect complement to his eyes and the yellow highlights his dirty blonde hair. Paired with his jeans, it's a striking look.

Brian flashes his flawless white teeth and walks to the front door. "Ready?" He squeezes my shoulder and I notice his bulging bicep.

I nod and grab my purse.

Ready or not, here we go.

We jump on the C to Greenwich Village, but I still have no idea where he is taking me. I am trying my best to enjoy the beautiful night, but heart palpitations and my mind's bombardment with thoughts of the impending "talk" are overbearing. Also, the chaos of the subway is never my friend. I hope I don't look as nervous as I feel.

We arrive at a place we haven't been to in years. It is a hole-in-the-wall Mexican restaurant we love. They have the best beef burritos in the city. The key is they put just the right amount of cheese, onions, and red sauce spice in them. My mouth waters thinking about it. Two days in a row of Mexican food, my second favorite cuisine. Yum! Italian is my first love, of course.

Just as we seat ourselves and I loop my purse strap on the back of the chair, I hear Brian call out, "Two margaritas, please." I look up and see him signaling with two fingers to the waiter.

I dip my head and whisper to him. "Jeez, can you be a little more polite?" I hate when he calls attention to us. I look around to see who's staring. He knows I like to blend.

"What do you mean? I said please." He has a blank look on his face and I think he is clueless, not just acting clueless. My embarrassment doesn't faze him, though. He's never affected by what other people think of him, so it never seems to click in his head that not everyone has his confidence. It would be incredible to have that sense of freedom.

"Nobody had a chance to come over yet, so give them a second." I'm tense enough for tonight without thinking the waiter will spit in the food of his annoying new customers.

"I'm sure he'll recover. You gotta chill, Rachel."

If he only knew how much that is needed.

After we order and start drinking those darn margaritas, I feel the alcohol taking off my edge. I can take some deeper breaths now and try to enjoy tonight. Well, as much as possible knowing what I have to face.

"How's that granola bar account at work?" I try to focus on any other topic.

He licks his salty lips. "It's goin'. Jake and I think we are winning over their brand manager with our mockups of kids diving into huge bowls of granola with flying breakfast bars around them. It's ludicrous, but the feedback has been positive so far. Maybe some of your clients can be in the ads." He squints his baby blues and grins.

"Yeah, because that would be ethical. Oh, and not at all a breach of confidentiality." I smile and take a sip of my liquid medicine.

He reaches over the table and grabs my hands. His are warm and soft, as usual. I feel tingles in my fingertips, but my heart also jumps. I slowly look up from my bowed head.

"This is nice, Rach."

"Yeah, I'm glad you suggested we go out together. It's been a while."

"Too long."

Butterflies fill my stomach. My hands feel clammy. Before he can realize my sweat glands are gearing up, I let go. I hear a screaming internal voice telling me to talk about another subject, quick. Come on, think. Um…ooh okay, I have it.

"So, you know how I finished reading the book set in Italy? Guess what I started reading about now."

"Oh, let me take one guess. There's some kind of anniversary coming up, I think. I mean, somebody keeps telling me about a ship that sank or something like that." He puts his index finger to his chin and crinkles his mouth to the side, in an exaggerated thinking expression.

"It's only the biggest shipwreck in history, but whatever." I roll my eyes and laugh.

"Wait, is it called the *Titanic*? Nah, you don't care about that. Your book has to be about something else."

"Wow, you guessed it. Gold star for you." I throw the straw wrapper across the table at him.

"I think I know you a little bit. The details you have told me can't leave my mind at this point even if I wanted them to."

"Well, everyone should know them. How the hell could something man-made be unsinkable? What were they thinking? They weren't prepared at all! Not enough lifeboats, crew not filling them enough with passengers, trying to make fast speed to America without—"

"I know, Rachel." He laughs. "I think I know everything there is to know without being a fan like you."

"I'm only a fan of the movie from the '90s. Who wouldn't be with Leo starring in it? Duh. But I'm just fascinated with the history of the whole thing. I can't be '*a fan*' of a disaster. That's sick."

"Oh, Leo. Oh, Jack." Brian raises his voice to a high pitch, lifts his shoulders, and tilts his head to the side. He proceeds to make kissing sounds. "Oh, I love you!"

"Stop." I laugh. But, is Brian my Jack? Am I his Rose? Stop. I need to take my own advice. Don't go there yet with thinking of us. Stay in the moment.

"Here's something I haven't told you. I came up with a term for my condition."

"Your 'condition?' I'm listening." He leans toward me like I'm about to disclose the winning lottery numbers.

"I've determined I have TOD—Titanic Obsessive Disorder."

He bursts with a belly laugh. "What?"

My eyes scan the room to see if his volume attracted any gawking. Good, it didn't. "With all the centennial sinking documentaries and books out there that I've been engrossed in, I figure it makes sense. And, it makes us silly therapists laugh. Maggie just says she's embarrassed for me, though." I grin.

"I don't blame her."

"Hey! Watch it, mister. I may not take you to the re-release of *Titanic* in 3D next month."

"I don't know what I would do if I couldn't go!" He puts his hands together in prayer form. "Please let me go and drool over Mr. DiCaprio with you."

"Since you asked so nicely, yes you may come to witness him in 3D. You lucky man, you."

"I'm just glad you are interested in something."

I feel like I've been kicked in the gut. What is that supposed to mean? I gaze into his eyes, frozen for words. Maybe he's not so clueless.

"What's wrong? I'm saying I'm glad you love it so much. Keep reading the piles of books you have. Keep telling me about your memories of checking out library books on the *Titanic* as a kid and how you remain fascinated. I'm looking forward to our movie date night. I want you to have a passion again."

A passion.

Again?

The more he speaks, the more I withdraw within myself. I know logically he is rooting for my one interest at this time, but it still hurts. He has noticed what I've been feeling. I didn't think I've been that obvious. But who wouldn't notice me not wanting to leave the apartment much, I guess? We used to walk in Central Park, ride bikes, and even took a few easy exercise classes. I bet that's why he's excited for the movie. I muster up words.

"Yeah, me too." My fake smile moves across my face. The shift in my mood is probably noticeable, but I'll try to keep up an act.

As dinner progresses, I keep him talking about himself, so we aren't focused on me. But all I can think about is the topic I would love to avoid. I thought the more margaritas I have the better, but they aren't washing away the nerves that constantly remind me of what I need to do, no matter how much I drink. My appetite is minimal and a major stomachache is present. I must find the courage to get started with the conversation before dessert time. Yes, that is my time limit. I've decided.

As soon as we order dessert, my heart beats faster and my palms sweat again.

Calm down, calm down, calm down.

This mantra isn't working. No! It's having the opposite effect.

"Rachel?" Brian raises an eyebrow.

I should be used to that look, but this isn't normal from him. Other people, yes, Brian, nope. Help!

My fingers tremble and my legs go limp, all the way down to my toes. Maybe I should try some deep breathing. *Go.* I attempt to inhale, but my lungs reject the air.

"What's going on? You look strange." He reaches out and puts his hand on mine.

Oh no, I can't hear anything. What is he saying? What's happening to me?

"Are you okay? Rach?" Brian's lips move but there's no sound. He leans closer to me over the table, our faces almost touching, his eyes wide and alert. He grabs my shoulders and shakes me.

Everything around me slows then the room spins and the lights go out.

Psst, here's where we started. It's so embarrassing, but read on. I'll imagine you holding my hand for support as I lay it all out for you and cringe.

My eyes open and I feel like I just had the best night's sleep of my life. But I'm not at home in my comfortable bed and this is definitely more like a nightmare. I gasp and try to sit up. I'm on the dirty, sticky floor of the restaurant. My head is still spinning but I keep blinking to try to look at the unfamiliar faces that surround me.

My gaze lands on Brian and I hold my breath. "What happened?!" My eyes grow large.

"You fainted. Are you okay?" Brian is on his knees, leaning over me.

"I, I guess." I rub my head. "Ow."

"You fell off the chair before I could reach you. Is your head okay? I didn't want to move you just in case. How many fingers am I holding up?"

"Two." The margarita signaling pops into my head. I shake it, both for getting rid of that thought and to be more alert. "I think my head is okay. It just hurts a little in this one spot." I place my hand over the crown of my head.

"Good." He takes a deep sigh. "You scared me to death!"

"I'm sorry." I accept a glass of water from the waiter. Another waiter tries to hand me a cold washcloth. I look up at the generous man and say, "I'm fine, but thank you."

Well, it's settled. I can't ever return to this place. I'm mortified!

I get up slowly and grab my purse from the chair. "Brian, can we get the check and leave now?" I need to leave yesterday if it were possible.

"Yes, let's do that."

He takes care of the bill while I walk to the front door to wait for him. I look back to make sure he sees where to meet me and wish I could disappear on this spot. Just let me sink into the earth and transport back to my bed.

He comes over to me a few minutes later, puts his arm around my shoulder, and leads me out the door. "Are you sure you're okay? Do we need to get you to a hospital?"

"I promise, but thanks." I lean my head on his shoulder as we start walking to the train. It feels like years passed from ordering dessert until now. I don't think I have ever been this embarrassed in my life. I am such an idiot. And…here come the tears. Hold them in, Rachel. Don't make it worse.

"So, what was wrong, Rach? Why did you faint? Have you ever fainted before?" Brian is going a mile a minute with the questions as we walk, which doesn't slow down my heart rate or breathing. I can hardly verbalize my racing thoughts at this moment, never mind try to translate them to another person. I separate myself from him to get some air.

"No, I never have. That was so scary. I can't believe what happened!" I speed up my pace, leading him to keep up with me, unable to make eye contact. I'm such a fool. Who faints like that in public? Oh. My. God. "Let's just get home."

Focus remains on my feet, speedily moving toward the comfort of my apartment. In fact, I refuse to let my eyes off of my feet. They are safe to look at and help me to see the stable ground below. If looking at the ground means I'm not lying on it again, that's a plus.

"Why don't we just get a cab? I don't know if going on the train is the best idea for you after what you've been through tonight. You don't even like it when you're feeling good."

"Uh, yeah, that's a good idea."

He places his hand under my chin and gently moves it up so I can make eye contact with him. "Let me help you. Just let me. I want to."

My eyes fill with tears again.

"Thank you." I sniffle and look down.

Once I am sitting in bed under my silky sheets and fluffy comforter, surrounded by soft pillows, and drinking warm mint tea Brian brought me, I have clearer thoughts. I am breathing deeper now. Ahh.

I can't believe I nearly had a panic attack for trying to start a conversation with this sweet, caring man. Wait, was that a panic attack? I shut my eyes tightly to banish the thought. If I think about it more, I'll have another attack for sure. Next thought, please.

When I open my eyes, I see Brian staring at me. He slips into bed next to me and asks, "Are you absolutely sure you are okay? That was a nasty fall."

"Nasty in more ways than one. I'm permanently scarred from

touching the germs on the floor. There aren't enough times I can wash my hands." I pretend to gag.

"Yeah." He laughs. "Well, let me tuck you in so you have sweet dreams. We can figure out things more tomorrow. You should rest tonight." He brings the comforter up to my face and pats it around my upper body so I'm snug.

I smile at his show of support and nod. "Thanks again for being there for me tonight. I'm glad I didn't have to deal with that alone. I'm lucky to have you."

But will we last forever? It's torture to stop the thoughts. I sigh and roll over to get the remote. "Want to watch a movie? I'm not ready to go to sleep yet."

"Maybe *Titanic* is on!" he jokes.

"We can only hope."

I channel surf until we agree on a movie. My mind continues to drift, though. I love that we had time together tonight. The warmth from it felt familiar and safe for a moment or two. I must admit that I also love the attention from him at home. I just wish I didn't faint to get it.

## Chapter 3

Feeling confused and sweaty, I open my eyes to see my family room. I rub them to make sure they aren't lying to me. I am in my apartment in 2012, not on the *Titanic* in 1912. To orient myself, I drop a foot off the side of the couch and make sure I feel the hardwood floor. That's definitely floor, not freezing water.

It's all coming back to me now. Oh God. It's been over twenty-four hours since my embarrassing—and now this. A girl can only take so much.

"You're up early for a Sunday." Brian appears in front of me holding a mug of steaming coffee.

I let out a groan and blink with force. My eyes feel like a thousand pounds.

"I didn't want to wake you to come to bed when I got home last night from playing poker. It was late and you looked like you were in a deep sleep."

"Yeah… I had a wild dream that I was on the *Titanic*."

"Well, I can see why. Looks like your, what was it, TOD is acting up?" He laughs.

I grin and sit up, wrapping my blanket around me. "I *have* to stop reading about the *Titanic* or watching *Titanic* related movies or shows so late at night. I've been having more and more dreams about the ship, but none as vivid as this one last night. I was a passenger!"

He sits down next to me, after moving a few *Titanic* books out of the way. "It's no wonder when you put this into your brain before bed. Look at all this." He waves both of his palms over at the special editions of magazines, the coffee table books, and the novels that support my habit.

"You have to hear about this dream, though!"

"I'm ready. Do you need some coffee for this?"

"I'll never reject that." I smirk.

He gets up to go to the kitchen.

I turn around on the couch and start spewing.

"Okay, it was freezing and I was walking along the rail of a ship I knew is the *Titanic*. I could feel the smooth, white railings. It was weird because I knew I was dreaming, but it felt so real!"

"Oh yeah?" Brian hands me a warm mug of energy and sits next to me again.

"Thanks. Yeah, I knew it was going to sink, but I was pretending to enjoy the day with family and friends, like everything was normal."

"Wait a second. Why would you be on a ship? You hate cruises."

"I know! I was thinking that in the dream. Get out of my head." I point to him as if threatening him. He smiles then I go back to staring into space to recall the experience.

I wrap my blanket tighter around me as I think about tightening my long winter coat in the dream, to shield myself from the frigid weather.

"I was definitely a first-class passenger because of my upscale beaded dress and heels. And you know I think heels are from hell for their discomfort and the attention they draw, so you know this was not reality."

Brian nods and raises his eyebrows.

"Anyway, the dream skipped to me being in my huge suite, with luggage everywhere; trunks and old-fashioned suitcases as tall as me. Then, there were ornate sconces, elegant linens, and European paintings. My parents were in the room with me, but they weren't my parents I have now. My best friend from high school was there too. I don't even know her anymore. It was so strange." I crinkle my face.

"That's how dreams go." Brian takes a sip of his coffee.

"So, we were unpacking and I knew it was the first day of the voyage. But I also knew the ship would hit the iceberg and sink that night, even though it was four days from then in the real timeline of events. Then, my friend pulled me by hand to the Turkish baths almost instantly."

"To the what?"

"Oh, they were like a modern-day spa. The dream kept flashing to different parts of the ship. Like I was taking a personal tour. And everyone kept talking about the beauty of the ship and how lucky we were to be sailing on it. I knew otherwise but remained silent."

I gulp my coffee and continue. "The day seemed to last forever, as they do in dreams. We were wandering around aimlessly and chatting politely to strangers, when the ship struck something. We were in the hallway at this point, where there were no windows. The jolt made us all fall to the floor. Everyone started to panic and even though I knew what was happening, I was scared too. It felt *so* real. The time had come, and I knew it. So, I rushed to my suite with my friend to tell my family what just happened, but nobody was here. Where were they? I needed to find them and get off the ship asap! I knew what the lifeboat situation would be like in a few hours."

"If anyone knows, you do."

I barely hear Brian's comment. My heart is beating fast remembering what it felt like to be in the dream.

"My friend and I frantically ran through the decks, calling out my family's names. Everyone else was running around and screaming as well. Logically, it must have been hours later, but it felt like seconds. I was carrying one modern day suitcase that had essentials in it. I knew I needed it. Finally, we found my parents. They were standing by the edge of the boat and smiling, looking completely calm. Next thing I knew, we were walking onto a lifeboat. We were going to survive. Then, I woke up."

I fall back into the back of the couch and bow my head. Why do I feel guilt for living when it was all just a dream? I wasn't on the ship.

Brian chimes in, "That was something, Rachel. It sounded intense."

"It was." A tear comes to my eye. "People must have been so scared. I can't continue to think about it because it makes me too sad."

Brian bends toward me and tries to look me in the eye. "It was just a dream. You are safe here."

Okay good, he said it too. It feels good to hear it, even though I know the truth already. "Yeah, I'm just tired. I should know better than to stay up, but I couldn't stop. *Titanic* sucked me in once again."

"When did you get home?" Brian asks. "You don't like to stay out late."

"I know. Maggie also sucked me into staying out with her." I roll my eyes. "I love her, but you know how it is."

"I do. That Mags. Well, let's eat something and you can fill me in on your night."

"Sure, but first tell me about your night." I follow him to the kitchen and sit on a bar stool at the counter. Harrison wakes from the sound of the stool screeching on the floor.

"Sorry, Harrison. You can go back to your much needed rest now."

He yawns, rolls over, and follows my instruction.

I'm guzzling my drink this morning. Maybe I need some water. I'm too old for this night owl business. I get up to fill a glass with water while Brian starts pulling out way too many ingredients for my non-morning mind to comprehend. He starts whipping up another complex breakfast I've only ever seen on TV.

"What are you creating today?" The cool water soothes my dry throat as I swallow.

"I want to try an eggs Florentine omelet with a peach pie smoothie."

"How do you come up with this stuff? I'm lucky if I can crack an egg."

"You are one strange Italian. Don't you all like to cook?" He widens his mouth in a playful teasing smile and moves the blender close to him to continue his preparation.

His comment sends me inward. I have always felt like somewhat of an outcast outside of my family, due to my looks alone. Add on my lack of traditional Italian interests like cooking and the ability of socially superficial conversation and I'm finished. Brian knows this but speaks mindlessly so much of the time.

All of these thoughts send a sharp pain to my chest. Who says heartbreak isn't real? I miss Grandpa even more in these times I'm reminded of my differences to normal society. He was the sole person in this world that completely understood me.

I touch my tangled hair and push it back over my shoulders with a scowl. I look as far from being an Italian woman as one could get and it's so unfair. Aren't Italian people always dark skinned with dark, shiny, straight hair, like my dad and Dylan? All the people I've known who are Italian looked more like a stereotypical Italian person. I can sometimes hide my internal awkwardness, but I can't hide how I look. Well, not without gobs of hair product and makeup.

When Grandpa died in my freshman year of college, everything in my little world started to change. My life lost color as the years went by and now I'm here, feeling more lost by the day. My heart sinks and I look down. Will I ever feel truly happy again?

"Rachel." Brian snaps his fingers in front of my face.

I look up. "Yeah, sorry." Come back to the present, Rachel.

"Do you want a straw for your smoothie?"

"No, that's okay." I twirl my pajama pants string and take a deep breath.

After a few more minutes, he sets breakfast in front of me and comes around the counter to join me. "Dig in."

I need to change my thoughts so I don't stay stuck in them. Do some therapy on yourself, Rachel. "Tell me about your poker night." I take my first heaping bite. If anything can help me get unstuck, it's this food. Thank God for a man who cooks.

"It was fun. Ignacio kept winning and we accused him of cheating. But we all know he's just a good player. We like to give him a hard time."

"That doesn't sound like you guys at all." I giggle. "Oh, by the way, these eggs are to die for."

"Try the smoothie."

I take a sip and my mouth is sent to sweet sugarland. "How did you get it to taste like the crust is in there too?"

"That's a chef's secret."

"I won't be trying it out anyway." He's already made that clear. I mumble, "It's delicious."

"I'm glad." He continues to chew.

"So, what else?"

"There's nothing much to say. Just the regular guy talk." His voice deepens and he grunts. "Booze and babes, the usual."

"Uh-huh. Pu-lease."

"I'm sure your night with Maggie was much more interesting. It always is with her." He sprinkles Tabasco sauce on his plate to dip his eggs.

"Yeah." I chuckle. The thought of Maggie can always bring a smile. "Well, she was the epitome of sparkle and glamour, as usual, so we were quite a pair."

"What was it this time?"

"Oh, she was single and ready to mingle. She wore a skintight, apple red dress, which was more like a long shirt if you ask me, with what had to be five-inch heels. She always looks gorgeous, don't get me wrong, but then there's me in my ballet flats, black work slacks, and a high-necked bulky sweater."

"That's my girl."

"She met a guy who was in a class of hers at our college," I say with my mouth full of smoothie.

"An old New York City University grad? Nice. How long will it be until she finds a minor flaw in him, makes a big deal about it, thinks that she can't live with it, and moves on?"

"Probably as we speak."

We both grin.

"Nah, Ray seemed pretty nice. Maybe he will last a little while longer. I hope for her sake. She deserves a great guy."

"Like me?"

"Yes, just like you." I know it's true but what makes me feel it's not? There's no reason to feel unstable in my life. That's what irks me the most. Why can't I find a reason for this emptiness in my spirit?

He gets up from his seat to rinse his plate. "What are you doing later today? I need to go into the office for a little bit." He grabs my plate from across the counter, since I'm done eating too.

"Thanks for cooking and cleaning." I can barely gather enough will to do my minimum responsibilities. If he didn't cook, I bet I'd be eating frozen meals or starving most days.

"No problem." He throws a dish towel over his shoulder. "So?"

"I think I better catch up with Maggie about her new love interest." That's what a good friend would do and I'm going to try my best to be there for her, even though I only want to veg on the couch all day with *Titanic* documentaries and cuddle up with Harrison. "When I left, she was still talking with him, so I'm sure she has a lot to fill me in on. I'll give her a call."

"Okay. Will you be home for Sunday dinner?"

"I wouldn't miss it."

"Great. I'll come up with something I haven't tried before. Maybe we can have a redo from the other night."

"Anything but Mexican."

"You got it."

After showering, I don't feel any rejuvenation in my mood. What will it take to knock me out of this funk? Nothing sticks anymore.

My dream last night isn't helping my cause. Somehow, it's making me feel like there is urgency about facing my fears today. Not tomorrow, today. I can't shake the feeling of being on that sinking ship and needing to do something to survive the disaster.

My pulse is speeding up and my breath is getting shallow as I think about it. The images, sounds, and sensations are still realistic. Seeing the fear on the passengers faces, hearing the screams from the ocean, and feeling the boat tilt makes my heart feel ready to burst out of my chest. Faster and faster, it keeps speeding up until I think I'll have to breathe into a bag soon. Does that even work? I will not have another panic attack!

My knowledge of therapeutic interventions pops into my racing mind. Grounding will help. Feel the floor. I shuffle my feet. Bring attention to how my hand feels on the sturdy wall. I rub it. Breathe in the spices from breakfast. I inhale. Look at the navy blue bedding. Breathe in through my nose, breathe out of my mouth. Repeat.

After a minute of breathing and focusing on my senses, I'm feeling less likely to faint. Maybe this dream is a sign. Maybe it's helping to push me into having the dreaded conversation with Brian that is inevitable. But first, maybe I should have a trial run with Mags about it. I need to get on a lifeboat before the (relation)ship sinks in my real life.

# Chapter 4

S till in my robe when Brian leaves for weekend work, I glance outside my bedroom window for the first time today. It looks a little colder than yesterday. People are in snow hats and walking fast, probably to avoid the strong wind I see blowing through the trees. I hear the whistle through my poorly insulated window. The sight and sound send a chill through my body. On instinct, I squeeze my robe around my throat. That's how this time of year is though; one day it is gorgeous and warm enough to wear light spring clothes and the next I find myself needing multiple layers. I don't think I'll leave the apartment today. No, I know that I won't.

Harrison's bell on his collar keeps ringing. What is he up to now? I turn the corner to see him on his back with his catnip filled mouse toy between all four paws. He grips it with his front claws to bring it closer to his mouth, then tosses it just far away enough to pounce on it and toss it around more. I wish I had his energy. Maybe there's catnip for humans.

I drop on the couch and let my head rest so that I have a perfect view of the ceiling. I stare at its blank white canvas enough that my eyes glaze over. What will I do this afternoon? I'll call Maggie later, but what do I do right now? My thoughts are interrupted within seconds by repeated pounding knocks on my door.

I sigh, having to gather all my strength to get up.

I push myself off the couch and stagger toward the sound.

"Rachel! Rachel! Come to this door."

The familiar voice prompts me to increase speed. "Coming Maggie."

When I open the door, I see my bestie bearing gifts. "Here." She shoves a coffee in my face. "I took a guess that you'd need this after last night." She pushes past me and enters.

"Thanks. I'll never reject caffeine." *This* may be the human catnip. I take a sip and savor the warmth running through my bones. It feels good to be filled with something, even coffee, for a brief period.

Maggie makes herself at home in the family room, kicking off her shoes, throwing her coat on the ground, and pulling up a blanket when she sits down. "I know you don't love it when I drop by unannounced, but I took a chance. I had to drop off dry cleaning on the corner so I stopped in your favorite cafe."

"Thanks so much. And it's okay. I was going to call you, err, soon anyway. I would love to hear about what happened last night."

"Yes, girl. That is part of why I wanted to catch up. We kind of got sidetracked once Ray entered the picture. Sorry about that." She grits her teeth and lowers her lip.

I respond to her remorse. "No worries. So, tell me all the details."

"Wait." Her eyes scan my body up and down. "Why are you in a robe at two o'clock, missy?"

I look down at my apparel choice of the day. "I don't know. It's cold out and I don't want to go anywhere. It's Sunday. Why get dressed?"

She squints at me. "Uh-huh. This is even more antisocial than your usual. I don't like it."

"Everything is fine. Now tell me about last night. Ray was a cutie. I loved his dark brown eyes." I raise my eyebrows and use one of my therapy techniques to focus back on her.

"Yes! I'll drink his hot cocoa anytime."

It worked. "And what does that mean?" I tilt my head and furrow my brow.

"He's a fine Black man for this fine Black woman." She shimmies side to side and runs her hands down her body.

I shake my head and grin. "Oh my gosh. Okay, continue."

"Well, you know how irresistible guys are always gay, married, or have girlfriends? I swear, you are so lucky to have Brian. Anyway, Ray's free and clear. I can't believe it. And to know him from way back in the day, that's just icing on the cake."

"Yeah, that's astonishing."

"We're probably meant to be." She drinks her coffee and looks out the window.

"The odds are low to cross paths with any old classmates, I'm sure. This is a huge city. Running into him is a win." My comment leads her to turn her head back to me.

"Yup, so after you left us, we talked for hours and exchanged phone numbers. The martinis helped to keep the conversation going." She laughs. "He hasn't called me yet, but it hasn't even been twenty-four hours."

"Um, yeah, I think you're good." I remember the aggravation the three day rule brought in my dating days. Now I feel like an old married lady with no ring to show for it.

"I'll keep you updated. Now back to you."

Damn. She's doing my tricks now. She's known me too long. "What?"

"You can't dupe me. Something's been up and I'm here to force it out of you. That's why I said I was partly here to tell you about Ray. Didn't you wonder what the other part was? Hmm?" She turns her head to give me the side eye.

I look down. "I don't know." I play with my robe, pulling the belt tighter.

"You *do* know. Spill."

"I guess I don't know where to start." I pause. "Well, I had a horrible dream last night about the *Titanic*. I was on it." I pause again and stare into Maggie's eyes. "I think I'm sinking in reality."

"What are you talking about?" She moves closer to me and leans her chin on her hand, elbow on her knee.

I look away again. "In the dream, I was a passenger and knew the ship was sinking, but I felt helpless. I tried to act normal, even though I knew disaster was coming. I eventually got into a lifeboat, but the metaphor has to mean something, right?"

Maggie takes a deep breath as her eyes grow large. "What you always tell me is the dreamer is the only one who knows what the dream means. What's your interpretation?"

"I—"

"Come on. Just tell me." She dips her head lower to look into my downward eyes.

"I think I'm in a rut and I can't seem to get myself out of it. I don't feel like my old self. I don't even know what's happening with Brian and me. I mean, why have we been dating this long, live together, and yet still aren't moving forward?"

"As in getting engaged?"

"Yeah. What's the hold up? We're a couple that sails smoothly down the middle of a calm, boring river." I make a straight line with the palm of my hand. "There's a total lack of passion to be intensely affectionate or argumentative. No waves or even ripples take place in our river. We get along fine. So, isn't that a good thing?" I feel tears building up in my eyes.

"I don't know, honey. I'm no expert in this area, but I would think some passion is needed for a lasting relationship."

The blood rushes from my legs, leaving tingles from hip to toe. That's exactly what I never wanted to hear.

She continues, "Brian's a great guy. He is everything a woman would want in man. He has a great job, is hot as hell, and isn't all into your business like some guys out there. But he's also not as emotional as you. You knew that from the start."

"That's the problem, though. I don't know if he is losing interest in me or what. He's not an expressive guy, but he used to be more, I don't know, interested in me in some way. I feel a difference. I actually planned to talk to him about us on Friday night and you won't believe what happened."

"Oh yeah?"

"Yeah." I feel nauseous thinking about it again. "I made a list of points I need to tell him."

"Of course you did. Go on," she jokes.

I smile. "I had it in my purse and was prepared to whip it out once we ate dessert. But as soon as we ordered, I had a panic attack and fainted!"

"What? You did not. Oh girl, that's horrible."

"It was. I ended up on the dirty floor with everyone staring at me." I automatically make a gagging face.

"Your worst nightmare."

"Basically. So, I decided I need to approach him today."

"I feel like an ass. How could I be so into finding my man that I had no idea you were feeling like this about yours?" Maggie gives me a tight hug.

"Don't beat yourself up. I bet Brian doesn't even know there is a problem. But I need to face this today. No more waiting for me. I'm bringing it up at dinner tonight." My stomach remains in knots.

"We need to find some way to get you back on track. I don't want to keep seeing you sad like this."

I thought I was putting up a good act for everything being normal in my life. When is my life ever normal, though? I'm a fool for convincing myself I was making an Oscar worthy performance with people like my best friend.

"As you like to say, this is a mission. It's mission *Get Rachel Out of Her Slump*. Now, let's make a plan."

"A plan?"

"Yes, you want to talk to Brian tonight so let's make sure that happens. I know you love to spell out every word and movement when you're anxious. We can role play what you'll say."

"You love me enough to help me. That means a lot."

"Of course. I'll always help you. We're on a mission." She winks.

"Okay, how can I bring it up to him?" I look back toward the counter, having an urge to get my pad of paper and pen to write step by step notes.

"You just spit it out. Say, 'We need to talk.'"

I get up to retrieve the beloved list in my purse and bring back the pad and pen, just in case. I look back at Maggie as I walk to them and say, "That doesn't sound like doom is coming at all."

"Hey, you gotta be real here. No use in beating around the bush."

"I know you are right." I come back to the couch and start reading out the points.

"Okay, how's this? 'Brian, we need to talk.'"

Maggie deepens her voice and says, "About what, apple of my eye?"

I laugh. "Stay on track!"

"All right, all right." Now in her own voice but acting as Brian, she continues. "What do you want to talk about, Rachel?"

I look at my list. My hand grips it so tight it's getting creased. My fingers are already getting sweaty and I'm not even here with Brian. Gather courage, Rachel. I breathe in then exhale, saying, "You work so much lately. I wish we could spend more time together."

"I need to keep my job, so what do you want me to do?"

My heart speeds up pace. "Time out." I make the universal signal with my hands. "You're making him sound defensive. Do you think he would be like that?"

"I don't know. It just came to me. I think he'd say something like he has to do what the job requires. Blah, blah, blah, some stuff like that."

"Yeah, that does sound like him. That's not the biggest deal anyway. It's my starter point." I clear my throat and go back into the mode. "Well, we used to be more affectionate. And you used to call me pretty. You haven't said it at all lately."

She touches my shoulder and peers into my eyes. "You're always beautiful to me. I don't know what you are talking about."

"You used to kiss me more. Initiate things." I look down and away from Maggie's eyes.

"Things?"

I know Mags wants me to say dirty *things*. "You know, things," I whisper.

She gives up and stays in character. "I'll make a better effort with that. Now that you told me about it, I will pay more attention to you. How does that sound?"

"Um, Mags, I don't know if he will be that easy-going about it."

"First you think I'm being too defensive and now I'm too easy-going? Come on, my friend. Help me out. I'm tryin'!" She laughs.

"Sorry! I know you are doing your best Brian impression. None of us can get into a man's mind."

"Ain't that the truth?" She nods her head.

"This is too hard to predict what he'll say. Let's stop."

"No, Rach, you got this. Just finish your list. I'm dyin' to know what's left." Maggie, being the wonderful friend that she is, forces me to face my anxiety.

I look at my points once more. "Why don't we go out much anymore?"

"We just went out Friday night."

"Yes, but that was rare. I remember we used to have date nights, and day dates for that matter, all the time. I want that again with you. I miss you." A tear rises to my eye and out so fast I don't have a chance to fight it. I quickly rub it off my cheek.

Maggie's face drops. "I would love to do that too. Where do you want to go? Let's go tomorrow after work."

"I'd like that. Even if we just spend more time together here, I'd love it. I read and watch TV on my own so much. I would like you to be with me. Remember how we used to read together on weekend mornings? You with your business books and me with novels…or *Titanic* books of course."

She laughs. "Oh yes, I do remember. I used to like that too. Let's start that again."

"Maggie, do you think he would say that? Give in so easily to what I want?"

"I think so. He's a simple man. And I'm sure he wants it too. What else would he say?"

"Yeah, I guess. I want to make sure I think of all possibilities before I have this conversation."

She looks up and to the side. "Hmm, well he could say he doesn't want to do more with you or he can't because of work. Maybe something like that? What would you say then?"

"I understand work obligations, but if he doesn't want to be with me, that's a different story."

"I'm sure it's not going to be that. He's not so stupid that he'd get on your best friend's bad side." She puts up her fists and lets out a belly laugh.

I love when she gets a kick out of her own jokes. "Let's hope."

"What else? I think I see one more point on there." She moves her head closer to the paper trying to read through the back.

"This is the big one. I crossed it out, but I probably should bring it up." I take a deep breath and go back to the pretend conversation with Brian. "We have been dating four years. I would love to talk about marriage soon."

"Oh." Her eyes widen.

That's probably what he would react like with this last point. I force myself to push past my desire to run into the bathroom, lock the door, and never come out again. "Do you ever think about it?" I enlarge *my* eyes, conveying to continue immediately or I may still flee.

Maggie nods, widens her eyes again as well and says, "I have thought about it but didn't think that you wanted to get married right now."

"I think I do." My hands shake.

"You think?"

"I should probably not be so unsure with him, right?" I ask Maggie.

Also coming out of character, she responds, "I wouldn't be. Do you or don't you?"

This seems like an uncomplicated question. I should have no ifs, ands, or buts about it at this point. My heart screams at me, saying, "Yes you want to get married, you idiot." I want it, but my head says to stop and consider the facts. Like, why hasn't he asked? Is something wrong with him? Is he dying? Oh my God, what if he's dying and he hasn't told me. Argh! Stop it. Who am I kidding? Of course I want it. We don't have to get married soon, but to at least know that's where we are headed is important to me. I guess I wouldn't be bothered that we haven't talked about it if I didn't want it. I decide on the obvious answer.

"Yes, of course I do."

"Okay then. We can go look at rings if you want. Let's go to a few jewelry stores this coming weekend. What do you say?"

My heart returns to its average beat with this soothing thought. That should clue me into what I want in itself. "Sounds perfect." I smile. I have a hint of hope that he would be on my same page, like Mags pretended he would be.

"I love you, Rachel." Maggie makes kissing sounds. "Let's get married and have dozens of kids."

"Mags! Seriously, do you think he will want to move forward?"

"I'm sure of it. What reason would he not want to? It wouldn't make any sense if he doesn't. He lives with you and you've been together forever."

"Yeah, you have to be right. But is there anything else we aren't thinking about that he may say?"

She breaks the silence after what feels like five minutes. "I think no matter what happens, you'll have a good outcome. You're Rachel and Brian. You guys are made for each other."

I smile ear to ear and give her a tight hug. "Thanks for helping me sort through this mess in my head."

She shakes her head and points to mine. "I wouldn't want to be in there, but I'm glad to work through the cherished list with you."

"No, you wouldn't want to be in there, believe me."

"Do you think this conversation will help you feel like you're out of your 'rut?'"

I take a second to think, but words fly out of my mouth to convince myself. "Yes, it has to be the problem. Everything else in my life is set."

"True. I hope the chat does help you get back to the old Rachel I know and love."

"I do too."

If that's possible.

Now that I have a plan, I can try to relax, at least physically, because my thoughts never stop racing. I'm so lucky to have Maggie as a friend. She helped me today more than she knows. Well, she probably knows since she knows me well. I learned that once again today. She had to force information out of me, but I have a feeling she wasn't going to leave until she found out what was happening. That's my Mags.

"Well, I'll leave you to it." She gathers her thrown about items and walks toward the front door.

"Let me know if Ray calls," I say.

Before she closes my front door, she says, "You'll be the first to know after me. See you later."

"Bye."

After she leaves, I curl up with a book about the behind the scenes of the movie *Titanic* and try to forget about dinner tonight for a little while. I've spent so much mental energy on the situation already and need to save some or I'll chicken out from pure exhaustion. I refuse to let that happen.

The night should be fine. No, it *will* be fine. I repeat the mantra in my head. And the most important aspect of my plan? No fainting will occur. I make myself that promise.

# Chapter 5

Growing up, Sunday dinner was always reserved for family, and even though I didn't get the cooking gene, I've always wanted to continue that tradition with my own family. Thankfully, Brian likes to cook and is happy to make sure that eating "lotsa pasta," my family's phrase, lives on. We've modernized pasta Sundays to include any Italian-oriented meal in our household.

I sit down and Brian puts a steaming bowl of parmesan risotto in front of me before joining me at the counter. If I don't do this now, I'll just delay it again.

"Brian, I need to talk to you about something important." I blow on the steamy risotto on my spoon.

He looks up from his bowl, his brow furrowed. "About what?"

I take a quick bite and swallow, working up the courage. "I don't know where to start…"

"What's wrong? Are you okay?"

I take a deep breath. "I haven't been feeling as connected with you."

Brian doesn't move.

My heart beats faster and I push through the building anxiety. "I feel like you work all the time. Like, all the time. There's barely any time left for us. And now I think I'm too used to you being gone so it's kind of weird when you aren't working late or are home on the weekends. That isn't good. Don't get me wrong. I love that you're ambitious, but sometimes I feel like you forget about me. Or maybe you'd rather be at work than home with me."

Brian opens his mouth, but I hold up my hand to stop him. If I let him talk, I may lose my nerve.

"We used to be so affectionate, but now we hug on occasion and rarely kiss. And you used to tell me I was pretty at least once a day. Am I horrid now? I mean, I know I'm not all into clothes and makeup and stuff, but you fell in love with me for some reason. And I'd think you are at least a little attracted to me, right? It makes me feel better about myself when you compliment me."

Brian sits back in his chair and folds his hands in front of him.

"Date night was a great idea, but how often do we do that anymore? And please, let's not talk about Friday night. I want to go out to dinner more, walk around the city, and find some festivals to attend. Where is the Brian who used to surprise me with dates more than just once a year?"

Brian cringes, jerking his head back.

I may have gone too far with that one. My emotions are getting the best of me. Scale it back, Rach.

"And finally, how long have we been together now? Are you ever going to propose? Did I do something to turn you off? Do you not want me as your wife someday? Are you even thinking about proposing? I feel like I'm spinning my wheels here, so give me a clue." There. I did it. It's all out.

My worries kick into overdrive and my stomach churns. I sit back in my chair and wait for him to process everything I just spit out.

After what feels like a century, he looks straight into my eyes and says, "I feel the same way."

My entire body tenses and a million thoughts course through my brain. Is that all he's going to say? Is he going to break up with me? What's he thinking? Should I keep talking? What else could I say?

He folds his arms on the counter. "Rach, I work that much because I have to. What kind of boyfriend would I be if I wanted to be away from you more than I'm with you? I have a lot of responsibilities at work and sometimes need to put in a little extra effort to get things done. You know I also want to move up in the company. I can't stay in this position forever."

And…I suck.

I unlock my eyes with his and look down. "Okay, that makes me feel a *little* better."

"As for not showing any affection, you can't place all of that blame on me."

My jaw drops and I look up at him once again. "W-what do you mean?"

"How many times have I wanted to have sex and you turn me down?"

"Well—"

"You can't say you don't do that. You never start anything either. I don't see you jumping up to hug or kiss me when I walk in the door. So yeah, I haven't thought about getting that close lately. That doesn't mean I don't think you're pretty, though. You're beautiful. Nothing could ever change that. And I have said it recently, but you can't hear me. I can get better at saying it more often, though. But you don't see what you do, or don't do, anymore either."

Tears stream down my face and into my risotto. "I guess not." I hadn't considered his perspective at all. Maybe it's time I listen to him, instead of focusing on myself.

"This isn't a new thing. It's been happening for a while now. At first, I wasn't sure what to think and probably pulled away from you a bit. I wasn't sure if you were angry with me or if something else was wrong. The date the other night was me trying to reconnect. I don't want this distance between us because I do love you. And maybe I don't always show it in the right ways, but you haven't been yourself for a while, and I wonder if you even recognize that."

"This is a lot to take in. I didn't know you noticed stuff was different too."

"I'm not blind. I'm human. And a normal guy…with normal urges." He reaches over and pokes me in the ribs.

For the first time since we sat down, I crack a small smile.

The corners of his mouth curl into a frown. "To tell you the truth, I have been kind of worried about you. Have you noticed how reclusive you've been?"

"You know I'd rather stay in than go out into the city—"

"Stop right there. That is not the woman I met years ago. You were the one who got us tickets to every event that looked interesting. You used to love experiencing this city, but I can't tell if you still do. Now, you even complain about going out with Maggie and she's your best friend. You'd rather hide in the apartment and read. And you just said you want us to go out more, so you don't even know what you want."

My mind races and I struggle to keep up. He's right. It's time to ask the million-dollar question.

I stare down at my risotto. "So, do you ever think about marrying me?" My words crawl out.

"Yes!"

I let out a sigh and my chest loosens a little.

"Rach, I love you to death. I hope you still know that."

I nod once and grab my glass on the counter.

He continues, "I've seen my friends propose, get married, and some even have kids. Don't you think I want that for us? I know what I want, but I am not too sure about what you want."

My glass drops out of my hands and tips over. "How can you possibly think that? It's all I think about. Every day, I listen to Annabelle talk about her glorious life with her perfect husband and their ideal house and all the fun coupley stuff they do on the weekends. Don't you think I want that life too?" I reach over my plate for a towel from near the sink so I can clean up my mess.

Brian takes the towel and wipes up the spill for me.

I drop back into my chair, rub my tears away, and shriek, "We have

47

been together all these years and still can't communicate effectively. I might not be alone in my misery, but you shouldn't be either. Instead of talking about it, we're fighting."

"Rachel, I want to be with you forever. I want to have a family with you. I want to propose to you right now. But do you want to know what's holding me back?"

My shoulders droop and I can barely speak. "Y-yes."

"For being a therapist, I don't understand how you can have no idea about yourself."

He pauses.

"I think you're missing something in your life that I can't fill for you."

My eyes crunch down in confusion. I wasn't expecting that. "Huh? You know I'm in my own thoughts all the time. All I do when I am not at work is to think about my life…almost to an unhealthy level."

Brian raises his eyebrows. "You are in your thoughts all the time. *And* I think you have this huge hole inside of you that you expect me to fill—or expect it to be filled when we're married. I can't complete you. You have to figure yourself out first."

How many times have I heard Annabelle say she tells her clients something similar? But I haven't connected the message for myself yet. "What…am I…missing, though?"

"I wish I could answer that question, but that isn't how it works. Until you can fill this empty space within yourself, I don't think we can move forward together. I am scared that this hole is starting to swallow you up." Brian stops and grabs my hand, pushing aside his bowl to rest his elbow on the counter. "You're not alone, but again, I can't do this for you."

I'm trying to process everything that's been said. It's like I'm drowning and can't find a way to the surface anymore. This is the worst Sunday dinner of my life.

*Chapter 6*

"So, tell me about the convo now! You've made me chase you all week," Maggie says.

"Sorry. It's not you. I just need time to think through things and try to figure them out for myself."

"Yeah, I know, I know. Miss do-it-all-on-your-own." She takes a bite of her peanut butter and jelly sandwich.

I unwrap mine from the wax paper. "How much detail do you want?"

"All of it! Don't make me beg."

We sit down on a bench. Spring is in full bloom and Central Park is full of people out for a Saturday morning walk. The fresh air and kindness of my bestie to drag me out of my apartment for an impromptu picnic and girls' day may be just what I need to feel some relief. I hope.

"This week feels like a blur. Ugh." I think back to try to remember what I've half obsessed over and half tried to block out of my mind. "Our practice conversation didn't prepare me as much as I would have liked."

"Oh no." She furrows her brow.

"Yeah, we couldn't predict that he would say he felt the same distance I have been feeling."

"What?"

"Yeah. We went through the work topic and that was no biggie.

49

He just needs to work, plain and simple. It isn't about me. But then he said how our lack of intimacy is not all his fault and, get this, that he's been worried about me."

I look at Maggie's face for a validating reaction to my shock, but it remains flat.

"Mags? Isn't that ridiculous?" I need her to be on my side. I need her to say she hasn't noticed any difference in me. Come on, Maggie, say it. Please!

"Well, I can't disagree with Brian." She looks down and takes a deep breath.

I remain silent.

She reaches over and lays her hand on my knee. "Look, I know you love your cozy nights in and don't need as much social time as me, but you've been even more reclusive than usual lately. Harrison gets you all to himself. I want some Rachel for me."

"That's what he basically said, minus the Harrison part." I slump in my seat. My sandwich isn't as appetizing anymore.

"We care about you. That's all. It's hard for me to see you in this 'rut,' as you call it."

"Brian said there's a hole in me that he can't fill. A hole! I'm defective once again."

How many times in my life have I felt abnormal? Oh, let me count the ways. This brings me to every memory of wanting to stand in a corner and escape the world when I was a kid, surrounded by cool, pretty, athletic people, while I was the nerd who read and kept to herself. It wasn't easy to talk to other people and make friends. I'm not outgoing and sure wasn't in my youth. Now my boyfriend thinks there's something wrong with me.

"You aren't broken, boo. But what do you think he means? Did he tell you more?"

"He said he wants to marry me, but that marriage won't fix what I may be missing. That he can't be my solution so we can't move forward with engagement yet. I know that, but didn't think…" I can't bring myself to finish the thought. It's like I'm in a cheesy rom com movie. Yeah sure, a guy will save me and we will be married happily ever after with all my problems disappearing into thin air. Old Rachel would have never thought that way. I have an urge to scream for what I've become but I push it down. I don't need people thinking someone is getting assaulted.

"And this week we've somehow been even more distant than before the *open communication*." I can't help but roll my eyes as I emphasize that phrase with sarcasm. "That's a new goal with us. Anyway, Brian heard my points and has said I look beautiful a few times this week, and I've tried to hug and kiss him more frequently, but it's our silence otherwise that bothers me. I've been so lonely. At least we aren't fighting, but a fight may be better than this lack of emotion. I've never felt so awkward in my life, and that says a lot. Even with both of our efforts, the metaphorical wall remains between us."

"Let's knock it down!" She punches and kicks the air.

"I don't know how. I thought couples feel closer after they have a deep discussion like we did, even if it was only one talk. But reality strikes again and works against my logic and professional training. I want to hide. Was all I ever learned in school a joke? Maybe I am not even a good therapist." Well, one thing I learned is true. Situations and feelings do get worse before they get better.

"Don't pick apart your competence as a therapist. You work with kids, not couples. And you know when situations are personal, we all have blinders on. We can't help ourselves sometimes. That's why I'm here. I want to sort this out with you." She starts eating her chips without missing a beat.

Somehow the immediate chomping causes us to laugh, cutting the tension. But my thoughts persist.

Should I tell her what I have really been thinking? Admitting it out loud makes it too much of a possibility. I can't tell her I'm worried

I'm on the verge of the "D" word. Rachel, you have no right to be depressed. You have your basic needs met, live in a dream location, have a successful therapy practice, and have a wonderful boyfriend. But even when Brian tried to cheer me up with talking about going to see *Titanic* in 3D soon, I faked an excited reaction. My true reaction felt blunted. That must mean something. I want to feel the passion about everything again, instead of this sense of dragging through my life.

I look Maggie straight in the eyes. "If I don't figure out how to feel more like my old self, will Brian leave me? Will we not be together anymore? Not live together? I can't comprehend that world. I—"

"I have to stop you." She pushes her palms toward me and swallows her food. "You are talking yourself into a spiral."

"I just expected him to propose any day now, you know, pre-*the* discussion. But instead, he is...what? Waiting and seeing what will happen? Analyzing how I will act day to day and seeing if I pass his imaginary test?"

"No, stop. For real. That's not like Brian and you know it."

"I know." I dip my head. "I'm all worked up."

"I gather that."

"My life feels like I'm stuck on an endless conveyor belt in an abandoned factory. When I'm alone at work, all I can think about is being at home. When I am at home, all I can think about is going to sleep. But when I try to go to sleep, all I can think about is waking up to everything being okay. Then it starts all over again the next day. I'm stuck."

"I wish I had the perfect answer to fix this for you, Rach." She looks into the sky and leans back. "Maybe we need to get together one of those lists you always talk about doing. You're such a list girl."

"A list of what, Mags?" My interest is piqued at the mention of the word "list."

"What makes you happy, what used to make you happy, and what you think makes others happy."

"That could be a start. I do like a list." I smile.

"Ooh, what about how your life would look if you were happy?" Her eyes widen.

"That's actually a really good idea. It's a quintessential therapy question."

"Well, there you go. Think on that."

"You know I couldn't stop thinking on that now even if I wanted to." I grin.

"Oh, I know." She laughs.

I'm lucky to have someone like her. Not everyone has a Maggie in their life, so thank God I do.

After we separate to go home, I start brainstorming for my happiness list on the walk. The first idea that comes to mind is a special person. Of course, it's my grandpa.

I wish he were around to talk to me now more than ever. He would know exactly how to help because he always understood me. I barely had to speak about a problem for him to know what to tell me. He wouldn't feel like I am damaged, broken in half and incomplete, like I feel about myself. What I need is a hug from him and to feel that comfort and assurance that everything will work out well. I close my eyes a second and imagine how it would feel right now.

Think about something else. I miss him too much to continue down this road, but the universe is working against me. I walk past a street performer playing guitar and am sent right back to when I listened to Grandpa play his guitar. My chest feels heavy, and I lean on a streetlight. I crave his singing and playing and could use it now more than ever.

The old Italian songs he knew so well were always a comfort to hear. I couldn't understand most of the words, but I got the point of them through their expressive tone. That is what music does; it's a universal language. All the songs were about love, from what he told me. He translated some of the songs' lyrics at times and it always came down to love, family, and relationships. I sometimes heard him singing them to my grandma, even after her death.

I close my eyes again and smile. I should listen to our song tonight, "Mambo Italiano" by Dean Martin. It's an Italian American one we always danced to when it was on his favorite radio station. Maybe remembering our silliness can break the suffocating silence at home as well.

I walk into the apartment, ready to make my list.

"Hey. You were gone for a while. I was starting to get worried."

Brian sets his book on the armrest of the couch as I take my shoes off near the door.

"Oh, well here I am." I give him jazz hands and giggle.

He smiles. "And I'm glad. Do you want to watch a movie?"

I can make my list tomorrow, I guess. What's one more day? Time with him is important, especially right now.

"Sure. Do you have one in mind?" I sit next to him.

"Not really. You pick." He hands me the remote and puts his feet on the coffee table.

I scan through the channels and land on one of my favorite movies. "What about this one?"

"I'm not really into chick flicks, but if you want to watch, go ahead." Brian shrugs.

Ten minutes pass and Brian gets up and disappears into our bedroom with his book and without a word.

So much for watching a movie together. I could have made my list. Instead, I remain in place and pull my feet underneath me on the couch, wrapping myself in my blanket as I start to rub it.

Harrison climbs onto my lap and I stroke his soft, long fur until he falls asleep, almost immediately. The fortune of being a cat.

A few minutes before the movie ends, Brian returns. He picks up my feet, sits down, and sets them on his lap.

What is happening? I squint my eyes while I stare at him, but he doesn't see it.

Instead, I say, "I'm glad you are back. You missed all the fun, though."

"I think I've seen this one enough." He rolls his eyes.

"Oh, sorry. You should have said something. I would have changed it to another movie."

"Don't worry. I'm into my book anyway. What did you and Maggie do today?" His fingers glide over my feet in a gentle massage.

"She's such a sweetie. We went to Central Park, had a picnic lunch, and talked a lot, then stopped for ice cream on the way home. I really needed that."

He chuckles. "Ice cream is a cure for everything."

"You got that right. She didn't tell me much about Ray, but I guess things are going well. If she's not complaining, it's all good, right?" I smile.

When the movie ends, Brian slides next to me and kisses me, sending warmth throughout my body. Time seems to stop with his soft lips on mine, making me forget how long it's been since the last kiss like this.

"I love you, Rachel."

My heart jumps. The worry from me not being home, the massage, the kiss, and now this statement. I stare into his eyes and say, "I love you too, Brian."

He turns off the TV, grabs my hand, and leads me to our bedroom.

More unexpected time together begins.

Maybe due to the combination of the exhausting conversation with Maggie and how my night is shaping up, I doubt I'll have problems falling asleep tonight.

# Chapter 7

L ist time is here. Brian's visiting his dad for this Sunday afternoon and I have the place to myself. Come on, Rachel. You can do this. The idea of making a list is usually energizing, but the theme of this list feels like I need to climb a mountain.

As I sit at my tiny table where my laptop lives while not on the coffee table, I stare at the blank screen. I feel like I am in an episode of *Sex and the City* and I am Carrie, needing to write but having no idea what to type. There isn't a writer for the Rachel show who can swoop in and provide my dialogue and future life events. The white page remains in front of me, taunting me with its blinking cursor.

My fingers finally type *Things in my life that make me happy*. I put a bullet point below the title. So far, I can only think of two topics that never fail me, Harrison and researching the *Titanic*. I love getting sucked into the culture of the dissipating Edwardian era and all of the lessons people learned from human arrogance and poor planning. I can get lost in another time period and retreat from reality. Could I be any more pathetic that these are my top joy points? At least there's Harrison, a living being.

I know there are people in my life who bring me happiness, of course, but can I put them on this list? People equal the possibility of negative feelings and interactions. The risk of pain. I do feel pleasure with my support system, but they aren't bliss twenty-four seven. Not that I would expect that. It's impossible. So, can I add them on my list? Nothing and no one are ideal. If that were the case, Grandpa would still be alive. He would have been my number one point on this list.

It's like there's a battle going on between my head and my heart. My head knows I have a pretty good life and many aspects that should lead to delight, but questions why I feel empty. My heart knows the real answer. It just hasn't let my head know the truth yet.

After about thirty minutes of trying to fill out this page, I remember one of Maggie's last suggestions. She said to write about what I thought others feel happy about in their lives. Let's see, before I type it out. I daze out the window at the passing clouds.

Annabelle is happy because of her loving husband, her magnificent house, her job, and all their travel. I'm sure it takes more than that for her positive demeanor. Well, she is an easy-going, fly-by-the-seat-of-her-pants type of woman so maybe that freedom brings her glee. I can rule this out for myself. Next.

Maggie seems happy when she is flirting with guys or making an influential move at work. She loves fast food and bar food (the greasier the better), late nights, sexy and tight clothes, and getting me into uncomfortable situations which make her laugh. I giggle. Oh, that Mags.

Brian is happy when he is with his friends, reading, when he is successful at work, and when he is with me...or he used to be. I don't even know anymore. I think it's still true. I hope.

I look back at my computer screen and type what came to me for my loved ones. It is so much easier to write about other people. I try to push myself to continue with focusing on me, but I can't think of anything else to add to my two points. Maybe I need a break.

I open up my email. There isn't too much going on since I last checked, but something on the side of the page catches my attention. One of those sponsored advertisements pops up about searching for ancestors. Ooh, it's free for thirty days. Hmm, that sounds like it could be interesting. I never thought about my family history beyond the few bits of information I overheard or learned through the grapevine. What do I have to lose at this point? Plus, it would give me a break from the depressing manifesto of others' happiness when compared to mine. I click the ad.

When I type in the first person who comes to mind, my grandpa of course, and click search, my mouth drops open. So many Salvatore Granzas populate! This is wild. Where will I begin? I guess I have to start clicking on each person to see if the entry is my Salvatore's information.

But wait, what year was he even born? I search for the calculator in Google and figure out he must have been born in 1902 from knowing his age and the year when he died. Yeah, I have no math skills. You got me.

When did he arrive in the United States with his dad and Great-Uncle Vince? Why didn't his mom and sister come with him? I remember him exchanging letters in Italian with them and later with his half-sister, so I know they still lived in Italy. I always wanted to know what they said in those letters, but he wouldn't tell me. My heart feels like it's sinking into my stomach. He was my hero and yet I lack so much basic information about him. I don't even know when he became a US citizen. That's life-changing information I should know. My head falls into the palm of my hand.

"Vaffanculo!" Swearing in Italian always helps a situation.

What kind of a granddaughter am I? I'm a sham of a granddaughter, that's what. It can't be normal that I don't know any useful information about my idol besides his birthday year, which I had to figure out.

Maybe I need to call my parents to ask some questions before I try to go further on my own. My dad should know information about Grandpa's life, I hope. But that call will have to wait because I can't tear myself away from this site. Even just exploring what it offers piques my attention. There's a way to build a family tree, contact pages for people who have connected through the site, so many fascinating documents, and even pictures. There is some DNA section as well where they'll match you to family members who have already taken the test. Dare I say, this is fun? Yeah, that's right, fun. No, more like it's amazing.

Before I realize, hours have flown by and Brian's walking through the door.

"Hi, Rachel." He stares at me and slowly approaches. "What are you doing? You look like you've seen a ghost."

I make sure to get up, blink a few times, and give him a tight hug. "You won't believe what I've done all afternoon."

"I'd love to hear about it over dinner. Come on, let's get you out of here." He extends his hand for me to accept.

I reach out and give a squeeze. "It would probably do me good to leave this table I've been glued to, right?"

"Right. Now, where do you want to go? Obviously Italian since it's Sunday?"

"Obviously."

I take a huge bite of crusty white bread topped with a gob of butter. I didn't feel hungry until we had food in front of us, but now I can't wait to get my mountain of fettuccine.

"You can sure put that bread away. Where does it go?" He looks underneath the tablecloth.

I shrug and keep swallowing. "How was your dad?"

"He's good. He's remodeling the basement, so I helped him move furniture upstairs."

"You're a good son." I bite off another chunk.

"Aw-shucks." He swings his arm in jest. "Thanks." He smiles and finally butters a piece of bread for himself. "Tell me about this afternoon. Sorry I had to take that call on the walk over here."

"It's fine. Well, I stumbled upon an ancestry database and started researching about my grandpa."

His eyes enlarge. "Really? That sounds like something you would like."

"I guess you can say that because I kind of got lost in there with strangers' files. I can only imagine when I find my grandpa's information. There were US censuses, naturalization papers, phone book pages—"

"What do you mean when you find your grandpa's information? Isn't that why you were on there?"

"Yes, but that's the problem. I'm realizing I know few concrete facts about his life. If they had a way to search his favorite food, music, or phrases, I'd be golden. Wait, I guess I already know those loves though. Anyway, he was extremely secretive about his life before his time in the United States. None of my family knew the reason, but it was a given norm. Nobody ever questioned it."

"That's sad none of you know about that part of him. I know how much he meant to you."

"Yeah. It is sad. Why was I so stupid to not ask him about his youth? Like, why did his dad choose Philly to settle in? How does that happen?"

"Because no teenager thinks of asking these questions. Don't be so hard on yourself."

"I guess. Ugh. Another mystery I thought about is why the women family members never joined the men here in the United States. Grandpa, his brother, and dad never saw them again. It's heart-breaking."

Brian opens his mouth to speak but closes it.

"It's hard to find words." My eyes droop.

"It is. I think that it happened more than not. The men in my family came to the US to find work and get a place to live. Then, the women came. That's what the family lore is, anyway. It was typical for that time period and maybe even now in some families."

"I can't imagine people being split from loved ones. He never even met his younger sister, but he talked about her just as much as the older sister he knew when living in Italy."

A rush of warmth shoots through my body and feels like it wakes up my brain. My heart beats faster as I feel a spark of the old Rachel's passion in something. Nah, it's more than ever before. This may be Rachel 3.0. The idea of focusing on my grandpa and solving old family mysteries at the same time needs to happen. It's more than a want, it's a need. Oh yes, I need to know those answers and need to know them asap.

"How will you find out anything if you don't have facts to enter on the website?"

"I have his birthday so, that's something. I'm going to see if my dad knows more. I can't stop my brain from working overtime with all the unanswered questions I have. I think I may have another 'addiction' forming. Are you ready?"

"Will I ever be?"

"No, but I'll tell you anyway. I may have FHOD—Family History Obsessive Disorder—as well as TOD."

He rolls his eyes and laughs.

"Hey, the TOD doesn't just disappear since FHOD joined the party."

"I am so happy to see you animated about something. I think this could be really good for you, Rachel."

"Thanks. It's remarkable to even be on the path to gaining more facts about my family. How did I never think to research my history? There is a potential to find out all about our family secrets just by putting in a little research time. So worth it."

As we lay in bed to go to sleep tonight, Brian leans over to kiss me on the cheek. I turn my head and catch his lips. He smiles, closes his eyes, and hits the pillow.

I see him holding his smile, which spreads to me grinning.

I close my eyes and let my thoughts drift. It must be the magic of pasta Sunday that sent me, and us, on this new course. I know there's a long way to go, but after crying spells in my office this week, a new low, the only way I can go is up. Please, God.

It dawns on me that this little project may be something to help me with my black hole of emptiness. How could finding out more about my grandpa be anything but fun?

*Chapter 8*

"Hey, Mom." I drop onto the couch and press the speakerphone button.

"Hi, honey. You are calling on a Monday night. What's wrong?"

Brian smiles and starts washing the dishes from dinner.

"Nothing. I'm doing okay, I guess. I was just wondering if we could come visit soon."

"You don't sound good. Is everything really okay?"

"Yes and no. It's been a while since we've been out there, and I want to talk to you both about our family's history. I've started researching Grandpa but keep hitting a brick wall. I want to know more about him and Great-Uncle Vince, and their dad. The Granza family in general." Messing around on the site all day long between clients didn't get me one step further than yesterday. How is it this hard?

"Oh. You would leave *the city* for a little while? I may be speechless."

"Mo-om!" I roll my eyes, which is basically my autopilot move nowadays when I speak to her.

"Your dad and I would be happy to share what we can about Grandpa. That sounds like a nice idea, honey."

Mom doesn't sound nearly as thrilled with this as I feel she should be. In fact, she sounds outright bored with the idea.

"Helloooo? Mom, this is an *awesome* idea. I'm glad you want to help, but why aren't you excited?"

"Oh, I am, Rachel." It's never good when she says my name. It usually means my whiny teenage voice has crept out and aggravated her. "I just don't want you to get your hopes up. Grandpa kept his past private for a reason. I don't want you to dig up anything that he wanted to keep buried."

Who would discourage their child from researching their family history? Something is strange here.

"Do you know something?"

"No. But if I did, it wouldn't be my place to share it."

I take a deep breath and exhale slowly, gritting my teeth. "Um, okay. I'm interested in Grandpa's life. He was my world and I think finding out about his past could help me with my future."

"I know, I know. Well, just come out this Sunday and we'll go from there. I'll ask Dylan to come over for dinner. Maybe we can have cavatelli, bread from Mario's, and your favorite dessert."

"Cannoli?" My mouth waters and I lick my lips. The rest of the rigamarole left my brain for a second.

"Of course. Okay, well, see you then. Remember to email me with the time your train comes in and I will ask Daddy to go and pick you guys up."

"Okay, I will see if I can switch my clients around on Monday so we can stay the night. I'd rather do that than come home so late."

"Whatever you would like."

"Love you. Thanks, Mom."

"Sure. Love you too."

I hit end on the screen and wonder why she isn't as enthusiastic as I am. What a weird conversation with her. Maybe she doesn't quite realize how much I need this little project. And I do need this. Not just want this.

I'll have to try to force myself to relax tonight so I can forget about her reaction. I could go back to my research but would just end up at the same impasse, finding all the Granzas who aren't part of my family. That's a waste of time. I'll get the information I need this weekend and will know more about Grandpa then. A week more won't kill me.

Brian walks over and sits down next to me. "You don't seem very happy that they're willing to talk about your family."

"I am, but you heard Mom. She clearly isn't interested and is just placating me." I pull Brian's arm around me.

"I'll go with you…if I'm invited."

"Of course you are invited. But I will be trying to stay into Monday. Can you miss work?"

"Maybe I can go in late. I can figure it out. I can't miss Sunday dinner at the Granzas."

"Sounds good to me. Thanks." I smile as he grabs the remote off the cushion.

"What should we watch tonight? Something *Titanic* related again?" He smiles.

I shake my head. "You can pick."

I slide my blanket over me and try to concentrate on anything but my mom.

# *Chapter 9*

Sunday morning finally arrives. How am I this elated to *leave* the city and go to Philly? People try to *come* to the city. Changes are happening all around. But will they remain?

"We're on our way, Rach." Brian taps my lap and exaggerates a smile.

"Yes, finally! This week dragged on and on. Ugh." I need this train to get to Philly fast. Like, in warp speed. That isn't asking too much, to expand the limits of space and time.

I slouch into my broken-down seat and try to get comfortable for the hour and a half ride. Brian's eyes are closed, his usual move. How can he sleep anywhere? It must be nice to be that relaxed.

Looking around the train car, I see that everyone seems peaceful though. Some people are already listening to music through their earbuds, reading newspapers and books, and busting into their snacks. Meanwhile, I can't stop shaking my leg. The energy has to escape somewhere, I guess.

I pull my legs up on my seat to sit cross legged and force myself to focus on my '90s pop playlist. Prince will help me out today. I discreetly mouth the words to "Diamonds and Pearls." Good thing I'm sitting by the window because Brian obstructs passengers from seeing me. But this doesn't last long anyway.

My mind drifts to the food I hope that will be at my parents' house. Since they have frequented their local Italian deli since I was a baby, I know exactly how the pepperoni and provolone will taste on their butter crackers; like perfection. I could taste them in my imagination.

Grandpa used to bring me a plate filled with stacks of the combination, just for us to share. His slippers dragged on the floor as he called out for me and pretended to hide the plate from the others. I can still hear the sliding sound and feel the childish laughter.

How I wish he would be there today when we arrive. I'd watch him, Grandma, and my dad eat the hot peppers, Grandpa's name for jalapeños, while they sniffled and had watery eyes. Mom and I always laughed at the absurdity of their actions because who wants a burning mouth? I guess I do now that I partake as well.

Dad or my grandparents always said something to the effect of "That's a good pepper," with flammable mouths mumbling barely audible sounds. Next, they'd take turns blowing their noses. Then another person would chime in with, "Yeah, but could be hotter." And this was all said in seriousness.

I laugh and notice Brian looking at me from my peripheral vision. "All okay?"

"Yeah, sorry. I didn't mean to wake you up." I look past him to see if I was loud enough that other people also noticed. Thank God, it doesn't seem so.

"I was just resting my eyes."

I grab his arm and squeeze. "Rest your eyes some more." That's his code phrase for sleeping that he doesn't know I've decoded.

After a few minutes the train comes to a stop at a station. As I click play to resume my music and glance outside until we move again, my body freezes. I don't hear any music playing. I only see the slender man with straight brown hair and dark skin who looks just like Dylan from the back. My brother can't be here. Turn around, Mister, turn around! No!

I get as close to the glass as possible without touching the dirty thing and try to will the man to turn around. I know I haven't seen

Dylan in a long time, but I would still recognize my own flesh and blood, right? Even if I wish I could erase him from my mind. I know that's harsh, but it's true.

Ooh, that would be just like him to show up on my train unannounced. He loves to hassle me. Ever since we were kids, he's had it out for me. I shake my head to try to stop the memories.

The man outside my window finally turns around and peace is restored in my body. I feel my heart rate slowing back to normal and I can breathe deeply again. But I haven't thought about my mom's mention of inviting Dylan to dinner today until now. Damn it! How did I gloss over that from our call? Old habits die hard, and blocking him out is one of them. I have too many other things on my mind to clutter it with someone who dislikes me.

Talk about a mood changer. Think about something else, anything else. Okay, how about the information I'll get from Dad. He must know everything I need to enter in my searches. I bite my lip. Will I have all the answers I desire? Will I have none? Stop with the black or white thinking, Rachel! Gray thoughts, gray thoughts, gray, gray, gray. Think of possibilities.

My attention goes back to my music. Come on, George Michael. Come to my rescue and distract me.

I thought this week was slow, but this ride may have it beat. Please step on it, Conductor.

We step out of 30th Street Station and see my dad waiting near his car, a big grin on his face. I love seeing that smile. It always makes me feel safe.

"Hello, strangers." Dad opens his arms and wraps me in a giant bear hug. His familiar cologne graces my nostrils with nostalgia. He turns toward Brian and repeats the action. Italian and Italian American men don't seem to care about restrictive American social norms for showing affection to other men.

American Brian, on the other hand, looks like he's in excruciating emotional and physical pain with this interaction. His stiff reciprocated hugs to my dad provide a hilarious comical viewing experience. Even though he has been subjected to the Granzas' affection for a long time, he's clearly still not used to it.

"You two ready to go?" Dad opens the trunk.

We drop our bags inside and climb into the car.

The short drive to my parents' house is racked with unpleasant memories. I always dislike being in my old neighborhood. It's where all the self-doubt, feeling different than everyone else, and daily overwhelming desire of bursting into tears started, long ago. Not much has changed over the years—for me or the neighborhood.

The split-level houses look the same as they did a decade ago, most with dingy, old red brick or deteriorating siding. At least the spring flowers add a pop of color that is otherwise lacking.

As we turn the corner and my childhood home comes into view, my anxiety skyrockets and I start counting backwards from ten to gain calmness. Ten, nine—argh! Oh, stop, it Rachel. Don't live in the memories of the past. Eight, seven—well, at least when they are negative—six, five…

I reach number one as we get to our driveway. Nothing looks new on the outside of my old home. I'd wage a bet that few changes have occurred inside as well. My parents pride themselves on their lack of remodeling unless absolutely necessary. Must be a neighborhood pact.

I open the door from the garage and step inside the familiar house, the smell of my mom's cooking smacking me in the face. That can ease anyone's anxiety and to this Italian girl, there is nothing better than the smell of garlic. I recognize the old Italian tunes floating through the house with the scent. The mandolins, accordions, and smooth voices fill the air.

"Well, if it isn't the big city people," Mom quips as she pulls me in for a hug. Just like that, she has the ability to make me feel irritated and loved all at the same time. Are all mother-daughter relationships like this or is it just us?

In the small kitchen, she stands at the stove, her simmering pasta sauce behind her. "Water, tea, soda…what you want?" Mom asks in her faux, though accurate, Italian American accent. She says that being married to my dad for over thirty-five years gives her that privilege. And she lives in Philly, which is populated with many Italians. I guess the dialect was easy to pick up with those factors in play.

I take a slice of pepperoni from the platter on the table. Even though there are countless Italian delis and bakeries in the city, the food is never the same as it is at home. It's the taste of home.

She wipes her hands on her full-length red apron. "You know what they say. You can take the girl out of Philly, but you can't take Philly out of the girl. I'm glad you're eating."

Upon entering the Granza house, one has no choice but to saddle up and eat… All. Day. Long. For as long as I can remember, there's been a huge sign in the kitchen that says "Mangia" in the same bright green, white, and red colors as the Italian flag. The word should be on the country's flag for how much we value it. Eating is an experience and not just a basic need.

"I'll leave you two to chat in the kitchen with Mom." Dad grabs a handful of appetizers before he escapes to the living room.

Brian gives me a deer-in-headlights look as he chooses to follow my dad. He's told me several times that he's always torn between wanting to bond with him and being too scared by the thought. Maybe he's afraid he'll be crushed in another hug.

When the TV goes on, the music stops. Sportscasters' voices replace the crooners from the 1940s and '50s.

Not even a minute later my dad yells to my mom. "Hun, can you bring me the snacks?" This is one dynamic that has always bothered me about my parents—their 1950s roles. Music from the '50s, good.

This, bad. My mom goes right along and serves my dad, and he enjoys every second of it. I think he expects it too. They never realized this wasn't a good example to set for me when I was a child.

I bite my tongue and keep my thoughts to myself though. Whenever I made sarcastic remarks about this behavior as a kid, I always got the same response, so I gave up a long time ago and internalize my frustration instead. I know it's not the kind of relationship I want—nor the one Brian and I have.

I peek in the living room to check on Brian and Dad. At least Brian looks comfortable. When there is something to take over his stress of thinking up topics of conversation with Dad, like the TV that's saving him right now, he does well. He sits on the opposite end of the couch from my dad, with closed body language and staring at the TV. His legs are flat on the ground and his hands are folded in his lap as if he is praying. Maybe he is.

Dad spreads out, moves his body position to having one leg on the old rectangular dark wooden coffee table and one on the ottoman, remote in hand, with a smile on his face. Does he realize how Brian feels? I bet not a chance. He never has a smile when someone else is uncomfortable. That is not like my dad at all. He wants everyone to feel at home.

I drop into a kitchen chair at my grandparents' old white and red Formica table my parents inherited and take a few deep breaths, exhaling slowly through pursed lips, to gain composure before I jump into my starter question.

"So, Mom, when do you think we can all talk about the details I need about Grandpa's life?"

"There's plenty of time for that later."

"Why can't we talk right now? Nobody is doing anything important," I nudge.

"I am just about to start the soup for dinner. Want to chop some veggies for me?"

Not really, but if it helps move things along, why not? I've already waited this long, what's another hour or two?

Before I can take a step, I'm blindsided. "Hey, little sis." Dylan picks me up, throws me over his shoulder, and runs a few laps around the kitchen table, knocking chairs astray.

"Stop! Stop! I'm gonna barf." I pray all the good food I've been eating doesn't pay me a repeat visit I'd never forget.

"What is your problem? You are no fun." He drops me onto the floor and stomps away, pushing chairs out of his path and leaving as quick as he came.

"Hey, Mom." I groan. "Why must he always make such an entrance? It's just so embarrassing."

"It's the way he shows his love for his little sister. You should go and talk to him while I get the last things ready for dinner."

"What would Dylan and I ever have to talk about?"

"Well, he is a history teacher. Maybe he can help you find some of the info you're looking for?"

"I never thought about that. I can't believe the state allows him to teach kids." I look down and mumble. "Maybe he doesn't act like a stunad there."

"Don't call your brother an idiot."

Oops, she heard me.

"Now, go, go. I'll handle the chopping." She waves me along as she straightens the chairs.

Entering the family room, I notice that Brian looks positively bored out of his mind by now. His eyes are glazed over and he's leaning on the arm of the couch with his head on the palm of his hand. He only cares about when the Phillies play, so that must be why.

Dad is catching Dylan up on what happened in the game before he arrived.

To ease Brian's discomfort and provide a little moral support, I sit on his lap. Listening to the details of baseball, which I don't care about, is fun for all of three seconds.

"So, Dylan...um...how's your class?" Dylan teaches eleventh grade and I never have any idea what to talk about with him so I'm thankful for the suggestion from my mom.

"It's cool. Getting to the end of the year. Same old." He keeps his eyes on the TV.

"Okay, good. Well, let me ask you something, since your specialty is history."

He looks my way. "Huh?"

"Did you hear me?"

"No. I try not to." He smirks.

"Yeah, same here. *Anyway*, do you know anything about ancestry research?"

"Like what? Using Google?"

"Please be serious for a second. No, like finding old documents and information, when you have very little to enter."

"Not really. But ask me about World War II. The laws that came as a result of it is on Monday's test and it's also my favorite war."

Of course he loves war. He creates a battle every time I see him.

"All right." I don't know why I try. He can barely tear his glance away from the game. It's more important than his sister.

How I wish Grandpa and I could do our secret handshake in front of him right now. That always angered Dylan. I know it's horrible of me to want to aggravate him, but look what happens when I try to have a real conversation. Whenever he'd see us go through the ridiculous steps of our shake, he'd practically push me aside to get Grandpa's attention and try to make him do it with him. Grandpa never conceded. That was *our* thing.

Be the bigger person, Rachel. Well, that isn't hard. I sigh.

"Dinner is ready!" Mom's voice echoes through the house.

Four voices respond in sync. "Be there in a minute!"

The years may have flown by, but some things never change. Our loud Italian voices being one of those things. Stereotypical? Yes. Realistic? Yup.

Granza Sunday dinner is officially commencing, a top pride of anyone in my culture. The traditional Sunday dinner in an Italian house consists of what a typical American family would consume on a big holiday, so the thought alone makes my stomach rumble. The meal is enormous, and we make no apologies about it.

Our first course is always Grandma's soup. Her recipe is not quite the same as when Mom makes it, but it is still tastes better than the concoction I would make. The rib meat, carrots, celery, onion, and garlic blend to a level of perfection, especially with hand grated Romano cheese on top. Ooh, it's time. I take a large sniff before eating my first spoonful.

All of us enjoy a tiny glass of red wine tonight, as is typical for even kids during Sunday dinner in Italian households. Sometimes children as young as eleven drink alongside their family, a tradition that started when the water quality in Italy wasn't extremely safe. Adding alcohol to water killed the bacteria, so it was a flawless solution. Immigrants kept the practice of allowing the youth to sip wine moving forward and I'm glad. Once Dylan and I were old enough, we had our own shot glass sized table wine to consume. When my friends would join us for dinner, their comments were surprising to me and brought it to my attention that my family had a strange custom. Add it to my personal list of being abnormal.

I take a bite of heaven. By this I mean hard, crusty white bread with real butter. I could eat the whole loaf by myself. Sometimes Grandpa and I would, in fact, eat the whole loaf by days end. How have I not come for dinner in such a long time?

The main course is—obviously—always some type of pasta. Tonight, a glorious cavatelli pasta, my favorite, sits on the table in front of me. I always struggle with deciding whether to have it with the most amazing sauce my mom makes or plain with butter and that

Romano cheese. Yes, we put it on everything. This time, I can't pass up the sauce, or as Grandma called it "gravy."

In the typical European way, we eat salad after the main dish. Marinated chickpeas in extra virgin olive oil, vinegar, salt, pepper, and oregano round out the Sunday dinner as the dressing and a topping. It's perfection.

Between bites, the dinner conversation consists of generic topics—weather, friends, jobs, etc. My dad is a quiet man, just like my grandpa was, but at the dinner table, he talks more than in any other setting. Family dinners were always meant for quality time, and he makes sure this value is carried on with us.

I look around the table and the impact of how much I miss our family dinners hits me. I need to make sure Brian and I eat together more often—at our counter not on the couch—so we can have this meaningful time. We already don't talk that much, so we don't need the TV putting more distance between us.

As dinner continues, I feel it's actually going okay. I could almost push aside the fire inside of me to launch into my quest for our family history with the amazing food we are experiencing. Almost.

"Hey, guys?" I ask. "Can you help me clean up? I've been waiting for a cannoli since Mom mentioned them the other day."

Dylan groans as Brian stands and gathers plates without missing a beat.

I think how Grandpa was our family's official dish dryer. Grandma handed him the newly washed dishes, he dried them, and eventually put them away. I'll embody that ritual tonight in his honor. Maybe that will be my new role when I visit for dinner.

Before starting in my new job, I grab the cannoli and set them on the table, then grab the cups for the cappuccino. There can't be a better combination in the world. The sugars in both must complement each other to form one enchanting experience—and I need all the magic I can get.

*Chapter 10*

**"S**o, what do you want to know?" Dad sits in the chair next to me at the table, sipping on the rest of his cappuccino.

"Everything you know." My heart races. Oh, please don't faint, Rachel.

He chuckles. "Well, your grandpa came to the United States with his dad and brother when he was fourteen years old. Uncle Vince was a few years older…maybe two years? They came to Philly after entering through New York, then started their tailoring business. That was the family business in Genoa, but they wanted to start a new life in America, as most Italians did then. They thought they could have more success in this country. Your grandpa's dad, my grandpa, died when your grandpa was a teen, but I don't know how young he was at the time. As far as I know, they had no family here yet so most of their time was spent at the shop. They learned English quickly and were able to grow their business. I'm not sure why, but your great-grandpa left his wife and daughter in Italy. Your grandpa never wanted to talk about it…or much about their journey in general." His mouth curls in his pause.

I jump in. "Okay. I calculated Grandpa was born in 1902. Is that right? What was his dad's name? Why did they come to Philly and not stay in New York if they didn't have family here?"

"Whoa, Nelly, slow down there. I think your grandpa was born in 1902, yes. So, he came to the US around…1916 then." He looks up in thought. "Age fourteen, born in 1902. Yes, that's right. That would

76

probably mean Uncle Vince was born in 1900. Probably."

"Thanks, Dad. This helps. Oh, what was Grandpa's dad's name?"

"Gino. Gino Granza." A slight smile appears on his face. "What a great name."

"Are you kidding with me? That's your name!" I tap his shoulder.

"I am not joking. That really was his name. I was named after him."

"I can't believe I never knew that. What a great bit of info."

Mom had conveniently escaped the kitchen at the beginning of our conversation but is now back at the sink. "Mom, I never knew Dad was named after Great-Grandpa."

"Oh, yes, dear." Could she sound any less enthused?

"Okay…" The sarcastic teenage voice sneaks out again and she notices.

"I'm sorry, Rachel. I just don't feel it's right to dig up the past," Mom says.

I feel immediate anger ready to burst out of me. "Wait, what? Why would you say that?" I scream, my voice loud and shaky. I didn't realize how much anger I held over her apathy on the topic.

She looks shocked at my differing emotions. "Calm down, honey."

"Stop calling me honey and dear! I am not your honey and dear right now. How could you be so disrespectful to our family? You don't even want their names mentioned!" I shout, tears streaming down my face.

Brian and Dylan run into the kitchen.

"Everyone just wait a second now," Dad adds. "People have a right to their opinions, Rachel. Don't talk to your mother like that. Charlotte, explain to our daughter why you feel this way."

"Yes, let me hear the reasoning behind your insanity, Mom." I wipe tears from my face, but more replace them.

"Rachel, don't go using your psychobabble in this house. I just feel that since Grandpa never wanted to talk about them coming to America, why should we want to? He was so proud to be an American.

He didn't like to bring up the past and if anyone else brought it up, he looked so sad. I never wanted to hurt him. He would be displeased to know you're sticking your nose where it doesn't belong."

"My nose should be exactly where it is!"

"Yeah, on your ugly face."

My dad points to the hallway. "Dylan, leave."

And he does, miraculously.

I take a second to mindfully breathe in and out before I answer. Say it calmly, Rachel, calmly. "I think Grandpa would be honored that I want to know more about him and our family. I know he would be on my side, as he always was with me. Mom, I am sorry you feel this way, but I'm going to continue my research. There has to be more to this story. Something bizarre must have happened for his mom and sister never to have come to the US. I am going to get to the bottom of it...for me and for Grandpa."

She shrugs and turns away. "I can't stop you. Just be careful."

I lower my eyebrows. "What do you mean by that? Be *careful?*" So much for staying calm.

"God is watching. And so is Grandpa."

"OH. MY. GOD!" I can't contain myself.

Mom throws the sponge in the sink and leaves the room.

Dad and I stare at each other, mirroring puzzled looks.

Brian is speechless and his body's turned to the side, looking like he wants to head home now to avoid another awkward Granza family moment. This isn't the first argument he witnessed between my mom and me, but it could be one of the loudest. He just wants everyone to get along, he's said in the past.

"I don't understand why she can't be happy for me." I fall into the chair and grab another cannoli.

Dad places his hand on my arm. "Sometimes your mom has... different thoughts, but she does mean well. She's just trying to honor your grandpa and keep you from going down a dead-end road. I think it would be fantastic to find out more about our family and I think that my dad would want you to do whatever you feel you need to do."

Knowing Dad thinks Grandpa would be okay with my research, a sense of tranquility washes over me. If he didn't want to talk about his past when he was alive, that was his choice, but now it is my time to find out the real story.

"Wait, what do you mean about a 'dead-end road'?"

"Researching family history is hard work." He shakes his head. "I don't know if there's even a mystery to solve, but if so, don't you think that it will be extremely difficult to find out the facts?"

"I am ready for that possibility." I nod once and take a bite of cannoli.

"That's true. Nothing will stop you when you get interested in something," Dad reassures.

Brian kisses me on the cheek and leaves the room again, still refraining from adding to the conversation.

"So, Dad, how old was I when Great-Uncle Vince died? I remember him waving outside of a home, wearing some sort of blue outfit. That's my only real memory of him."

Dad nods. "Your mom always says she can't believe you remember that. You were about three years old. We were leaving his nursing home."

"That means he died in 1983, or around that year."

"Yeah, I guess that's right. Too bad you didn't get a chance to know him. He was my favorite uncle. He was the greatest."

"He sounded as sweet as Grandpa. They must have been best friends."

"Definitely." He pauses and looks me straight in the eyes. "Your grandpa was such a strong man. He came to this country as a poor boy and to help build a successful family business, not even knowing the language. And look where we are now. You went to college and live in New York City. You always made him proud. What a long way we came from the old country where business was tough, not like the opportunity of having an American business."

I reflect on his words for a moment. "I wish he could have seen my success with school and my career though."

My dad grabs my shoulder and gives it a gentle squeeze. "He does."

"Is there *anything* else you can tell me?" I know I sound desperate, but I am.

"I don't know why they chose to live in Philly. That's one mystery." He looks up in thought. "You already know Grandpa and his sister wrote to each other for the rest of their lives. They wrote in Italian, so I never knew what the letters said. He wrote to his half-sister too. Sometimes they would talk on the phone. Now that I think about it, I don't know either of their names. That never occurred to me."

Both of us remain silent a moment.

"Oh, one more thing. I remember it being important to your grandpa that he came from northern Italy."

"Huh?"

"Yeah, he would always say 'northern Italy' when anyone asked where we were from originally. It was never 'I'm from Italy.' It was 'I'm from northern Italy.' I never really understood why."

"That's strange, but okay. Yeah, I think I remember that too. Hmm. Thanks, Dad. At least I have something else to work with now."

"Let me know what you find out. Don't worry about your mom. She'll come around."

"Brian, I've got the bed in the basement ready for you."

He responds from next to me on the couch. "Thanks, Mrs. Granza."

Dad, him, and I caught a re-run of *I Love Lucy*, a favorite classic we have in common. Thankfully, Dylan went home earlier so we watched in peace. Ahh.

"Goodnight, Mr. Granza," Brian says before we part ways for the night. Since we're not married, we have to sleep in separate rooms—a Granza house rule.

I take my time getting ready for bed in my old room. All the information Dad shared is making my head spin, and I find myself having a lot to think about from the evening. Laying in my teenage bed, complete with the cranberry and forest green accessories that threw up all over my room in the late '90s, my mind is flooded with thoughts of my early years.

My bed faces my childhood closet, so I stare at some of my long-forgotten clothes. There are dresses from weddings I was obligated to be in—the brides always lie, they are not dresses I can wear again—to everyday clothes to other formal clothes. Man, I used to wear some ugly stuff in the '80s. There are colors I would never wear now. Bright red? Orange? Even yellow. What was I thinking?

The outfits that stand out the most are the ones Grandpa tailored for me. Sometimes, he made pieces for Dylan and me in his spare time. From scratch. Just for fun. I mean, who did that? He could whip up any piece of clothing—or mend, hem, shorten, take in, loosen, or whatever else the garment needed. He was a magician.

No other kids I knew had someone with this skill in their family. My mom's friends always asked if he was available to help out here and there. The choice of doing things for free or asking people to bring their clothes to the store and pay was a hard one for him. His heart didn't want to charge people, but his business, home, and bills required it.

Grandpa often joked that I should have taken over the family business instead of going to college. I knew Italians want to pass on their craft to the younger generations, but he knew Dad wouldn't want to do it. And Dylan would never have considered it. I was left as the last option in our family. I still hope I didn't break his heart by declining his flattering offer, but I didn't see myself happy in a career like that. So, there was one minor dissimilarity between Grandpa and me. If it disappointed him, he never let on. He always accepted me no matter what decisions I made in my life. He valued independent thinking, since that was what he had to do as a young man.

The fabric arts gene may have been left out of my DNA, but the tradition of hard work did transfer to me. I know I made Grandpa proud when he was alive. He knew about every single school performance and good grade, and he showed his pride with a huge hug and peck on the cheek—and Grandma too, of course. Their acceptance of me, no matter what happened, was so comforting in my youth. How I could use that now in my life…

A quiet knock at the door pulls me from my memories.

"Coming." I jump out of bed and open the door.

"Shh, not too loud." Brian whispers. "I wanted to say that I was proud of you tonight. It kind of turned me on to see you so passionate about something again. The old Rachel is back…or at least on her way back."

"Thanks." I grip the door tighter.

"Hey, you wanna—"

I bend down to grab a decorative pillow to throw at him. "No! My parents are down the hall. Are you losing your mind?"

He puts his hands up like he's guilty. "Just thought I'd try."

"Go to bed, Casanova."

"'Til tomorrow, I guess." He puts on an exaggerated sad face as I giggle and shut the door.

This morning at breakfast brings an interesting vibe. Mom is busying herself cooking a large American style breakfast of eggs, bacon, ham, toast, and coffee, while Dad is reading the sports section of the newspaper at the table. Neither of them are speaking to each other, but this is not unusual for the Granza morning ritual. Dad is not quite a morning person. Like father, like daughter.

As Brian and I come into the kitchen around the same time, I think how grateful I am that Dylan went home last night. That gift will bring me a little harmony this morning. Sad, but true.

Dad's consciousness strikes when Brian's chair makes a loud screech upon pulling it away from the table. "Oh, hi kids."

"Morning, Mr. Granza."

"Hey," I say flatly, including both of my parents. I can't put my finger on it, but something about the way my mom is cooking seems strange. She looks up and smiles at both of us briefly, but her usual sparkle when cooking, a little bounce of some sort, is absent. This morning feels different. With all my training to observe others' behaviors, I have learned to trust my instincts when I notice a changed sense with someone. My non-therapist friends think I overanalyze, but as time continues, they see more and more that I am spot on.

I go over and hug my mom. Maybe she is still distraught from last night's, err, spat. I may have been too rough on her. I still have it on my mind, but was able to get a good night's sleep and woke up ready to move forward. The disagreement between us was one of many in my lifetime, and I am sure many more to come.

"Hi, Rachel. Did you sleep well?" Mom murmurs out, while flipping the bacon forcefully.

I make sure to stand next to her and give direct eye contact and a smile. She manages to smile back and appears happy. I'm glad. I don't want to leave on that note.

The chit chat lasts through breakfast. Nobody mentions the family history topic, but it is all that I can think about this morning. At least I am leaving on good terms with my parents. In a few hours, we will be back in the city and I will be back on my search.

# *Chapter 11*

W e walk into the apartment and I turn on the computer right away. I can't wait to research again using the new facts my dad gave me last night. I've used multiple sites for my searches, but Ancestry.com has international information, just what I need. That's my first stop. I type the website into the browser and grab the list I made on the train ride home.

*Family facts*
- *Grandpa was born in 1902, died in 1998*
- *Great-Uncle Vince died in 1983, probably was born in 1900*
- *Grandpa had a sister and half-sister, names unknown*
- *His mom and sister never came to the US (why?)*
- *Grandpa came to the US with his family in 1916, age 14; Great-Uncle Vince at age 16 (probably)*
- *They were from Genoa, Italy (northern Italy- very important!)*
- *My great-grandpa's name was Gino*

These ancestry sites are confusing. I swear a million names come up when I enter my grandpa's name. I have a little more to work with now, but there are still so many fields as options to narrow down the results. Do I enter in exact years? Allow date ranges? Set it to exact names? Let it choose alternate spellings? Which type of record do I want to find? Do I try birth certificates? Marriage certificates? Death certificates? A census? Oh, the options.

I start by entering Grandpa's name and birth year, knowing the year is accurate now. One thousand one hundred and forty-seven results populate. That's nothing compared to the first searches I did so I can handle it.

Hmm, the 1940 census looks like a good place to start. It just released today the site states, so it's the newest census available to view. What luck! Maybe it's a sign I'm on the right track. I read there are rules for when censuses can be released, for privacy purposes. Well, I'll take whatever's offered.

As the image of the 1940 census loads, my heart pounds louder and louder. My grandpa's name is right in the middle of the page. "This is amazing! There he is! There's his name!

"Salvatore Granza." I can't help but yell it out. A sense of relief washes over me. I instantly picture his face. Oh, how I miss him.

Next to his name, there is a *lot* of information that I didn't realize would be on a census. It shows all kinds of elements of his life, like his education level ("4," meaning fourth grade), place of birth ("ITALY," spelled in all capital letters, making me feel its importance), residence ("Philadelphia, PA"), and job ("business"). My grandma's name is there too. Under "Children," my Uncle Tonio is listed as a four-year-old child. My dad wasn't born yet but would be soon after this year. So, there is the little family, all existing together in that 1940 census.

Great-Uncle Vince is listed under Grandpa's immediate family as well. There's a woman's name after his, which had to be his wife. More children are listed after them. Wow, that is a lot of people in one house. My grandpa and his brother worked together *and* lived together?! I can't imagine that much time with anyone—especially not *my* brother. I'd die. But, I wish that time was able to come to life for a minute. Even a second. I'd take a flash in time to be able to see them and meet those I never did, co-existing together in harmony.

I don't expect to see Great-Grandpa Gino's name on the census, since Dad told me he died shortly after they arrived in New York. There's a part of me that mourns not having proof of his existence. I'm alive, so obviously he lived, but still, I want to see the documentation for the purpose of pleasure. Maybe I can find him in an earlier census.

My mind wanders to how life may have been for my family in 1940—the long hours at the tailor shop, the crying kids at home, the packed house, and many mouths to feed. My family had one of the strongest work ethics around, and now I know they must have had plenty of patience too. Patience doesn't come naturally in my personal life, maybe because I save it all for my clients. Add it to my list of needed self-improvements.

I try to look further back in time, but the 1930 census isn't providing any new information. The same family members were together at that time. The next census I analyze is from 1920, and this one leads to something captivating. Now that I know what to look for, I easily find my grandpa and his brother, but *only* them. Was their dad already deceased at that time? Even though I never got to meet him, I feel another moment of sadness and loss. I can't imagine growing up without a dad. Grandpa was so young at that time and to not have his dad after traveling from a foreign land—I can't fathom it. He was only eighteen years old in this census year.

The other interesting piece of news here is that Grandpa and Great-Uncle Vince are listed under another person's family name in this census—the Serafinos. Who were they? Did we have family in the US after all? Why wouldn't my grandpa's immediate family have lived alone? Great-Uncle Vince was surely old enough at that time. I mean, they had the tailoring business that Great-Grandpa Gino started here.

As the search goes on, I realize I keep thinking of more and more questions, but the answers aren't there. When I find one bit of information, three more questions come to mind.

# The Difference

Before I know it, it's time for bed. Family history research is the biggest time sucker I've ever experienced, which is all fine and dandy, but I want my answers now. Remember, patience.

*Chapter 12*

t feels like I have been away from work for years, but it's only been three days. When I walk into the office, Annabelle's wacky outfit of the day strikes me as...pretty? Her sparkly pink bangles and hot pink heels make me smile. Most days, I cringe at her clothing choices. *What* is happening to me? Her office is the epitome of disorganization though. To be able to have it all together but also be this chaotic blows my mind.

My workload is light today because of a few no shows to appointments, so I'm able to sneak in some random ancestry searches between clients. I can't say it's the most productive way to search though. This project is the ultimate internet rabbit hole. But something tells me it would not be professional to ask a child to wait to pour their heart out because I need to search for another name in my family line.

*Hold that sadness inside about being bullied, little Aiden. I need to just check one more thing over here.*

I giggle at the absurdity.

Even though that doesn't happen, the pile of client notes is happening. Every little thing I do requires a note for insurance purposes. Calls, referrals, sessions, consultations, parent contacts, teacher contacts, and treatment planning all require documentation. It stacks up quickly. I wish I could devote twenty-four seven to my new cause, but life isn't that luxurious.

I hear a loud thud and a flutter of papers from Annabelle's office. I'm sure another pile of folders fell from her desk.

She barges in moments later, never remembering I don't like that, and sits down on a chair on the other side of my desk. "Hey, I saw your door is cracked so I thought I'd—ohhh, sorry. I did it again." She starts to get up, but I hold out my hand.

"No worries. I just haven't slept well so I'm a little out of it. Sorry if I look like a mess."

"Please. Have you taken a gander at my office today? Hurricane Annabelle tore through at a Cat 5 level today. I need professional help to organize it. And you never need to apologize for anything. You know that." She kicks off her heels and gets cozy in the chair. "Why didn't you sleep?"

"I think I did sleep, but I don't feel rested. It's so annoying— among other stuff." I don't dare make eye contact because she's too good of a therapist and she'll be able to read my face.

"So, what are you talking about? Spill it."

I didn't plan on having any deep discussions today, but I've worked with her long enough to know she won't give up that easily. "I just haven't felt much like myself lately, well, for a while." I scribble as I talk.

"We all go through changes, my friend. It's okay."

"No, I think it's been a little more than normal bad days and life changes for me. I think I may be almost mildly depressed, stuck in a rut. Whatever it is, I feel like I need to take action or I'll get worse and might not realize it." I pause to see if Annabelle has caught on yet, but lose my nerve and hurry on. "But I found a new hobby that has been helping me a lot. My spirits are higher and I've got something to focus on again."

There, I said it. I feel relief in being honest with her. I don't want to be fake anymore.

She leans forward in the chair. "Oh sweetie, I had no idea. I'm a horrible office mate and friend."

"No, Ann, don't go there. Unless you knew to look for something, you probably wouldn't see it. I love seeing the kids and try to be my best self when here. Poor Brian takes the brunt of it. And Maggie. And my family. Ugh." I cover my face with my hands. "I'm so irritable outside of work and I hate that about myself. But I get all anxious and…"

Annabelle brings me the tissue box and gives me a hug. "I'm here for you. Just know that. And all that guilt is just part of the deal when you feel this way. You know that too, but I'm reminding you." She bends down to try to make eye contact and flashes a slight smile my way.

"Thanks. Like I said, I started doing something I think may help. I just get shaky sometimes, with fluctuations in my mood. It's so exasperating, but now I understand my clients a lot more."

"What are you doing for the new hobby? Can I help in any way?"

"You're so sweet. I'm trying to find out about my family history. My grandpa never spoke about his childhood. I think if I can learn a few things about him, it will help me to have a firmer sense of myself. You know how much I looked up to him."

"Oh, yes! That's great. I'm so glad to hear you have been doing some self-care. And as for however you think you are acting with your loved ones, I'm sure they understand. Don't let that guilt consume you." She laughs at the clinical sternness of her speech, I assume, and it makes me giggle a little as well.

"You're the best. Thanks. I'm glad I told you."

"It's the first step in healing to admit the problem." She laughs.

I flash a toothless smile, still heavy in my heart from saying my status out loud.

"But seriously, Rachel, you know you can talk to me any time. I can always use a distraction. Maybe we can go to lunch together more often. We can try to set our schedules to coincide better. Or, ooh, we can try to go out after work or on the weekend—"

"Annabelle! It's still me and the normal Rachel doesn't even have the desire for all that. Well, only sometimes. But I do appreciate it.

Maybe if I can get out of my head a bit more, I'll take you up on that."

"Okay with me. I just want to help you to steer clear of the slippery slope. You don't have to deal with this by yourself. I'm here. Please talk to Brian and Maggie as well if you need to. You are far from alone."

"Thanks. I think if I didn't change something in my life and find this new interest, things would have gotten worse. So, let's continue to hope I find more answers. I have glimpses of happiness and want that all the time again."

She hugs me again and looks directly into my eyes. "Yes, I believe you will."

"Keep telling me that!" I need to tell myself that as well.

I will know the answers. I will know. I never needed an encouraging mantra as much as right now.

Ah, it's finally time. I'm in my pajamas, have my herbal tea, and my laptop is ready to work.

My only plans for tonight are to comb through the search results for anyone with the surnames of Granza and Serafino combined with the first names that I recognize from the census records. I have to make sure more paper trails lead to my family, and God forbid not another Salvatore Granza.

As time ticks on, I am seeing how easy it is to go down the wrong path in Genealogy World. Welcome to the amusement park where time is lost and rides lead you in circles. Enjoy.

Before I know it, there could be a whole line of people who aren't related to me because of one person with a similar name on my list. I don't want to fall into that trap. And, let me tell you, Salvatore Granza is like John Smith in the Italian world—so common that it would be simple to mistake another man for the right Salvatore.

There are so many strange forms that populate here tonight.

What *are* these? Some files look like pages ripped straight out of an old phone book, ragged edges and all. The poor person who had to scan all of these in here. Jeez.

This is another weird document that keeps coming up for me. It consists of only last names and occupations—some are jobs I never even knew existed. Brogger? Packman? I assume that's not related to the game. But anyway, there are multiple Granzas listed in these papers.

Guess what name I can't find, though. Those elusive Serafinos. Is looking for them a waste of time? I hope not because I have to find out why my grandpa was listed with them in that census. It just doesn't make sense and this is yet another unanswered question.

The process of searching for answers is a huge mess, feeling like more than I can handle right now. I shut my laptop and rub my eyes.

"Oh, Harrison, it's time for bed." I give him a quick pet and go to my bedroom.

Virtual ancestry documents are scattered across a sea of confusion, sucking me below sea level and I need some air. I plop down on the bed and sigh. Family history research is exhausting.

There are so many routes to take. Some lead to nothing, while some lead to information that could be helpful, but I never know right away. Still others must lead to what I believe is the pirate's treasure on the deep-sea floor. I will find that chest, damn it. I will.

Cue the mantra.

# Chapter 13

Saturday comes faster and slower than I imagined. Although the week dragged, it also flew by because I was so busy at work and exhausted at home. I had to DVR numerous *Titanic* specials because of my new rule not to watch *Titanic* related shows after a late hour, as well as continuing to search and search…and search for family information. I will be set with so many *Titanic* programs about its one hundredth sinking anniversary this weekend that I will have shows to watch for a month. Maybe more, if I'm lucky.

No, seriously. How can I pass up the countless facts I could learn? There are shows about how the *Titanic* was built, why and how it sunk, how researchers found the wreckage on the ocean floor, people protesting the visitors there, and many political undertones of the time like class separation, coal strikes, and more. And don't even get me started on new theories about how the disaster could have ever happened in the first place. It's way beyond simply hitting an iceberg, believe me. There are new theories for how it could have happened, including my *Titanic* idol's miraging theory. Oh yes, I have a *Titanic* idol. Are you surprised? His name is Tim Maltin. Look up his research. You'll be fascinated for hours, I swear.

I take the TV remote and lay on the couch, cozy under my knitted blanket and ready for documentary action. Spoken like a true nerd, I know. Harrison comes over to share the warmth, so I invite him on the couch by patting the extra space.

I'll allow myself to get sucked into the mystique today to try to relax from the week. I have to prepare for tonight's extravaganza anyway.

"It will be a TOD day, Harrison," I say and hug him, now laying in front of me on the cushion.

My excited heart beats faster as I think about diving into a TV special or two, or three, or four. I continue to pet my little buddy and take a deep breath. What a switch from most of my week.

"Rach, look at you!"

I twirl in front of Brian and try to hide my smile. "This old thing?"

"I'm glad you are feeling more festive tonight because I took the liberty of making reservations at…a restaurant."

"You can't say the name? It's a surprise restaurant?"

"Someone at work told me about this Italian place near the movie theater. I looked at their menu and thought you would love it."

"That's a lot of effort for tonight. I, um, thank you." My mouth hangs open.

"I know seeing *Titanic* in 3D means a lot to you, so I wanted to make it even more special." He stands and wraps his arms around me then gives me a quick kiss before pulling me to the door. "Let's go. We don't want to be late."

When we get to the restaurant, I sigh a breath of relief. It's quaint and a little fancier than I expected but feels like a perfect choice. Wait, am I dressy enough though?

I play with the anchor charm on my necklace and move closer to Brian so he can hear me whisper. "I thought you said I was dressed nice tonight."

His brow furrows. "What do you mean? You are. That is a nice dress."

"You know I don't like to stick out. I might have chosen something a little more upscale if I knew about the level of this place." At least I threw on my silver chain necklace.

"You're fine. Don't worry. Let's get a table." He rests his hand on the small of my back and leads me to the hostess stand.

How does he not understand?

My cheeks heat up as I smooth my dark gray dress in an attempt to make it appear less casual.

When the hostess notices us, I swear she looks me up and down. Or maybe it's just in my head.

"Reservation for two," Brian tells her.

"Name please?"

"Brian."

Without a smile or change in her unenthusiastic facial expression, the hostess looks at her book on the stand. "Follow me." Miss Personality leads us to our table and drops a menu in my hands as soon as I'm seated.

"See why I made a reservation? There are about six tables in here so I wanted to make sure we could get in and that your night is flawless." Brian's bright eyes have no trouble catching the light above us as he smiles, pleased with his planning.

I return the smile and let out the breath I'd been holding, thankful I'm able to hide part of my outfit under the tablecloth. I look down at the menu and notice today's date printed on the top. Not only is this restaurant Italian, but they create menus each day, which means fresh ingredients and new ideas.

Glancing back to today's date on the menu, a chill travels throughout my body. Today marks one hundred years since the *Titanic* hit the iceberg that sank it. The people on the ship would have received menus that night that read "April 14, 1912." Obviously I knew this fact, but seeing the date in writing, even with the year 2012, makes my chest hurt.

"Rach? What's happening over there?"

"Oh, I, I just noticed the date printed and it...never mind. All is okay."

"If you say so. How about ordering bruschetta? I bet they grow their own tomatoes here." He looks around as if searching for a rooftop garden.

"Sounds good." I smile. "You'd love to see their garden, I'm sure."

"In fact, I would, Ms. Granza." He smiles as well.

Being with Brian in this environment, on this night, for this occasion, feels serene. I'm happy. Dare I proclaim that?

After our order is taken, I wait not so patiently for the delicious food to start rolling in. Not even my excitement for the movie can take my appetite away. "I hope they bring the app soon. I'm starving."

"Aren't you always?"

"Pretty much." I nod my head.

"So, what's happened with your research this week?"

"Not as much as I would like. I haven't been able to find any new info yet." My face drops.

"You will."

Does he know my phrase? "I hope so." I pause. "Oh, but there was a family listed in a census with my family who I never heard about, so maybe we did know someone here in the US. I almost forgot to tell you." I'm so focused on my grandpa that it slips my mind sometimes.

"Good news."

"Yes, salute." I hold my wine glass up to clink it with his glass. "I'm glad we are here together now."

"There's nobody else I'd rather watch over three hours of a ship sinking with than you."

"How romantic." I flutter my eyes to add to my sarcasm.

"Oh no, did I spoil the ending?"

"Yes. You jerk. I keep hoping it doesn't sink." I laugh and grab a slice of white bread. Brian pushes the tiny bowl of the mixture of olive oil and spices closer to me so I can dip my slice.

Three doughy slices later, I put down my fork after finishing my last piece with my lobster stuffed ravioli in lemon butter sauce. "I can always tell when the pasta is freshly made. Who told you about this place?"

"Jason."

My eyes enlarge. "Well, he deserves a prize. I knew I always liked that guy."

Just in time to keep the food high going, the waiter brings us dessert menus. I hold back a scream as soon as I spot a special choice. Instead, I whisper-scream to Brian, "THEY HAVE SPUMONI!"

Brian's face lights up. "Why do you think we came here?"

"Oh, I hope they have *real* spumoni."

He chuckles. "I called ahead of time to make sure it's the way you like it. I think the menu is just for show."

"You mean *actual* spumoni and not the fake crap, right?" I tend to get a little too animated when it comes to the right way to prepare Italian food. "People should not be able to call their knockoffs 'spumoni.'"

The waiter sets two dishes on the table and I gasp.

"What's wrong, miss?"

"Oh, sorry. I am just excited that this is true spumoni." I stare at the plate, mesmerized by the culinary gift in front of me. Hopefully the waiter doesn't take me as rude that I'm not looking at him, but I can't get out of my bubble at this point.

"Thank you, sir," Brian says to the waiter and gathers our useless menus.

I pick up my spoon, my mouth watering. "The time has arrived." Before I can take a bite, I examine each layer. "The colors *are* precise. I see the pieces of pistachios in a green layer, chunks of cherries for the pink middle layer, and bits of chocolate for the last third. And it's sliced and served on a plate, not in a bowl, as is correct. And no chocolate drizzle on top. Puh-lease, that's sacrilegious."

Brian rolls his eyes. "I told you. Now eat and stop analyzing before it melts."

My first bite is heavenly. Angels must have brought it down to this restaurant from the skies above. It has the perfect creaminess and sweetness in each section. They do it right at this place. I feel proud, even though I had nothing to do with making it. Only my people could create something so delicious.

Even after a perfect Italian meal, Brian and I have no trouble making room for movie theater popcorn. As we stand in line, my eye is drawn to the *Titanic* posters and cardboard cutouts. The building excitement feels so foreign to me that it's a bit scary.

Walking into the 3D theater, holding the precious tickets in one hand and popcorn in the other, I feel my heart beat faster with every step. We are about to see *Titanic* in 3D...with Leonardo DiCaprio...in 3D! Choosing our seats is important for the cinematic experience—not too close to the screen, not too far, and in the middle of the section. Brian likes an aisle seat, but this is my shindig tonight, so I get to sit where I want. As the theater fills up, I am glad that nobody sits next to me. I need my space and want to stay in my own little world. The only exception might be a little snuggling with Brian.

I look around before the lights dim. The moviegoers all look so young. This is probably the first time they'll see the movie in a theater. They were probably in elementary school when it was originally released in 1997. Everyone needs to see this movie on the big screen at least once—and in 3D it's even better. It's a basic human need. Eat, sleep, see *Titanic* in the theater.

Finally, the opening credits start and the title *Titanic* is sprawled across the screen, with the dark blue water of the Atlantic in the background. Chills fill my body as the iconic song plays. It's haunting and sad, yet a perfect melody to set the mood. I slouch further down into the plush red theater chair and let my mind wander to the world in the movie, both 1997 and 1912.

When the final scene ends, I realize I have been practically holding my breath for the last hour. I breathe in the moviemaking beauty with a deep intake of air. Oh, please stay in my memory forever, especially 3D Leo.

I'd sit here and watch it again if they would let me, but when I see everyone in the theater getting up from their seats, I know I should too. Brian's what-the-heck-are-you-doing look also convinces me. I follow him down the steps begrudgingly, toss my popcorn bag in the bin, and sadly exit out the door. It's over. My head dips, but my mind doesn't stop reviewing the masterpiece.

I've watched this movie dozens of times and am always able to enjoy every moment of it—even the sorrowful ones. Watching in 3D was a whole new experience though, almost overbearing. It was so large and so real; so heartbreaking. I can't imagine losing a love like Rose did when Jack died.

Every time I watch *Titanic*, I fall in love with the sets, props, and costumes all over again. They are so accurate that I can imagine myself in those circumstances, which is part of what makes it eerie. The disaster could have happened to anyone. The movie truly is a work of genius and I agree with the many Oscars it won the year of its release. Leonardo DiCaprio should have won the Oscar for best actor as well. What happened, Oscar voters? Come on!

The word vomit begins as we exit the building and start our walk home (because how would I ever hold all this in?). "What captured my fascination this time was seeing the modern-day underwater scenes of the wreck. The 3D aspect of the movie made all the difference for the viewing experience. Don't you agree?"

"It was awesome. The fish around the cameras looked like they were swimming right toward me."

"Exactly! Also, the motion of the camera moving through the rooms of the ship made me feel like I was on that deep-sea rover with the explorers. Like I was *in* the movie and part of their world."

"With Leo! Oh my God." Brian imitates me with a high-pitched voice.

I punch him in the arm and giggle. "Well, it was a thrill we could see it in this format and that they re-released it."

"And how about that dinner? I did well." Brian puffs out his chest and shimmies.

"Yeah, the surprise dinner, the out of this world food, the best movie, and last but not least, the us having time together part." I grab his hand and we swing our arms as we walk.

Our closeness tonight feels like we have a chance to survive as a couple. At least I feel closer. I *think* he does too. Fingers crossed. Putting my arm around him in the movie had to show my feelings because he later did the same. I think we have been more affectionate in general since the talk. Right?

I push aside my doubt and allow a soothing warm wave to flow through me. He is my Jack. Yup, he just has to be. I am sure. Can that sureness stay with me please?

I guess he did feel the closeness because as soon as we enter our apartment, he guides me to the bedroom. I know what this means.

"Um, Brian, I feel strange about having sex when we just saw a tragic movie about love lost. How can I forget about what I just watched?"

He stops walking, lets my hand loose, and turns around to face me. "The ship didn't really just sink, you know. That happened a long time ago."

"It is real to me right now because the event did happen, no matter when. It isn't like we witnessed a movie about a fictional event. I'm not heartless and can't move on easily from three hours of gut-wrenching distress." Our new open communication seems to be the way to go. Lay it all out there, Rachel.

But his face grows red. Oh, this isn't good.

He takes in a huge breath and releases it with force. "What do you mean? Should we mourn the tragedy?" he raises his voice.

"I don't know." I look down. My voice gets softer. "It's the centennial and I feel weird being intimate in this time of loss."

"Rachel, you are really illogical. You didn't know any of those people. I thought I was reading your signals right, but it's fine if you aren't in the mood. I know this stuff means a lot to you and it is your night." His voice remains loud, but a notch calmer. He gives me a tight hug then walks to the bathroom.

So, is he annoyed with me or not?

Brian is an understanding man and I am fortunate for that. It just feels wrong to celebrate, in a sense, when one hundred years ago so many lives changed from the wreck. He has to understand that, right?

I go over to the bathroom to hug and kiss him again. His reception is flat. Huh?

"Brian, I'm sorry! I don't want the night to end this way. Please don't be mad at me." I wait, staring at him as he washes his face and prepares his toothbrush for use. When he puts down the toothpaste, I think how it would shoot out everywhere if the cap wasn't on. He's slamming everything.

"It's fine, Rachel." Only his eyes turn toward me but don't meet mine, while his head remains down and away. He brushes aggressively and acts different than what he verbalizes. 'It's' obviously not fine.

"I don't know what else to say. I enjoyed the night. I really did. It was amazing how out of the way you went for me and I appreciate that so much. I can't force myself to get into the zone after such a heavy experience." A tear drops from my eye, but I don't want him to see it. I turn my face away and wipe it fast.

"Don't worry about it. Love you." How could he have no emotion in his face? His body even looks deflated.

He walks to our bed. Whipping back the covers, he drops in and turns on his side so he can't see me anymore. I'm standing here lost for thoughts and words. I still can't read him. Is he just tired or something? This is out of character.

Why do I always mess everything up? Brian doesn't completely understand me, but he does the best out of anyone. If not him, who does understand me then? He *gets* me most of the time at least. That is something. Maybe I am *ungettable*, after all. Except by Grandpa.

Stop it, Rachel. I need to tell myself to stop letting my mind go into catastrophe mode. He loves me and we will get through this shaky time. He still wants to spend time with me. Tonight shows that. I'm not completely awful to be around. Am I?

But what if his actions are band aids and they are not allowing me to address the real issues? What if there *is* something truly wrong with me? Do I need medicine? Therapy? But what even is the issue anymore? There isn't an issue! My life is great. Ugh, I don't know. It's too much.

I go to the family room and turn on the TV to watch something before I go to bed. I need a transition time from the emotional waves of tonight. Reviewing it in my mind is draining, so I have to try to tune out.

I force myself to watch something light and happy on TV because I already broke my late-night *Titanic* rule and don't want to watch any more on the topic tonight. My mind can't take it. And Lord knows my heart can't either. I don't want any more of those lucid dreams.

# *Chapter* 14

We have plans to go to the 6th Avenue Chelsea Festival with Maggie and Ray today, but after how last night ended, I'm not in the mood. I know I better get in the mood because it's happening.

As I continue to lay in bed my mind races, reflecting on last night and what it means. It is always so up and down with him—with us. And I know I cause a lot of the shifts. Do nights like last night push him further away? Does he still want to be with me? What do I want? This is all too overwhelming for the morning. I need a coffee the size of the *Titanic* to get me through right now, so I crawl out from under the covers and shuffle into the kitchen.

"Hey."

Brian looks up from his laptop. "Morning."

"I'm sorr—"

"Don't worry about it."

"Okay… Um, are you still going to the festival?"

"Why wouldn't I be?" He keeps his head down and types.

"That…never mind. Okay great." I try to carry on as usual, but my voice is three octaves higher. Grabbing my coffee and popping a quiche Brian made into the microwave, I stare out the window.

Brian's silence is torturous, but I don't want to cause more ripples and ask about his feelings again. That will just annoy him further. Last night warned me of it. I know what I can say.

"I wish I could tell Maggie about my research today."

"Why can't you?" This causes him to look up.

Uh-oh, did I hit a nerve I wasn't aware of? I thought this is a safe topic.

"I want to be able to say every last bit to Maggie. I can't lay out all the details when we are walking around with you two guys." I muster up a laugh to give off a this-is-a-normal-reaction vibe.

He rolls his eyes.

So, he didn't buy it. Oy.

"Please, respect my wishes."

"I don't get it. It's strange you wouldn't want to talk about what's up and that's what's up." He folds his arms across his chest.

I feel a challenge energy coming from him, which is unusual. He's the calm one. Crap, I really upset him last night.

"I just want to have a deeper conversation than throwing out pieces of my story. We need to go to lunch or something. You know, some girl talk stuff," I re-emphasize but keep my tone light. He has to understand that.

I grab my food and a fork.

"I mean, if that's what you want, but it just seems odd to me."

Ouch. *His* re-emphasis isn't good. I pause and take a deep breath.

"It's just me. You know how I am." I honestly could just tell her some of the story today. He has a point. It doesn't need to be a big to-do.

"What, worried about everything, everyone, and everything in between?"

I hear the metaphorical record screech to a stop, like in the movies. Too far, my man, too far. Now it's on.

"Brian, please? Just…please." My words are short and pointed. "It's important that I tell my best friend when and how I want to, that's all." I am trying hard to keep the pleasant tone, but the frustration keeps building inside and I have an urge to dig my feet in further to my stubborn desire.

"Whatever, Rach. It doesn't matter to me. You're the one making this a huge issue. No one cares."

"Oh, that's nice. And I don't believe you! Of course she cares. Nothing means *anything* to you!"

"Rach—"

"Don't worry about it," I mutter as I stomp to the bedroom. The tears start as soon as the door shuts.

He yells out, "I didn't mean that," but I don't respond.

I set my food on the nightstand and curl up under the comforter. Harrison snuggles next to me. "How could he think this isn't so major for me that I would want to spit it out in sections while pre-occupied? Why does he view it as such a superficial topic that doesn't deserve a full-on conversation? *Everything* means something to me so if this isn't the way I want to share my news, it won't be the way it happens. And he should respect that."

Harrison can't be bothered, keeping his head resting comfortably on my lap.

"Trying to find out more about myself through my family history is important. And the information I find could help me heal and feel like Grandpa isn't gone. How can he say nobody cares? Doesn't he want that healing for me, for us?"

Harrison meows and jumps off the bed, clearly not interested in listening to my monologue any longer.

I sit up and notice my laptop on the bench in front of the window. Nothing is going to stop me on this mission. Not even Brian.

"Rachel! Brian! Over here!"

Maggie and Ray are standing next to an adorable pink hamburger food truck, waving. The decision about what to eat will be easy, it seems. I break the silence of our walk to the festival by asking Brian,

"Is that okay with you?"

"Yeah, burgers sound good." He smiles and crouches down to lock eyes. "And I'm sorr—"

"Don't worry about it." Now it's my turn to keep him from apologizing. "Let's have a good time. I was being silly anyway."

"I can't imagine you being that way." He smiles.

"Good thing we are almost near them," I whisper an imaginary threat and shake my fist.

A walk helps to clear my head sometimes. Being in the fresh air puts things in perspective. I need to stop overreacting. Gosh, Rachel. Get it together.

It seems like it helped Brian too. I don't plan on rehashing the fights—plural, ugh. If he wants to talk later, fine, but if not, I'm just going to try to be a good girlfriend.

Open communication is to be determined by this lady for what it just put us through.

"Normally, the line takes forever to get through because they're so popular," Maggie explains after a few minutes of standing together. "I can't believe we only waited fifteen minutes. Good thing we jumped in on it though because I need to eat."

"This is record time?" I don't want to tell her this seems like a long wait to me. I need to refuel after the night and morning I had as soon as possible. Oh well, we are staying in line, obviously.

She nods.

Luckily, it doesn't take too much longer before we are able to devour the sought-after food. People are right to wait, I have to admit.

"Hey, have you heard what going to be built over there?" Maggie says after swallowing a mouth full of sweet potato fries and motioning toward the old railroad tracks.

"Huh?"

"There's going to be an elevated path along the tracks. It will be called The High Path. No, wait." She squints and looks at Ray who shrugs and takes another bite of his burger. "Oh. The High Line!" Her hand rises and the last few fries are lost from her knocked tray.

"Cool." I show the same level of enthusiasm as if she has told me a hardware store would be built there.

"Do you not get what this means?" she says, still enthused.

"No, sorry." I look at Brian and Ray for a clue but gain nothing.

"More stores, restaurants, beautiful sculptures along the path, and who knows what else. It will follow the Hudson. It's supposed to have pretty little park benches where you could look at the river or the city. I think it will be the place to be. If you don't want to be there, then poo on you." She blows a raspberry at me.

"Okay, okay. It sounds neat."

"Neat? Oh, Rachel." She shakes her head.

"Sorry," I say while amping up my ability to pretend to be excited with her. "I do think that will be great for us to have here."

I notice Brian and Ray wandered away from this conversation to check out some fabulous looking produce. Now's my opportunity to fill Maggie in on some current events.

"Mags." I speak softly.

"Rach." She matches my tone and dips her head to make eye contact.

"I want to let you know some stuff."

"Ooh, tell me the deets." She locks elbows with me and leads me further from the men.

"Since we last spoke, so much has happened. I started researching my family history."

"You what? *Niiice.* What are you finding out? Any celebs in your bloodline?" Her face lights up.

"Not yet." I giggle. "No, it's become something that brings some joy to my soul. It happened by chance because of your list suggestion."

"See, don't I know you or what?"

"Yes, you do. So, I haven't learned much yet, but I'm not going to stop until I do. I realized my grandpa never wanted to tell us about his journey to the US or anything about his childhood."

"That's weird."

"I know. I even visited my parents to see what they knew about Grandpa's story, but no luck. I mean, I got more basic info like the year my family came from Italy, but nothing mind blowing."

"Nothing juicy is what you're telling me."

"Nothing juicy." I laugh.

"I see a little twinkle in your eye when you talk about this project. I want you to keep doing this, or whatever it involves, because I don't ever see that sparkle in you anymore."

My heart sinks. My face must show my mood shift because she reaches out to hug me.

"Now, there's no need for all that sadness. I love ya."

"I'm so sorry for being such a lousy friend lately, Mags. I really—"

"Be done with that. I won't have any of this sorry business. We all go through phases and you've been there for me when it was my time. Think nothing more of it. Let's think about how my girl found her happy activity we hoped for."

"Yeah, it's frustrating when I don't find what I want, or to not even really know what I'm looking for, but every tiny bit of my grandpa's story makes me feel closer to him."

"I'm so glad for you." She peeks over my shoulder then whispers. "Now what about you and Brian? How's it been?"

I glance over to him. "Well, if you would have asked me a day ago, I would have a different answer. We're hit or miss. We've been a little more open in talking, a little more affectionate, and have had a few dates. But I hurt his feelings last night and he was still angry this morning. So, overall…I don't know. Probably better than not. Does that answer your question?" I chuckle.

"Yes, that was very clear."

I glance toward the guys once more before leaning in close to

Maggie and lowering my voice. "There is so much more to tell you, but I can't right now."

The guys appear with a few shopping bags.

Brian opens his to show me its contents. "I have fresh veggies for dinner. What should we do next?"

He looks emotionally lighter, which shopping for ingredients can do to my man. I'm thankful he doesn't want to run away screaming from me anymore today. Err, I think he doesn't.

"There's a coffee kiosk over here, and a bunch of art stands scattered around. And I know you can smell the pastries and baked breads surrounding us," Maggie replies.

"I'm good with any or all of those choices, but especially the food ones." I grin and start walking toward the coffee aroma, ready to check out the options.

# Chapter 15

I drag through my apartment door for what seems like the millionth time in the last few weeks. These kids are zapping more of my battery than usual. When it's low to start with, I guess that isn't too hard.

The end of the school year always raises their energy level so I should have been prepared. They've been cooped up in those classrooms all year and are more than ready for the long summer break. The hot June temps must add to their burning need to be outside and in water of some form; pools, the beach, or at least running through a sprinkler.

Harrison's already sitting by his food bowl and giving me a longing look. "I'm coming, little guy. Momma had to work late again."

He meows and drops to the floor, resting his head on his paws.

Before even taking off my shoes, I reach for his dry food and fill his bowl.

"Here you go."

He continues to lay while he digs in. Talk about having the life of luxury.

I glimpse at my laptop on the table and take a deep breath. I want to continue my research, but have to prepare for the summer therapy conference coming up next month. Why did I have to go ahead and become an ADHD expert? Usually I can just attend workshops, but this time I need to speak in front of way too many people since the organizer wouldn't take no for an answer. She was so sweet, and convincing, darn it. I do like presenting on behavioral techniques and how to engage parents in treatment, but I'd rather be able to stay home and keep working on my ancestry. My one-track mind does that to me.

Once I settle down on the couch, hair thrown in a bun and face washed, I dive into a loose plan for filling my three hours of presentation time. Making a list is always a great way to start planning. My trusty pen and pad never let me down. Let's go.

Out of nowhere I hear, "Hey Rach."

I'm awoken from my internal world and it takes me a second to register someone's talking to me. "Oh hey. What time is it?"

Brian peeks over the couch. "Late. What do you have going on over here? It looks like your bookshelves exploded."

"They did." I laugh. "I had to look through some books for my conference. Time flies when you're having fun."

"Yeah, I was thinking about that conference of yours. What do you think about me going with you?"

"Oh." My head jerks back and my eyes enlarge. "You would want to come to Orlando in the middle of summer? You do know it's probably 200 degrees, right?"

"I thought it would be 300 degrees, so what a relief." He gathers a stack of books from the couch and sits next to me. "Seriously, wouldn't that be nice to have a familiar face there?"

"Of course, but you can't be at my presentation, you know."

"Yeah, and that's fine with me. I don't have a burning desire to learn about therapy. It would be nice to see you at night, to have dinner together or something. I have plenty of work I can do while you are busy changing the world."

I freeze. I didn't picture being there with him and any time my plan changes, I need a minute. I know, I know, it's a good thing that he wants to be there, and I shouldn't need any time to respond with a resounding "Yes" or a "I thought you'd never ask!" But even in normal

Rachel times anxiety stops me in my tracks.

And why is it always him who thinks of these dates or dinners? I'm never the one who suggests an event together, yet I called him out on not having enough quality time together. I can't seem to get out of my bubble. He's the kindest man alive and I'm the worst girlfriend in the world. I'm trying to be the best girlfriend. Argh. And there's the black and white thinking again. Double argh.

No, Rachel, don't get sucked into the guilt spiral. Stop! And P.S., think gray.

"Sure, that would be great. I didn't book my plane ticket yet so we can look at flights this weekend. I'd love to have you there."

"All right, Mickey Mouse, here we come."

"Uh, stop right there, buddy. There will be no Disney adventures for this woman."

"But it's right up your alley. Crowds of people, noisy, and energetic. I thought you would want to see the head cheese. Oh, well now I don't know if I still want to go."

"Uh-huh. Yes, that sounds just like me. How you know me so well after all these years."

I fall into his lap and give him a hug. He squeezes me tighter and we both laugh.

"Let's celebrate with some pizza. Have you eaten?" Brian says.

I look at the clock and realize it *is* late; already 9 p.m. "Oh, wow. No, but now that you mention it, I'm starving." Funny how my stomach can be triggered by knowing the time.

"What a shock."

# *Chapter 16*

I swallow my sip of coffee and almost miss the coaster as I put down the mug. The computer screen has all my attention.

I figured I would take a short break from planning my presentation, but who I am kidding? When I mess around on these ancestry sites, it's never short enough for a break. But the project keeps pulling me in like a magnet. I didn't expect to find this though.

Sophia Pescetti's family tree has a Gino Granza *and* a Salvatore Granza. This has to be my family. My heart starts racing.

I scroll up to try to find names I have never heard, not only regarding my family but in general. Anselmuccio? Villana? Whoa. These names are one of a kind. Well, at least nowadays. Who knows if they were as common as the more modern-day Christina or Jenn back in old times? My hands hover over the mouse before zooming in for more names and information about the names, I mean the people. My family.

"Isabello." That rolls off my tongue nicely. "Isabello." I have to repeat its melodic pronunciation. And that one's not too strange of a name. I've at least heard of the name female version Isabel.

But people actually had names like these in Italy? How unbelievable. My mind drifts to images of medieval castles, horses, and men in suits of armor. They roamed along the vineyards and rode those horses over the rolling hills of Italy. Or maybe near the coast, trying to stay away from the cliff's edges along the sea. I bet there were sword fights and duels all the time. Yeah, like my family would have been nobility. *Tsk.* They were probably the staff living in a shack on the property. That's okay though. They still would have had tasty food from foraging the land.

Maybe my family made clothes, even back then, just like my grandpa. I bet it's in my blood. Although, a sewing machine and I never got along so maybe that's not totally true.

Still, what a world that must have been. These dates go back as far as the 1700s on Sophia's tree. I quickly type in "18th century Italy" in Google to view this time period of my family's life.

The age of enlightenment. Ah. Philosophers spoke about new ideas and the Baroque period of music was in full force. I wonder if Anselmuccio knew Vivaldi or Bach. I bet they were all hanging out together, messing around on the harpsichord. Yes, of course. Anselmuccio helped Bach compose all the time. "Ha." The giddiness is real, people.

But I struck gold here in my research, thanks to Sophia, whoever she is. Maybe I can find her and meet her, since we *are* family. That will be my goal after finding out about my grandpa. Right now, I need to keep searching for his information though. I can't wait a second longer or have any delays if I can help it. I'll come back to you, Ms. Pescetti, don't you worry.

I start copying all of my new family members to my tree. Each one I bring over to my chart feels like I'm introducing myself to them with a virtual handshake. Hey, Matilde. What's up, Giovanni? Maddalena, have you met Alessio? I'm sure you would get along.

Harrison rubs along my leg. I pick him up and give him a huge hug.

"I'm finally getting somewhere!" I lift his long-haired furry paw to high five him. And…he's done. He jumps off my lap and gets comfortable by the window.

Maybe FamilySearch has more information from Sophia. I've only set up an account on there and haven't explored it too much yet.

Supposedly they have a large Italian registry, I've heard. Well, heard meaning saw on Google searches. I switch from Ancestry.com to there and type as fast as my fingers allow to log in.

After three tries, I finally remember my password and get in, grateful not to be locked out. I don't have time for that. As I type in Sophia's name, my heart speeds up.

Darn, nothing populates for her. There's a Sophia Pesci. It's a close enough name to investigate. but quickly scanning the entry, I see she can't be my Sophia. This person is much older, according to the birth date. I wish the US would release a more recent census for public viewing, but that won't happen until 2022 and it's only the 1950 one. It would make things so much easier for a girl on a mission to have census' until 2012. Hello!

Okay, I'll come back to my Sophia. I type in Villana Lionardo and wait for entries to arise.

Nothing.

Hmm, how about Anselmuccio Lionardo? Did I spell it right? I click back to Ancestry.com to make sure. I double and triple check my spellings of both unusual, yet gorgeous, names and try one more time. Yes, those are the correct spellings. As I hit search one more time, I think I stop breathing a second.

What? Nothing again? This is so weird. Take a deep breath, Rachel. In and out. In and out.

I type in a few of my other new family members' names as well, but there's still no luck. Maybe I need to change the spelling. Yes, that's it. Anselmuccio can easily by typed in wrong by someone entering the data, even the wonderful Sophia. Come on search, come on. But once I click the submit button, there are still no entries that populate with my ancestors. Sure, a few names pop up that are close, but they still aren't my people. They have other surnames or correct surnames and incorrect given names. I wish this was an easy task, but there wouldn't be genealogists in existence if it were simple.

Well, I can always start my own tree on this site. That's what I will have to do. I will enter my new family information from Ancestry. com and create a tree. Maybe FamilySearch sends hints like Ancestry. com does once I have some names in there. Then, I may even get new information.

Yes, this is the plan. I better get to it so I can keep the momentum going. I feel a surge of energy wash over me that feels strangely familiar. I remember having energy once.

# Chapter 17

The humid July Florida air hits me in the face as soon as Brian and I walk outside of the Orlando International Airport doors. I can feel every strand of my hair frizzing up and preparing to be one big poofy mess. Good thing I don't wear makeup because it would be running down my face within seconds.

"Whoa." Brian looks at me with raised eyebrows.

"Yeah, we thought the city was stifling." I try to flatten my busting out curls as a preemptive move, but they refuse to be tamed. "This is why I don't leave the apartment in summer."

"Only in the summer?"

I see him smile, but my face remains flat. His statement strikes me in my chest and I freeze. We just arrived on a semi-vacation and he's giving me a dig? I don't need that. Not cool, buddy.

But he's right. That's what I dislike most. I know getting out of the apartment helps. I know I used to go out more and want to do more around the city. But all that I know doesn't matter. It's what I do that matters...or the lack thereof.

Please know I'm trying, Brian. I'm really trying. Ugh. Every time I find something in the ancestry research, I feel hope that things may change in my life; not just for me, but for us. I have so many more moments of feeling like my old self too. That has to count for something. That must mean something.

"Rachel?"

"Yeah, err, let's get the car. I have to check in at the conference in a few hours and I can barely breathe through this heat." No need to cause an argument. Push it down and continue on, Rachel.

"You better put on SPF 1000 sunscreen here."

I glare at him. He doesn't know when he's already on the other side of the crossed line.

"I'm just *kidding*." He rolls his eyes.

"I know." I rally a smile, but my heart sinks.

He's telling the truth about kidding. I really do know. He doesn't seem to realize these little comments hurt, even though they aren't meant to cause harm. He would never try to hurt my feelings.

Eh, I don't need to start this trip with that kind of open communication. The kind about how he has two strikes already in the first minutes of being outdoors in the Sunshine State. Grr. And we see where it got us the last time.

Maybe I'll toughen up over time. Maybe when I'm back to myself I won't be this sensitive. I cross my fingers hidden behind my back.

"Let's get moving." I smile more fully this time and play off my internal battle in a hopefully believable manner. My feelings are not his fault. This is all on me.

Phew. I'm relieved that my presentation is over and I'm back at the hotel. Those three hours felt like six, but at least people enjoyed it. So many people thanked me at the end that I think it's safe to assume. I almost got teary eyed for the gratitude. Even though I needed to take time away from my family history search to prepare for this lecture, it was worth it. Maybe many kids will be helped with my suggestions and they can succeed in school and at home. That's part of why I love my job, no matter how my mental state is at the time. And altruism is proven to help the "D" word.

But now I can try to relax and recharge. I rub my face and push back my curls from my forehead.

"Want to go to the pool?" Brian moves the curtains aside and looks out the hotel room window.

I stay in position, laying on the bed, fully suited since plopping down the second I entered the door. Baking in the sun isn't my idea of fun or relaxation, but I've been irritable since we arrived yesterday and need a change in gears. I swear it's the heat. It makes my patience the size of a mini cannoli. And nobody likes a cannoli that size.

"Um." I look over at my laptop I planned to use for more ancestry research. "Sure, that might be nice."

Can my face fake genuine interest? I hope so.

"Great, let's change." He jumps into action.

By the time we make it down to the pool, the only place left to sit is in the shade. Perfect for us Northerners, even though I've already slathered on a pound of sunscreen in the room. I can't do that down here while everyone looks at the scene. I can hear them talking now. *Ooh, that pale girl will be burnt to a crisp today. I feel bad for her later. Hope she has some aloe in her bag.*

"Come in with me." Brian reaches out his hand to invite me into the cool blue water.

I grab it. "Yes please." I squint up at the sun through sunglasses and under my hat's brim. Maddone and Mamma Mia! I may melt if I don't get in.

We ease into the pool from the beach entrance. "I've never seen a pool designed like walking into the ocean."

"That's how they do it down here, I guess," Brian says then dips below the water. "Ahh, it's refreshing."

"Yeah, it is." I keep my head above water, but take pleasure in the decrease in body heat at least.

We linger in a quiet corner and sip from our water bottles.

"It's beautiful here, Rach." Brian leans back on the side of the pool, elbows up on the deck.

"I could never live here. My blood's too thick from the north. But I have to admit it's nice to get out from being confined in our apartment and also see some palm trees."

"Well, nobody forces you to stay in there, you know. We live in a place where there are constant activities, but *someone* wants to sit at their computer for all of their free time. I wonder who that can be."

"Hey, you're lucky I'm not on it right now." I giggle.

"Oh, am I?" He splashes me.

"Aaah!" I splash back.

I feel like a kid at summer camp. But the silly elation fades as fast as it came when I think how this summer isn't that different than the last few years, pre-project. Again. Dread washes over me, along with another splash from Brian.

"What the hell, Brian?"

"You looked like you were in outer space, so I brought you back. It worked, didn't it?"

"For the moment." I tilt my head in exaggeration.

"So, seriously though, how are you feeling down here?"

"In the pool? We just talked about this. How are *you* feeling?" I use my therapist voice.

"No, I mean about us."

A bundle of nerves shoot from my heart to my toes. "Come again?" I didn't expect this question, especially not in a pool in sizzling Orlando. Why is he asking? Have I been that horrible to him in this heat? Oh no. Would he say he's leaving me when I'm in a bathing suit? Nobody should be broken up with while in a wet bathing suit. At least let me be in a cover up or a towel. Have some decency, man.

"I just want to have that open communication you love."

Argh, the new catch phrase in our home rears its ugly head. "Uh-huh." My wheels are still spinning.

"I've noticed you have been happier lately." His eyes show longing and his voice is soft.

"I've been okay. I mean, finding my family's tree already put together like a solid puzzle has been a peak of the last few weeks. And I think I'm feeling better here and there. More often than in the past."

"Yes, I see that and I'm glad to hear you feel it. But I hope your happiness is more than just that. I'm hoping I contribute to it." He stares into my eyes.

Does he? Can my mood really be dependent solely on a stranger's discovery of our family? No, it can't be. I know my ancestry is a main focus in my life right now, but let's remember the whole point of it; to feel full and alive again. And Brian is a large part of having a vibrant life. Even in our minor ups and downs in the last few weeks, err, months, okay, okay, year, he's a welcomed constant. He feels safe and warm, even when I scare myself. He's my Brian.

"Of course you do. You are my partner in crime. My better half. Usually that statement makes me sick, but in this case it's true. Nobody is as kind and wonderful as you."

"Oh, stop." He pauses and pretends to blush by patting his cheeks. When I don't speak, he says, "No, that really means go on."

"Brian, Brian, Brian." I shake my head.

"Okay, enough sappy stuff. We are officially on vacation now that your presentation is over."

"I should attend more sessions, but eh, that's all right."

"I encourage you to play hooky. Stay in the pool, have a drink. Now, where do you want to eat tonight? While you were away, I asked the concierge—"

"Oh, aren't we fancy now. 'I asked the concierge,'" I say in a snobby sounding voice.

He pretends to ignore me and purposely continues. "—for suggestions. I know you're always up for Mexican and there's a place on I-Drive that makes all their food from scratch. The fajitas look outstanding. And they make the guacamole tableside."

Almost before he can finish the sentence I say, "I'm in. I can use that guac. The spicier the better. And I want a homemade taco." But just as the words leave my lips my annoying mind links Mexican and fainting. That won't happen again. I'm in a much better place now. I'll be fine. I better be fine this time.

# Chapter 18

"No!" I push the laptop away from me.

I thought the Florida trip sealed the deal with me being on an upswing in my mood, once I cooled down from the inferno inside and out. I especially felt relief after valuable time with Brian, my successful presentation, the glorious tacos, and the even more glorious refrain from fainting. But the high and the streak of prosperity from the family tree seems to have run out as quickly as the sun fried my northern skin. Oh yes, we all knew it would.

I just spent weeks creating my family tree in FamilySearch and making sure it parallels the one in Ancestry.com that I perfected from Sophia's information. It's been so much fun to see it all come together and has given me more energy and motivation with the project and in my life in general. Brian and I have been smooth sailing lately too. I'm digging out of this hole I've been in. I can feel it. August has been a good month all the way around. I should have known the other shoe would drop eventually.

Now that my tree finally matches the Ancestry.com one, I stumble upon this, this catastrophe! I lean closer to the screen to try to wish it away. What is this new ship manifest Sophia submitted to her tree today? It can't be right. Gino and Salvatore couldn't have been on the SS Ancona in 1908. That's eight years prior to when Great-Grandpa, Great-Uncle Vince, and Grandpa came here to the US. It doesn't add up.

Sophia must have made a terrible mistake. Maybe I need to get ahold of her and inform her. That wouldn't be awkward. *Hi, you have never met me and I'm your cousin, I think, but you have mistakenly added a document that can't be correct so please remove it, so our trees can be perfect.* She would probably block me forever.

A sinking feeling weighs down my chest, as a horrible thought rises to the surface. I don't want to believe this. It can't be. No, shove it away. But my effort isn't working.

I have to admit to myself that I never saw Great-Uncle Vince in Sophia's tree.

How did I miss that fact? I was so excited for the other people and all the new family members I was virtually meeting that I forgot about sweet Great-Uncle Vince.

My head falls in my hands.

I drag the laptop back to me so I can comb through her tree one more time. I skim through all the names and see the information I've already analyzed to death, hoping for reassurance. Her family has to be my family. All the other facts line up. But Great-Uncle Vince isn't there. It's one hundred percent true.

After a few frantic minutes, I realize the hideous truth. This tree isn't my family tree. How could I have not seen it before? How did I let Great-Uncle Vince slip from my mind? *I'm sorry*, I mouth to the sky, in hopes he knows I didn't mean to forget about him.

I'm such a fool, copying a stranger's family tree into my account. It looked like it was accurate though. I thought it was a sure thing. I fell for a rookie mistake.

Tears gush from my eyes. I don't understand why this is so hard. I look to the ceiling again for the heavens beyond, ready to plead. Again, I mouth my words. *Grandpa, if you can hear me, and I believe you can, help me out please. I want to know your story, our story. Help me find it. It would mean everything to me to know more about your journey and what made you the man I adored.*

Well, back to square one.

Time keeps slipping today and the wall between me and knowing Grandpa's past grows taller. It's like there's an imaginary evil brick layer getting a kick out of laying more and more bricks on top of one another. There's no limit to the height and he's overjoyed to keep stacking them, as high as the endless sky. I can almost hear him laughing. Muhahaha. Stack, stack, stack.

No matter how much I keep pressing on and trying my best to figure out this mess, I'm going in circles on these sites and so far, have no forward motion. I keep going back to Sophia's tree and trying to find a way it can be mine as well. But it's not. I need to say goodbye to her and all of *her* relatives. Nice knowing ya, fake cousin.

Maybe I need to give up for today. I need to stick to that thought of how a walk and getting out of here in general has been helpful in the past. Leave this room, Rachel. Another day will be easier. The information will come on another day. Another day, darn it. It will come.

I dive for my phone on the couch, find the number I want, and hit send.

"Maggie, are you free to hang out?"

"I may need a doctor to check my hearing because are you calling and asking me out? Rachel wants to leave her apartment?"

I sense the excitement in her voice, despite the sarcasm.

"Yes, I would love to grab some lunch at Luigi's deli and vent to you. Is that okay?"

"I'll be there in five."

I take a swig of water from my glass, grab my keys and wallet, slide on my flip flops, and get the heck out of this apartment.

I adore living where everything is so close. This is what I dreamed of as a kid in the suburbs of Philly. Now, I'm living it. Appreciate that more, Rach. I touch my fingers to my temple wishing to force that thought in my head in a more permanent manner.

Chelsea has my favorite street to walk down in all of New York City; Cushman Row. I'm glad it's on my path to Luigi's. This street has a series of pre-Civil War era, Greek Revival style red brick row houses, each with their black wrought iron rails next to steep steps leading to their elaborate front door entrances. The woodwork, often highlighted in whitewash above the multicolored doors on the street, show their owners' unique style. The door frames contain old world details one doesn't find in today's architecture; simple and beautiful, which I admire. No need for flashiness here.

Also, nearby, in multiple directions, I can walk by grand Gothic or Romanesque Revival style churches anytime. Maybe I'll do that for a long and leisurely walk home. The dark gray stone for some of the churches, once white and clean, along with the stained-glass windows, are now weathered in appearance. How did they look when brand new, before the grime of the world set in on them? We all were like that at one point, then we decay over the years.

Before I realize my feet carried me to the deli, Maggie is walking toward me.

"Hugs, friend." She embraces me with a warm, strong embrace.

"Thanks for coming. Let's eat."

"You don't have to ask me twice." She smiles.

Ordering is fast, thankfully. It's part of why I love this Chelsea deli staple. That and the tasty sandwiches. So, we grab a booth and get comfy. I unwrap my sandwich and take a huge bite into the crusty Italian bread. The salami, prosciutto, mozzarella, and fig jam sandwich is the cure to all that ails me. Yeah, I wish it were that simple.

I force myself to stop eating after a few tasty chews so I can release what I need to share with Maggie.

"Ooh, Rachel, that sucks. I can't believe it wasn't your family on that tree."

"I fell into the trap of being too excited before confirming the info. I swore I wouldn't do that and I did. Stupid me."

"No, it was excited you, not stupid you."

"I guess. But now it's almost like starting over. I can't find anything about Grandpa or the others before they arrived in the US. I want to know how they got here, what their life was like in Italy, to see the names of more family members…" I feel the tears gathering behind my eyelids.

"I know you do, boo. I know. This is a difficult project to take on. If it were easy, everyone would do it." Maggie reaches her hand across the table.

I grip it and sniffle. "Yeah, I have thought that too. I wish I could pay a genealogist to do it for me."

"Where's the fun in that anyway?"

"True. But I'd get my answers."

"Well, keep that as an option. You could always save up for it."

"Yeah. The block in my flow is beyond frustrating. I felt so good making progress. But it was false hope."

"I hear ya. But you gotta keep trying. You have to keep hoping. That's the only way this will get done."

"But what if I never break this research wall I've hit?" I see the bricklayer smirking in my mind's eye. Grr.

"You'll bulldoze it down if I know you. Just like you are doing with the Brian wall. We just don't know when they'll be flattened. But it will happen." She winks.

That new image strangely comforts me. I move the foil down on my sandwich to prepare for another bite. Keep going, Rachel. You have to for Grandpa, and for yourself.

# Chapter 19

"Harrison, where do I look next?" I ask, as if he knows what to tell me. Instead, he bats the leg of the chair with his paws. I lay my head in my hands and rub my face. Weeks have passed, yet again, since any leads. And the lead I thought I had slipped through my fingers. Deleting my tree from FamilySearch felt like my soul was dying. Taking off each person, one by one, in Ancestry.com's tree was more of the same. I had to say goodbye to all of those people I called family for a short time. Bye Matilde and Alessio. Bye to all of you who I loved for a short but magnificent time.

I keep repeating steps that aren't getting me anywhere. Where are you hiding, Granza family? A deep breath fills my lungs and I try to release the frustration as I exhale with a groan.

Needing some outside air, I grab my keys and head out for a walk. I have to take action. I have to do something different than the monotonous pattern in which I'm stuck.

The heat of the concrete New York summer finally lifted and everyone's out and about to enjoy it. Look at all the happy people, strolling along with their dogs and boyfriends on this sunny September day. I wish I could walk Harrison like those dogs over there. I refuse to be one of those people who walk cats on leashes or push them along in pet strollers, though. I feel like people would judge me. I guess it wouldn't matter at this point.

As I walk toward the Hudson River, an old tune pops into my mind. "I love you a bushel and a peck. A bushel and a peck and a hug around the neck…" My grandma used to sing that song to me when she was helping me go to sleep. I feel a smile rise to the surface as I approach the river.

A person's brain does the strangest things. No matter how much I study people in my profession, I still will never understand how these thoughts randomly occur. Where do these ear worms come from? I haven't heard that song anytime recently, yet here it is, in my head on repeat.

A bench along the water looks like a great place to sit for a minute, as the song continues to play only for me. The memories of Grandma and Grandpa in their home, smelling like bread and garlic, comes to mind. My mouth waters for some of Grandma's "aioli," a garlic and olive oil sauce mixture for linguini, formally called aglio e olio. I deeply breathe in the air in hopes of breathing in the scent of the food in reality. That would be nice.

A small ship passes by the abandoned docks of the Chelsea Piers in front of me. Somehow and again randomly, Ellis Island materializes in my thoughts. Oh…my…God.

"Why haven't I thought to go there yet?" Okay, now I am talking to myself in public. I look around and fortunately it is pretty desolate here, as usual. Phew.

I haven't been to Ellis Island in years. It was a yearly school trip for all Pennsylvania youth in fifth grade. While I remember thinking it was interesting, I never thought about going back as an adult, and not at all for my current undertaking. Didn't all ships from Europe land at Ellis Island back in the day?

It's a real lead! Also, I think, this has to be a sign from Grandma and Grandpa. Ellis could be where the information I need resides. Of course, they would connect with me through music, a value that runs deep in our family.

Speed walking home, running up the stairs of my building, and continuing to run to the computer, I type the words "Ellis Island" as fast as possible into the search engine. Their hours of operation will work well for me to visit next weekend. I wish I could go tomorrow but it's not possible with work.

Oh, it looks like they have some information about immigration on their site. And about their exhibits, of course. There's a space for research right in their building; more than what's available on their website. But they do have a database of ship manifests and people's names online. Wow, how did I not know all of this?

Let's see… I type in "Salvatore Granza" and hit enter on the search button. Hmm, nothing comes up. I type in "Vince Granza" next. Nothing again? I pause a couple seconds and think I must have to search his full first name, Vincent Granza. Nothing yet again. Huh? More frantic now, I try entering "S. Granza" then "V. Granza." Nothing!

"Argh!"

As I scream, Brian walks through the door, looking startled and on the defense. "What?! What's wrong? Is someone in here?" He looks around, ready to defend us.

"No. I just came to yet another disappointment in my searching." I answer while tears build up in my eyes.

"You scared me, Rach!" He takes a moment to catch his breath. "Glad you are okay. Don't worry, you will find something soon."

Yeah right. I roll my eyes. "Sorry if I scared you. Well, I was looking on the Ellis Island website and got nowhere, yet again," I say with an even more edgy tone. "But I am just going to physically go there. Maybe it's easier to find information in person."

"Cool. I'm surprised you hadn't thought of that already."

"Why do you have to rub it in? I know! I can't believe I missed this huge opportunity that is down the road from us. Well, a road and the harbor." Adrenaline courses through my body. I don't need any discouraging comments from him.

"I'm not. Jeez. Calm down." He walks into the bathroom.

'Calm down' ranks as number one for phrases not to say when another human being is angry or anxious. But I force myself to focus on my trip to Ellis Island soon. It will be ok. *I will know.*

# Chapter 20

A gust of wind sends a shiver through me as I step onto the shaky ramp of the ferry at Battery Park. I grip my hoodie tighter around my neck. It's unusually cold for an early fall day so I'll make my way into the enclosed area to stay warm.

I look around and realize there are hordes of people going to Ellis Island today. Maybe it's like this every day. Who knows? This New Yorker doesn't. Waiting outside didn't seem as overwhelming as being on this boat with the crowd. Well, at least it's not as tight as the subway. It will be fine. The ride is only thirty minutes and there's no wretched smell. Score.

I scoot across the bench to make room for a few more people, who smile and nod their heads in gratitude. The engine is revving up and we are getting ready to take off, I think. Awesome, let's do this thing.

I twist my body around to watch the waves from the ferry as we make our way to the island. They're mesmerizing with their smooth cylinder-like flow. Did Grandpa and the rest of our family sit by the window and watch the glistening water as they sped to this destination from Italy? Did they stand on the deck? Did they wave at immigrants on other ships, like the movies portray? I envision many ships coming in at the same time with people en masse emptying out on the Island. Seeing land for the first time since leaving their countries had to be exhilarating for everyone. Starting the sought-after American dream was at their fingertips and about to be reality. My family made that dream happen.

But how did my family feel about leaving the women of the family? My grandpa and Great-Uncle Vince must have missed their mom and sister. Although my mom can be annoying at times, I would have been devastated to leave her behind, an ocean between us, not knowing when I would see her next—if ever. And especially as a child. There's no way I could have done that. I can't imagine how Great-Grandpa Gino felt either. Leaving a wife and child must be one of the bravest acts a person could do.

My grandpa was a strong and courageous boy for coming to America with his dad and brother, at only fourteen years old. I don't know if he worked in Italy, but I assume he must have with stating to the census taker that he only had a fourth-grade education. I wonder why he stopped going to school. Add it to my list of questions. Anyway, he wasn't sitting around the house doing nothing with that good old Italian work ethic. I know he would have been working right away in America too. I'm sure that was part of the deal with his dad. And knowing him, he would have wanted to work, learn, and contribute to the family in all ways.

Grandpa in his teenage mind probably also wanted to explore his new city on his own, thinking about what to do and what to see first. I bet he couldn't wait to run free after being restricted on a boat. I know the clients I see at that age would hardly be able to contain their energy. They often fidget with an object in their hands and are restless in their seat. I can only imagine the excitement of finally being on the land where my family talked about being able to live after such a long journey.

And I wonder what the conditions of the ship must have been like. While I'd like to think they were clean and safe, I fear they weren't always that way. Were there really rats, like the movie, *Titanic,* showed? God, I hope not.

What did they have for food on the ship? Was it basically stew and water? And how did they entertain themselves? Did they read or play cards? Oh, I'd love to know every. Single. Detail. Once I find out the ship's name, I can try to find out all of those features of their ship.

The ferry bumps against the dock, waking me from my daydreamy thoughts. When my three family members arrived on their ship from Italy, they must have been in awe, seeing the beautiful Statue of Liberty right there on the next island. They had to be thinking about all the opportunities that lay ahead for them in their brand-new country. I imagine they must have been scared too. Such a mix of emotions.

I wish Grandpa and I could have revisited the island together. Maybe seeing it as a museum and an educational site would have been gratifying for Grandpa. Just seeing how far he came must have made him proud, despite never returning here.

Before I get up from my bench, I look up to the boat's metal roof and send a message to him. *I am proud of you. I'm grateful for your bravery. And I miss you.* I sigh.

Walking off the boat and onto the sacred land of Ellis Island, I am struck by the beauty of the buildings—red brick and flawless white accents along the corners, windows, and doors. Multiple towers climb toward the skies with what seem like copper dome peaks matching Lady Liberty. What did the buildings look like in 1916 when Grandpa arrived? Were they similar to what sits in front of me or have the buildings been remodeled since then? I follow the crowd into the main building and spot a man in a blue vest. He must be an employee.

"The information counter is to your right and the maps and headphones for self-guided tours are to your left. Please help yourself."

I smile at him and walk to the display of maps, ready to explore on my own. English version, check. My thoughts would drown out any audio tour so this will be fine.

As I walk into the large main room and look at the map in my hand, I see I'm in the holding room, where many immigrants had to wait. It's a beautiful room...now. Back then, I bet it wasn't charming to those awaiting their life in a new country. Large dome windows scallop the top of walls covered in ivory subway tile. Two huge American flags are angled toward each other in the center of the grand room. As I lean on a post and stare out one of the tall windows, I wonder if my grandpa saw the same view—the Statue of Liberty standing proudly and waiting for him once he was able to leave this place.

A hallway off the holding room leads to medical exam rooms and overnight rooms, which look more like jail cells. There's even a small courtroom for the unluckiest of the newcomers. To be faced with more delays after they arrived here must have been torturous.

I shudder. I hope my family didn't stay here long. The pictures throughout the museum show people looking absolutely miserable, lacking smiles or any ounce of excitement. The long trip overseas had to be grueling with long days, rough conditions, and anxiety through the roof. Well, that answers part of my questions from the ferry. And I don't like the answers.

Walking through the displays of the now-turned museum, I find a section for multiple ethnic heritages. The one for Italians has information that makes sense with something Dad said the night he gave me information about our history. The sign states that upon arrival to the United States, the Italians were classified by not only country of origin, race, and other physical features, but also if they were Northern or Southern Italian.

I stop reading a moment and take in what I'm seeing. Grandpa stated he was from northern Italy many times, I remember now. I thought it was a strange addition to whatever he was saying in the moment, but never thought it was a cultural norm in Italy and definitely didn't give it more thought until Dad reminded me about his insistence recently.

Reading more of the signs, I see that the Northern Italians were associated with more wealth and education, as well as business owners. The Southerners were poorer and typically farmers. Grandpa grew up needing to define himself based on location, even though he seemed to be a combination of the qualities; part of a business owning family but still poor. I wonder what those identities meant to him. He didn't know how to *not* be defined by them, I guess.

Now what in the world is this? My eyes bug out when I read that some of the documentation of immigrants included descriptions for skin tone like fair, medium, or dark. Stop. I can't believe this. These words were used on actual legal documents? I feel sick to my stomach. Why was so much in history based on how someone looked? How did this ever matter for any group of people?

With these ludicrous and unnecessary descriptions of immigrants, there was more fuel to the fire for discrimination in their new home. I've read that in the late nineteenth century and into the early part of the twentieth century Italians were perceived as dirty if having dark skin, and that people went as far as lynching them. People viewed them, err, us, as lazy, ignorant, and criminal. This was a problem in the US countless times in its history and now I know how deep the racism existed for more diverse groups than I realized. The arbitrary standards were disgusting. Although Italians still have stereotypes in America, it isn't to this level. And sadly, so many other groups of people still face racism and hate crimes in America daily.

I shake my head as if that can fix the centuries of wrongdoings. My heart feels heavy and my shoulders slump. I take a deep breath to try to carry on.

After I get my legs moving again, I take in the rest of the information on the signs, thankfully including much less difficult facts to absorb. Oh, I need to go outside to find my family name on the memorial wall. I should have started there. Stupid, Rachel.

I push through the doors leading outside and venture to the glowing metal walls. The walls are massive, extending in multiple sections with what looks like a million names. Where's the "G" section? Hmm.

I spot it and rush over to see my family name. There are Granzas listed—but not my Granzas. No Salvatore to be found. How could that be? I look left and right, trace my finger along the etched names, and hope to see what I need. The list of names goes on and on. Italian, Irish, German…but my family doesn't appear anywhere here. Disappointment and confusion visit me once again.

I fall back on the wall, hoping the next time I turn around my family will appear. Dreams are free, after all.

I take one last glance. Nope. Still not there. This doesn't make sense. I exhale so heavily my lips flap.

Time to move along to the cafeteria, then. Energy is needed for the hours of research ahead of me. I pull the door open and view the menu above the registers. Oh, they have some appetizing choices. I'll take that ham and cheese sandwich with jalapeño chips on the side. And a Diet Coke. That will recharge my battery. I'll scarf down the goodies so I can keep going on my adventure.

Soon enough, it's time to find the research room. I'm a pro at eating in five minutes flat. Did you have any doubt?

As I walk there, I think how it's sensational to be in the same corridors as my family nearly one hundred years ago. And now I am researching that journey in the same place. If they only knew the irony.

The room of computers is easy to find. I spot a pleasant looking white-haired lady sitting at a welcome desk. She looks up when I stop in front of her.

"Hi. I want to find my family information…" My face flushes and I have trouble making eye contact. I suddenly feel like this is a strange statement. But this is the exact reason people come here. Stop those negative thoughts.

"Of course. Pick any computer you'd like. If you need any help, please let me know."

Phew.

"Thank you." I walk to the closest seat and shake the mouse as I sit down. Okay, here I go. I type Grandpa's name into the search engine. "Come on, Ellis Island computer," I say in the quietest whisper possible.

Whoa. A lot of Granzas came through Ellis Island. I see only one "S. Granza" so I click on that entry and hold my breath. And… it's not Grandpa. This guy didn't even come from Italy.

Keep trying. Keep going.

I glance down at my watch. An hour has already passed and none of my searches helped my cause. I entered all possible combinations of Salvatore, Vincent, Gino, and Granza that I could think of, and still nothing is right. If it's not the year being wrong for the immigrant's arrival into the US, it's that the country of origin is incorrect. Or the spelling of their name is odd in some way. Or whatever other stumbling block arises. How can searching for this information be so hard in this day and age?

I can't take the disappointment much longer. The roller coaster of a lead and a chance at Grandpa's secretive past being revealed then loss and emptiness are trying for anyone, including a certain lady trying to make a U-turn from mild depression. I thought coming to Ellis Island would be fruitful since the idea to come was a sign from my grandparents. I know it was. It was so clear, it had to be. The song and the thought of this new path for my research could not have been false hope. No!

"You look like you're about to give up. Can I help you search?" The employee is standing in front of me.

I blink in succession to come back to the present.

"I can't seem to get anywhere. I've been trying to research my family for months now and can't find any new information." Speaking the words feels like a thousand daggers in my heart. Do not cry, Rachel.

"Oh, yes. This is so common you wouldn't believe it." She flashes a reassuring smile.

I let out a deep breath as that glimpse of hope sneaks into my body again.

"Let me see what I can do." She grabs the mouse and asks, "What is your family's surname?"

"Granza. Given names of Gino, Vincent, and Salvatore. They came over from Italy in 1916."

We search together in the same ways I had been searching when alone. The fact that she isn't getting anywhere either makes me feel a strange reprieve, if only for not being a total stunad. Her sighs and other sounds of surprise contribute to my comfort as well. The loud and obnoxious ticking of the clock on the wall, however, does not. I feel like we are racing against that clock. I kind of wish this whole thing were a time limited test. Then I could have closure at a known time.

"Are you positive that your family came through Ellis Island?"

The question drives fear so deep I feel tingles in my limbs. "Yes, in 1916. Didn't everyone's family come through here?"

"There were many ports at that time. They could have come through Boston or Washington, DC—"

"They definitely came through New York. I know it." I don't mean to cut her off, but this has to be the port of entry for my family. Right? My grandpa always said, "When I arrived in New York, blah, blah, blah." Tears well up in my eyes and I wring my hands together as I wait for her response.

"Okay, dear. Let me see." She walks over to her desk and flips through a binder. Not glancing up as she comes back and just missing walking into a table, she squints and says, "You'll have to excuse me. I just started here a month ago." She fumbles through the pages in the binder for another few seconds. "They give us this guide to help people in your situation." Turning to another probable unhelpful page, she continues, "It says to try different spellings of your name. Have you done that?"

Oh, wait. "What do you mean?"

"Well, in historical records, you always have to try different spellings for names because sometimes travelers were not understood by the people recording their names in the log books, or maybe they purposely shortened their name in order to have a fresh start in America. Think about how the people documenting names were trying to communicate with people from all over the world. All of those accents they must have heard. Never mind those who didn't speak any English at all. Sometimes those writing in the logs made mistakes. And those mistakes last forever in the books and now in the databases."

My jaw drops. Why didn't I think of that? What does it mean for me? Is our family name even correct? My throat feels like it's closing. Does this mean I have to start my research over? Months of work for nothing? Again?

"Uh-oh." Brian walks over to give me a hug as soon as I enter our apartment and he sees my face. "What happened at Ellis?"

Tears stream down my cheeks. "I found nothing. Nothing! I even got help from the person who worked in the research room. She said to try alternate ways to spell my family name. I thought that must have been the problem, but that didn't even help. I don't want to give up, but I don't know what to do now."

"I know this was a huge disappointment for you, but we'll figure it out. Just try to relax tonight." He hugs me tighter and rubs my back. "Maybe you could talk to Annabelle tomorrow when we go out to dinner with her and Peter. She may have more ideas. She's a smart woman."

"Noooo! I totally forgot about that dinner. I don't want to go out tomorrow at all."

"Let's just go. I bet you will feel better tomorrow."

"Have you just met me? I don't think I will be magically okay by tomorrow night. But whatever. I shouldn't agree to do anything social these days."

He gives a sympathetic look and walks into the other room. Brian knows now to let me be alone to gather myself.

"Sorry, Brian," I say as he gives me space.

All I can do is wash my face, put on pjs, and curl up on the couch. This day must end. What started with such promise is ending in complete disaster.

*Chapter 21*

We meet Annabelle and Peter at a restaurant of their choice, as planned. I like being with Annabelle, but not on a night near of one of my year's lowest points. At least she knows what I am going through *and* the burgers are supposed to be excellent here. Food always helps the old mood.

When we walk into the restaurant, I spot them, side by side like they are on a first date. They are the married ones yet look like new lovers. They ooze happiness. And is that an actual holding of hands? Oh gosh, I can't take it right now. The more I struggle emotionally, the more I withdraw from others, especially Brian, and the more guilt I feel. I grab his hand in protest of my usual reaction and continue to walk toward the lovebirds.

"Hey guys," Peter says getting up to hug us hello. Annabelle follows and I turn on my all too familiar fake persona right away. The 'everything is great Rachel mask' is a common occurrence in the last few years. I think I even have Brian fooled sometimes. Maybe.

"I'm ready to eat. How about you?" Annabelle taps the menus at our seats so we could order and get the night started, I assume.

"Oh yes, you know me." I smile, let go of Brian's hand, and slide in my chair.

"I already ordered a bottle of Cabernet, if that's okay with you two," Peter says.

"Sounds good to us, right Rach?" Brian's baby blues sparkle in the restaurant lighting.

"I love it."

After choosing appetizers and meals, Annabelle whispers to me "Are you okay?"

Damn. Maybe I am not a great actress after all. Keep my day job, I guess. I answer semi-truthfully. "Yeah, I just have a little headache." Okay, not truthful at all. You got me.

"Oh, I'm sorry. Want some medicine? I have some in here somewhere," she asks as she frantically looks in her huge red zebra patterned purse. She has to match her red sequined cocktail dress and black patent leather four-inch heels, I'm sure. That makes me chuckle at least. I have to love her.

Still giggling, I say, "No, don't worry. I'll be okay. But thank you." I refuse to let my moodiness ruin the evening and I sure as heck won't dump my issues on her at a couples' dinner.

The guys carry on in conversation throughout dinner, always able to hit it off with no issue. They have a lot to talk about, both being in similar career fields. That's a relief for me at least. Sometimes partners of friends are such duds that Brian doesn't want to meet up with them. Peter is pleasant and dare I say, normal. Ah, there's my favorite word again.

At the end of the meal Annabelle and I indulge in a shared slice of black forest cake. I think how it's not *that* awful to be here with them tonight. Is it the chocolate speaking? Nah, it's because I enjoy being with Annabelle.

But her and Peter look so meant to be. Their behavior is a reminder about my questions for my own relationship. I am happy for them of course, but also always think why can't that be me right now? Unless it is how Brian and I feel about each other, and I just don't realize it. Why do I confuse myself so much?!

"Rachel, are you good? Want any more to drink or can we close out?" Brian asks.

"I'm fine." I grab his hand again and squeeze it. He squeezes it back. I listen to the voice within that tells me it feels right. *We* feel right, so what makes me constantly question our relationship?

Back at home I hug Harrison for a solid minute. He must be in a good mood. Maybe he finally caught his tail in play tonight.

As he jumps out of my arms, I go to the bathroom and get ready for bed. No matter how much I try to hold on to the reassuring feeling at the end of dinner, I struggle to push past the spiral of doubt and guilt.

Brian touches my shoulder while I brush my teeth, giving it a little love squeeze. I don't even notice right away. Images of Annabelle and Peter touching each other lovingly or looking into each other's eyes run through my head on repeat. They are so connected.

"Brian," I say as I crawl under the covers in our bed. "I just want to say I'm sorry I'm not like Annabelle."

"What? I need more words, Rachel." He turns to face me and slides across the sheets to be next to me.

"I just feel bad that I can't be my old self all the time. Looking at how Annabelle and Peter are always in sync, I feel awful that I am not like that with you right now. Consistently. But you know it's all me and nothing you have done, right? I know I'm tough to be around with my raging emotions or lack thereof sometimes. I don't know why you stay with me. I don't know, I just want to say I'm sorry."

He squints his eyes and tilts his head. Maybe he has lost hope in us or gotten used to the lull by now. Maybe he is planning his quick exit tonight and a bag is packed and ready in the closet. I'll wake up to a Dear John note on the counter with a mug set out for my coffee, because he is that sweet of a guy. He wouldn't leave me without taking care of me, even if only for one last sip of his love touched coffee. Maybe—

He cuts off my thoughts, thankfully. "Rachel, I don't want anyone but you. I'll even take you with your moodiness, though it makes me want to scream sometimes. I want us to work. I thought we talked about this already."

"We did, but I just want you to know I'm trying to change. I'm trying to fill that hole in me. I'm in progress. So please know that. I want things to be how they were when I wasn't on the verge of depression or…in actual depression."

I hate admitting this. I hate that I have let myself fall in this hole so far. I see how easily it happens now for clients. This whole experience is horrible for me, but constructive for them because now I can truly understand their situation even better. I would never want this, of course, but I'm still trying to see the positive in all of this mess. I'm going to be an even better therapist.

"I think you are adding more stress to yourself than you need. We will get through this. Let's just go to sleep for now." He kisses my lips then slips back to his side of the bed.

He isn't shocked by my use of the "D" word. He knows me better than I think. That's what happens after a long time together, so I shouldn't be surprised by his lack of surprise at my words.

Strangely enough, his ending of the conversation feels needed. There's nothing else to say at this time. There's only action to take. I hope to be me again someday and I'm going to keep trying to get there.

Brian and I can make it through this phase. I know it in my heart we are strong and we are a good pair, so I have to stop fighting with myself. I'm hereby declaring to myself that I will try to stop this back and forth worry about us. I don't have the energy for fighting the truth. And that's just dumb. I'm choosing a different choice, just like I would tell my clients.

Putting aside all of my flooding thoughts, I follow Brian's wishes and simply say, "Love you, Brian." I grab his hand once again tonight. He grips it in return.

# Chapter 22

Annabelle calls out to me from her office as soon as my client exits the waiting room door at our lunch hour. "Hey. You free?"

I walk over and sit down on her couch. "Yup. What's up?"

"I want to check in because I felt like the mood was off last night."

Oh. I wasn't expecting this. And saying *the* mood, not *my* mood. Hmm. She chose her words carefully. She's good.

"I've just been a little discouraged about my family research." I still can't bring myself to tell her the part about my friendly envy of her soulmate and her. Plus, I'm making a different choice now so there's no need. Brian knowing is enough. Yes.

"What's happened?"

"You know how the last thing I told you about was that I was going to go to Ellis Island? I was sure that my family's information would be in their database. Every family from back in that day came through there I thought. Well, not mine apparently. I always have to be the different one." As I say that last line, my eyes fill with tears. Good thing I never wear mascara.

Getting up to grab a tissue for me, she replies, "Oh sweetheart, that is awful news. I would be so upset too."

"I just have to brainstorm what to do next. It's like every angle I turn there is another roadblock."

"That is how that kind of thing is, I've heard. I haven't spoken to anyone doing it, but you know, it just seems like it would be that way, frustrating and all. I mean, why would companies advertise hiring their genealogists if it was easy work?"

That fact hits me again, giving me slight relief. "That's what I've thought. Thanks for reinforcing it, Ann." Still crying, but less so now, I get up for my own tissue this time. "I'm supposed to help other people crying at work, not be the one crying."

"You are human. It's okay. Now, let me know if I can help at all. I don't know a thing about that whole process, but I'm here for you. Wait, let me see if I could find something here." She shuffles the pile of items on her desk around, then looks in a drawer of her file cabinet. Lord only knows what she is searching for, let alone if she will ever find it in that tornado of an office.

After a minute of tsking and sighing, she gives up. Her attention span won't last much longer, despite her kind heart and intention. "Oh, phooey. I can't find it. I wanted to give you that friendship magnet you gave me last year. It said something about always being there through thick and thin. That applies from me to you as well and you could use it now. It's just right for this particular dilemma."

I can't help but smile. "You are a thoughtful soul and the greatest co-worker. Thanks, but don't worry. I know you are here for me. It is just that nobody can do this for me. Well, except if I hire someone, that is."

"You'll get through this."

"Thanks. Okay, I need to make sure I leave enough time to eat my lunch and be put back together before my first afternoon client arrives for their session."

"Yes, me too. Later."

I go back to my desk and turn on some R&B music to enjoy while I eat the sandwich Brian made for me this morning. He always makes our lunches fresh in the morning, so we don't have soggy bread. Today's turkey and cheese on wheat has a special mayonnaise with dill herbs. It's so tasty I forget about my issues for a second. Just a second.

I need to remember the points that bring me relief, like that one about how I'm tackling this adventure on my own as a non-professional genealogist. Go me. Maybe I should make a list later. Yeah, a list of feel-good thoughts so when I feel sucked into the abyss, I can pull myself out. Like I need another list. I'll remember this stuff. And I must pull up my appointment calendar now anyway.

"All right, who's coming in next?"

It will be eleven-year-old Cole, a sixth grader whose parents are newly separated. He isn't acting out or anything, but his parents want to make sure he is doing well, not just putting on a front for them. I can see through an emotional disguise with these kids as easy as seeing my reflection in the mirror, and he isn't acting.

This is only the second time I am working with him, so we're still building a rapport in order for him to trust me. I plan to try to color with him while we speak because he loves art. It'll get him talking more and I can get information from what he draws. Setting out some coloring pages and blank paper, I reach for my bucket of crayons and colored pencils and place it on the center of the table.

After this preparation and glancing at last session's note, I feel a sense of calmness. At least now I can concentrate on my work. Maybe I needed a tiny cry at work. Or Annabelle's words. She is a therapist after all.

# Chapter 23

The changing season is yet again upon New York City, which is taunting me with a reminder of the last few months' research being all for nothing. The last time the trees showed their evolution, it was spring. I had no idea what the following months would include, but as time progressed my mood followed suit with the flourishing trees and flowers. From the normal Rachel doldrums, the crescendo to excitement, hope, and most of all, some deeper meaning, to the present free fall. Now, the trees are going dormant in the nearing winter, matching my history search. I feel a pain in my heart for the lack of progress. With each leaf falling to the cold, hard ground, more of my expectations also plummet. Once again.

This weekend, however, I try my fortune at what may be a last possibility for answers. I read about the National Archives near Battery Park being another option for a database of ancestry records. Brian offers to go with me but could only supply a few hours at an inconvenient time with my schedule, due to his work schedule. It is better I go alone anyway. I don't want him to experience the probable failure that meets me there and my mood not being able to survive it in a socially appropriate manner. Crying and cursing under my breath wouldn't help our relationship status.

Walking to the Archives from the subway stop nearby, I get a chill that is like no other I've had in my entire life. It shakes me to the bone and wakes up all of my senses. My nerves are at full alert, shooting unknown signals to my toes. I look around, as if I'll find a reason.

Having been a New Yorker now for years, without the luxury of suburbia's car transportation door to door, I am not that affected by its cold weather, and especially not fall temperatures, so what's happening? I walk faster to the building. Get me to the warmth.

The chill lingers a few more minutes, despite my speed walking. When I finally reach the door of the Archives building, the heat from inside washes over my entire body. The drastic change makes me shiver again, right in this spectacular foyer. I hope I am not getting sick. I probably am, with my luck.

The foyer is a grand area, with what looks like gorgeous early twentieth century details from floor to ceiling. My mission, and my physical reactions, escape me for a moment as I am awestruck by the room's beauty. The gold lined wall sconces, decorated ceilings with attached ivory sculptures, and the beautiful banister details on the stairs are breathtaking. The old buildings in the city are all stunning, but this building is on another level. Okay, enough distraction though; back to business. Where are the research rooms?

Once I find them, a room attendant greets me kindly and offers any assistance when and if he is needed. I smile in an awkward manner and choose my seat. This time, there are at least four other people in the room, unlike the Ellis Island research room. Four other hope-filled people on similar journeys, like the one that consumed me almost this whole year, are right here with me. Maybe they had some success on their research travels and now's my time.

First, I search the correct spellings of my family's first and last names, each and every one, then the alternate last name spellings. It is so routine by this point I can practically do it with my eyes closed. It takes a few hours to get to the point where I can conclude I am still on the wrong path, searching each tiny lead and being led to dead ends. Yes, the records are correctly brought up for my family once they were in the US, except still not for Gino for some reason. I want to scream. I can't even find the vessel that brought them to America. I just don't understand.

With my head resting on the palm of my hand under my chin, I go somewhat delirious and type arbitrary Italian sounding combinations of words with my last name. I try Granzafina, Granziatti, D'Granza, and so on.

What's this? The name on the screen makes me stop in my tracks. My foolish game of desperation has led to a fascinating find. Allegranza populates as an actual last name. Huh? Wait a second here.

I type in my grandpa's full name and hold my breath.

There it is.

The words "Salvatore Allegranza" appear on the screen along with the information stating he immigrated from Italy to the US *"through New York ports."* Eee! His birth year is correct. His death date is also true. Home addresses. Check.

I keep scrolling to confirm every fact listed. This one hundred thousand percent has to be my grandpa. Yesssss!

I navigate back to the main search and see another Allegranza. Vincenzo Allegranza. Great-Uncle Vince's name was Vincenzo, not Vincent! The Italian version of Vincent was needed all this time. Of course! I feel like my eyes grow larger than my head. These records are my family's records. I am too excited to feel stupid for not having thought of these alternate spellings. Hmm, that's weird for me. Anyway, the right files exist. My family is documented as arriving as immigrants in New York.

But wait, there is still no date of entry, actual port of entry, or ship listing. This dance I'm doing of a step ahead and two steps back has to stop. I quietly groan.

But as soon as I feel the annoyance building, a chill goes through me once again. This time, I realize the sensation is a definite sign. Grandma and Grandpa sent that chill through me outside as well, I know now. It has to mean I am on the right track, even with the questions that remain. I will never doubt their signs again, as I did for Ellis Island. I guess it just takes time to get the reassurance sometimes. They are making me work for it. The Italian work ethic persists.

*Please forgive my haste and ignorance, Grandma and Grandpa. I just want to know you more, Grandpa. I won't give up the search.*

"I found something! I found my family in the records today!" I exclaim upon Brian setting one foot into our apartment.

He looks at me with bright eyes. "That's great news, Rach. What did you find?" He takes off his black leather messenger bag, light fall jacket, and loafers while petting Harrison as he greets him at the door.

"I know now that my last name is supposed to be Allegranza." I pause for his reaction before continuing, but my eyes get wider by the second.

"What? I don't understand. Supposed to be?" Brian walks over to me and sits down on the couch.

I speak with increasing speed. "Remember how I was told to look at alternate spellings by that lady at Ellis Island? Well, I started adding prefixes and suffixes to my last name and this is what I ended up stumbling upon. I don't know why it was changed to Granza, but I know for a fact that it was changed. This is definitely my family. Even one record for Grandpa and Great-Uncle Vince's known US address showed up with the new, or I mean old, last name. The original surname hasn't been on any other documents I've found. Not on newspaper announcements for events with the business, not for burial records, and not even Grandpa's cherished naturalization papers. All other documentation shows the name Granza."

"That is really something. I am shocked too, but more happy for you. You are getting somewhere, Rach."

"Yeah, I was losing faith recently."

"Uh, you think? I try to leave you alone when you are in those moods, but I also do keep an eye on you."

"What do you mean you 'keep an eye on me?'" I am riding high on adrenaline so I'm careful to stay in check with my tone. Choices, Rachel. It's cute he cares so much, but what does he actually mean?

"It's part of my job as being the world's best boyfriend to make sure you are okay, that's all." He brings his arms up like he's God as he speaks the words 'world's best boyfriend' and it makes me laugh.

"Well, you aren't the *best*, but you know, you'll do." He grabs me and tickles me as I playfully scream to stop.

I don't even get the chance to tell him about the knowledge I gained about Great-Uncle Vincenzo (how wonderful to know and to say his real first name now) before we find ourselves acting like Annabelle and Peter. Finally. My mindful choices lifestyle may be helping us after all.

# Chapter 24

The recent mounds of snow lessen my guilt of not wanting to leave my home. While most people dread the coming winter, sometimes I think it could be helpful for perspective, even when not trying to solve all these mysteries. The weather is a perfect excuse to stay in my soothing space and have a moment of gratitude. Even sludging through the snow for work, I end up in my comfortable office. I need to embrace these thoughts more often.

I love to stare out of my window at the white, fluffy flakes floating down while I sit in my warm apartment, cozied up with my fuzzy blanket on the couch. I pull it tighter around my body, sit up straighter, and position my computer on my lap.

Since the new/old last name reveal, the ancestry databases have become my friends again. Gino has entered the building! I do an upper body dance of joy. There's no shame in this game.

Gino's date of birth and his Italian business records are right in front of my eyes once again. I keep bringing up his beautiful name, appearing in someone's perfect cursive handwriting. It's the most gorgeous view in all of New York City. Every document shows him living in Genoa, or as the records state, Genova, Italy. He was born and raised there from what I can conclude so far. Any other documents though? Well, they're still in my hunt.

What's beyond amazing is that I now know the names of my great-grandmother and Grandpa's full-blood sister. Francesca can finally be declared my great-grandma and Antonia my great-aunt. Isn't that exciting? I squeal internally every time I think about them.

Beyond the birth and death years of my family members, well most of them, ugh, there still isn't much more information I can find. I can't break a second metaphorical wall that's present now. Those bricklayers are still hard at work.

Even with knowing our true and original last name and confirming birth dates, I still can't find some family members' baptism records, marriage records, and death records. These documents would reveal a treasure of family information, such as addresses, names of the generation before my great-grandparents, and who Grandpa's sisters married. My family *had* to be members of their neighborhood church in Genoa, knowing how religious they were, so why doesn't that information appear?

I reach for my steaming coffee and take a second to sniff the hazelnut creamer before taking a sip.

My fingers drift away from the ancestry search engines and type the word "Genoa" into Google. I guess my fingers know I need a break from chipping at the wall.

Images of Grandpa's hometown flood the screen. My God, those lush green hills and those rocky cliffs set against the dark blue sea. The Mediterranean architecture in the warm tones of the color spectrum force my eyes wide open. The photos are true eye candy. Okay, the most beautiful site in the city today may be these images. I was wrong.

I open my Pinterest page and immediately start a Genoa board. The photos from there are too gorgeous not to keep coming back to in the future. But what's this? Genoa is known for pesto and focaccia bread. These are two foods I can't live without. Often, I eat them together. Of course, I hone in on the food.

Leaning in to this sidetracked journey for now, I take a large bite of my biscotti. Its sweetness matches the moment.

More and more information populates on Pinterest. They know

how to capture my attention and suck me in. This pin leads me to an article that states Genoa was a major seaport and maritime city for centuries. It must have been easy for my family to leave Italy from that port then. How convenient. It looks like there is still a lot of trade that goes on there today too.

I need to make sure to save all the information I can find about Genoese culture. *I'm* Genoese, after all. Italy is a country that I only dream of visiting so I've never researched anything about it. I should have looked up information about Genoa years ago. How has this thought never crossed my mind? I curl my lips and ball my fists at the thought. The next book I read will have to be about Genoa. Or at least fiction with the story set there.

What about the early 1900s in Philly, Grandpa's new city? Rapidly typing those phrases into the search brings up a whole different vibe. Oh, these pictures are much darker than the glistening Genoa shots. I don't know if I want a board like this in my Pinterest account.

I type in "Italians immigrate to Philadelphia 1900s" on Google instead and click enter. Well, there is a lot to sift through here.

Okay, it was more of a popular destination than I thought. This first article states many Italians immigrated to South Philly in those years, which is consistent with the wave of Italian immigration to other areas of the US at that time. Little Italys formed and jobs were booming in the careers that Italians were already trained in from Italy.

Skimming more, I see jobs were plentiful in factories, but the specific work our family did—tailoring—was one of the listed necessary occupations for South Philly. What a perfect opportunity for my family. Their knowledge was needed. Maybe that's why they settled there. Hmm.

The demands of America's progress included the skills of Italians. My people! I take in that thought and hold the pride close to my heart. Grandpa's family trade was essential to keep America growing.

In these old photos, the fabric merchant shops look like they were close in proximity to tailors. Did they all have certain districts or something? The shoemakers on one block and the butchers and bakers on the next? Maybe businesses that didn't complement each other as much didn't need to have these connections. But maaaybe I'm just making up stories. The proximity is an interesting idea to remember when searching for information in the future, though. It may help me somehow. I grab my journal to jot it down. The facts are starting to add up so much that I need to keep track. I don't want to forget anything.

I finish the rest of my biscotti and smile at Harrison. The sound of my movement casts his attention my way. But as soon as we make eye contact, he meows.

"What, little man?"

*Meow.*

"I'm busy over here. If you want more attention, come over and sit with me." I pat the cushion next to me.

He puts his head back down.

Looking back at my screen, I don't recognize any storefronts as Grandpa's store in these photos, but I'll keep exploring. I only saw a few pictures as a child, but I think I'd remember. That would be pretty unbelievable if any photos of his store exist online. Maybe I can catch a glimpse of the inside someday.

Oh gosh, what are these photos? They speak a thousand words. I see why the phrase is true.

Glum looking new Americans working in dirt lined streets is not a pretty picture. Their faces convey a hard life, full of long days and less than exciting work. Maybe I am reading into the images too much, but my heart breaks for them. How spoiled we are now, due to these ancestral angels that paved the way for easier times for us. I can't believe Grandpa had to live in those hard times. It must have been challenging to earn enough money to survive in a new country and to eventually help feed a whole family, be it his family of origin or creation. I pray that behind the straight faces and apparent discomfort that the photographs show, there was true satisfaction and fulfillment for their achievements.

The rows of wooden crates of fruit and vegetables lining the streets show a hint of home that was brought with the immigrants. People were carrying wicker baskets as their shopping bags of the day, dressed head to toe in what looks like peculiar clothing for today's standards, though I doubt they were for back then. Man, it must have been hot in the summer. The landscape in general looked dusty and soiled, and so did their clothes.

Now here are happier people. I click to enlarge this photo. Musicians look like they were playing their mandolins and accordions at a festival. Maybe these images demonstrate what was the start of the Italian festivals I grew to know, which I loved attending as a child. Their pride shows through the faded photos, over one hundred years earlier than today according to the date written on the photo. There is always a large saint or a Virgin Mary statue carried at the front of the parade that starts the festivals the information states, which is also pictured here. Another photo's caption reads that the "festas" gave the Italians a sense of being united and that there was a comfort when at the festivals because they shared a similar identity in this new land, even when I now know they were looked down upon for what seemed like strange beliefs to others.

As I continue to view the pictures, my perception morphs. Maybe they weren't miserable and overworked people. Well, probably overworked, let's be real here. But maybe they were serious in the pictures because they had a lot at stake and they took every minute in the United States as a chance to succeed; to make it at their jobs, with their families, and even for their celebrations and traditions to persist. And they had a lot to celebrate, finally living in America.

Oh, now what's this? Okay, this is the last bit I'll allow myself to dive into today.

"I swear it is, Harrison," I say like he can hear my thoughts.

How could I not read about the Italian language dwindling with the immigrants in America? It's one of the fastest dying languages? No, this can't be true. I honestly haven't heard it spoken by anyone too much in my life, but what I have heard was beautiful.

Reading more, I see that when immigrants came to the United States, they were desperate to assimilate, and often abandoned their home language. They would change anything about themselves to be a true American. They not only wanted to learn English but wanted to forget their old language when conversing with others in the new land. One quote is from someone who said their mom would get scolded by her Italian immigrant parents for speaking Italian. They would say "Soltano Inglese," or only English.

My mouth drops open.

Did that ever happen with my dad? I doubt Grandpa and Grandma would penalize him for trying to speak Italian. Right?

Was this why Grandpa never wanted me to learn Italian? Never wanted to be called Nonno, like many Italian grandpas? Not that I pushed either issue, but I remember trying to read a letter or two of his, between his sister and him, and he wouldn't let me. He would just say it wasn't important and don't worry about it, while grabbing it out of my hands. I always let it be, without a thought as to his reason. And, of course, he was called Grandpa to me, so that wasn't a big deal. But wow, he wanted to be American with all his heart.

Well, I'll end this round of research on that note. An exhausted sigh escapes. It's a lot of emotional information to take in for one night. I rub my eyes to gain some visual clarity. The screen sometimes does a number on them.

I move my laptop to the coffee table, place a throw pillow at the arm of the couch, and plop down to lay flat.

With the plethora of images whirling through my mind, I want to focus on the beauty of Italy and the promise of Philly that my

Grandpa must have had. That foreign land of South Philly is only thirty minutes from my childhood home, jeez. If I knew back then what I know now, I'd have been down there all the time, taking in the sights. I'll visit what's left of it someday. That's in my power and darn it, I will make that a reality.

# Chapter 25

When lunch time comes, I stroll along the Chelsea sidewalk near my office to meet Maggie for lunch, lost in thoughts, as usual. Today I am especially absent from the moment. I've been forcing myself to try to stay present all morning with my clients so now I declare permission to myself to let my mind wander. Ahh. I exhale a large breath.

I wrap my oversized scarf around me once more to shield myself from the chilling wind blowing through the streets. My curls must be popping out of my ponytail since I forgot my snow hat at home. I'll look like a lion with an unruly mane by the time I arrive at the diner.

People rush by to escape the temperature, from the looks on their faces, but this is a needed break for me. It's been hard to focus since all I can think about are the scenes I viewed last night. What was life like for my family living in Philly long ago? If it were just Grandpa, his dad, and Great-Uncle Vince in a tiny living space, without the added Serafinos? I allow myself to slip even farther from reality and let my daydreaming take over.

Young Grandpa, adolescent Great-Uncle Vince, and Great-Grandpa Gino were in their little apartment. The boys were quietly reading books at the brown nicked up wooden kitchen table. Only three chairs existed, instead of a more common set of four.

Their dad was cooking food for them. Was it dinner? Yes, dinner. The linguine was about to be thrown into the large black pot on the stove. Sauce was simmering on the other burner. There were only two burners. Stirring from one pot to the next continued back and forth for a few moments.

Great-Grandpa Gino scurried from the stove to the window briefly to close off the cold breeze flowing in through the bright yellow curtains. The whole room was beige, with paint chipping everywhere and visibility of rust-colored walls underneath. The room was dark with the weather's dreariness and didn't have any decorations. The only light seemed to be from the curtains.

No fridge was in the room, so a stick of butter was sitting on the tiny balcony of their wrought iron framed fire escape. Maybe it was so cold outside that the dairy had a chance to survive. How did Great-Grandpa afford the ingredients to even make dinner for the family when conditions looked so meager?

They spoke few words to each other until it was time to eat. The food opened the floodgates, though. Each boy was trying to out-talk the other.

"Let me tell you about my day at school today," teenage Grandpa said.

Then, Great-Uncle Vince responded back, "No, I have so much more to tell you." He rose out of his chair, but immediately sat down when Great-Grandpa gave him a look. That's the universal look from all parents to sit and eat.

Great-Grandpa Gino smiled at him, taking a seat and letting the boys verbally fight out their position in the storytelling line. But when dinner was done, he insisted on them cleaning up then going to bed right away. It was past dark now and time to sleep.

There was one light for the entire apartment, and it was small and dim. Everyone slept on the other side of the room, not having another room in existence. The boys had to sleep together in a twin size bed, while Great-Grandpa Gino had his own bed, atop theirs, bunk bed style. Sheets were thin and dingy white, but they did have a heavy gray blanket and pillows.

Despite the bleak surroundings, all of my family members appeared happy. What a strange juxtaposition to imagine, but I have an overwhelming confidence that it was accurate. They loved spending time together and it showed in their smiles and energy with one another. Their daily routine was stable and secure for the teens.

As they went off to sleep and their dad read at the table, I wonder what tomorrow would have brought for them. Work I'm sure, but what else? Conversations with good neighbors? Written letters to and from their mom/wife and sister/daughter? I just hope they had the closeness I imagine and that they were happy.

I am long overdue for a grilled cheese sandwich and fries and this 1950s style establishment is the best option near my office. Maggie orders her standard tuna melt and we enjoy our Diet Cokes, sitting on the turquoise pleather seats near the jukebox. Elvis belts out "Teddy Bear" and I almost sing along. What a reprieve in the middle of the day.

"You are sure talking more with your hands today than usual," she says while chewing her first bite of the melt.

Laughing because it is true, I respond, "Well, that's me, as you know. Give me a break."

"Mmmm-hmmmm." Maggie can draw out her words like no one else, adding extra special sarcasm and drama just for me. "So, let me tell you about Ray." She's a to-the-point type person and today is no different. I love the lack of small talk. "He's been surprisingly good to me. He opens cab doors for me, makes sure I am satisfied with the food when we're dining out, and generally does all the chivalrous things any woman would want…"

Uh-oh. "What?" I say in a way that braces myself for the "but" that is coming. This is Mags and about a romantic interest, after all.

"See, he's great, but he does this thing."

Busting out laughing, I say, "There's the 'but.' Oh, God. What is it now?"

"I know, right? It's always something," she says matter of fact then continues. "But Ray always wears his sunglasses. Even indoors."

"Oh, no, you have to be kidding!" I scream across the table, but not loud enough to cause a scene. "He wears sunglasses. The horror of it all!" I make sure to act dramatic back to her, of course.

Cackling now, Maggie corrects me for my exaggerated response. "No, you don't get it. We don't live in Hollywood. Why does he insist on always having his sunglasses on, even on gloomy days? It isn't summertime anymore, so what is his deal? It's just weird. I don't know." She drops her head down.

I have seen this situation more than once with her, so I expect some strange trait she dislikes in her current dating partner, but I don't expect this reaction. I have never seen her this affected. She must really like this guy, so I change my joking tone. "Does this mean you will be breaking up with him? Is this the deal breaker this time? I'm so sorry he does that."

She looks back up at me. "I am going to try to be an adult this time. I like everything else about him, well, for the most part. I mean, he hums a lot, but that doesn't get on my nerves as much as the sunglasses. It's just...odd."

"Well, I can name a few things about you that he may think are strange." I wink in a purposely creepy manner so it's obvious that I'm kidding. I want to bring up her mood like she's done for me countless times.

"Like what?" She retracts her chin. Her brows furrow at the same time.

Oh, I'm not as obvious as I thought when I try to be creepy.

"How about that you bite your lips when you are thinking? That you start singing song lyrics when people say certain phrases? That you—"

She stops me by holding up her hand and rolling her eyes. "Okay! I get it. I am not perfect, I know."

"No, those are just your *things*. Your cute little quirks. They aren't bad, but maybe someone would think they are unusual, like you do with Ray's quirks."

She nods and looks like she's processing what I said.

I continue, "Well, look, Ray seems like a good one. I like him. Brian likes him. You like him! Just don't let his eyewear preferences get in the way of something real."

"It does feel real this time, doesn't it?" she says looking to the side and still appearing deep in thought. She takes a deep breath and says, "I'll do my best."

"So, this was what you needed to tell me?" I couldn't help but laugh again. You gotta love her. I do.

"Well, yeah, what did you think? I mean, come on. It couldn't be something you would think is big, Miss I'm So Deep I'm Finding My Roots." Maggie flashes a mischievous side smile, squinting with one eye.

The rest of the lunch hour ends up consumed with me updating her on my ancestry search, making plans to hang out soon again, and touching on Brian issues, questions, changes, improvements, and whatever else fit into the time frame of lunch that still lingers. This time with Mags is just what I needed to carry me through the rest of the day.

Walking out of the diner and back to my office, I review my next client's treatment plan goals from memory. It is always good for my mood when I can get out of myself and my own concerns, if only for a few hours. And now I feel like I can carry that on and be more present the rest of the day. Well, I can aim for it anyway.

*Chapter 26*

This month brings colder fall weather and even colder attitudes from me at times. It must be a post quarter life crisis. Yeah, I made the term up, but it's probably true. Well, it needs to end already. I'm tired of it. I demand it leaves now. Uh, pretty please?

It's time to try something I haven't done in the past. Yes, I'm still attempting to follow my own advice. That's what I help the kids with at work; if someone keeps trying an action that hasn't worked in the past, why the hell would it work now? By the way, I do not swear in front of them, so just take that word right out of there and imagine it otherwise. And just like the kids, I must be missing a change that's in my power, so think, Rachel, think.

Come on. You can do it.

I shut my eyes tight and put all my effort into this intention for what seems like hours, though it's only minutes.

Hmm, what about the Catholic churches in Genoa? I wonder if I'll get anywhere by researching the churches that existed in the early 1900s. I'll go directly to the source, since I can't find any religious documents on the ancestry sites for my family. Yes! I know for a fact that my family was Catholic, like many Italian families back in the day, so I can bet on that at least. This can be a whole new route to try for family information. *Thank you, God, Grandpa, Grandma, or however I got this idea.*

After a few minutes online, I see that Genoa seems bigger than

I thought, so narrowing down its churches may be a challenge. Even navigating the Italian websites are a challenge. Grr. Sometimes the page doesn't have a button to translate the content, and I don't know Italian, so I don't know what is written at all. The page could say, "Stop looking for something you'll never find, you American idiot. Find another hobby," for all I know. To avoid that negative focus, I push forward and try to piece together the phrases from internet translating sites.

Oh, now I see. Yay, translation website. It looks like only two churches existed in Genoa during the time my grandpa was a child. I wonder if he lived nearby also. I'll write that down in the journal really quick. Okay, come back to that, but first, stay on this track.

Maybe I'll contact the church staff directly and see if they have any answers for me. I click on the email address on one church's website and compose my query on whether my family's records exist there. Oh, I better include a translated version of my narrative. What if the staff member doesn't know English? I cut and paste my letter into the translation website then repeat the steps in reverse. After both the English and Italian versions of my email reside on the digital page, I click the send button and feel a sense of accomplishment.

Scanning the website of the other church option, I find that it doesn't have an email address, only a snail mail address. I grab a piece of paper and a pen to write an old-fashioned letter, copying my email content exactly, in both languages again. As fast as I can move, I lick the envelope to seal it, triple confirm the mailing address, and set it by my keys so I can mail it tomorrow morning. I wish the mail carrier could pop by a second right now.

I also wish I could call the churches, so I don't have to wait for responses. I don't have an international plan on my phone, though. And again, I don't speak the language anyway. Argh!

Since I'm on a roll otherwise, where else could I look online for places in Italy that may have records? I sit back down and think. The screen stares at me.

Maybe the city hall or a newspaper archive site. I have seen an advertisement about a newspaper archive online here in America. Well, anything's worth a try.

I search a while for both. What a shock. Another void. The Italian city hall doesn't have records online and no newspaper articles populate with any family member's names. I am getting nowhere fast yet again. I think I'm a master of that now.

No, choose to concentrate on the positive. I made a step tonight that may pay off. I'll have to hold out hope for a kind church employee to answer my email or letter. I just wish for it to be sooner than later.

*Chapter 27*

So, here we are. Christmas Eve at my parents' house. How did the year go by swiftly, yet painstakingly slow? Actually, that seems typical lately.

As I sit at their kitchen table, I take in the aroma of the holiday food and listen to songs from Bing Crosby and Lou Monte in the background. Dominick the Donkey always makes me laugh. I'll be a kid at heart forever when that's playing.

Staring into the living room, I admire the soft-appearing Douglas fir, complete with the angel from Grandma and Grandpa's old artificial tree. Dad insists that their topper will always be the one we use on our trees. I agree with this tradition, of course. She shines atop the sparkly tinsel and colorful lights as if confident in the miracle of Christmas. Why can't she bring me answers as a Christmas miracle?

I reflect on how the days have inched by since I wrote the letter and email to the churches in Italy and how I haven't reaped any rewards for my hard work. I'll take anything at this time; a pointer in another direction, a lead…anything. I check my email spam folders obsessively every day and make sure to get the snail mail as well. And there's always nothing. I am sure *someone* has to have written back and either it got lost in the ocean crossing or in the internet servers somehow.

I am so sick of waiting for a next step. At least my torturous delays haven't been affecting me as much with Brian. Making different choices and trying to focus on logical, positive thoughts has helped me and therefore us, especially when the Christmas spirit takes hold. I'm glad I can remind myself that I enjoy this time of year, and that I can finally use some of my therapy techniques on myself.

Brian's right by my side today, as usual. Tomorrow we will visit some of his family, but I'm thankful that he gladly spends the large Italian holiday of Christmas Eve with mine. Well, he would be a fool not to spend it here, with the incredible food we prepare.

The Feast of the Seven Fishes is an Italian tradition that my grandpa carried on and my parents continue to engage in as well. Right now, there are seven types of seafood being prepared, in addition to homemade soup, Grandma's "aioli," tossed salad, and crusty bread. I imagine the explosions of taste and let out a satisfied sigh.

Brian looks over at me, mid-cutting of the bread.

We exchange a smile and he goes back to his much-enjoyed task.

Baccalá is the staple fish every year and it's making this year's appearance across the room. It's the one smell in this kitchen that I'm not too thrilled about. I never think it's that tasty, but Grandpa demanded it every year, and other family members still like it. So, it continues to be made in his honor. I'll drink my eggnog to drown out the odor.

Speaking of sugary treats, the desserts are plentiful in the Granza household, of course. Cheesecake and a variety of Italian cookies are the most common sweets to have on this holiday. Pizzelles are always one of the Italian cookies my mom makes. The crispy vanilla flavored flat cookie, shaped like a snowflake and topped with confectionary sugar, is easily my favorite cookie in general. I look over at them on the counter, ready to be devoured. I'm coming for you, babies.

Brian jumps right in today to help my mom, but she knows I would be more of a hinderance than a help to her smooth flow. I have my hands full trying to put up with Dylan anyway. He's in the living room with Dad, where I generally hang out. He throws in stupid comments here and there to try to irk me, but I am not allowing it today. Literally. I left the room to come and sit here. I'll just ignore him, unlike the attention seeking eight-year-old he acts like.

But after only a half hour, Dad calls out, "Rachel, come in here again."

"Yeah, we miss youuu," Dylan adds.

Fire fills my chest at the sound of his brattiness.

Parents always want the kids to get along. Grr. Well, it's Christmas Eve, so I'll try to make him happy. "Coming."

As soon as I sit on the couch, Dad turns his body toward me from the other end. "Tell us about how your family research is shaping up after you found our original last name. I still can't believe that one. When I told your Uncle Tonio, he was also in shock."

"Aww, I hope they all have a great Christmas in sunny LA. I wish they lived here. Anyway, thanks for asking. Yeah, it's pretty amazing."

I will still ignore Dylan's comments, but so far, he hasn't made a peep. Does he want to hear how it's going also? I furrow my brow in caution but proceed to spill all the details.

My dad's face drops by the end of the short summary of progress, or lack thereof.

It feels like validation for how hard it has been to get to the reason Grandpa never wanted to talk about his youth. I'm sure Dad wants the information just as much as me. And, my dad could usually fix anything for me when I was a child, but adult issues are a whole different animal. I can see him racking his brain for an easy answer to solve all of my adult problems, now and in years past. He opens his mouth and holds back from speaking multiple times for this problem's solution. I know he has no idea what to say to help his little girl, but his desire to help is bursting from his insides. "A" for effort, Dad.

He finally finds the words. "I think you will get there. You will find what you want. I guess it just takes time, honey." I can see his metaphorical heart breaking for me when he gives up the brainstorming and makes that statement. He knows I always reached my goals in school and in my career, but this goal is more out of my control, making it my first—and hopefully last—feeling of such immense failure.

"I just wish I knew *how* to move forward. I am waiting for a letter of some form that may never arrive. My past and future seem to be in someone else's hands and that isn't okay with me."

Letting out a loud groan, Dylan blurts out, "Rachel! Why are you so dramatic? I don't even understand why this is that important to you. Can't you just be normal like everyone else and not care about the past?"

I clench my jaw as heat sparks up in my chest. He said the magic word. The negative magic word, that is. I will never be "normal," like I always have tried to be. I open my mouth to speak, but all that comes out is a tear from my eye. He's impossible to ignore.

In the most obnoxious voice, Dylan carries on saying, "Poor little Rachel, who has the life and still complains about it. Enough already. We are all sick of your privilege."

Now, dad chimes in, "That's enough, Dylan. Leave your sister alone. This research means a lot to her because Grandpa meant a lot to her."

"He always loved her more than me, so whatever." He kicks the ottoman in anger.

The fury in me rises within a millisecond. If it were tangible, it would shoot to the top of my fiery red hair and burst through my head to the ceiling. "YOU WILL NEVER TALK ABOUT GRANDPA NEGATIVELY AGAIN."

I let out a scream and continue, "He loved you, just like he loved me, although I don't know why. That man didn't have a bad bone in his body, and you have no right to assume anything about him!" The rage isn't fading. The tears flow and my whole body shakes uncontrollably.

Dylan yells, "But isn't that what you are doing? Aren't you assuming he would want you to find out about his past? You heard Mom back in the spring when she said how she didn't think he would want his history known since he never told us himself. Leave it alone and get on with your own life."

This statement strikes me dead in my heart. To *get on with my own life* is something I am trying to do, but I am convinced that finding out about my role model, and other family members, is the only way to carry on with larger meaning. I feel ungrounded because of the mysteries of the past, which paves the path toward my future. To understand my roots is to understand myself. And I need to understand myself because my relationship also depends on it. There is no way around that. Ugh, look at me convincing myself about the validity of this mission. I hate that Dylan does this to me.

And what was that about how he thought Grandpa loved me more? Is that part of the reason Dylan has always had it out for me? My child therapist hat goes on and I think of him as one of my clients. Everyone was loved by my grandpa and if Dylan didn't feel that same love I felt from him, did it affect him by feeling jealous? Maybe the jealousy is a mask for his pain.

My heart goes out to my brother for a moment. Thinking of him as a hurt child instead of a tantruming one has new meaning. He may be carrying around a boy who wanted more attention than he thought he received.

Besides this information Dylan revealed, possibly by accident, he also knows how to hit my triggers just right. I may not have been *normal* in my school days, but I think I blend in pretty well now as an adult. I hope.

Oh, darn it, Dylan. I don't want to think about that part of the past. I'm in my old home, where I should feel safe. Grandpa accepted me as I was, even in my awkward years. So there, Dylan, he loved me more than you so deal with it. Now I am also an eight-year-old spitting lies. I know that would never have been true. Worse yet, I have sympathy for his perception on his experience.

"I need some air." I go out the front door to gather myself and break my circular thinking before dinner. None of us need two bickering adults who should be able to get along after all these years.

As I sit down on the front steps, the motion detected Santa Claus belts out a "Ho, Ho, Ho" next to me, inserting a much-needed bit of humor in this moment.

Be the bigger person, Rachel. It's a holiday, after all.

The absence of my grandparents at the dinner table always feels wrong, but today is a holiday so that fact feels more present. They were central to our celebratory gatherings. Grandpa would get out his huge wooden cutting board and slice through the crispy, yet doughy, fresh bread he baked that day. Grandma would put the grated cheese, butter, crushed red pepper, hot peppers, and a carafe of red table wine in the middle of the table on a Lazy Susan. We all prayed before the meal and dove into her soup.

At tonight's dinner table, the air is strange with a silent combination of sadness, frustration, and pure tension. Brian is the one to break the ice. "This meal smells delicious, Mrs. Granza." He makes sure to flash his wide, beautiful smile in her direction. "I am so honored you had me over again for Christmas Eve."

"Yes, Christmas Eve," my mom goes on to say. "Let's remember that this is Christmas Eve. So, whatever is happening away from this table, leave away from this table. We are a family and we are going to pray, eat, and enjoy this holiday, as we always do. And Brian, you are always welcome."

"Buon Natale," Brian says smiling as he raises his glass.

A second of hesitancy reigns before everyone returns his sentiment. We've taught him well if he now wishes us Merry Christmas in Italian.

"Buon Natale," all of us repeat while raising our glasses.

After my dad prays before the meal, he follows "Amen" with "Mangia." Now we are officially able to eat. It's about time. I can hardly stand the delicious smell of the food anymore without pouncing on it.

And by the time we slurp through the soup course and start on our traditional Mediterranean olives and roasted red peppers with shrimp and scallops to follow, we are conversing in a usual manner, until—.

"Why don't you just go to Italy instead of waiting here for answers and responses?" Mom spews the words out with such ease and assumption, like it's a typical thing to travel across the ocean on a whim.

I stop mid-chew.

This is her first response after my dad told her about my genealogical roadblock? Hands down, it's the most shocking statement from her in my life.

When the meaning of her words hit me further, oh yes from the person who tried to convince me not to go on this ancestry mission, my eyes squint, my face crinkles, and I bust out laughing. She has to be kidding with what she just said. "Oh, okay mom. I will book the next flight over there. I'll get right on that." I say, still laughing.

Brian breaks the trend that is transpiring and chimes in with his two cents stating, "Hmm, actually that isn't a bad idea."

Laughing at both of them, yet more curious, I ask, "What? How is that even possible for me to do financially? That's why older people go there in retirement. Italy isn't cheap."

"Rachel, why are you fighting this idea. Haven't you said that it is your dream to go to Italy, let alone now to go where your family is from and where you have learned so much about?" Brian says in a convincing argument.

"Great, now the princess will get to go to Europe, while I eat school cafeteria lunches." I knew it wouldn't be long before a comment came from Dylan.

"I'll go just to piss you off, Dylan." Stop it, Rachel. You are thirty-two years old, not eight; I reiterate to myself.

"Ha, ha," he utters.

I'm sure his reaction is more than his usual Dylanness. He has to be a little resentful that I may go to our homeland. But that would

175

mean he has a heart. Tough call.

I think the wild idea over a second longer. Maybe it does make sense to go to Italy and be able to go to the places where I need more information. But to refrain from seeing clients for therapy while I am away means no income, plus I would be spending more money while being over there. That would be challenging to finagle.

"Rach, I think you should do it. Just 'get on with your own life,'" Dad says, smirking and looking at both my brother and me.

With his blessing in this idea, I inch even more toward a "yes."

"We planned to give you money for Christmas this year so use it for flight money," Mom adds.

I do have savings and a nice cushion every month anyway. My parents' money could seal the deal. But, my stomach aches with the idea of traveling to Italy alone and over the large, dark, cold, Atlantic Ocean. The idea always scares me for some reason.

"I don't think I could do this by myself. And Brian you can't come with me, so I don't know if I could go." My chest tightens and my throat feels like its closing. I don't like making large decisions, let alone this sort of decision.

"How do you know I can't go with you? If we time it right, I am sure I could get some time off from work. And I am sure there is a down time for tourism there, so it could be affordable. We can at least search out possibilities." Brian is endlessly reassuring and realistic. And so darn calm.

That is true. We could at least investigate it. And this *really* qualifies as doing something different to try to get different results. My physical issues of the moment subside as *I will know* pops into my head. This is better than any gift I'll open later with my family. This is the treasure of a chance to know my grandpa like I never imagined, in his homeland.

"All right then. Let's look into traveling to Italy." I can't believe what I just said.

*Chapter 28*

A fter searching for reasonable flights to Italy every day since Christmas Eve last week, it appears as though we have to fly by mid-April or after late September, or it's entirely too pricey. I guess the school schedule and warmer weather makes it ideal to travel in the middle of that time span. I can't imagine waiting until fall though, almost another year, to move forward with my search. No thanks. But wow, this trip is going to be a reality. We can do this.

As for hotels, staying slightly outside of the city limits looks like a possibility of more affordable prices, but I'll see what I can find. I'm bookmarking this deal, though. If we stay a week, we will get a night free at this certain hotel. And they serve a true Italian breakfast daily. The advertised flaky croissants and foamy cappuccino are calling my name. *Rachel, come eat and drink me. We want to see you soon. Don't wait a year. We are ready for you now.* I'm in, food.

My list of hotel possibilities and airline choices kept growing every night this week, as well as the food I want to try, like genuine Genoese pesto and focaccia. More choices are better for everything, I guess, but the imaginary list is getting to be so long that I have to stop myself from ogling the scrumptiousness and make a decision about flights and hotels soon. Food can wait because I'll probably want to try everything when I'm there. That list would be endless.

"Hey," I call out to Brian from the couch. "I need you to help me help myself over here. It's getting out of control."

"Coming in a sec." I hear him washing his hands in the bathroom.

"Do you think we should go to Italy in spring or fall?"

He sits next to me and tosses a throw pillow in his way onto the ground.

Say spring, please.

"Spring."

Whoa did he hear my thoughts?

"We will have to go in March or April because I need to travel to Seattle for work in fall and I don't know the date yet. After that, it would get a little too cold to enjoy it there, right?"

"Yeah, and I can't wait that long."

"And I don't want you to wait that long." He smiles at me and props his feet on the coffee table.

"And I thank you for that. I also thank you for sticking with me through, you know, all this mess." I fall onto his lap and curl up in the fetal position.

He taps my butt and says, "Rachel, there's nowhere else I want to be."

"Me too." I put my arms around his waist.

He brushes my hair away from my face and stares into my eyes.

I hope we can stay on this good path beyond the holidays. He's not perfect, because nobody is perfect, but I know our rockiness has been because of me. I got us into this mess, and I want to continue to make efforts to get us out. He means too much to me, and I mean too much to me.

"Okay!" I belt out. The decision is made. "We are going to Italy."

My brain is frozen in both shock and excitement. I'm staring at the computer screen, searching for actual flights for our Italy trip, while Brian watches an awfully loud action movie behind me from the couch. There are no more lists of season options for flights, only choosing from my list. I'm deciding the flights we will take, whoa. This is the real deal, even though the real deal is surreal. Yes, I mean that rhyming statement. Ha.

I can't waste another second and need to book our flights before I bust. Our—Brian and me! I'm so glad he's coming with me. I hope Italy lives up to how it looks online; like a movie set. A pristine, magical place. A place that can continue to help a fluttering couple finding solid ground again.

Wow, flight prices drastically decline on March 31. Why? I look at the calendar and see it's Easter day. That's against my logic. Maybe nobody wants to fly on an actual holiday, so the airlines drop prices? Hmm, that does make sense. But as I look at the choices of flights further, I feel a knot in my stomach, half for the thought of being able to book an actual flight to my dreamland and half for thinking of breaking the news to my parents that we won't be having Easter dinner with them. I am an adult, needing to make the right selections for me, though. They'll understand. We could always celebrate on another day. Eek.

"Brian?" I call out in rushed words. Harrison is curved around the chair leg at my feet, probably due to their warmth. When I speak, he cracks open his diamond eyes in a groggy displeasure then goes back to sleep. I bend down and give him a quick pet to ease his disturbance.

"What's up?" Brian says while tearing himself away from the newest car chase scene.

"What do you think about us going to Italy the week of Easter? On Easter? It would work well for my job because with the kids being out of school for Easter break, I usually have appointment no shows and cancellations anyway. Also, look at how much the prices are in our favor." I point to the rates.

He's taking a long time to form any sort of sentence on the matter. "Wait." He grabs his phone from the coffee table and scrolls in his calendar app. "When is Easter?"

"March 31."

"That would work for me, but leaving on Easter day, though? With your family and all?" He sucks his lips inward and raises his eyebrows.

Sweet Brian knows my family by now. The implications of missing a major holiday are numerous. The guilt given by my mom then part of my conscience for eternity is enough, let alone that I may hurt my parents' feelings, even though it's not personal. It's a major Italian faux pas to miss family time on a holiday and we already missed Easter last year when Brian's extended family visited his parents, basically requiring our presence. The second year in a row where we will have to celebrate Easter on another day probably won't bode well for the Granza parents, but it may have to be the way life goes again, unfortunately.

"I...I think it would be fine. Let's just do it. They *have* to understand... Right?" My mouth stretches and draws back, showing my teeth. My confidence in my family's acceptance of us not being together on Easter again is shaky, but I know in my heart they will recognize the circumstances and want this trip for me more than having one dinner with them.

"Yeah, I think so. Okay, one week in Italy it is," he says while lifting me off the ground and spinning.

The synchronicity feels relieving, as our hearts beat together as one in this moment, through his tight hug.

He stays for the official "click" of the purchase and we smile at each other.

"The flights are bought."

I look at the screen, my finger in mid-air an inch above the mouse for a few more seconds while I grip the sides tightly. If I had a mirror to see myself, I think I would see my eyes open as wide as possible. It is done. We are *really* going to Italy.

# Chapter 29

I t doesn't take long for panic to set in for me. Approximately ten minutes to be exact. That must be the amount of time it takes for the adrenaline to leave. Is that a scientific fact?

Anyway, after I text Maggie and make sure to tell my parents the news another day, racing thoughts blindside me. So. Many. Racing. Thoughts.

I have never flown overseas. I've never flown somewhere so far from home. Oh no. My breathing is getting shorter. My heart is palpitating. How do people get around there? Is there a subway? Do they have cabs? What do people wear? How cold will it be? Do they speak any English there at all? The questions are endless.

"Rachel, what's going on?" Brian comes over again and rubs my back. Sitting with my legs on the chair and hugging my knees must be giving away my current state.

"I just got scared, no, terrified, about how much more planning needs to be done. We are going to another country! Not just New Jersey. And I don't have that much time left."

"Well, sometimes New Jersey does feel like another country," he jokes, but must realize the intensity of my feelings because his effort at humor and his smile fades. He puts his arm around me. "We have plenty of time. Don't worry. It's months away and I'll help you out with any planning you need."

I get up and pace back and forth. "Thank you. I know that. It's just that we will need to know so much to get around there. And I must be prepared with all of my questions and research in order to find out more about my ancestry. I have to find out more and in fact, I have to find out everything!" My words almost jumble together as the speed of my speech increases and the tone in my voice rises.

Brian catches my eyeline and grips my arms to stop me from pacing. "Breathe. Please just take a breath. It is going to be fine. I promise. You aren't going alone, remember? I will be there to help you navigate. Whatever we need to do ahead of time, we will. It's okay." He holds my gaze until I take a couple deep breaths, then drops his hands and steps back.

"I won't be alone. That is true." My breathing steadies and my heart rate slows. I am not alone in this. The thought is sinking in for the first time. I feel like I've been doing all of this solo, but I haven't. Brian has been with me the entire time, supporting me and being there for my ups and downs. Tears start coming to my eyes but with joy this time. "I'm so glad you are going with me."

He bumps the top of my head with his palm in a playful motion. "Let's just take it one day at a time. This is fun, remember?"

I chuckle, but my head is still swimming with ideas. I sit down and grab my pad of paper and pen. "Yes! You are right. And you may have saved me from another panic attack."

"Glad to be of service. Come on, Rach, we will be fine. We will figure out every single thing every single time." He returns to the couch to relax.

I feel my heart beating steady and in control once again. His reassurance is always appreciated, but especially in these freak-out moments. And I shouldn't be feeling anything but elation. Gosh, Rachel, you are going to Italy! It's a dream and dreams should not cause stress.

"Okay, first things first, let's get passports this week. We will need to add the numbers to the tickets online." I write a bullet point on the paper and the words "Get passports" after it. This is such a Rachel move, getting down to logistics, instead of focusing on the fun. But planning *is* fun. "Step one is done, but we have approximately one hundred more steps." I turn and smile at him. I hope he knows I'm kidding. Well, partly kidding.

He returns my smile and nods with a sigh.

I will be able to do this adventure. I have Brian by my side. And hopefully Grandpa pulling for me from above.

# *Chapter* 30

As I wake up on January 31st, I smile before I even open my eyes. Two months! Two months until leaving for Italy. It's typical lately for my brain to be full speed ahead the second I become conscious, but Italy has me in overdrive. It's been hard to concentrate on even reading for pleasure this month because all I can think about is the trip.

Even though it is early in the morning on a work day, the surge of energy drives me to pop out of bed and look at the weather today. The gray cloud-covered sky and bare trees as its companion can't even take away my uplifted mood. This is strange for me, but I'll take it.

I grab my pen and paper from the bedside table and plop back down on the bed. My to do list travels around my apartment with me so I can jot down thoughts. I can't forget anything for this once in a lifetime trip. Let's review.

*Things to do to prepare for Italy*
- Get passports ✓
- Flights- booked ✓
- Book Hotel Pace ✓
- Add passport numbers to flight info
- Read whether car rental is needed/ how do people get around the city?

- Talk to Mags about taking care of Harrison
- View the schedule of bills for home and office/set up payments
- Stop mail delivery
- Plan emergency contacts for clients while away
- Exchange money for Euros

I wish I could check off more points right now, but the passports, flights, and hotel are the only points that are definite. I love how the hotel is near the central area of Genoa, which seems like an easy location to travel to all of my destinations. The pictures online and the reviews make it appear like a dream. I wonder what our room will look like. And what the food will taste like. And what the people will be like.

*Purr.*

Harrison interrupts my daydream in the best way.

I roll over to pet him, and he also rolls over on his back and stretches all fours.

"Yeah, that's a good stretch, Harrison." I rub his belly.

Well, I better get going today. Let me waltz over to the kitchen for my coffee Brian left in the pot. Dragging myself there has faded away in the last month.

I sip my steaming goodness and walk over to my closet. The last few days have me craving brighter colors in my wardrobe for some reason. I feel like taking small fashion risks even. What's that about? The rich aroma from my coffee fills my nostrils as I scan my closet for an acceptable sweater. Maybe I'll try mismatching my purse and my shoes today. Outrageous, I know.

I wish I could feel this motivated more consistently. I still have my moments of feeling blah, but mostly have been feeling like I have—I'm afraid to say it—more of a purpose of some sort. I can't quite put my finger on it, but I feel lighter in a way. Maybe even less restricted by me not getting in my own way.

Take when I told my parents about missing Easter again, last night. Yes, I avoided the conversation for weeks and finally got the gusto to spit it out. It was silly of me. I need to face my fears.

Turns out that we'll be able to celebrate Easter a week early, no problem, despite hearing the tinge of disappointment in my mom's voice. "As long as I can make your favorite, Pizza Rustica, I am okay with celebrating early," she said. And that's a wonderful send off for me.

Focus, Rachel. Back to what I need to wear today. But hmm, I may need a tiny shopping trip. The weather in Italy around those months could still be cold, so I may as well get a few new items.

I set my coffee on the bedside table, grab my phone, and text Maggie that we'll need to go shopping. Now I wait for the response, still not getting ready, but oh well. I roll my eyes.

> **Maggie:** Rachel wants to shop?! What is happening in the world right now?!

There it is. I knew it.

> **Rachel:** Yes, she does. I figure I may as well pick up some things, so no time like the present to start.

> **Maggie:** I'll text you later to set up a time.

> **Rachel:** Ok.

I reach for my plum V-neck sweater, cream colored lace scarf, black slacks, and flat black boots. As for a purse, all of mine are neutral so I can't mismatch after all. Maybe I'll buy a non-neutral purse when I shop with Maggie. Mmmaybe not.

I look in the mirror to fix my hair and decide to keep it down, but with a thin black headband to keep it out of my face. There, done. Not too shabby.

Finishing my coffee as I walk out the door, I almost forget my coat, so I swipe it from the bench and leave my mug. I wouldn't have gotten far without that warmth.

Once I get downstairs, I see the thin layer of sparkling snow on the ground. As I start my walk to work, I notice the quiet slush sound my feet make. It doesn't annoy me. It doesn't make me worry I may have to change my shoes or socks when I get to my destination. I just enjoy the brief sinking in when the snow is thicker than I thought.

When I get to my office, Annabelle calls out, "Sixty!" a new morning tradition we started as a countdown to the Italy trip. Hey, I can be more present in moments *and* countdown for the future. That's allowed.

"Yeah, sixty days too many," I reply in my pretend exaggerated frustration, changing the day's number to the correct one for the time.

We both laugh, without fail. It doesn't get old.

Despite my higher mood more days than not and my consecutive humorous exchange with Annabelle, I have to admit, I still don't want to spend my free time with her and Peter. Don't hate me! Brian and I have been doing better in our relationship but seeing them together still is a little too much for me. They are just so damn happy. Like, no hiccups ever and no problems at all; movie romance happy. I dislike admitting it, but I'm glad she stopped asking for all of us to spend time together. Maybe she is giving me space. I hope she's not aware of how I compare my relationship to hers. That's not her fault, it's mine. I'm getting there with my relationship security, but it's too soon.

"What's on tap today?" she asks. "I have way too many people on my schedule. And it's so dreary outside. I just want to be lying in bed watching TV all day." She's so bubbly in the morning, even those words have zest.

"Who are you, me? I don't think I could ever see you just laying around, relaxing."

"Well, you know, I have my chill days too," she says and grins.

Sure, Annabelle is human and has down time, but she also could brighten up a room ninety-nine percent of the time. Today she is decked out in a yellow dress, with long gold chains of varying lengths, diamond patterned cream-colored tights with black gemstones on the points of the diamond shapes, and maroon knee-high boots. It takes so much energy to even think about all those items, let alone wear them.

I walk to my office to turn on my computer. "So, can you meet me for lunch one day next week? I want to run through some plans for when I am gone," I call out.

She pops her head in the door frame and says, "You mean, when you are gone in fifty-nine days or less?"

We both giggle.

She continues, "Doesn't that seem a little far away to be talking to me about office issues? It's fine and all, especially to have lunch, but you know me, and I'll probably forget much of what you tell me by then."

"True, true. Well, let's just eat together and as we get closer, I can talk to you about clients' needs. Like, will you be their crisis contact if something happens and they need a therapist?" I accidentally slip in a question.

"Love it," she says while going back to her office. "I can handle that. Even if they are kids. I mean, you don't expect many crises, right?"

"Isn't that the definition of a crisis, not to be able to expect it?" I laugh.

"I'm just kidding," she yells out.

"Are you?" I joke because I know she is kidding. She's more than capable of crisis work. My kids would be in good hands. But I still hope nobody needs her.

Okay, it's showtime for today. Let the day begin.

# Chapter 31

My eyes widen and my heart stops in syncopation as I see the Italian word "cattedrale" in the sender line of one of my emails. That's the Italian word for cathedral. This is an email from one of the churches in Genoa!

Clicking the open button as soon as my fingers can move leads me to see a bunch of words in, you guessed it, Italian. Oh, hurry up, Rachel. Cut and paste into Italian to English translation in Google. And enter.

Monday, February 11, 2013, 1:03 p.m.

**Subject:** Seeking information about my family

**From:** Allesandro.Pastorino@CattedraledeiSanti.com

**To:** Rachel.Granza@myemail.com

Greetings Ms. Granza. We are sorry that we are just now responding to your email, but we had a change in office staff over the past few months. Let me introduce myself. My name is Mr. Allesandro Pastorino. I am the person that handles all church correspondence.

I looked through our church records recently and I am sorry to tell you that I do not see anybody having the last name of Allegranza. My search was thorough, as I asked another church member for assistance. We both concluded that your family did not attend our church in the past.

You are always welcome to visit if you come to Genoa. Our

church staff would love to meet you. I am sorry that you could not find the information you were looking for at the Cathedral of the Saints, but may I please suggest that you contact the Cathedral of St. George? They have the longest history in the city, since they are the oldest Catholic church in existence for our area.

Please let me know if I can further help you. Good luck with your undertaking. It was a pleasure to try to assist you.

Kindly,
Mr. Allesandro Pastorino
Cathedral of the Saints
www.cattedraledeisanti.com

I fall into the back of the couch.

They don't have any information on my family as being members of their church. Ugh. I purse my lips.

I'm forty-nine days from being there, so I still have time to receive a response from the other church. This nice man even suggests it, so I must be correct that my history exists at one of the churches. The oldest section of Genoa isn't that big.

I guess if I don't receive a response from the Cathedral of St. George, I'll visit when we are there. There's no way around it. That's the church.

And if the Cathedral of St. George is not where my family worshiped, I will have to make it be their place, damn it. It just has to be.

# Chapter 32

Arriving in Philly's 30th Street Station forty-three days away from going to Italy is long overdue. I need to see my grandpa's old stomping grounds and this cold, but sunny February day is the time.

The train ride was not so sunny, though. With this thick sweater, the heat was in overdrive and I couldn't get comfortable the whole time. I didn't have a chance to eat much before leaving, so I snacked on a tiny bag of mixed nuts I picked up in the station, needing a pound more. The combination made me feel sick. Heat and hunger, yuck. I am more than ready to get some fresh air.

"Finally, we are outside again."

"Is that Rachel or an imposter?" Maggie laughs.

"Well, my God. That was a ride from hell." I look up at the clear blue sky and take a huge whiff of…urine. "Ew. I guess we need to leave the train station."

"Yeah, come on." Maggie yanks my arm and hails a cab to bring us to Philly's Little Italy.

She's talking a mile a minute on our ride, but I am in more of a contemplative state, taking in all the sites. What was the ride like for my grandpa and his family when they arrived in New York? I don't even know how they traveled from there to here. It must have been grueling to travel long distances in those days. Then there's me, who got crabby for the comparably slight discomfort on today's train. *Sorry, Grandpa.*

Driving into the Little Italy vicinity, I have vague memories of some of the sites from when I was a child. Maybe Grandpa showed us his old business, or even still owned it at that time. Maybe he showed us his first apartment too. I don't remember and I wish I could. But this time, I am looking at every inch of the places surrounding us.

We're dropped off at the Italian Market, which looks like the hub of the entire area. I read how this market and Isgro Pastries are still huge tourist spots, and I can see, I mean smell, why. The flavorful cuisine's aromas hit me as soon as I open the car door. I take a large sniff and beam from ear to ear. "Mags, we…are…here."

After experiencing the brief olfactory food coma, I realize I need to get some actual food into my body. "I can't wait to explore a little, but first things first Mags; we have to find somewhere to eat lunch," I say rubbing my stomach.

"I'm into it." She takes her phone out of her purse, ready to search reviews, I know.

"Are you okay with getting quick slices of pizza somewhere? Let's come here after we have eaten so we can take our time and walk through the whole area. I can't handle the temptation of being in here without having eaten anything yet."

"You know I will eat whatever, wherever," she says while starting to scan her search results. She looks up at the street sign and confirms, "This place on the corner has good ratings, so you want to check out the menu in the window?"

She can eat "whatever" yet only when from a place with acceptable online ratings. At least it makes us have better odds to have a good meal though, so I don't mind. Oh, my Mags.

We walk over to glance at the menu, but I'm already convinced that I'll stay. I just need something as soon as possible.

We are seated at a picturesque, but also stereotypical Italian table for two with a red and white checkered tablecloth. I love the tradition. Straightaway, a waiter comes by with water and tray of shakers filled with parmesan cheese, crushed red peppers, and garlic powder.

"Two slices of cheese pizza for each of us, right?" I ask Maggie not to delay at all.

"Yup, let's do it." She hands both menus to the waiter and he's off to put in the order.

As we sip on our water and talk about our plan for walking around after lunch, Maggie surprises me with news about her and Ray. "You know how I was telling you about some things about him that bother the livin' hell out of me?"

Amused, I answer, "Yes, of course."

"Well, I decided that's all fine now. Well, not *fiiine*, but at least all right. I've been enjoying our time together a lot and I have slowly moved on from some of that BS I was stuck on. That was old Mags anyway. This new Mags is trying to be a proper adult." She straightens the imaginary collar of her shirt.

Even more entertained now, I say, "Uh-huh," while shaking my head in hesitant agreement.

"So, that's it. I just wanted you to know what's up since we haven't been able to hang as much lately. I really am falling for this one, Rach."

"I am so excited to hear that! Also, I guess I need to wish you congratulations on your adulthood?" Smiling, I wait for her quick retort, but it doesn't happen. She seems to be in her own pondering state of daydreaming. When I snap my fingers close to her face, she comes back to me.

"Thanks for saying that. I'll keep you posted."

The thin crust cheese pizza is everything I hoped for in this Little Italy. Being a true New Yorker now, I have high expectations for pizza. Not only do we have mouthwatering slices in New York's Little Italy, but also in the city in general. Philly doesn't disappoint, though.

We're almost finished eating when I notice a bulletin board in the corner of the room. There's neighborhood announcements, flyers, and business cards. And I see posters for the South 9th Street Italian

Market festival I went to as a child. "Mags. Oh wow. Look." I point to it.

She looks over her shoulder and reads out the title "Everyone's Italian." Then, she looks at me and says, "Great. That's settled. I'm Italian." She smiles, taking a sip from her straw.

"Well, you are sure welcome to be Italian, but what I'm trying to show you is that the poster is advertising the festival I used to go to when I was a little girl. Grandma and Grandpa would take Dylan and me many years in a row. We would walk around to see all the craft booths and I remember being mesmerized by all the colors and sparkles. Ooh, especially when I got my face painted."

"Aww."

"We also ate so much our stomachs hurt. Lots of fried dough. You know, the kind with sauce and grated cheese on it."

"Yes, ma'am." Resting her chin on the palm of her hand, Maggie continues, "Rach, it sounds like you have fantastic memories here. I'm happy to hear that for you." She reaches over to my hand and grabs it, squeezing it as a sign of support.

"It happens in May. I might have to come back for the festivities. And see, they even have a Saint processional." I motion to the picture next to the flyer. "I don't remember that from when I was a child, but I read about it online. Italians brought that tradition to the States. I could see one in person soon."

Mags and I both walk over to examine the pictures on the posters for a closer look. One shows a picture of a huge Saint statue adorned with excessive amounts of gold being carried by many people, with money pinned to the statue's garb. I touch the photo and say, "I read this was a practice carried over from the homeland to show the prosperity of being in the United States. The immigrants were proud to show they earned money and could send it home to their families in Italy, so they celebrated by pinning it to the statue, which usually was donated to the church."

"Sounds fun. What's this though?" she asks pointing to a picture of a pole with people piled one on top of another.

"Ha. That's the greased pole! It's an old Italian tradition to see who can get to the top. The participants win prizes. I don't really see the thrill, but it's customary."

"Rachel, this place has such a good vibe. Like, the whole area down in South Philly, not just this restaurant, you know? I feel it."

"Yeah, I know. It feels comforting here."

She agrees by a head nod and we go to the table to wait for the check. It is time to explore a little now. My stomach is ready and so am I.

Walking to and through the Italian market makes me think of items my grandparents would speak about often. Cured meats are hanging in shop windows everywhere and Catholic saints and the Virgin Mary decorate many a vendor booth. Green, white, and red Italian flags hang throughout the market, with Italian music providing candy for our ears.

On the sidewalk, there's a small Italian flag colored newspaper stand. It's the only one there decked out in the traditional colors. I peer inside and open the door. This is a newspaper just for the Little Italy section of the city. It is still in production. How amazing.

I show Mags and she finds it "adorbs" as well. Flipping through, I see certain businesses highlighted in articles, as well as advertising the festival. They even have a section for an "Italian Recipe of the Month." How cute it is to see an older Italian woman holding up her wooden spoon with one hand and pointing to a pot on her stove with the other hand. I bet there was something good cooking in that pot.

I stuff the newspaper in my purse to stop myself from reading it more so that I don't waste precious time. We came to shop in a few stores and explore, not to read. I can do that later.

There aren't that many stores, though. Little Italys in the United States have been decreasing in existence and in size. New York has one of the biggest areas, and it isn't even that big anymore. So, I want to contribute to the success of at least one store and buy something as a memento of this trip. When I find the item that's a must have, I'll know right away.

And it doesn't take long. "I found the perfect souvenir," I call out to Mags. My new magnet will kindly remind me that the nicest people have "a root in the boot," decorated with a tri-colored map of Italy on it. I can look at it every day on our fridge and remember this special day.

Before buying it, I see a postcard near the register that sparks a memory. There is a picture of a bocce court on it. Grandpa loved that sport. He told me it was something he did as a young adult with the neighborhood guys. My dad even got in on the action sometimes as a kid. And, yours truly also dabbled in it.

I went with him many times to the Italian American club, where there were bocce ball courts available for use, as well as someone always around and willing to be a partner in play. Throwing the marker ball was my job; a real honor. Then, we both would throw our bigger bocce balls to try to get closest to the marker ball. I became semi-good at my underhanded throw, I must say. How I wish I could live in those carefree times again.

As I slip my new magnet into my pocket and walk out of the store, I think about how strange it is that items like these can be bought in a place where families traveled thousands of miles to live many years ago. They came to survive and knew of no luxury items. Souvenirs? They would laugh in confusion. I bet there wasn't even the idea of a souvenir back then. They would never believe it if they were told of what the future would bring. If I could only have one conversation with Great-Grandpa Gino... I'd tell him this and so much more.

"I think we make a right there to get to the old tailor business," I mention after walking a few blocks. The red brick buildings that line the street somehow make me feel closer to my grandpa, like he is walking with me. He used to walk on this same path, I assume. Oh, how I wish he was walking next to me at this second.

The estimated address of his old business isn't far from the corner. But where's the building? Stopping at the dilapidated construction in front of me, my heart feels heavy. There are barely four walls standing anymore. The brick walls are at all different heights and crumbling from the top down. I think this place must have meant everything to my grandpa and Great-Uncle Vince, and probably to their dad as well. Now it is as if it never existed.

For the building to be in this condition, it must have been abandoned for many years, maybe decades. There's been so many businesses in general that have come and gone in the new land of the United States. My family had a part in that cycle. Did any other line of work take the place of Grandpa's tailoring services here and go out of business as well?

"Oh wow, Rach. This is… Wow." Mags breaks the silence. "Did you ever visit here before? It isn't that far from your parents' house, right?"

I continue to stare, but answer, "No. Or, I don't know. But it isn't far, yes." My thoughts are jumbled and exit as barely sensical answers. I don't want to see my grandpa's once-dream in this state.

"When you came to the festival as a kid, did you ever come here?" Maggie asks.

"I—I don't know. I wish I knew. But, it just wasn't a thing to visit these places with him. When Grandpa was alive, we just went on with our current lives and he would talk about when he closed the store years before, but he never said much more. He was such a quiet man. I didn't even think to ask these questions because I—I don't know," I repeat. My chest aches. A tear rolls down from one eye. The exhilaration of being in the area has deflated like a popped balloon.

Maggie hugs me and remains silent. "I didn't expect to have this sort of reaction here. Maybe in Italy, but in Philly?"

"Don't you always tell me you can't control your emotions? That they come and go like, what was it, waves in the ocean? I think you need a bit of your own medicine right now."

I grin for a second. "Yeah, I do. Thanks. I am so glad you are here with me."

"Me too. I wouldn't miss it. I mean, you almost didn't invite me, but whatevs."

"Brian wanted to come and you know we're trying to make us stronger."

"Likely story. Your best friend will just be waiting on the wayside. Don't worry about me."

I laugh and push her shoulder.

"Come on, take a picture. I know you want to," she says.

I snap a picture of the ruins before moving on to our next intended stop. I can take solace in knowing I can return here any time that I want. It's fine...

As we walk to the resident address listed for Grandpa and Great-Uncle Vince on the 1920 census, I realize it isn't that far of a walk from his old business address. In only two blocks from the old shop, we arrive at what must have been his home.

I look to the right and the left of the building to make sure his house number falls between them. Huh?

A fresh coat of white paint disguising the probably once beautiful bright red brick doesn't cover up the shocking size of the building. I peek around the side and notice how narrow the building's width seems. What looks like a complex of apartments now must have been a house back then in order to fit all those people in it, right? I can't imagine housing, what, at least five to seven people in a small city apartment? My family and the Serafinos all lived there.

"I wish I could see the inside of one of these residences," I say, still awe-struck. "The tiny windows don't allow for much to be revealed to outsiders."

"Yeah, I don't think that will happen anytime soon." Maggie's tone conveys her empathy.

"Yeah," I utter while looking all the way up to the top of the three-story building. "Let's go up to the residence list to see if the apartment numbers are listed."

"Yup, there it is; number 115." Maggie re-confirms what I see.

Grandpa lived in an apartment with all of those people, not a house. This isn't the way I imagined his home at all in my imagination. Sure, in some romanticized versions, but not in reality-based daydreams.

"Yes," I finally respond.

My mind races to schemes that may allow us entry to the building. On TV that happens all the time. People ring the doorbell and before they know it, they are inside searching their old residence, with friendly new owners allowing them to roam wherever they want. But we can't just knock on a stranger's door and ask to see their apartment. That isn't even safe. I will have to settle on walking in Grandpa's shoes, so to speak, and imagining what his early life would have been like out here from the street.

"Wow. This is where it all started. This is where Grandpa lived as a teen, new to the country, the language, and the customs. In a way, I come from here as well. This is where I started."

"You know it." Maggie pauses speaking, allowing me to take in the moment. She knows me well and knows what I need. She also knows when I need to be pushed to move on. "Are you ready to start heading to the train station?" She gently grabs my arm in a tight and reassuring embrace. "We don't have that much more time before our train leaves."

"Yeah, I am ready." I take a large, deep breath. "This was a millimeter of a taste of what Italy may be like, so I can only imagine the feelings that will flow over me when I'm there." I steal a few more seconds of staring and manage to say, "Let's go home."

I leave my grandpa's probable first American home with a sense of connection to the land. This land provided him, and therefore me, the opportunity to have my current life. It's an incredible gift that I haven't thought about quite enough in my life, but I can change that from this time forward.

# *Chapter* 33

Today is the day that I've been dreading. Day thirty-seven until the trip. Yeah, I had a great experience in old Little Italy and yes, I am about to head to my ancestral homeland, but today is a double whammy for Anxiety Girl. Where's my cape?

February 23rd is not only my birthday, but the five-year anniversary of when Brian and I began dating. How would that sort of thing *not* happen to Rachel Granza? I don't need attention from either "holiday," so since they are combined it's my personal hell.

Let's take the birthday topic alone. Guess who's a huuuge birthday person. Yup, my sweet Brian. No matter how many times I reassure him that I don't need to do much more than a quiet meal together, at home even, he makes a big deal out of it. In the past he's invited friends to celebrate, he's bought gifts that, while thoughtful, are unnecessary—and that was just for the birthday part.

Don't get me started on when I turned thirty. Can we say surprise weekend itinerary? Just thinking about it makes my heart palpitate. It ended up being wonderful, of course. It was the surprise part that shook me the whole time. I always appreciate his efforts, but I wish he would save himself the trouble. If being thoughtful is his worst quality, though, I'm one lucky lady.

Combining my birthday with our anniversary means I will for sure have a celebration bigger than I prefer, especially on this milestone anniversary. Thank God it's not also a milestone birthday.

My soul would explode.

So, I know I can't escape the celebration tonight. Fine. I have to admit, there's the tiniest, itsy bitsiest part of me that feels we should celebrate a little bigger tonight for getting through this fourth year of dating, but as soon as I think that, the anxiety whips me back to my typical desire for, say it with me, no big deal. Imagine what would happen if I let him really go wild with the "holidays." My God, I'd be on the news or something every year, with all of New York City singing "Happy Birthday." There are birthday people and non-birthday people, and we are one of each. I don't know about the anniversary people categories. I haven't made them up yet.

Anyway, at least I know what to expect tonight, dinner at an American bistro and an off-Broadway show. It's some small production, one I haven't heard of, but that is excellent with me. What matters most is that it's just us tonight, the way I like it.

I pick up my drink from the table, but before I get the glass to my lips, Brian stops me.

"Wait a second there, birthday and anniversary lady. We need to toast to you and to us."

"Of course." I smile.

We gently tap our glasses together and say "Salute" in unison.

I take my first sip and close my eyes to savor the taste. The Chianti sends notes of fruity pleasure down my throat. "Ooh, this is good. Do you like it too?"

"Yes, it's great. And even better because of the company." He reaches across the small table for two and opens his palm, gesturing for me to lay my hand on top.

I grip his hand.

"Rachel, you've been doing so much better lately."

Um, huh? That's abrupt, mister. I cringe and my hand tightens. He squeezes back, possibly thinking I'm tightening it as a positive response to his statement. I should have known he'd want to talk about the shape of us tonight, but that's one part I didn't expect, like a stunad.

After my self-labeling, comes the guilt. It's been a while, you rascal. I hate that I've caused him so much heartache that he starts our dinner conversation in this way. I hate that I've changed our home's atmosphere and maybe even his happiness because I couldn't get myself together. I hate that I've caused him any worry or added extra stress in his life. But instead of saying all of that and risking the floodgates of tears from opening for the thousandth time in this past year, I simply respond, "Oh, how so?" I think I sound convincing, but he knows me just as much as I know him, so we'll see.

He goes on, smiling ear to ear, which sends a ripple of delight through my body. "You seem like since we have decided to go to Italy you've been in such a better mood overall. A more stable mood. I know you had some disappointments, but I'm so glad to see you getting back to yourself, overall." He pauses and turns his face slightly away from me, crinkling his eyes and waiting for my reply, it seems. Does he think I'm going to hit him or something? Calling me 'stable' does make me want to punch him in the face though. Okay, not really, but the truth hurts.

"Yeah, it's fantastic that we are going. I think I have felt better, especially since Christmas. I'm trying to be okay, you know. I don't want to be like how I've been and especially don't want to take things out on you. I've been trying to do some therapy on myself. You know, a technique or two." Or five million.

What a mature response, though. Go, Rachel, go. Good job at holding composure while using that good old open communication. I feel like bumping my fist in the air.

I continue, "I think being able to go to Italy gives me a purpose of some sort. I need to find out the reason Grandpa never talked about his childhood and I think the chances are better there than anywhere. So, you know…" I look down and push around my utensils on the table with my hand I released from his. I can't believe I just said such a cheesy statement about purpose out loud.

He dips his head down to catch my gaze, puts his fingers under my chin, and slowly moves it up. Continuing to use his sparkly blues to pierce into my eyes, he replies, "Oh, I do know. And I know you know I am here for you. You haven't pushed me away as much, and that's a relief. Please let me *go* on this trip with you. I don't mean physically. I mean to let me in. I want to help you. I want you to find what you need to find when we are over there."

He's pouring out his heart while my heart jumps in a tangled array of emotion. How can it feel ready to beat outside of my chest surrounded by a familiar warmth of safety all in one swooping moment? I know I won't faint at least. I can't and won't allow myself to repeat that past madness. You've got this Rachel. Keep moving forward.

I nod in response.

"Rachel, I want this year of you being thirty-three to be your best year yet. And this is another year of us being together as well, at least it looks that way."

The small question in his voice gives me a sinking feeling in the pit of my stomach. I despise that I confused him with my personal problems and my own confusion about, well, myself. He doesn't deserve that.

"Brian, I am *so* thankful for you in my life. Sometimes you just have to give me space to process things on my own. I won't always have the answers for how I feel. In fact, I can't always express them verbally, especially in the moment. I didn't even know some of what I felt and that what was building was largely related to the lack of identity I had about myself. I thought that years after Grandpa died, I had been able to move on and regain feeling grounded. But I wasn't my normal self for so long that I forgot what my normal felt like at all. I hope the trip can bring that feeling back. And help me to be even better than before."

"I do too and I think it will. But, what about the us part?"

Damn. He isn't going to let me off the hook.

"I think we've been good. I do feel closer to you and more like how it used to be. And I love you to death! Just keep giving me time for getting myself together. That has to come first."

"I agree. You have to be okay so we can be okay. You know I love you, Rach." He shows his pearly whites.

I take in a deep breath, knowing he does want to continue to be together. The marriage question still lingers, but we'll figure it out. Step one is me being me. Step two is us being us. Step three will get decided when it gets decided. What I know is I'm happy in this moment.

"Let's get on with our night. I'm looking forward to that play." And I am now. A tiny weight has been lifted off of me. It's a birthday/anniversary miracle.

# Chapter 34

*Italy Must Do's*
- *Visit church (Cattedrale di San Giorgio) - baptism, marriage records?*
- *Find city registry (Comune di Genoa Anagrafe) - birth, death records?*
- *If get the address, go to Grandpa's childhood home*
- *Explore city- see the port where Grandpa left?*

The list. The Italy list. Italy! I keep staring at it more and more as the days approach and today's no different.

"Brian, can I run through some stuff with you?" I call out from the bedroom.

"Yeah, sure." He yells back. Walking in the room and sitting on the bed, he asks, "What's up?"

I hand him my list. "Here's what we absolutely need to do in Italy. In exactly fourteen days."

"O-okay." He laughs and reads the points. "Sounds good to me."

"The 'Things to do to prepare for Italy' list is almost complete, you'll be happy to know."

"That does give me relief. I was worried."

I hear his sarcasm, but only chuckle and continue with what

I need to release so I don't burst from anxiety and excitement. "I'm gathering a pile of what to take to Italy and I'm going to start packing." I point to the bench by the window.

He furrows his brow. "You do know there's still time right?"

"Only a few weeks. May as well get the show on the road."

"Uh-huh." He lays down on his pillow and puts his elbows behind his head.

I lift up the new shirt I found when Maggie and I went shopping for more spring-like and untypical Rachel-like clothes. "What do you think?"

"You bought a yellow shirt?"

"Well," I say and analyze it. "It's pale yellow."

"No, I mean, that's great. You are venturing out of your colors *and* the country."

"Yup, and you'll see more unlikely clothes on the trip. And look at this." I dump a shopping bag's contents next to him on the bed.

He rolls over and starts lifting each item. "A new purse?"

"A metal strapped purse. Nobody can cut that off of me."

"We aren't going to war, Rachel, just Italy."

"You never know. We'll probably look like tourists, so we can't be too careful. That's why I also picked up this identity theft wallet. There's one for me," I toss him a wallet, "and one for you."

"You shouldn't have, but thanks." He places it back down on the bed.

"No problem. The rest are Italian outlet adapters of course."

"Of course." He nods his head. "Now why do we need them?"

"Haven't you researched at all?" I put my hands on my hips and smile.

"No, that's covered by my girlfriend."

"Ha, yeah. They are needed to plug in devices because Italy's outlets are different than ours."

"Ah, well that's good to know," he replies.

"Oh," I run to the closet. "I also picked up these walking shoes because I plan to be walking a lot."

"Well, I'll do my part and convert our money to Euros this week. That way it can be another task completed for you. Tell me if there's anything you need done."

"I appreciate that."

"So, Annabelle's got my clients handled if needed, she knows she can reach me on your phone, since you have international calling, and Maggie has Harrison's needs squared away."

"Spoiling him and catering to his every whim?"

"Exactly." I take a breath and laugh. "She'll come here twice a day to take care of him."

"That's really nice of her."

My eyes widen. "I know."

"And last but not least, I have a question for you."

"Shoot."

"Dov'è il bagno?"

"What?"

"I learned common Italian phrases that may come in handy. Plus, of course, I downloaded a translator app on my phone, just to cover my bases. I wouldn't want to be ordering chicken brains instead of chicken breast. Do Italians eat strange food like that? I hope I won't find that one out, you know, the hard way." I pretend to gag.

"So, what was that question? Doves and bags?"

"Yes, I asked if you like doves and bags." I sit down next to him and laugh. "I asked where to find the bathroom, I mean toilet. That's what they call the bathroom in Italy."

"Well, congrats, Rachel. Now you won't be left wandering the alleys of Italy having to find a corner to relieve yourself." He pulls me onto him.

"I don't plan to have to do that, you weirdo." I plant my lips on his and he rolls over on top of me, and the items for Italy. "Ouch." I pull out an adaptor from my back.

"Oh, sorry about that."

"I think I can forgive you."

And for the first time in as long as I can remember, *I* initiate physical time together.

# Chapter 35

Walking into my parents' home, my mom shouts, "Well, if it isn't the world travelers." A little razzing is expected for this once in a lifetime trip in seven days. One week! Dad hangs his car keys on the rack and scatters to the living room while Brian and I set down the Easter loaves of bread on the kitchen table, which he kindly made for us. They look so delicious, I wanted to eat all of them as soon as they were ready yesterday. The traditional circle loaf of braided, ring-like Italian bread has colored eggs in the middle, so they also look gorgeous. This year he made one mini version for each of us, each with our favorite color for the egg at the center.

My mom comes over to hug us.

"Good to see you guys," she says enthusiastically.

"Yeah, thanks again for celebrating Easter early with us. Buona Pasqua."

"Happy Easter to you also, Rachel," my mom replies walking to the sink. She dips her head and starts rinsing bowls she must have used to cook the meal.

I know this isn't ideal for her, so I'm thankful she's willing to change the Easter celebration again this year, especially when she was far from giving me her blessing for starting my genealogy endeavor.

She continues speaking in a forced cheerful tone, "It's wonderful we get to celebrate early," and smiles.

She's trying.

"Brian, how are you, honey?" Mom asks.

"All good on my end, Mrs. Granza. Thanks for having us over. We wouldn't want to miss celebrating with you."

"Us too, dear. We wouldn't miss it for anything, so here we are." She looks over her shoulder to speak and continues washing the bowls. "Next Sunday, we will be praying for your safety while having a, you know, low key Easter dinner with Dylan."

Dad jumps in, "He can't make it today. I should have told you in the car."

My heart leaps, but also, surprisingly, a tinge of sadness follows. What the hell is that about?

"Why?" I ask.

"He had a school field trip that he couldn't get out of this weekend. You know how he volunteered to mentor that club at his school. They had a competition this weekend. He sends his regrets." Dad looks like he means it. Like Dylan would have meant it. Please.

The thought of him being a mentor to children terrifies me. I hope he is a different person at work—aka a sane person. But, he did kind of reveal more about what's behind his nastiness with me that last time I saw him, so...

"That's fine. It will be nice to have a peaceful dinner, just the four of us. But, you know, I will kind of miss his snide remarks today." Maybe the realization I had last time we were all together will settle in me. I have a soft spot in my heart now for him. I hope the same happens in his heart for me.

Taking my first bite of the Pizza Rustica slice during dinner, I think I am having an out of this world experience. The flavors blend in a divine combination in my mouth as I chew. The delectable main course is the traditional Italian Easter pie, and no Easter holiday is complete without it.

"Mom, this is remarkable! I taste every bit of the soppressata, pepperoni, ham, and prosciutto. That's all the meat in here, right?"

"Yes, you are right." She smiles wide.

I examine the layer between the two homemade pie crusts. "And if I remember correctly, not that I can see them, but there's ricotta, mozzarella, provolone, and Romano cheeses?"

"Right again. Now if you'd only try to cook."

"You wouldn't want that. But, what did you do differently this time? New spices?"

"It was made with LOL, of course." She beams.

"What?"

"Lots of love."

Brian and I both giggle. She must be trying to sound knowledgeable about pop culture.

"Well, I don't know if my palette is just preparing for authentic Italian food or what, but your food tastes better than usual today, Mom." I can hardly stop eating to speak. No time to waste if I want seconds.

"So, what will your week look like when you are in Italy?" Dad changes the subject, unfazed by the superb cooking of his wife.

"I can show you my Italy must-do's list after dinner if you want," I mumble through the food in my mouth.

Chef Brian goes straight to his most anticipated aspect of the week. "I can't wait to have some true Italian wine and bread," he says with a mouth full of the latter. All acceptable in the Granza house. Don't ever stop eating.

I chuckle at Brian's food obsession, obviously relate to it, and turn back to my dad. "I first plan to go to the church that must be the one our family attended. I think I will have luck with their records there, if anywhere. Those hopefully will lead to more information I haven't been able to find online. It just has to be the church since the other church responded that they didn't have our family's information. I want to sort of retrace Grandpa's steps while I'm there. You know, to walk on his path a little on his home soil."

"Yeah, that too." Brian grins.

Dad chimes in, "I really hope you can find out more too. You will have to tell me everything you find. I miss my dad."

"He was a great man," Mom says. "I'm glad you are going and doing this. I know how much you loved him, and how much he loved you."

I nod my head. Warmth washes over my chest. My mom is finally in agreement with my mission? Maybe that's Grandpa's work from the beyond once again. He must have sprinkled her with knowledge that I need his information.

She continues, "Rachel, you have to give us all of your flight and hotel information. And do you know what to do if you have an emergency over there? Do you know the phone number for help? And what if you get sick? You'll need to find a pharmacy. And—"

"Mom, I got it covered. Don't you think I looked up all of that info? You know me. I'll write down the flight and hotel details for you before we leave here though."

I know she's showing her motherly care and concern. She just wants to make sure we are healthy, safe, and that we have set ourselves up for a great trip. And we have. Would I have it any other way? Not a chance.

"Yeah, believe me, Mrs. Granza, she is more than prepared." He raises his eyebrows.

I smile and sit up straighter. That's right, I don't leave any stone unturned. Err, as far as I know.

"You guys be careful over there," Dad says.

"Oh, we will be," I reply.

"And you call us collect if you need to. Anything you need, we will help you. I'll jump on a plane right away if I have to," Mom adds.

I laugh. "Thank you. I know you would."

"I'll be back," I say, mid near-suffocating hugs from both of my parents.

"I know," they say in unison, dipping their heads.

"We just love you, okay?" Mom adds with a tear in her eye.

They hug Brian and keep saying their goodbyes.

"Have a great time. And remember, don't leave one detail out in telling us about the old country and our family," Dad requests. "Brian, you take care of our little girl."

"Oh, I will, as always," he replies.

"Love you guys," I say while stepping out the door. We want to walk to the train station in this crisp spring air tonight.

"Love you too," they say at the same time, and wave bye.

Although it is dark and mildly cold, I sense a bright and balmy change in the air. Flowers and trees will bloom soon, and I want to bloom with them. I hope this will be my time, need this to be my time to flourish.

I grab Brian's hand as we walk. He looks at me and squeezes it tighter. We are a team on this fact-finding journey. And soon we will be detectives together in a foreign land. We will get to the bottom of this mystery. *I will know.*

# PART II

GENOA

# Chapter 36

I t's the date I've been unknowingly waiting for my whole life, March 31, 2013. Zero days left. It feels surreal that today is finally here. The countdown is complete.

My thoughts are on Mach speed as we race around the apartment so we can leave on time and probably exacerbated by the shock (fear? anxiety? both? other feelings?) that we'll be in Italy today, well technically tomorrow since the flight is overnight. We won't be landing on actual Easter, but close enough. It's the most special Easter of my life.

"Harrison is all set with enough food for today," Brian yells out from the kitchen.

"Thanks," I say, coming back to the present. "Maggie will be over later. I hate when I've had to board him in the past, so thank God for her." I can't bear the thought of him lying in a cage all day, bored and sad. My child can't be cooped up like that. Harrison will be even more thankful than me for Maggie's loving services.

But, I think he senses a change is coming. I can tell. He's looked up at me with wondering eyes in the past few days. My heart breaks for leaving him. Ugh, if I could take him with us, I would.

"Yes, she's a good friend," he says.

"The best." Gratitude fills my heart.

Even though I've planned for weeks, there's always last minute business before a trip, a huge dislike for this planner. Trying to keep us moving, I grab my purse that contains all of the necessary travel items.

I check one more time to see the printed flight e-tickets, passports, and the itinerary with all necessary details, like our hotel I can't wait to see. Eee! All secure and in place. Check. I grab my kelly green wool peacoat that Maggie convinced me to buy and my carry-on bag filled with books and devices for all of our entertainment needs.

Glancing in our bedroom one more time and hoping to come back to it with much more knowledge than I have leaving, I grin. I have faith it will happen and need to hold that sense close to my heart. Grandpa will help me. I know it.

Harrison waits in the door frame and stares up at me. I walk over, pet him with my free hand, and scoop him up. "Love you, little guy. See you real soon. Mags will take good care of you."

"I have our suitcases, Rach. Ready?"

I put Harrison down and say, "Yes, ready." I smile larger than I have in the past year. "Let's do this thing." We are going to Italy.

My first breath of Genoese air leads me to close my eyes and inhale deep into my abdomen. I'm smelling the most gorgeous scent in the world; my homeland. We. Are. Here.

I am standing on the land where my ancestors are from and where they actually could have stood decades ago, though before the airport existed. My feet are planted on the concrete in the most grounded, mindful manner I have ever felt. I am in I-T-A-L-Y!

The loud urban noises make themselves known when I come back to outwardly focused consciousness. Wake up, Rachel. I blink several times. Reality strikes that we are standing on the curb of the arrivals terminal and we need to make our way to the taxi stand.

"There it is, Rach," Brian gently guides me to the right post by holding my arm. I silently follow, and continue to take in the surroundings. Good thing he is here to lead me at this point. After the long flight and my current dream-like state, I need his help to stay alert.

I look around as I walk with him and hear people speaking in charming Italian, or English but with elegant Italian accents. Signs are in Italian and English, but I focus on the Italian verbiage. "Benvenuto," or "Welcome," is everywhere. I treasure seeing "Benvenuto a Genova" and mouth the words to retain them. This is ah-mazing!

Although I've learned a few common phrases in Italian in the last few months, I don't know if we should try to speak in the native language or try English and hope that people understand. Hmm, I remember seeing in travel blogs that it would be best to ask people the phrase "Parla Inglese?" first and wait for whether they realize we don't know how to speak in Italian, so then they hopefully speak in English. At least it will show them we tried to speak their language. Okay, that sounds like the plan. I'll push past my fear of looking like an idiot to be respectful. I refuse to be *that* American (you know, the people who are so rude they assume everyone speaks English. Gross.).

Continuing to take in the sounds of the Italian language on the radio while in the cab, I'm strangely reminded of being home in the city. There are often times where I'm surrounded by people speaking another language, be it people on the street or owners of a store I enter. Sometimes it would take a while to hear English, which is wild, right? Lately, people speaking in their native tongue has led me to think of my ancestors living in their new land of America. Maybe I had a fleeting thought before this year-long journey, I don't know. Foreign languages are just the sounds of the city, so they weren't something that stuck out to me most days. But now, everything is different.

In my favorite Chelsea Italian market, I enjoy the Mazza family's communication with each other every time I'm in there lately. I never paid attention before my mission. There were countless times I was picking up ingredients for Brian, or getting a quick snack, and heard them squabbling in the beautiful Italian language. I always thought their animated gestures and speech were humorous, though. And if Brian's with me, he's quick to say I'm the same way when I'm irritable, except that I express myself in English. Can you believe that? Ugh, I guess he's right.

As we drive, I witness the most majestic snowcapped mountains in the distance, transitioning to lower rolling hills. They form an elegant frame around the cityscape of buildings, homes, and businesses in the foreground. We haven't even been outside of the airport for five minutes and I'm awestruck. I think I would be shocked by Genoa's beauty even if I didn't have ties to it. It is that breathtaking.

The main road we're traveling on from the airport is a large highway, along the coast and the old Genoa ports. Scooters and cars whiz by us from all angles in a mass rush to get to their destinations. Thank the Lord I am not driving. Talk about anxiety provoking situations. I am sure my wide eyes are giving away my fear of crashing into a car and plunging into the sea, over the cliffs. I hope the cab driver doesn't see them and keeps his eyes on the road, though. Eek, he better be!

So far, Genoa looks like a typical big city, but with a feel of aged elegance. How strange that it's boisterous with all the traffic, drivers honking their horns, dogs barking, ship noises, and faint live music, yet is also tranquil. The juxtaposition is a mix of the old and new world.

I wonder what it's like on a non-holiday because today's the day after Easter, a major national holiday called Pasquetta, or Little Easter. I read that Easter is the second largest holiday for Italians and that on Easter Monday people are not obligated to be with their families. They are free to be with friends and to venture away from home, unlike the actual holiday of Easter. Often, the major cities in Italy hold festivities with egg related games, picnics, and food, food, food. Oh yes, the festas occur in the homeland too. Well, that makes sense for how they began in the US then.

As we drive, I want to keep an eye out for stores selling chocolate. I saw some mouthwatering pictures of the largest chocolate eggs I've ever seen in my life online. Do I have a Pinterest page for the holidays of Italy and Genoa specifically? Of course. A small human could fit inside one of those eggs so I had to pin them. Oh, and there are prizes inside the eggs too. How much fun that would be for a child…or an adult named Rachel?

Driving by a few parks, it looks like people are enjoying the sunny spring weather. I put down my window more and breathe in that Genoese air again. I want to be on that picnic blanket, by the colorful blooming tulip patches. If this door wasn't locked, I can't promise I wouldn't escape to do so.

I fight my urges and we're at the hotel before I know it. A tinge of exhaustion rolls over me as I get out of the car, but the next wave is a surge of a second wind. No time to rest, we are finally here.

Wow. I look up at the four story hotel and admire the sun soaked yellow painted stucco, age cracks and all. "Brian, look at our gorgeous hotel," I say and point.

He pays the cab driver and pushes our suitcases toward me. Looking up a second, he says, "Um, yeah, it is nice. What's nicer is that it has a bed. I'm exhausted. Can we relax in the room for a little bit before we go out?"

I see the fatigue in his drooping eyes. He has done so much for me over the past year that I can't ever say "no" to him again for what he wants. Well, that's an exaggeration, but this time I can definitely give him what he needs.

A couple hours later, with a nap and some snacks recharging our batteries, nighttime is upon us and we're ready to explore this great city. "Brian, are you ready for our first proper Italian dinner?" I say as we step outside the hotel lobby doors. Italy may be an energetic hot spot for me because I don't remember the last time I felt this alive.

"Yeah, let's do it." He grabs my hand, fingers intertwined.

We walk a short distance from Hotel Pace and I'm hit with the aroma of true Italian food. "We must be walking in the right direction. It's going to be hard to choose where to eat with all of the choices."

"My stomach can't take much dilly dallying with the decision." He rubs it with his free hand.

"I know what you mean." Mine responds to his by rumbling and growling. "I am glad that places are even open on this holiday."

"You got that right."

As we walk by a couple apartment buildings and down narrow alleyways toward the scents filling the air, I notice a group of four older men playing cards. Trying not to stare, but allowing curiosity to surface, I look closer, slowing my walking pace to a near stop and leading Brian to give me a "What the hell are you doing now?" look. Staring into his eyes, I say, "Sorry, one sec."

I recognize the game by their motions and appearance of the card patterns they are making. The men are playing Scopa! That Italian card game is something I have completely forgotten about in my adulthood. A memory of Grandpa and Grandma playing the game pops into my mind, with those strange looking small Italian cards that I see again in front of me. They don't have numbers, just symbols, unlike American playing cards. They were so tiny for Grandpa's big, strong hands. I want to hold all of the suits of cards and shuffle them through my hands. I always thought the pictures of the swords, cups, coins, and clubs were adorable and cartoon-like.

I'm trying to sneak a peek, but uh-oh, the men catch me gawking. One of them says something I don't understand, but he sounds welcoming, so I creep closer.

"Buonasera," multiple people say one right after the other, smiling and making eye contact with both Brian and me.

I reply with the same greeting, which I know is traditional for wishing others a good evening in Italy. They must know by my one word and awkward smile that I don't speak Italian. So, thankfully, they switch to speaking to me in English, with their dense, yet adorable accents.

"You like to play?" one man asks. I'm not sure if he is simply asking if I like to play Scopa or if he is wondering if I'd like to play with them.

Trying to look normal, I reply, "I'm sorry for interrupting. I just noticed you are playing Scopa and it reminded me of when my grandpa used to play it with my grandma, when I was a little girl."

Their warm smiles grow even larger.

"Well, your grandfather must have been a good Italian man," one man says while making the Italian hand gesture where the thumb and fingers are pinched together and shaken. "All Italians play Scopa. And the best people even play Briscola." He has the hint of a wink. I love the ease of bodily expression with my people.

"Oh, I've never heard of Briscola, but maybe he played that too. I don't think I ever played Scopa with him, but seeing you play makes me want to know how."

"Well, you are welcome to sit down and learn. It is very easy. Come on, sit," another player encourages while getting up and walking toward extra chairs behind the group.

I look at Brian in yearning, but nod because I know our stomachs need food. I'll have to look up information about the game later. We aren't even in Italy a day yet and I am already finding a connection to my grandpa. It must be a sign.

"Oh, that's okay, but thank you so much. We are on our way to find a place to eat dinner right now. But it was nice talking to you. Have a good game." I wave for some reason and feel ridiculous.

"Ciao," each of them call out, then get back to their game.

"Ciao. Grazie." I walk away with Brian as I thank them.

"That was a game your grandpa played? Nice."

"Yeah, it was wonderful to see. So unexpected. What a gift." Is this place real? I may have to pinch myself.

Walking further down the alley and turning right at a fork in the cobblestone path, we find a restaurant that can be a possibility for dinner. "This place looks good," Brian says while he eyes a menu on the restaurant window.

"Sure, fine with me," I reply. "I don't think any food will be bad here."

As soon as we are seated and given menus, we are asked about our water choice. "I want to try sparkling water," I reply to the waiter, which I read is the standard preferred choice in Italy.

Brian chooses the same type of water.

Almost instantly, the waiter brings our own individual bottles and exits again. We glance at each other with confused expressions. "How strange," I say.

"Yeah, it sure is." Brian picks up and examines the bottle.

"Well, I guess they can't keep sparkling water in a pitcher to refill glasses, like restaurants in America do for the flat water. It would lose its bubbles within minutes. But what's ironic is that in America, this water would cost more money than flat water, however, in Italy they're about the same cost. Well, at least at this restaurant. But see, I am blending in as an Italian."

"Spoken like a true Italian woman." Brian smiles and drinks his special water.

Scanning the menu still, I say, "The first meal I order in the homeland has to consist of pasta. It is a must."

"Agreed. All of their pasta is made fresh in house the menu states, so who can resist that?"

"Not us."

When we finally have the pleasure of eating our meals, I'm taken to another dimension. The mussels and clams compliment the house's spicy red sauce on the spaghetti. I think there's a hot red pepper olive oil mixed in there because I see the tasty flakes. I swirl the noodles around my fork and take heaping bites.

Brian's meal also looks extraordinary, with sausage and peppers in a mound on top of fettuccine piled high on his plate. I have to ask, "Can I try a bite?"

"Of course." He pushes his plate near me. "Have two or three bites."

And I do. "It's outstanding, just as I would have expected a meal to be in Italy.

The portions are not the gargantuan American sizes either, which is refreshing to see. Since pasta is their primi, or first course, that makes sense. They need people to save room for the secondi and most Italians must eat an antipasto, or appetizer, in addition. I need to train my stomach to eat "as the Romans do." Err, Genoese.

Once the waiter knows it's our first night in Italy, he brings us complimentary Limoncello to have with our traditional northern Italian Easter bread dessert, colomba di Pasqua.

"Brian, can you believe this?" My eyes bug out.

He takes a bite as I continue to admire it. "Now this is good. I wish I knew their secret."

I finally dive in, nodding my head and widening my eyes in agreement from the first bite off my fork. I want to swim in this batter. I want to roll around in the almond slivers they use to garnish it. But I guess eating it will have to do for now.

"The almond flavoring tastes especially fresh. They must make it from scratch too." He holds the bite in his mouth a second and stares into the distance.

He must have sensational taste buds to know that kind of information.

"I'm sure. I especially love that it's in a dove shape. That's traditional for this holiday, I read. What a kind waiter to bring us this fresh Limoncello too. It's sweet, not bitter, like I thought it would be."

"I can't believe you never had it."

"Yeah, it isn't something I thought I would like, but I was wrong." I hold up my glass and tear myself away from the bread for a second. "Here's to new experiences and opening our minds."

Brian leans toward me. "Rachel? Is that you?"

"Yeah, it's just the new and improved Rachel. At least, I'm getting there."

We salute with our drinks for the first time in Italy.

Shortly after dinner, it's time for bed. We are both ready to drop from fatigue. The time change between New York City and Genoa is six hours and we are up waaayyy past our bedtimes. I'm sure the food coma doesn't help. But it will help us get a good night's rest for our first full day of exploration tomorrow.

Our lips meet to kiss good night and before I know it, the pillow feels perfectly soft, and...

*Chapter* 37

A s much as I would like to have an ordinary, touristy Italian vacation, that is not the reason we are here. And who am I kidding? I have never been normal by social standards a day in my life. Why would this trip be any different? We woke up today ready to hit the road for the genetic adventure. Mission *Family History* is in effect, as official as possible.

Our first stop this morning has to be the church. It doesn't look that far from the hotel according to the map, so we leave the hotel and enjoy the journey by foot. We are not in the true urban part of the city, so we'll be safe as pedestrians on this route.

In the bright spring daylight, the friendliest looking tan and red clay buildings on more cobblestone streets appear as we walk, as if they hid last night to get a good night's sleep and returned to welcome us on our first day of business in their homeland. The green hills and gray mountains appear again in the sun. I missed seeing those beauties last night. Genoa looks like it was drawn in a children's fairy tale book, imagined instead of solidly in the real world. How can a real place look so quaint?

Vendors are in the streets, as well as many shops along the corridors. The shop owners all have their doors propped open. Little old Italian men and women are taking care of their shops by sweeping the stoops and cleaning the windows. The pride they have in their businesses is apparent.

The smell of baked goods dances through the air, as well as strong coffee. The mix of brisk air and goodies make my heart happy. I take a cheerful deep breath, which is becoming a habit here, and keep putting one foot in front of the other, which I hope will lead me to the point of knowledge I've craved all this time.

"Brian, look at those candies in the window," I blurt out as if I am eight years old again. Looking closer, though, there's a lack of the large chocolate Easter eggs I hoped to see here in Genoa.

"Well, let's go in," he says without much thought, and luckily no judgment since he enters the tiny store right away.

I gladly follow.

On various levels of shelving, there are what seem like thousands of candied fruits. Figs, clementines, apricots, peaches, pears, plums, mandarins—and the list goes on. The artistically placed goods fan out in multicolored glory. Reds, oranges, browns, and purples all glisten with a coat of white sugar under the store lights.

The counter display allows for customers to grab whatever they want to make their own personalized box. This would never occur in the US, since in my experience candy left out in the open is only seen in stores giving away samples. There's a pureness to this element in the store, a trust that nothing would be tainted. People would do the right thing and refrain from stealing or God forbid poisoning another's candy. It's not a concern. The store owner, I assume, goes about his business sweeping, and is unaffected when we get close to the selection.

"Scusi," I say to the owner as I attempt to try out my Italian. He stops sweeping and looks up at me. He must know I don't speak Italian because he answers in English. Damn, I can't fool anyone that I'm not Italian, nationality wise, anyway.

"How may I help you?" He leans the broom on the wall to give me his full attention.

I smile at his friendliness and say, "Thank you. I was wondering how much it would be to buy one piece of candy. Oh, and do you have any chocolate Easter eggs?"

"One piece of candy!" He throws his arms up into the air and frowns. "Nobody comes to my store and gets one piece. Why don't you buy one and take another for your fellow at least? And, no I am sorry I do not have any eggs left. They were more popular this year than I expected."

"Oh, you don't need to *give* us any. I can buy another one for him. And that's okay about the chocolate. I just figured I would ask you."

"I won't hear of it. Take whatever candy you would like, sir." He directs his eye contact to Brian this time.

"Grazie, sir," Brian shakingly replies and looks at me. He seems just as shocked as me with the forceful kindness.

We better accept it because the amiable man is not going to take "no" for an answer, so we both choose our pieces, me a simple apricot slice and Brian a clementine in chocolate that is filled with sweet juice. I can't wait to eat mine, but feel strange biting into it here and now. Brian, however, eats his while I pay for mine.

Walking out of the store, Brian comments, "I can't believe how many people have gone out of their way to show us a good time here so far. And we aren't even here twenty-four hours yet."

"That's Italy, I guess! The nicest people on earth." I say this as a joke, but mean it in truth. I go on, "I agree though," I say more serious in tone. "I am stunned at the relaxed nature here. It feels like a different world from New York City. It's so unhurried and as if the people take more time to enjoy their lives here. They seem to care about true priorities here, focusing on the small pleasures in life. And they want everyone to have that joy." I connect his fingers with mine as we walk down the street further. The physical contact feels more natural again and I find myself loving every second.

As we stroll down the old street hand and hand, I keep my hope alive, not only for finding out about Grandpa's life, but about our relationship continuing to grow. Maybe, just maybe, I do want to be proposed to by Brian still. Maybe.

There she is. I stare at the Cattedrale di San Giorgio in silence and stop dead in my tracks. I am hoping this sacred spot in front of my eyes will hold my secret treasure. Her black wrought iron gate that surrounds the property is propped open, allowing for people to have a straight path to her large dark wooden front doors. Just inside the perimeter of the gate, there are two waving flags, one Italy flag and one English St. George's cross flag, which is the flag of Genoa. I read about the St. George cross, red with a background of white, being a prominent symbol of pride throughout Genoa, since St. George is the patron saint of the city. Both flags grace the sightline of the beige church and add an extra Italian flair that sends pride throughout my body.

A cemetery is on the left side of the main building. The aged olive trees encase the area, disguising the tombstones and memorials so much that people may forget they are there and instead may assume the land is a meditation garden of sorts. You know, not the land of a million memories of their residents, lingering below the surface of the thick soil above them. Too dramatic? That *never* applies to me. Well, I love looking at old cemeteries and will make sure we take a walk over there later.

Now, don't get me wrong, I never go to a cemetery to visit deceased loved ones, but would go to view the typically decorative decaying tombstones. I know that's weird. Add it to the never-ending list. I just don't think that the tradition of visiting the deceased makes any sense because the people aren't there. It is merely their bodies that were laid to rest in that space, but their souls escaped long before their "final resting place." So, if you want to "talk" to a loved one, you don't have to do it at their grave. Do it anywhere you want. That's my belief anyway.

*Creaaak.*

The heavy doors make a sound as if announcing our arrival to everyone inside. Scanning the room side to side, nobody looks up. Phew. That is way too much attention drawn to me, even though nobody looks fazed.

But this church. This church! It's magnificent. I don't know where to look first. The cathedral is so grand that I feel four feet tall. The altar looks like it's a mile away from the entrance. The red cushioned pews are endless. There are two adjacent rooms, one on each side, veering off from the altar that also contain rows of red seated wooden pews. I can't believe all of the details and how they come together to create one artistic masterpiece.

Colorful stained-glass windows, Gothic in aesthetic, surround the entire sanctuary. Like, all the way around. They are spectacular. I've never seen a church come even close to the aged beauty of this one. As I look closer at the stained-glass windows, I see their unique dome shape, which has thick beige frames all around them. They tell visual stories of Christ's life above each huge rectangular clear window.

Frescos also grace the walls and ceiling. I look up and swing my head slowly around the whole area. The faded colors don't impact their luxurious nature one bit. These are true Italian frescos before my eyes, like I've seen in history books.

Brian and I both remain silent, in an understood respect of the space.

Once my brain processes the combination of beauty with history in front of me, I can finally mutter, "Wow." That's all I can get out. I have been in old churches before, having lived my entire life in the northeast of the US, but this one is definitely the oldest, and most stunning.

Brian nods in agreement.

A wall plaque in the entry way catches my eye. I whisper, "It was built in the fourteenth century. How amazing that a structure could withstand nature, wars, and who knows what else, all that time, and look as though it was effortless."

"Yeah, she does look a little timeworn, but not too bad for being such an old lady."

"Yup, not worn in the way I would have thought. The time has only enhanced her natural beauty, just as age brings delightful wisdom to humans." I suddenly feel silly for my emotional statement and look down.

Brian puts his arm around my shoulder and squeezes. "That's true, Rachel."

"You know I love rustic buildings. This is the perfect place for me." I release my momentary embarrassment and laugh, quietly.

We walk down the aisle together—whoa—and slip into a pew near the ornate baptismal font. Well-used Bibles and hymnals are stacked on the pews, leaving room for people to sit in between the piles. There aren't any racks to hold the books on the back of the pews, like in most churches I've seen in my life. Hmm, there aren't any kneelers either. I guess that is something for modern-day churches rather than this fourteenth century one. There are lightly padded square kneelers that hang individually from underneath the pews, though. They look uncomfortable, but comfort wasn't a priority back then I bet. I swear they must be the original kneelers, based on their centuries-old appearance. The amount of wear and discoloration make me want to dig into my DNA and try to sew new ones for them. But, as I glance across the aisle toward the pews in front of me, I see the bigger picture. The array of colorful pads all hanging happily as if dancing in the gentle air wait for their next loving worshiper. Their longevity feels beautiful and safe.

"Look at the kneelers," I whisper. "They each have a family crest, or some set of religious symbols on them as decoration."

"Maybe families donated them so their name was attached to the church," Brian responds.

I dip my head in confirmation. "Maybe. I have no idea. What if my family did attend this church and I have a family crest on a kneeler somewhere in here?" My heart beats faster.

"If that's the case, we can look or ask about it."

"Yes, for sure if we get confirmation and there's time."

My focus shifts to scanning the room for its visitors. A few people sit sporadically throughout the large space, with their heads bowed in probable prayer. I remember that yesterday was Easter Monday, so this place must have been hopping. I am not sure if today is representative of the usual amount of people that visit on a Tuesday, or less than typical due to probable recent visits.

After sitting a few moments, Brian whispers, "I'm going to walk around."

I nod and remain seated. The table of lit candles in the corner captures my attention with their moving flames. My legs carry me almost automatically to them, so I can honor Grandpa by lighting one.

I take the candle lighter in hand and bring two votive candles to life. The mini white candles shine in their tiny red transparent holders. *Please know I am thinking of you, Grandpa. And Grandma too. But, Grandpa, I hope you are okay with me being here.* My head remains bowed, my eyes closed, and my hands in prayer form. *God, please help me in my quest for truth.* I really need it.

Brian is taking his time, walking around the sanctuary and looking in depth at each stained-glass window scene. I know he is fine for a while and can find me later, when he is done. Spotting a staff member, I make my way over to him.

"Scusi. Parla Inglese?"

"Sì, signora." He smiles.

I'm in luck.

"Grazie. I wrote a letter to your church a few months ago and I never received a response. I am trying to find out if you have records for my family. Can you help me?"

He nods his head and keeps a straight face, but springs into action to help. He asks, "Can you follow me?" He starts walking before I answer.

Um, this feels weird to follow a stranger when I'm alone, but hey, we are in a church and I am going along with that Italian trust thing I realize must be the norm.

The staff worker finds a co-worker in this new room and holds a short conversation that I can't understand. I hear "no" and "sì" but otherwise, I'm lost.

My heart and thoughts race, adding a hint of lightheadedness to this situation. Breathe, Rachel. This could be it. I'm seconds away from an answer.

But this is taking forever. Argh! Just when I feel ready to burst, the co-worker walks over to where I'm standing.

"Buongiorno, signora." After saying good morning to me, he struggles through his English sentences. "Please here you will wait for me to letters." I don't quite understand but shake my head in agreement. I hear the word "letters," so I'm making progress.

The original helper clarifies what his friend is doing for me. "He said he has a stack of inquiries regarding multiple concerns from people and he wants to see if your letter is in there. He is bringing the pile to you so maybe you could find your own letter. It will be faster."

"Oh, thanks! Grazie. Okay, I will wait here." I'm glad he translated. But now I *really* can't wait to find out if my letter is in that pile.

"Prego," he replies. I know that means "you're welcome," so I smile.

He walks off and I am left alone in the nearly bare room, made of light brown clay on all four walls, ceiling, and floor. One lonely Easter banner hangs on the wall. There isn't much to look at, but the minimal decor feels right, as a needed opposition to the elaborate sanctuary of the room next door. The beauty in there can't be diminished by another room.

I sit down on the one chair available and stare at the small cart on wheels across from me. Brochures fill its racks. Maybe this is an informational space for visitors and the congregation, not just lost American souls.

Once the man returns, he holds a stack of at least fifteen letters out toward me, of all different envelope colors, sizes, and languages. He shuffles them through his hands.

There it is! I see my letter right away. I pull it from the pile and grin. But it hasn't been opened yet. My heart sinks. It's okay. I'm going to get to the bottom of this right now.

I hand him my letter, with a deep breath.

He opens it and starts reading.

Time feels paused.

"I am sorry we no write you. Sometimes we take long to respond since we do not have many here to work. I can take you to the record room and we see about family name."

Eee! "Sì, sì, grazie."

Now, I still have the Italian trust feeling, but I do think I need to tell Brian I am leaving or see if he wants to come. Disappearing for who knows how long wouldn't be a particularly kind act. He may want to help or to be a witness to whatever happens, as well. So, I hold up a finger to the staff worker and say, "One minute," as I speed walk toward Brian.

"Brian," I call as I get closer to him. He doesn't look up. When I whisper I think I sound loud. Is that an echo? Nobody is looking at me, though. "Hey, Brian," ever so slightly louder now. This time, I attract his eye contact, instead of the fresco of angels he was staring at intensely.

"Yeah," he says.

"I'm going to go down to the record room with a staff member. Do you want to come?"

"Sure. I can look around more later maybe. Let's go."

All three of us go down the spiral, narrow stairs. The dark

basement is cold and damp, filled with old dusty books on its many bookshelves. We stop at a table in the middle of the room while the man looks at my letter again and places his finger on the name and birthday of my grandpa, which I included for helpful information. He walks over to a large brown leather book that has the dates "1900-1905" embossed on the binding in gold and pulls it off the shelf. It almost hits the floor because of the size.

I slide my foot on the gritty floor, curling my toes.

He dawdles back to the table in front of us, looking like the book may take down his elderly body, and firmly sets it down. A puff of dust flies out from under the book. I turn my head and close my eyes, so I don't get a whiff. He isn't affected by my reaction and casually flips page after page until stopping on one for a minute. And…nothing. False alarm. He continues flipping.

At last, he stops turning the pages for a second and remains stopped. He motions for me to come closer and look at where his finger is pointing. I guess sliding the book over to me would be difficult and I don't blame the tiny man. Viewing the content brings tears to my eyes. But, for once, tears of joy. The document in front of me is Salvatore Allegranza's baptismal record. I know the Italian word "battesimo" from my online searches. Now it's my new favorite word.

I see Grandpa's parents' names, his birth date, baptismal date, and home address. What a gorgeous piece of paper. This aged brown page is more attractive than any aspect of the sanctuary above us.

"This is really it, Rachel?" Brian is the first person to speak during the whole time we are in the record room. "It's that simple?"

I laugh at the thought that this moment came so easily, but just say, "Yes," feeling a sense of peace. I don't think my voice ever sounded so calm. "Here it is." I can't stop admiring it.

Seeing my great-grandparents' names, Gino and Francesca, are treats to my eyes. I see their home in Genoa was Via Figura 3. Their home! Over one hundred years ago, Grandpa lived at 3 Figura Street.

And Francesca's name on this official certificate confirms my previous find in the records online.

I take out my journal of notes and mark down all of the information. I squeeze the pen so tight that the ink may explode on the page. At least this way, my sweaty hands won't cause it to slip and drop to the dirt floor.

I know that this basement also contains information in one of those books that will help me to know my great-grandma's next married surname. It must. Since my grandpa had a half-sister, she had to have gotten remarried. Ladies in those days didn't usually have kids out of wedlock.

I look at the shelves and wish I had X-ray vision. "Sir, can we also look for my great-grandma Francesca's second married name? Sadly, my great-grandpa never came back to Italy after moving to the US and I think she remarried."

"Yes."

No computer system helps us to sort through the stacks of books, but the church has an unbelievably detailed system all their own. The man is able to find anything through his own old-fashioned search, cross referencing in multiple books. It only takes forty-five minutes for the next stop on this train. Hey, it's quicker than the year I spent looking for documents like these, so fine by me. But how nice would it have been if these records were online? Anyway…

"Qui." The patient helper points in the book in front of us.

I look down for the new treasure he found. "Francesca Ricci. That was her second married name, Brian."

"I see that. Remarkable."

"Yeah, it is." I stare at the marriage certificate, known by the word "matrimonio," and write down her name for my records.

"One last question. Well, actually the second to the last." Oh gosh, I hope he doesn't make us leave. This is a goldmine. "I wonder what her daughter's name was. Can you find it?" Her name also needs confirmation, so I have to ask. I'm getting so brave in my thirty-third year of life.

After only a few minutes, he props open another larger than life book on the table. This time I back away on commencement, knowing the dust bunnies will fly out by the looks of the cover.

Again, he points to an entry on a page where he stopped flipping. "Angeline Ricci. Battesimo," he utters.

"Thank you! Angeline Ricci was Grandpa's half-sister. Got it." I write down this last bit of information. She's my other great-aunt. Wow.

"I can't believe all that you are gathering here," Brian says.

"I know." I turn back to the man and smile. "My very last question is about my grandpa's full blood sister. I think her name was Antonia. Antonia Allegranza. I want to make sure. Do you mind *one* more search?" I tilt my head and make begging eyes.

The sweet man that has been downstairs with us all this time says, "I do that for you" and flashes a warm smile. It's the first time he broke his flatness, although I could feel his desire to help the whole time.

He starts looking in his reference books for the last time. Twenty minutes pass with us watching him plugging away for us before he tells me, "I am sorry. Her only record here was damaged in water leak many years long time past."

My heart drops. I would love to confirm this last piece of information with my family's names, but I will have to find out another way. And I won't stop until I do.

"Oh, that's awful. Well, you have done so much for me. I cannot thank you enough." I get ready to leave by putting my journal back in my purse. I need to stop taking up his time.

He stops me from turning around by saying, "Scusi. Angeline's family lives in home on Via Figura and she comes here Sundays. Now, last name is Santoro. I save that for last to tell." He smiles.

Brian and I exchange confused looks. This is too good to be true.

"You mean, Grandpa's half-sister not only lives close, but lives in their childhood home *and* you know of her without even looking up congregation names?"

"Sì, signora," he says, nodding with bright eyes.

"Thank you!" I exclaim. "Grazie! Thank you for all of your help today. You spent so much time with us and gave me more information than I could have ever dreamed of in my lifetime. You have provided me with the next step in my journey."

He reaches over and kisses me on both cheeks, one at a time. "Prego."

Brian and I climb the stairs to leave the dusty basement and move into the sanctuary. The candles I lit are shining bright, so much that it appears as if they are the only two there—with their flames rising proudly above their holders. They can't be missed. I know my prayers are being answered and I know this is a sign that my grandpa is okay with me being on this search.

# *Chapter* 38

After yesterday's fantastic church outing, I needed to recuperate before venturing to Grandpa's childhood home. Even good energy is energy for this introvert. Plus, all scenarios must be thought out and all of my questions need to be in order for this possible meeting with Great-Aunt Angeline. I spent the night in what I call 'planning ecstasy,' after our second delicious Italian dinner. I just hope she still lives there.

This morning I feel refreshed and ready to see his old house. My journal is in my purse and ready to be filled out if needed. I even have extra pens, just in case I write so much, ink runs out of one—or two or three.

Leaving the hotel room, I say, "Brian, you know we need to bring something to her home, right?"

"Oh yeah, your rule. What are you thinking about?"

We start descending the stairs.

He always thinks a gift is an unnecessary "rule" of mine when I visit someone's home, he's told me. I was taught never to visit someone's house empty handed—always bring something to eat and if not food, at least something to add to their home decor. As Brian and I are together longer, he seems to understand my values aren't going to change. My rule feels like the right thing to do, so maybe he is not just giving in via defeat, but also agrees with it at this point in our lives. Fingers crossed. But what to buy her…?

"I don't know what a typical item to bring would be food-wise here, and I don't want to offend her. Maybe—"

He cuts me off, "How would you offend her?"

"I don't know all of the ins and outs of a culture sometimes. Even though I know a lot about being Italian, what if there is some weird thing about American strangers claiming they are family members who come to your house bringing candied fruits? Like, it means lock the doors because they'll steal all your valuables."

"Okay, Rachel. I do not think that cultural standard exists, but just in case, let's think of a non-offensive gift that doesn't scream 'run for your lives.'"

"Sounds good." He gets me, or at least plays along.

Walking out of the hotel lobby and down the main street, we stop at a bar to buy cups of espresso while we ponder the big decision. We act as true Italians by standing at the counter of the bar. It's funny that bars in Italy aren't necessarily for alcohol.

All the serving sizes for coffee are smaller in Italy than I'm used to, but espresso is the same size as the amount typically purchased in America. The size is the only aspect of similarity, however. And taste? Well, that's a million times better than at home. The typical Italian dark roast has a hint of bitterness but is also smooth and sweet. How can that be? The strength of its aroma sends warmth throughout my entire body, like a blanket placed on my shoulders from my grandma. Maria B.'s Coffee Café down the road from our apartment can't compare one percent of their blend to the blends we are sipping in Genoa. Sorry, Maria.

After a few minutes of standing at the counter, I still draw a blank for the gift choice. "I hoped the jolt would stir up an image of something to bring, darn it. I want to find the ideal gesture of 'hello,' 'thanks,' 'hey I'm your family,' but I don't know what would be acceptable. No, scratch that; it must be perfect. Nothing but the best for my family."

"Rach, why don't we just ask the guy over there?" He discretely points to the man behind the counter, currently wiping up spilled coffee on the floor.

"He looks too busy for us to bother him with this issue. I feel weird asking him this foreigner question." My breathing rate increases with the thought of looking incompetent in front of, well, a stranger in a strange town. Such is a usual feeling from yours truly.

"Come on, Rachel. It's fine." He doesn't talk further about it with me before he calls out "scusi," and waves his hand to get the man's attention.

I want to cringe. Let me sink down onto the floor and under the counter. Rachel has left the building.

"Sì, signore?" the kind man says as he drops his rag and walks over to us. We are always stopping people from cleaning, I guess.

Brian starts, "In Italy…"

No, he's not… I cover my eyes with my hand and look away from him.

He continues, unaffected. "Do people usually bring gifts when they visit another person's house?"

"Sì, signore, sì. They would not make a visit without a tiny present to show the honor of being at the person's home."

"Great, so what do people give as gifts here in Genoa?" Brian says in response to the confirmation of the validity of my rule.

"Oh, well you see, people bring everything. They can bring food, pastries, flowers, wine… Those are the most customary gifts. But do not give red roses. Those are the flowers of love." He grins, while looking between both of us.

Brian smiles, says, "Grazie for your time," and nods his head.

He turns to me as the man goes back to work and says, "See, now was that so bad?"

My knee jerk reaction is to scream the obvious answer, "Yes." And I do.

"Oh, stop. Now we know what to bring." He jabs my shoulder lightly.

"Yeah, but where do we choose any of those presents from? And I don't think I want to bring alcohol. What if my family member is the one Italian who doesn't drink wine? That would be my luck."

"Even though you are being, well, very Rachel-like, I think maybe we can stick to chocolate or pastries. Something like that can't go over wrong." He seems confident when he suggests these items, which calms me a notch.

This idea *is* on the right track for me. A small box of pastry or chocolate will be easy to slip in my purse and to carry to Via Figura today. "Sure, let's find some sweet treats. Ready?"

As we walk through the narrow alleys, on the same path as the day before, we smell the strong bakery scents whirling through the air once more. We follow our noses to a shop just around the corner from the main alley. I hadn't noticed this place yesterday, but today am called to it directly, upon the recognition of the sweet fragrance releasing from the store.

Our noses are correct. This store has two counters, one on each side for the length of the tiny room, each with three tiers of pastries of all kinds. Tortas, biscotti, and a variety of colorful cookies' beauty shines under the ceiling lights like diamonds. As if a spotlight goes straight to the sfogliatella pastries, I know that is my choice. Simple, easy to carry, and delicious. Sfogliatelle it is.

Now we have caffeine coursing through our veins—which I don't need being so nervous, but whatever—and we also have our gift, so our mission is afoot. Continuing on our now familiar trail, we walk toward the protruding cathedral that provided us with so much family information yesterday I feel like I should bow down to it in tribute. Just past the building, a dirt road continues into the hills. That is our path to take today.

Good thing I put on my new black walking shoes. All the gravel, dirt, and clay would have done a number on my light-colored shoes from yesterday. I can't meet my relative looking like a cavone. You know, I mean like a no-class fool.

As soon as we start on the inclined path, I realize these hills do not look as steep as they actually are, jeez! A tad out of breath, embarrassingly so, I look over at Brian, who is gliding along as if he was born for this terrain. He must feel my eyes glaring into him because he looks back at me and smiles before picking up his pace. Pure evil.

"Come on," he yells to encourage me. "We are getting there. Just a little bit more."

"Coming," I respond, swinging my fist like a champ. Of course, he doesn't see that or my eyes rolling.

Three fourths of the way up the hill, we finally see Via Figura. There are not many roads up here, so it isn't hard to find the street. The village is made up of tiny homes on large, spaced out green grass filled lots of land. Maybe there used to be farms here. There is enough room for them.

We are at number ten and need number three, so we keep walking on the route to Grandpa's old home, allll the way down the winding road. I gasp for air now and make a deal with myself to start exercising when I get home.

This is quite a trek from his church. How did Grandpa do it and how did the older people, like his parents, handle it? Or Great-Aunt Angeline recently? My gosh.

People are outside of their homes along the way, and they are friendly as ever. A woman hanging her clothes on a line smiles and waves as we walk by. Another woman tidying up a flower bed full of budding purple beauties calls out "Buongiorno," and we reply with the same greeting. Italians are always saying "good morning," "good afternoon," and "good evening" to us. So polite. So formal. So un-American.

After passing number four, the tip of Grandpa's tiny house's red clay roof shows itself, far in the distance. My heart leaps and my feet glide as easy as Brian's all of a sudden. The contrast of the house's white stucco walls and its forest green wooden door and window shutters feel relaxing in a strange way. Did it look this way when Grandpa was a boy? Would he have had this image in his mind while he crossed the large Atlantic Ocean with his family, never knowing if he would ever see it again?

Standing right in front of Via Figura 3, I stop to collect my thoughts. "Brian, do we just go up and knock?"

I've thought of every possible interaction once meeting my family, I think, but not this starting moment. There was no way I could bring myself to knock on a stranger's door in Philly at Grandpa's old home but will have to be brave now. I didn't travel all this way to chicken out. But eek.

"Well, that is usually the way it's done to have someone open their door." He puts his arm around my shoulder for support, with a sprinkle of his playful mocking laugh.

Speaking rapidly now through short breaths, "I'm nervous to meet her. Great-Aunt Angeline has no idea we are here, or even maybe has no idea about me at all. I don't know what she knows. What do we do?"

Brian doesn't respond with words. They won't calm me down so it's useless and he must know that by now. He walks to the front door, and I robotically follow, in a half slow and surreal, half fast and totally aware of the anxious moment state. I smooth out my hair that I bet is a mess and frizzy as ever as we approach the front door. I take out my box of sfogliatelle so it is ready to be given as a sign of goodwill and pray that it may help ease any awkwardness. This must happen, no matter my comfort level. Just as I am about to knock, the door flies open and a dark-haired boy, about seven years of age, runs out past us.

"Roberto, torna dentro adesso!" a woman screams from inside but doesn't appear in view. The boy continues to run to a shed-like building near the side of the house. He appears to be finding it humorous that his mom, I assume, is repeatedly calling for him because he keeps laughing to himself as his tiny feet carry him along.

He slips inside the shed for a moment then runs back to the house with a cannister in hand. The door is left wide open, so we watch him take the lid off the cannister and dump out toy figures all over the floor. Still unaffected by us, toys going everywhere, and a woman calling for him, he continues his plan. He did say "Ciao" upon passing us, so it's as if this is a common occurrence, to have foreigners on their doorstep.

Although he left the front door open, I figure I should still knock and maybe call out to the lady inside as well. Softly, I say, "Ciao," with increasing loudness over three times, until the woman comes over. When she appears, I realize the boy looks just like her.

She speaks in Italian, which of course we don't understand. It is so fast, but so beautiful. The blank stare must be sinking in because she pauses and asks, "Parla Italiano?"

I say, "No, sorry. Parla Inglese?"

"Sì. How can I help you?" she replies, smiling and giving a sense that we are not inconvenient to her at all. "Sorry if my son was rude to you. He does not always obey his mother." She looks at him to give him a disappointed look, but he still seems like he couldn't care less.

"Oh, no. We are fine. Do not worry. I just want to introduce myself to you." Knowing this person can't be Great-Aunt Angeline because of her youth, my anxiety dissipates, but my voice is still shaky. I continue speaking though. "I'm Rachel Granza and this is my boyfriend Brian Holden. We heard that Angeline Santoro lives here. Is she home right now?"

"No, I am sorry, miss. She moved a few months ago."

"Oh. That is too bad." Looking down, I am at a loss for more words, when Brian picks up where I leave off.

"That's okay. Do you know where she lives now then?"

"No, again sorry. I never knew the Santoro family. But you may try asking that neighbor over there," she says pointing to the house to the left and across the street. "They may know. I think they have been friends for a long time, so they probably have the new address." Her face shows true apology for not knowing where to direct us.

I want so badly to be able to see the inside of my grandpa's home. This is the first thought that comes to mind when the woman tells us she didn't know my relative. Oh, the hell with it.

I blurt out, "Ma'am would you mind if we saw the inside of your home? See, my grandpa lived here as a boy and it would mean a great deal to me to be able to see it. We traveled a long way to find out information about my family and also to witness some of his youthful experiences." I am going to go on explaining, but she stops me by placing her hand on my shoulder.

"Of course. This is no problem for me. Come in. My name is Cella and it is nice to meet both of you." She turns around to lead us inside, and as I look at Brian his eyes are wide with surprise at my courage, I assume.

I whisper to him, "Hey, I couldn't leave here without seeing it." He shakes his head in agreement.

The house alerts my sense of smell upon walking into the small family room in the front of the house. It isn't the smell of food, which is familiar to me in a home, but rather a smell from an old library. Older homes often have that sort of musty aroma, I've found. It is pleasant to me, whatever the smell is in this particular Italian home.

She proceeds to allow us a minute to take in the family room's scenery, with its two tan cloth recliner chairs and a small circle shaped side table holding an in-progress puzzle. Adjacent to this room, I see the kitchen with its royal blue tiled walls, only breaking in their pattern for a small yellow wood bordered window above the sink. The mountains and a rather large private vegetable garden appear in its frame, from what I can see at this distance. Viewing the bright green of the outside in contrast to the deep blue tile is stunning.

The appliances look older, which may mean they were Great-Aunt Angeline's property. A dark wooden four seater table is in another small room, off of the kitchen. Maybe that was her table too.

Cella kindly guides us through her entire house. The narrow hallway off of the room with the table leads to two more rooms and a bathroom. All walls are freshly painted white, with yellow wooden window frames and windowsills. This is like another scene from a book, for me. Which room was my grandpa's when he lived here? Maybe it was the room the little boy moved to play in now, which looks like his bedroom according to the toys everywhere.

As Cella takes us back to the kitchen of her new home, she talks about how she plans to decorate. "The furniture was sold with the house, so these colors and the decorating style aren't my choice. This is the reason no pictures are hung yet. I want to buy new furniture before I hang anything."

"That makes sense," I say. But, this has to mean the furniture and style was Great-Aunt Angeline's and possibly some of Grandpa's parents' items and decor choices as well!

"Would you like anything to eat or drink?" she asks.

"Water would be wonderful," I say.

"Yes, please, water." Brian agrees.

It would be offensive not to accept something to eat or drink, I know. And speaking of offensive, I forgot all about the box of pastry I am gripping tightly in my nervous hands. I hope there isn't wetness from my probable sweat. I awkwardly grin and give her the box with a heartfelt "Grazie" and continue by saying, "for showing us your home." She accepts and thanks us.

Cella puts the dessert on a plate and brings it to the table in the side room, motioning for us to sit. Even I can't eat at a time like this. Brian continues a conversation with her. I fade away from the moment.

Grandpa was here. In this home. I look around at the rooms in view. Many hopefully happy memories were made there, right there, and over there. He was taken here as a baby, and he left as a teenager, his home for all of his childhood. This is where he maybe last saw his mom and sister. The thought would be glum if not for it feeling gratifying to be sitting in the same room where this may have occurred. I'm closer to him this way.

I am near enough to the wall to touch it without being seen, so I reach out from under the table. I want to experience all that I can while I am here. Taking a mental photograph in my mind, I breathe in the smell of the old musk, make sure to remember the floor plan and colors of his house, feel the smooth, cold walls with my fingers, and become aware of my feet firmly planted on the ground. Remember this, Rachel. I know that I will.

I pop out of my daydream just in time to hear Cella ask if we want to see her back yard area, where the garden is located. "I was told the garden existed for many years," she says while leading us out the back door seconds after our obvious agreement.

This could mean it was tended to by Grandpa as a boy. He enjoyed growing fruit and vegetables when he was older, so maybe that was a joy instead of a chore for him. Maybe he wasn't made to do it, but offered.

When we step outside, I can't help but reach down and take a small handful of dirt in my hand as Brian and Cella walk in front of me. This ground bred my hero and I am not going to leave without adding it to my mental photograph. Cella doesn't see this, and I am glad. I let the dirt slide through my fingers, back to its origin.

The garden is rich with budding plump fruit, and hidden vegetables in the ground. There are fig trees that line both sides of the garden, extending from the house a good distance. In between the trees lays a well-organized maze of various wooden dividers and small signs, probably stating what the food is, but they are in Italian so I can't read them of course. I bet they are herbs, but Brian would know better than me.

I hear Cella's son call for her.

"I will be right back. You are all right to be alone out here?" She seems like she is only asking for politeness' sake because she knows we are of course more than all right on this beautiful land. Plus, it is wonderful to be alone for a second.

"Yes!" I smile and she runs inside. I am sure this is pretty typical for that rambunctious little one.

"Brian, I wish I could have been here with Grandpa to help him tend to his little ones. You know, his bambinos; vegetables, fruits, herbs... He was so talented and could grow anything, *anything*! And he treated all of them like his babies."

"I wish I could have known him. For all that you've told me about him, I probably would relate to him the most on his love of ingredients."

"Well, Grandma usually was the one cooking, but he provided her with everything needed that could possibly be grown."

"To have fresh ingredients would be wonderful. If we had the land, you know how much I would be growing? My meals would be outstanding." He smiles and looks up as if imagining the possibilities.

"Well, they already are outstanding, but yes, they would be even better. Imagine the Sundays we used to have as a family, which included a persistent smell all day long of sauce with garlic and onions simmering on the stove. By mid-afternoon, we were all ready for some of Grandma's delicious meatballs and of course macaroni."

He interjects, "Oh yes, the macaroni. Only you Granzas use that term so generously, I think."

"No! It's normal." I say with a muffled laugh. I know we aren't normal, which is maybe why I am not. See, it's in the blood.

"Mm-hmm." He smiles and turns to walk in the garden.

Following him and having an urge to share more memories, I continue. "Grandpa and Grandma were such a great team, also. He did all the growing and she would make the freshest meals, which is a large source of pride for any good Italian. She also would preserve and can the food. Did you know that? A vivid memory of my childhood includes going down to their basement and seeing the canned goodness. The jars glistened in the dim lighting and held the promise of one day being delicious food in my stomach. Sometimes these jars would be in my parents' basement as well, since my grandparents always gave away their crops to loved ones. My mouth waters just thinking about all the food they made."

Brian crouches over, inspecting the plants. "Rach, look at these tomatoes. They're huge!" He strokes them and I chuckle. He doesn't hear me at all. But, in his defense, I *am* rambling.

"Grandpa's tomatoes looked like that, but even more glowing red, plump, and shiny. That's why Grandma's sauce was so yummy. No other sauce I ever tasted was like hers because it had his tomatoes in it."

"Don't tell your mom that!" He laughs.

"My mom's sauce is delicious as well, but back then, when she had his tomatoes, it was the best." I stop speaking because his eyes grow twice their size. I gently push his shoulder in jest. "Yeah, we can't ever tell her. Maybe it was just that I could taste the love and care that went into those tomatoes Grandpa grew. Wait, that isn't making it any better. I'll stop now."

"Telling her would probably make her cry at the next family dinner."

"And not from the hot peppers," I joke.

"Ha, yeah. You love 'em."

"Guilty. I can't stay away from them now. I just wish I was able to taste Grandpa's home-grown ones. I didn't have the guts when I was a kid. But now I blow my nose and fit in with the rest of the family."

"Your parents find the spiciest ones I've ever had, and you know how I've tasted anything and everything. It's impressive." He walks over to the herbs and I follow, but I'm still in pepper world, mentally.

"I never understood the thrill as a child, but now I get it. I mean, they are so good that it is worth the suffering. And it is almost a rush of power or control to be able to eat them; to overtake them and win the imaginary fight. That's my professional psychological opinion anyway." He misses my smirk because now he's in his own thoughts, I see. Food is the only topic that can make him act like, well, me.

"Rachel, these smell so good. Come closer." He subtly grabs the back of my head and motions with his other hand to bend down. He gently takes one herb into his hand, rubs it, and brings it forward, toward my nose to help me to smell it.

My eyes light up with the memory of Grandpa's fresh and pungent herbs. "This one is basil?" I am not good at guessing smells, but I can try.

"Yes, good job. You get a reward." He hugs me tightly and lifts me off the ground for a moment. I feel like I'm flying, for multiple reasons.

"Grandpa grew basil and parsley, so I'm more familiar with their smell, I think. They went on and in everything, adding a special taste."

"Well, they do go on everything if you are an Italian-born person with a desire for Italian food." He smiles.

"Grandpa especially made sure his basil was up to par. It had to be his favorite spice. He loved it so much that sometimes he had to move bins of them inside to keep them thriving. Icy winters are not friends with basil. I know that much."

"No, they aren't. I may start trying to grow some in our apartment. I would have to see if they could be placed on a windowsill for light though. Is that okay with you?"

How thoughtful that he is asking my permission, but he doesn't have to; it's his home also. "Of course! I would love to be able to smell the herbs again. And I would especially love it if you put them in more of your meals for us. Wink, wink, hint, hint." He smiles in response.

"We just have to train Harrison to leave them alone."

"Oh yes. He'll be fine. He's smart," Brian reassures both of us.

I take his hand and lead him to one of the rows of fig trees. I feel like we are two kids loose in an amusement park without our parents. I hope Cella is still occupied a little while longer.

We walk closer to one tree that looks like it's been here forever, based on its height. I examine it for its beauty. The green leaves, the purple figs, and the deep brown bark complement each other perfectly. Touching a fig, I tell Brian, "Now this is something we haven't had at the Granza house in so long. I wonder why."

"Yeah, you will have to bring them for your parents one day. Also, we can get some and have them at our home if you'd like."

Of course, I have more to say about Grandpa's garden. I mean, come on, it's figs. They were his true pride and joy in his garden. And this place has figs for days.

"Yes. Grandpa told me once that Pennsylvania wasn't ideal for growing figs, so he needed to think creatively. Although they grew best in the ground, he told me he needed to grow some in moveable bins as well, like the herbs, for the cold winters. He covered the trees every winter, but it was too risky to only have fig trees in the ground and possibly not to have any figs. He loved them that much. So, he grew them in both the traditional way and in moveable bins. Wow, they were good."

"You know, I'm not certain that I've tried figs. How strange. I need to." He trails off, walking further down the tree path to the back of the yard.

I walk with him. "We need to fix that problem. We can make Italian fig cookies or fig jam maybe. I can still taste the sweetness and texture when I think of Grandpa and Grandma's concoctions, especially the cookies." People's minds are so powerful that visualizing something can feel like it is real. I've demonstrated this countless times with clients, playing the imagination game, as the kids call it, that I can do it on command and in an instant. This is a useful skill for me because I can return to any culinary time I want, and as an Italian American child I have plenty of times to choose from with the cooking that surrounded me.

"Those cookies sound great to me." He keeps admiring the property.

"The only fruit or vegetable that isn't here is grapes. Grandpa loved his grapes because then he could make his sweet wine. I'd always grab a taste. Luckily, the grapes from the northeast of the US are sweet, so it fits a kid's palette."

"Did you just use the word palette? You are so fancy in Italy."

"Yeah, yeah, yeah, well now that I have your attention again, I want to tell you about—" but I stop when I see Cella is walking toward us.

"I am sorry to both of you. My son needed help with something."

"No need to apologize." I smile ear to ear.

"Yes, we enjoyed being able to see your garden, so thank you," Brian adds.

I could have stood on that land all day. As we walk back into the house, I look around and take another mental snapshot of the garden. Check.

"Well, we don't want to take up too much of your time, Cella. Thank you for allowing us to see your home. It means the world to me." I lean in to kiss her on each cheek, as I've quickly learned is polite here.

She walks us toward the front door. "I was glad to do it. Have a good stay." She places her hand on her chest as a sign of care.

Walking away from the house, Grandpa's house, Great-Aunt Angeline's house, I realize overcoming my fear led to great treasure. I need to carry that souvenir home with me for life.

I stop at the road and Brian does as well. We both stare at Grandpa's house one last time. It feels like my home in a strange way. There's a feeling of safety I haven't felt since he left this world.

I need to carry that gift in my heart because it doesn't have to leave me ever again.

"I can't believe that just happened," I say to Brian.

"It was pretty unbelievable that she was so nice and allowed us in her house as complete strangers. These Italians are the nicest people I've been around in a long time. Take a picture, Rach."

"I know. Yes, let me do that. I knew I couldn't ask to take pictures inside, but I definitely need one of the outside."

I snap a shot and look down at my feet. A teeny smooth gray rock lay by them, just begging to be taken by me as a reminder of Grandpa's childhood land. I pick it up and slide it into my purse. Brian smiles when he sees my move.

"We can come back if you want. This doesn't have to be the one and only time we see his home, at least from the outside," he reassures me.

"I guess," I say knowing he is right. "Well, let's go across the street to that neighbor's house Cella suggested. It's the only one nearby so we can give it a try. Maybe they will know where to find Great-Aunt Angeline."

But when we knock on the door, there's no answer. Disappointment number one thousand, I think while feeling a drop in my gut. My mind automatically goes to negative thoughts, even after all of these magnificent experiences. But, now I am able to recognize it and pop back to gratitude because I just had the chance to see my grandpa's house; the one I dreamed of seeing for a long time.

Keeping some positivity, I say, "Let's get some lunch, down the hill. I have another idea."

# Chapter 39

This afternoon, we make our way to the city registry office, or the Comune di Genoa Anagrafe as the Italians call it, to find the new address of Great-Aunt Angeline. Oh, I hope we find it. I hope, I hope. We have to stay on this track because I am sure Great-Aunt Antonia has passed by now, but Great-Aunt Angeline is younger than Grandpa so there is still a chance for her to be alive.

Taking a cab to the heart of Genoa, from the more rural side where Grandpa lived, I notice a transition of the terrain and activity alike. A few basil farms are visible by car, spread out over the hilly land, with people in the fields tending to the crops, the "green gold" that turns into pesto. Donkeys are present on the sides of the narrow roads that line the fields, with who appear to be tourists on their backs while they climb up the hills to the farms. The smell of the basil in the air is sharp and enticing. I hope we have time to visit one during this trip. But, that is only if there is time. It can't be added to the priority list just yet. To the city records, Jeeves.

As we descend from the higher elevation to the lower more metropolitan area, mopeds speed by, traffic floods the streets, and plenty of yelling echoes through the air. Calling out from house to house across streets and alleyways seems pretty standard here. Most energetic shouters are older women, with much joy in their tones. Yes, a joyful yelling if that makes any sense. People also lean out of windows while they scream, making it almost humorous. It is just normal conversations occurring, I think, because I have no idea what they are actually saying. But with exaggerated arm actions as side notes, I enjoy every second of the show when we are at stop lights. Brian must have gotten used to the hollering in my home since he never remarks about it here.

Getting out at our stop, close but not able to be dropped off in front of the anagrafe due to road closure, I realize what this city is made of—a perfect mixture of old-world charm with modern touches of glamour. The government building's location in the heart of the city is a world away from where Grandpa lived. The tan and darker brown buildings that surround us look much more contemporary and similar to some sections of New York. There are no fire escapes on these beauties though, just clean lines with simple decorations. The pretty as a picture Mediterranean style buildings have tiled roofs and all, just how I imagined Italian architecture.

"All right, Rachel. Ready for this?"

"Ready."

Upon walking into the registration building, I see a front desk attendant and ask my now standard line of "Parla Inglese?"

"Yes. How can I help you?" she replies.

"Thank you. We are here to use the research room for public use. Where is it located?"

"Down this hall and to the right. You cannot miss it." She points and smiles.

"Thank you." I grab Brian's hand and we start making our walk back.

This building isn't as grand or elaborate as the archives building in New York, but still has a charm all its own. Its European flair, with pale green walls and touches of gold on the light fixtures is effortless and elegant. Only one small, narrow hall protrudes from the foyer, so the attendant is right; we can't miss the room.

"Let's sit here, Brian," I say finding two computers next to each other in the empty room. Good, we don't have to whisper.

"Okay, let's get to it," he says.

Examining the homepage, I see the ability to read all pages in translated English. Perfect! "Brian, click the translate button in the top corner." I point to it on his screen.

"Thanks. I think that will help just a bit." He laughs.

"At least now we have an accurate name to enter in the database, unlike in the States when I had been searching. I'm going to start by typing in the surname Santoro."

My search comes up with several listings, with the first being a listing for a newspaper article about the death of a Santoro family member. "Oh no, I think Great-Aunt Angeline's husband may be deceased. Here's the obituary and she's mentioned. His death occurred last year, the poor lady. Maybe that's why she moved from her house." Was it too painful to be in the home she had all those years when married to her husband? I would think so. My empathy is in overload.

"I have some info here that I think you already have. Birth date, marriage date, that kind of thing," Brian tells me.

"Yeah, what I'm desperate for now is the story of my grandpa, which means talking to her in person. I want more than just what shows on the papers." Is that too greedy? She better still be alive. I need her. Come on address. I feel like I'm a character in a movie set in a Las Vegas casino, rolling the dice. Mama wants a new pair of shoes, err, address.

"I know." His tone lowers.

But seconds later, he says, "Here we go, Rach. I got it. Here's her new address."

"What? Yes! Thank you!" I bombard him with a hug. "Team work."

We high five each other and I write down the address.

"Let's see if we can get directions from the hotel front desk attendant when we return there today. It's getting a little late now to visit her, don't you think?" He looks at his watch and frowns.

"Yeah, I think going to her home tomorrow morning would be better for all involved. I'm tired and I'm sure an older lady is tired later in the day. I want to ask *a lot* of questions, so I need her at her best. I know she was younger than Grandpa, but she is in her nineties, I think."

Saying her age out loud drives fear into my chest. What if she has memory problems? She is in her *nine-ties*. I didn't come this far, geographically and metaphorically, to be stopped now. Tomorrow, I sincerely hope to meet Great-Aunt Angeline, and to learn more of the Allegranza mystery. Please, oh please.

# Chapter 40

Leaving the anagrafe building, Brian and I stroll around the area before going back to the hotel. There's a piazza, or square, we saw down the road when we were dropped off at the building, so it wouldn't be out of our way to do something touristy. Just for a minute. Also, taking a tiny bit of time out of the many places we need to go for the mission is a nice break. But only because our priority of the day is done. I nod to myself for keeping in check.

Honestly, I can use the time to process everything we've learned and seen so far and hopefully to avoid the stress about what is to come; the unknown. Rachel does not get along with that well.

"Hey Rach, look at the fountain!" Brian exclaims as we approach the piazza. "It's the most extravagant fountain I've ever seen." His eyes are wide and his mouth slightly open in awe. I realize that I am looking at him more than the fountain because of his exaggerated response, but once I shift my attention to the striking beauty in front of me, I know why he is reacting in this manner.

"Oh...my...God. It's—wow. I love it." The fountain in the middle of the piazza almost leaves me speechless.

"Let's get closer," Brian says, walking rapidly to its base.

"Look at that pure white stone. They must have to wash it every day to keep it that clean." I walk up to the large sculpture, I mean fountain. It is a work of art. Hey, someone designed it.

"Yeah, that's Brac stone." He spits out that little fact like he's telling me the sun is in the sky. Oh yes, it's totally common knowledge. But he is artistically inclined, not only in the kitchen.

I shoot him a confused look and taunt him just for funsies. "Oh really? So, tell me more, Michelangelo."

"What? Like I can't know anything except the perfect slogan for exercise shoes? Maybe I researched a little for this trip as well," he says while giving a loose hug around my shoulders. "Brac stone is from Croatia and it is a white limestone. It is used all over Europe and is even the stone that was used to build the White House."

"No way. That's pretty cool. Thanks for the fun fact, Brian." I love when his geekiness comes out because it's rare.

I peer closer and see many coins in the fountain. Hmm, that tradition isn't just an American one. In fact, there is money from everywhere. I don't even recognize some of the types of coins. I wonder how many countries' money is in here.

"Brian, let's make a wish and throw in some coins. I think we are supposed to throw it over a shoulder though. Do you happen to know that fun fact?" Sarcasm is *my* specialty. He can't match that or my nerdiness, unfortunately for me.

"Let me look it up real quick. I wouldn't want to lead you astray, my darling." He is pretty good at sarcasm too.

"I'm glad your company paid for international data."

He keeps looking at his phone. "Always ready to be contacted by them. But hey, we get to use it when we need, so that's fine."

"Yes, what would we do if we didn't know the life altering answer to this coin question?" I laugh and he ignores me because of his focus. Are we blending into one person now?

"Turns out we can do whatever we want. Seems like the biggest consensus is that you would throw in coins with your right hand but over your left shoulder, while your back is facing the fountain. Really though, this guideline is only something people follow for the Trevi fountain in Rome. If you throw coins into that fountain in that way, it is supposed to mean you will return to Rome."

"So, it doesn't translate to Genoa fountains? I plan to return so I don't need to do that whole process, you know. But eh, may as well for fun." I dig some Euro coins out of my pocket and go through the proper steps. I am a rule follower of course. While I throw them into the fountain, I also make sure to promise myself that I will return to Genoa. For sure. No ifs, ands, or buts.

Brian doesn't take the same precaution as me and thoughtlessly chucks a few coins in there, straight on, facing it squarely. I hope he at least made a wish. Probably not, though.

I turn to walk away and he grabs my hand to stop me. He looks directly into my eyes and tells me, "You look so pretty standing next to this fountain. I want to make sure I tell you that."

"I... Thank you." I lean over to kiss him and my knees weaken with both passion and relief. I realize that I don't need him to tell me this anymore. I missed it for so long and now that he made a point to say those words again, I love them, but am also okay without them. Don't get me wrong, a girl likes to hear compliments from her boyfriend, but now the joy isn't because of desperation.

It is difficult to pull ourselves away from the majestic Brac fountain, but we continue walking in the piazza area. There are bars all around here and they look enticing for a quick rest. But then I remember the no stools and only sitting at a table if paying for it rule in Italy. Being active (yes, I am saying standing is active so sue me) in this culture is fascinating to me, coming from a lazier American culture. But, my desire to sit a second ceases when I see something that piques my interest.

"Ooh, a knick-knack shop. Let's go in," I say on impulse, pulling Brian by his hand.

The store is packed top to bottom with mounds of souvenirs. The Italian flag and its colors are everywhere, on every type of item imaginable. I can buy an Italian themed spoon rest as easy as I can purchase a simple magnet. And even though the famous sculpture *David* is in Florence, not Genoa, his likeness is on numerous items here.

"Brian," I blurt out with a chuckle, "look at that apron!" I point as if in fifth grade and continue to giggle. Brian's eyes grow wide and he looks uncomfortable.

"Um, yeah. That is…something. I love to cook, but don't think I will be wearing that while I do."

The bottom half of an apron shows the statue's nether region in large scale form, which would be in the exact right place to match the apron wearer. Smart idea, but nah. I give the designer credit for creativity, that's for sure.

"I'm going to get it for Maggie. It's just dirty enough for her. I want to bring her something for watching Harrison."

"Yeah, that's perfect for her."

Meandering through the narrow aisles, trying not to knock anything off shelves, my eyes spot the card decks. I walk over right away and can't help but pick them up. Having these special Italian cards in my hands is soothing in some strange way. It feels like a tangible connection to my grandpa. Turning them over, I see there is a description about Italian cards in general, and specifically northern Italian cards of this region of Italy. Skimming the information briefly, because I will surely buy these and read it thoroughly multiple times later, I learn that they originated from a Latin influence and some Italian cards are different than these, depending on the region. Also, they are similar to other European countries' cards, like France and Germany. Interesting. I have to buy them asap and learn Scopa with these babies.

Walking out of the store with the goodies, I daydream about playing Scopa like a pro. Grandpa would have been proud that I want to learn the game. I won't disappoint him with the skills I'll have someday. Maybe I'll be able to join a pick-up game with the elders in Genoa when, not if, I return. Look at me, getting all social and adventurous.

Walking around a little more, I hit a low in physical energy level again, but strangely enough continue to feel, dare I say it, happy. I'm just tired.

"Brian, let's get dinner. I think the excitement of the day made time slip away from me, and my stomach."

"I can eat."

"Look over there on the corner." He points and starts walking toward a ristorante.

Seeming perfect for a rest, we get a table, guzzle down what seems like a gallon of sparkling water, and eat focaccia bread from the basket the waiter set down on the tiny square table.

After ordering both of our pesto filled entrees, I blurt out, "Brian, remember I was going to say something more about Grandpa today at Cella's house?"

"Nope, but I am sure you do have many more details for me so ready, set, go!"

"Yes," I say, smiling and proceeding. "Did you ever think about why Grandpa was so big on growing his own produce?"

"Not really, now that you say it. So, tell me the analyzed reason, Dr. Rachel." He takes another chunk of bread and gnaws on it while I speak, with exaggerated wide eyes.

"Thanks for being interested." I laugh. "The intent was not only for the unprocessed taste in meals, but also there was a familial lesson probably taught to him about being able to depend on yourself for your food. At least that's what I have concluded from what I've learned this past year. The ability to spend less money on these products was part of the goal for financially poor Italians. The pride in creating nutrition for their own family was ingrained in most Italians of that time."

"That is surprisingly pretty fascinating. I bet that was how a lot of immigrants felt and why they farmed, even if only in their own back yards. You are making me wonder about my own family. Maybe I even come from a long line of chefs."

"Maybe. You can investigate it someday. I know a person who can help you," I say while pointing at myself comically. "I thought you would be interested in this food history. And I've never thought of all these things in the past because what child thinks in these terms? I mean, now as an adult, I even wonder how my grandparents afforded to buy a house. No wonder they never liked to leave it."

"What do you mean?"

"Being poor immigrants in the first half of the 20th century was a feat. Not only did they not have money to go on a vacation, but a trip away from home wasn't even in their world of ideas. Why would someone leave their cherished and hard-earned residence? And who would watch their home if they left? They couldn't leave the house dark at night. The burglars would most definitely come."

"Oh, okay Rachel." An eye roll follows, of course.

"No, seriously, that was one of the conversations I heard Grandma and Grandpa have with my parents. When Mom and Dad would suggest how nice it would be for them to get away, they shut them down instantly."

"People used to stay in their own neighborhoods more often than nowadays. I know that from my own grandparents." He looks behind him to see if the waiter is bringing our food, I think. He must be starving, or is bored out of his mind. Wait, just starving. I can tell by his eye contact. Therapist skills, you know.

"Yup, their place of happiness and comfort was that home I knew so well during all of my childhood. And their pride in home ownership couldn't be shaken. They worked so hard for that piece of American land. They also loved their Italian neighbors and community, all with their prized grids of vegetable gardens outside, their large white yard statues of birds, happy children, or whatever else, and most importantly, their last name's initial displayed proudly somewhere on their homes. The big 'G' was on Grandma and Grandpa's mailbox. It was kind of embarrassing, but now I understand it."

"Well, I'm proud of our apartment, and we don't even own it. I can see why they were that way. Maybe we will be that way with a house in the future." He raises his eyebrows and seems to wait for a response.

My heart jumps but my mouth doesn't open. I look down and manage to say, "Yeah… Many of those traditions and ways of life have been left at their old home. When Grandpa had to move in with us, he was too distraught about Grandma dying to do any gardening, even though Dad gave him full reign of the backyard. I don't want to think about that time period." I shake my head like I can shake the thought out through my ears.

Brian lets both lines of discussion fade away. "Let's think of how wonderful today was and how much we accomplished." He knows how to help reset me.

"Grandpa would have been happy, I hope, that I had the opportunity to see his original garden. I mean, probably… I think."

"I'm sure he would. That hobby and way of life was too large for him not to have wanted you to see every bit of it."

Feeling reassured, I say, "True. And what a day." I put my hand on my forehead as my eyes grow big. "Oh, here come our meals."

Seconds later, Brian barely mutters "Mangia" before his mouth is full of pesto fettuccine.

Back at our hotel, I go with my urge to make something right and answer Brian's statement that was more like a question.

I sit on the edge of the bed, twist to see him on the other side of the room, and say, "I just want you to know that I also hope we have a house together someday." I look away and shake my leg touching the floor.

He walks around the bed to face me. "I know." He leans down to kiss me then backs away.

"I'm glad. I don't want to set my expectations on anything so it took me a while to respond. I'm sorry, Brian. And that I left you hanging."

"No apology needed. I'm not going anywhere."

I feel my entire body relax, not realizing how tense I was seconds ago. "Well, in that case, want to be my Scopa partner?"

"I'll be your partner for anything you want."

# Chapter 41

"The best way to travel to this address is by taxi," the front desk attendant tells us this morning, looking at the address for Great-Aunt Angeline. "It's too far to walk and too complicated for visitors to drive there. The cliffs along the coast make it dangerous for out of town guests."

"We don't have a car anyway, so we will take a cab," I say.

"Good. Make sure to be careful, my friends. When you walk anywhere up there, you need to be aware of the steep slopes and loose gravel," he warns.

"We will be. Thanks for the information, signore," I say as we walk toward the door. There is no time to waste today since we have a long lost relative to meet. We step outside of the hotel and walk out to the busy street to hail a cab.

I tighten my new salmon colored floral scarf with my hand that's adorned with a near-matching delicate bracelet, which Maggie gave me a few years ago. I have felt the urge to dress more vibrant since being in this foreign, yet familiar land so I'm glad I brought the bracelet along with me. By the time I leave here, I may look like Annabelle. I giggle at the thought.

Getting in the cab, I realize and blurt out to Brian in a scream-like whisper, "OH MY GOD!"

"What?"

"We need to get a gift to bring, of course. I can't believe I almost forgot."

"Shameful, Rachel. You are a horrible Italian."

"Thanks a lot. Now, we have to ask the driver to stop somewhere on the way." Looking at the cab driver, I ask, "Scusi, signore. Parla Inglese?"

"Yes, ma'am. How can I help you?" He knows English well. Score.

"Are there any pasticcerias along our way? We need to stop to buy something for my family we are visiting, um, meeting today." I don't even have to think about what gift we will bring because when I find something that works, I stick with it. Pastry worked well yesterday so pastry will work today. I won't fix what isn't broken.

"Yes, that is no problem at all. There is one place that I love to go to so I will take you there. Aurelio makes the best pastry that I have ever tasted."

A few minutes later, we arrive at the pasticceria. "We won't take long," I tell our cab driver.

"I will stop the meter. Do not worry. Take your time," he says.

How Italian of him.

"You are so kind. Thank you."

Brian and I still rush like the Americans that we are, scurrying into the pastry shop. I don't want him to wait for us too long, plus I don't want to delay going to meet my family any longer.

This shop is pretty small, but still has a nice variety of sweets. I scan the room for the options. "The amaretti cookies look like the best choice. What do you think, Brian?"

"Didn't we have something like that at our Easter dinner? I loved them."

"Yes, exactly. They're a traditional cookie of this season. I like the crispy almonds on these. I hope I don't eat the box of them in the car."

"I'll hold you back," Brian jokes.

I walk to the register and see Aurelio, I assume, straightening up a back shelf. He notices me and comes over. "Buongiorno."

"Buongiorno." And that's where my words stop. I awkwardly smile. Just like everyone else, he seems to know I need English.

"Ready?" he asks.

"Yes, I'll take these."

He looks over my shoulder and waves to our cab driver who waves back. "Oh, you have a good one there."

"He is very nice. We got lucky this morning," Brian chimes in.

After paying and saying, "Grazie and ciao," we are back in the cab and on our way. We are *on our way* to Great-Aunt Angeline's now. I can't believe it.

Driving along the shoreline, I see numerous shipping ports and imagine one of them as being where Grandpa set off for his new life in America. I'll have to ask Great-Aunt Angeline which one he left from so we can visit it. What an opportunity.

Fisherman are scattered all over the water in their various sized boats, while the elegant city buzzes on around them. I wonder what their days entail out on that glassy Ligurian Sea, catching the fresh fish we enjoy in the local meals. Mmm, those meals.

"No wonder there is such great seafood here. Look at all that action down there," Brian comments.

"I was just thinking about it too. Fishing is one of the city's oldest livelihoods, I've read. The city was built around sailing and shipping."

"Interesting. Is there anything you didn't read about this place?" He smiles.

"Nope. I covered every inch."

"I'm not surprised." He laughs.

We drive higher and higher up the cliff, next to the sparkling cobalt blue water. Our hotel's desk attendant wasn't lying. This road is steep. But one sharp turn off the street leads to an immediate stop. My heart jumps.

"Here we are," the cab driver says to us.

Brian takes out money to pay him and I ask, "Can you wait until someone answers the door and you see us go inside before leaving?" I can only imagine being stranded here on the rocky cliff, where we can slide into that water on the loose gravel. Eek.

"Yes, I will do that for you. Have a good day."

"Grazie," both Brian and I say.

We walk up to the burnt orange painted two story home, with aged gray stone on the bottom level. Another anxious knock needs to occur on another stranger's door. I don't give it a second thought this time.

*Knock, knock, knock.*

A middle-aged lady answers the door, and guess what…she has curly red hair! I pause before being able to speak. My body is trembling, my eyes widen, and my heart feels like it's dancing. I gasp for air.

# Chapter 42

**B**reathing again, I surprise myself and speak first. "Hi, I hope you understand English." I end my statement with a questioning tone, thinking how I didn't ask in Italian. Uh-oh.

"Yes, I do. How can I help you?" she responds with a head tilt and a grin.

Phew, she must not think I'm a rude American. "My name is Rachel Granza. I am wondering if this is the right address for my Great-Aunt Angeline."

The moments between my words and hers feel like hours.

Her face brightens and her voice raises. "Sì, signora. She is my mother. She is here right now." She looks over her shoulder into her house. "I am Teodora. Come in and we can talk more if you would like."

It's happening. She's here!

Brian motions for the cab driver to leave by waving to him.

I hand Teodora the pastry box. "Thank you for letting us talk with you and your mom. This is for both of you." I motion to Brian. "And this is my boyfriend, Brian Holden."

"Grazie. And welcome, both of you." She accepts the box and leads us inside.

In a semi-daze, I tell myself *do not faint*. Legs, don't fail me now.

We walk into the small dark foyer, with just enough room for a small metal coat rack and a plastic tray for dirty shoes, and follow her to the entry of a bright, window-filled family room. She continues on to an older lady sitting in a recliner chair. She must be my Great-Aunt Angeline.

With immersive sunlight shining on my grandpa's half-sister, hope rises inside me. Teodora seems to explain who we are to her mom while my soul jumps for joy. I must learn this language to know everything said though, darn it.

As we inch into the room where she sits, she simultaneously puts down her book and looks me right in my eyes. Her face lights up as if she already knows me. I, on the other hand, start to cry. Oh, not just a tear or two, but a full on weeping. Tears of triumph stream from my cheeks to the solid oak colored floor. I take a deep breath in relief as my release continues.

Great-Aunt Angeline eases herself up from her soft looking floral chair, plods over to me, and reaches up both hands to my face, giving me kiss on each wet cheek. There doesn't look like any sign of surprise or fear on her part, just happiness to have this moment. The sparkle in her green eyes and huge smile tells me so.

A "hello" escapes me and seems unnecessary. "I can't believe we are here. I can't believe you are my grandpa's half-sister," I blurt out through the sobs.

"Half? I call him my brother. Family is family," she says while grabbing my hand and leading me to the nearby couch, motioning to join her sitting down as she continues to her chair.

"He said the same thing about you," I respond, still blubbering and finally wiping my eyes.

Brian sits next to me, smiling, and moves his hand back and forth on my arm. I feel both chills and a sense of soothing from his motion.

I don't know where to start. Here we are, with Grandpa's sister!

"Let me get you both a drink. Would you like some water?" Teodora asks.

"Yes, please," we both say, look at each other, and laugh.

Great-Aunt Angeline and I are silent while we stare at each other and smile. For me it's from being in awe. I hope she feels the same.

Being in sort of a trance state, I quickly try to ground myself by using my senses. I can feel my feet on the floor. I see the white room around me with its soft loveseat couch I am sitting on and the two recliner chairs. I smell a light scent of garlic in the air. The gorgeous blue sea shines through the large picture window at the back of the room. Voices echo in the background.

Rachel, be present now.

Teodora hands both of us glasses of water. I take a long sip to quench my dry throat. My racing heart and dry throat aren't going to help me get my answers.

Teodora inconspicuously sets down a box of tissues on the side table. Smart move.

I don't want to set my glass down on the end table, for fear of a water ring, so I put it on the ground.

Great-Aunt Angeline hollers, "Il tavolo va bene."

I look blankly at her. I understand the meaning only as she points to the table.

"I didn't want to leave a water ring," I tell her, apologetically, and grab the glass.

"Culaccino è bene."

Now I have another blank look, obviously. "Sorry?"

Teodora jumps into the conversation, or lack thereof at this point. "Mom, remember, English."

Great-Aunt Angeline smiles and nods.

"She basically said don't worry about a water ring, or 'culaccino.' See, you learned a new Italian word today. It means, how do you say—ah—a behind of the glass." She points to her rear and lets out a huge belly laugh, as if she said a swear word.

"Oh, thank you," I say with a grin and raised eyebrows. "I don't

274

want to offend anyone."

"No, never, bella." Teodora gets a big kick out of the miscommunication, I think. She continues to chuckle and Great-Aunt Angeline joins in.

I can tell that Great-Aunt Angeline is a spry older lady and Teodora is a ball of energy. I want to know so much more about them both right now. And Great-Aunt Angeline's swiftness in expressing her thoughts gives me hope I can be that alert in my nineties.

As the day goes on, we are able to expand our subject of conversation from glass butt bottoms and not have too many language barriers. We jump topics with ease, from where we live to aspects of our respective countries. I could spend all day drilling them about Italy, but I hold myself back.

I learn that Teodora is on the same generational line as my dad, which takes me a while to grasp. She feels like a first cousin to me instead of a second cousin, especially with her similar hair. Hours pass like minutes and there's a bond that feels effortless and familiar. I feel like a true part of this family. My family.

Sitting at lunch, I can't believe my eyes. This feast is the largest I've seen in my life. And it's just little old lunch!

"Thank you for inviting us to eat with you," I say wonderstruck by the spread. "It's an honor."

"The honor is ours," Great-Aunt Angeline replies.

"Yes, Mom is right. We can't let you leave without feeding you," Teodora adds.

"Thank you so much, both of you," Brian says.

I dive into the fried anchovies and mushroom stuffed eggplant bursting with parmesan and ricotta cheeses, while admiring the room where we are sitting. The gorgeous kitchen looks like it's straight out of a movie. It can't be more perfect. The old wooden table and the matching, yet distressed, chairs are close to yet another huge window overlooking the sea beyond the cliff. The kitchen walls are painted a light yellow color, which contrast nicely with the dark wood furniture and even the 1970s looking stove and fridge. Is it even possible to still have these appliances in working order? I also love the white lace tablecloth they use, again floral in design like the family room furniture, and gently conveying how many delicious meals have been enjoyed on it—based on the staining and discoloration.

I take my last a bite of the freshly baked bread and wash it down with red table wine. Not only did Teodora not know they would have company today and she still has enough food for two extra people, but she has enough for another family of four in addition to us. Mangia, for sure.

I feel a surge of courage with my newly full belly and ask both my new family members my first question. "Great-Aunt Angeline, do you know why your mom, my great-grandma, and your sister, Antonia, never followed the men of our family to the United States?"

"My mom always told me that she feared crossing the ocean too much, especially after what happened."

"What do you mean?" I sit up straighter in my chair.

"You do know your grandpa's father, your great-grandfather, died on the voyage to the United States, right?" She stares at me with a flat expression on her face, as I am giving her.

I shake my head slowly side to side.

"Well, their ship sank and Gino never made it," she looks down with drooping eyelids, "but at least the boys survived."

"What happened?! That's awful!" This can't be true. But I know she's not lying. What?

Brian stops eating and sets down his fork. He looks at me and grabs my hand for support. I squeeze it in fear of what will come next.

"They were on the *Titanic*."

# Chapter 43

S ilence.

Processing.

No…words…

"The *Titanic*?" Brian is able to speak.

"The *Titanic*?" I whisper.

Great-Aunt Angeline continues, "As I'm sure most people know, the ship sank and not everyone survived. Men were told to wait to board lifeboats, and they did not have enough boats. Also, the crew didn't use all the seats that were available on each boat, so the passengers had a low chance to survive. My mom always said she was shocked her babies made it, and thanked God for that blessing every day. She never recovered from her husband's death, even after marrying my dad."

I can't mutter any words again.

Brian asks, "How would a group of Italians be able to board a ship that left from England? How did they even get tickets for that ship?"

Still frozen from the new knowledge and barely hearing anything she said after the name of the ship, I sit patiently waiting for the answers and hoping my brain clears its fog.

"I thought you would have known the story. Oh, I am so sorry for being the one to break the devastating news to you that they were on that cursed ship."

I finally can speak again. "I didn't even know Great-Grandpa

Gino died before coming to the United States. My parents always talked about all three of them being in America. They must not have ever known he didn't make it there. What happened once Grandpa and Great-Uncle Vince got to New York then, without a parent? Wait, first tell us about the *Titanic*." I am rambling, as one would expect with this news. I can't even tie in how magnificently ironic it is that I have an immense interest in the *Titanic* and now *my* family were passengers on it. That is too much.

"Let me start at the beginning then. I will try not to leave anything out. From what my mom told my sister and I, her husband and my two brothers were sent to the United States to pave a path for her and Antonia to go and live there as well, after the business was established. Gino owned a tailor business here in Genoa, but over the years, more and more people left this area for better opportunities in the new land. It was a hard decision to make, but my mom and Gino decided they could live an easier life, financially, in America."

I am hanging on every. Single. Word. Brian looks as though he is also, though I barely realize more people are present than Great-Aunt Angeline and me. Teodora, on the other hand, goes to the kitchen to get more water for the table. I am sure she has always known this story and is not as interested.

Great-Aunt Angeline continues, "As it turned out, there was an extremely wealthy family named the Bastows who used Gino's tailoring services and they developed a close relationship after many years. This family traveled back and forth from their home, to here, to the United States, like it was going to the next town," she says while motioning side to side with her hands. "They had tickets for the *Titanic* and couldn't use them because of something that came up in their own business. The man gave Gino his three tickets, *in first class*, to travel to America on the world's most talked about ship at the time. Who could have passed that offer up? He even paid for their trip to one of its ports; a train ride to Cherbourg, France."

"France! Of course. That makes sense. I have some knowledge about the *Titanic* actually, so I should have known that port was the closest port of call. Excuse me, since my mind was stuck in first gear." My brain is at full speed ahead again.

How could my family have had such luck—bad? good?—as to get free tickets to go on the *Titanic*?!

Great-Aunt Angeline, even more robust than earlier, continues on, thriving on my thirst for knowledge, I think. And her memory is comparable to that of a much younger person, it seems. Every fact is making sense, based on my historical knowledge of the *Titanic*.

"I have letters from my brothers, which told Mom the whole story. The poor boys not only survived an unimaginable tragedy at sea, but then had only each other when they arrived in New York, and your grandfather was only ten years old, mio Dio," looking up to the sky as if praying to God. "Vincenzo was about twelve, I think. They were children, and women and children were saved first, as you seem to know."

"Wait," I interject. "My dad told me Grandpa came to the US in 1916 and that he was fourteen years old. That isn't true." I am not asking, but more conceptualizing out loud what the true facts are now.

"Brian, this is the reason I couldn't find the ship Grandpa came to New York on! Because I was looking in the wrong year, he was the wrong age, and the ship never even made it to New York!"

"That would do it." His eyes remain large.

I rarely see him in shock, but these facts have overtaken even him, I think.

"And my horrible math skills didn't help. How did I miss the age gap in the censuses? I must have been so focused on the other details and didn't realize the ages didn't match up to Dad's story. No wonder he only had a fourth-grade education. Ugh, I'll have to re-analyze everything again, but I guess it doesn't even matter now that I know what actually happened. Good thing I can calculate a countdown without any issues." I can laugh at myself now, at least.

Brian chuckles as well, but Great-Aunt Angeline keeps a straight face.

I clear my throat and get back to business. "So, they came to America on the *Carpathia*?" I ask her.

She responds with a slight head nod and raised eyebrows.

Brain chimes in, "Rach, Chelsea Pier is where you said the *Carpathia* arrived. All this time, we have been living a few blocks from where your family entered the US."

"You're right. Holy cow. I knew the *Carpathia* arrived at that pier, but wasn't as enthralled because it wasn't like the *Titanic* arrived there, right by our home. I always thought it was kind of neat, but not as fascinating as if the ship I was really enamored with arrived there."

"But you even told me once that one brown metal archway down there is the old pier landing for the shipping company lines for the *Titanic* and the *Carpathia*. You can sort of see the faded letters on it that make out both, what was it, White Star Line and Cunard Line, overlapped. See, I remember the stuff you tell me," he says and squeezes my hand he is still holding for support, sweat and all.

"It is pretty strange that blocks from where I ended up living is exactly where my grandpa and great-uncle arrived in the United States. They didn't come through Ellis Island, as I assumed. This family's history gets more wild by the day." My eyes grow bigger by the moment. "I definitely will have to go to Chelsea Piers when we get home. I need some time there alone."

Mind blowing fact after mind blowing fact keeps happening. The truth is refreshing, yet still a feeling of sorrow remains as an underlying current within me. All of those movies, documentaries, and books I have watched and read about the *Titanic* over the years, all of the times I have wondered about life on the boat with the class divide, the timeline of events, and how the families could cope with such a loss...and now I am one of the families affected. Yes, almost one hundred and one years later, but still affected.

I don't think I ever even told Grandpa about my love of the subject. It wasn't like I tried to hide it, but it was not something I was focused on when I was with him. Would he have told me about his experience if I told him though? I doubt it because he never talked about any aspect of his immigration from Italy.

"What happened when they got to the United States, Great-Aunt Angeline? And do you know why they shortened our last name to Granza?" I need to keep her information coming. I could have the rest of my life to process it, but need to know anything else she knows right now!

"Well, first, I do not know why your last name changed. I was too young to realize that and never knew your grandpa and Vincenzo any other way. Sorry about that. Your other question, though, I can answer. There was a family from here who were going to help out our family when they first arrived. Their name was Serafino."

"Oh! The Serafinos!" I call out.

Great-Aunt Angeline furrows her brow so I clarify. "When I had been trying to find out family information, I saw Grandpa and Great-Uncle Vince's names on a census under a family household named Serafino, and I was so confused. Also, I had no idea why Great-Grandpa Gino wasn't listed with them."

"Yes, my dear, this is why. The boys had to stay with the Serafinos for some years, at least until Vincenzo was an adult and could take care of your grandpa. They were only planning to stay a little while with them and make their way to New York City, to start a tailor business there. Of course, that never happened. But the boys did learn more about business from the Serafinos, and that is how they were able to open their business in the United States, once they were the right age."

"What a giving family; to take in two boys they intended as temporary guests." I have immense gratitude.

"Maybe deep down you wanted to help kids because your family needed help as kids," Brian concludes.

I smile and reply with a light-heartedly sarcastic, "Thanks, Dr. Holden," following in a serious tone, "But, yeah, maybe."

Hmm, I remember something I read about in graduate school. "You know, there is this phenomenon called genetic memory." I am shocked I can function at this fine-tuned sort of cognitive level at this time, but it's a day full of miracles. "The whole concept is something about how us humans have the ability to know things we never learned, only due to it being in our DNA. So, the desire to help children may be part of my genetic memory, in some way."

Brian agrees, "Yeah, that's what I meant." He flashes a smile.

Teodora chimes in, "It is like how our family are all hard workers and ethical people. That is something that is just inside you, and we don't all necessarily learn that from being taught by others."

"Exactly. It's imprinted on us and in our DNA," I beam with pride. "And, maybe I'll never know why our name was shortened. Or maybe I'll keep looking for the reason, you know, in the future once I can catch my breath." I widen my eyes and look at Brian.

"Yes." He mirrors my expression and smiles.

"I am going to get some things to show you. Want to move to the other room again?" Great-Aunt Angeline politely asks. She must have thought this conversation is too off topic, or that the younger people are talking hooey.

"Sure, let's do that." I would move to the moon with her to keep listening to stories about my family.

"Teodora, do you need help cleaning up?" I ask.

"No, bella, but thank you." She smiles. "You are a guest, even though you are family."

That statement touches my heart and speaks to a longing I've had so long at this point, even before I knew I needed it.

Great-Aunt Angeline brings a box to the family room and sets it down on the coffee table.

"I have letters from your great-grandpa, grandpa, and uncle in here. Also, photographs and your Great-Grandmother Francesca's journal," Great-Aunt Angeline tells me.

"Oh, wow." My eyes are stuck wide open.

She takes out photos first. "Look at me as a young girl." She points to a black and white photo.

I examine it and see a familiar face. Before the wrinkles and gray hair of time, I see…my face. "You and I could be twins!"

She laughs. "Yes, I knew the second I saw you that we are family. I had those same freckles on my nose." She reaches to her nose and rubs it. "They have faded now, but you can see them if you really look."

I lean into her and look at her face. "Yes, I can." I touch mine as well and smile. Suddenly, they aren't so bad.

"I had hair just like you too. Look." She points to another photo. "I wish these were in color, but I know you believe me."

"Yes, I do." Now I rub my hand on her arm for a moment. It's soft and warm.

Regardless that by the time color photos in the box show Great-Aunt Angeline's hair had turned gray, her hair was, yes, red and curly in her younger years. She retains her beautiful big green eyes today, which are glowing in the color pictures. Even at this moment, her eyes twinkle and stand out from the bordering crow's feet in the room's natural light. Her daughter, Teodora, sure has "our" hair and eyes as well. I am definitely not alone anymore with my features, pale skin and all. And now I know the features must be inherited from my maternal great-grandmother's side of the family, carried down with Grandpa straight to me. I never thought I would find out anything, let alone unbelievable facts and see so much proof that I belong.

I'm also looking at pictures of Great-Grandpa Gino, Great-Grandma Francesca, and Great-Aunt Antonia for the first time. Grandpa's family. My family. I burn them into my memory. I couldn't forget them if I tried. Maybe she will let me take pictures of the old photographs with my camera, though.

Seeing any photos is beyond all expectations I set for myself on this ancestry journey. To be able to put faces to the names of people, even family members' names I just learned on this trip, is the gift of a lifetime. Plus, look at all of the cousins I have! I want to meet every one of them immediately. I hope that can happen someday.

Best of all, looking at all of these nuggets of gold show me that I'm not an oddity in the world anymore. I blend in, so to speak, with my own family, but don't have to blend because I *fit* in. The lack of desperation to fit in is a welcomed change I want to hold close to my heart. I feel free from my own ridiculous notions and enjoy a surging sense of peace from being part of the strong women in my family. Maybe I can just be me and be okay with it. Why do I have to be like everyone else in the world anyway? I'm me, and that's wonderful.

Great-Aunt Angeline pulls out a stack of disintegrating envelopes tied together by a red ribbon. "These are letters from Gino, your grandpa, and Vincenzo."

Even the mere thought of them trigger my eyes to fill with tears. I look for that nearby box of tissues and grab one to dab the known forthcoming waterfall.

Seeing my family members' words in their own writing on the outside of the unbundled letters now bring on those waterworks full force. Brian places his hand on my shoulder and squeezes. I put my hand on his and pat it.

Grandpa's letters, out of any of them, have a profound effect on me, of course. His signature that was on every birthday card I ever received in my life from Grandma and him is right here in front of me, only in a more youthful version. I reach out and touch one, but don't pick it up.

"It will not bite you." Great-Aunt Angeline smiles and picks it up for me, then hands it over.

I hold it a second before opening the ripped open flap. Pulling out the aged, folded paper, I see the letterhead reads, "On board RMS 'TITANIC.'" My breathing rate increases and my hands shake.

Teodora comes back into the room and sits on the opposing seat. "Would you like for me to translate the letters for you?"

I look at the writing in my hands and realize it's not in English. I was too focused on other details. "Yes, please." I hand it to her slowly.

One by one, Teodora starts translating the letters in the box for me, reading them aloud.

April 10, 1912

Dearest Mother,

Dad, Vincenzo, and I have made it safely on board the RMS Titanic. Although this is our first night, I know it is going to be a wonderful voyage. I still cannot count my blessings enough to think that we are in first class on this fabulous ship. I miss you and will write again soon. Say hello to Antonia for me.

Love,
Salvatore


April 11, 1912

Dearest Mother,

We have been enjoying our time in first class on the Titanic. Dad, Salvatore, and I cannot believe all

of the luxuries that first class people have on board.
Do you know they have a special string quartet that
plays while we eat or walk along the deck? Rich
people have music for everything! We are acting as
though we are one of them. Hopefully, nobody knows
we are not. Tell Antonia hello from us. We love you
and miss you.

Love,
Vincenzo


April 12, 1912

My dearest Francesca,

Our sons and I have been doing well
aboard this luxurious ship. I have never seen
anything like it in my life. I wish you were
with us. Maybe the Bastows will give us
another round of tickets soon. They have not
been spending as much time in Genoa as they
have been in their hometown in England.
Then, you and Antonia can come to the
United States as well. I love you and miss
you dearly.

Love,
Your husband Gino

April 13, 1912

Dearest Mother,

We have been having a grand time on this ship called Titanic. We were able to try out the gymnasium equipment and also the Turkish bath. I feel like the luckiest boy alive. We will soon be in New York City. Only a few more days. I don't know what I am more excited about, the ship or going to America. Soon we will be saying hello to Miss Statue of Liberty. I can see her in the distance now.

Love,
Vincenzo

April 14, 1912

My dearest Francesca,

The boys and I are still doing well. We attended the church service this morning,

which gave us a feeling of being at home
in our own church. People do not seem to
know we are not usually first class travelers.
They treat us like all the rest. I am glad to
be blending in with them. The suits I made
have us fitting in just fine.

Tonight, after the boys are asleep, I may try
watching the card players in the smoking
room. Do not worry, I will not be
smoking. Nor gambling. We need all the
money we have to make it in America and I
intend to save every cent. We all send our
love and will write to you soon.

Love,
Your husband Gino


April 16, 1912

Dearest Mother,

I do not know if you heard what happened, but
the Titanic sank yesterday morning. I cannot
believe I am writing this to you. I also cannot
believe I need to tell you that we think Father died

in the sinking. Salvatore and I have not seen him aboard the rescue ship, the R.M.S Carpathia, so we believe he may have perished in the Atlantic Ocean. Salvatore and I were lucky enough to get on lifeboats because we are still boys and look younger than our ages, I am sure. They only allowed women and children on them. We tried, Mother, we tried so much to get Father aboard the lifeboat with us. We miss him terribly and are still holding out hope for him to appear upon arrival in New York in a few days. I think ships went to look for people who did not get on the lifeboats. Do not worry, Mother, Salvatore is safe with me. We will be fine when we get to America. I will write to you soon.

Love,
Vincenzo


April 18, 1912
Dearest Mother,

We arrived in America today. We do not have Father with us, as Vincenzo told me he wrote to you a few days ago. Father still has not appeared anywhere that we know and we fear

he is not going to be in New York. Mother,
we really tried to have him come with us in
the lifeboat, but the men would not let it
happen. We miss both of you terribly. But do
not worry, we will be meeting the Serafinos
soon. We will be fine in America. We will
send money as soon as possible. I love you
and Antonia and I will write soon.

Love,
Salvatore


April 30, 1912

Dearest Mother,

Vincenzo and me are settled in with the
Serafinos. They have shown us nothing
but kindness in their home. Even though
we could not take our sacks of personal
items with us the night of the sinking, the
Serafinos have provided us with everything
we need. Vincenzo and I are trying to help
out with household chores and anything
else they need, to show our appreciation for
them letting us live with them. They are also
teaching us about the tailoring business in
America. We are slowly learning English and
I want to tell you a new phrase I learned;
"Hello Mother, I love you." I am doing well.

*Vincenzo is also doing well. Give Antonia a hug for me. I will write to you soon.*

*Love,*
*Salvatore*

When Teodora stops reading at the last signature from my grandpa, I sit in silence a little longer.

"I know these must be hard to hear for the first time." Great-Aunt Angeline speaks in a quiet tone.

All I can do is nod in agreement.

The recounting of the details of the shipwreck would be difficult for any empathetic soul to hear, let alone when they include loved ones. Oh, the horror the boys went through that April night in 1912—from not knowing what was happening, to having to leave their dad and hoping he would be on another lifeboat safe and sound, to realizing they would never see their dad again. Madone and Mother Mary, the terror that must have set in to have been entering a new country parentless, where they needed to learn the foreign language. Did they even know the Serafinos before meeting them in the US? No wonder Grandpa never wanted to talk about leaving Italy. No wonder he never would consider going for a visit. No wonder Great-Grandma never wanted to come to the United States. She was probably terrified to leave land.

The letters are heartbreaking, yet show such strength and resiliency. Those kids had to carry on without their dad. It never ceased to amaze me when I learned Grandpa came to America and didn't know English, but now that I have the whole story I am in awe times a million. I finally know his story.

And how Great-Grandpa Gino talked about blending in with the clothes…that blows my mind too. Is that another family trait passed down; the desire to be unseen? Maybe it is more of the genetic memory concept. I'll have to research that idea more.

As if the letters aren't hard enough to process, Great-Grandma's journal lies ahead; the last item in the box. The grief she must have went through is astounding, especially still caring for her present child, Antonia. The fear she must have had, the loss she experienced, the heartache that I bet never healed. I cannot imagine.

She never saw her boys again, though I know they wrote to each other. But she never could see or speak to her sweet husband, Gino, anymore. Yet, she went on. She survived and thrived. She was able to remarry, and even had another child, Great-Aunt Angeline, who of course personifies what her name means; an angel. But I am sure the pain of losing her Gino in such a traumatic way never left her soul.

I feel guilty for "reading" another person's journal, but am glad to have the opportunity to get to know my great-grandma a little more. I think she would have wanted her family to know our story, I hope. I cross my fingers in my mind's eye.

"Would you like me to read my grandmother's journal now? Are you ready for more?" Teodora dips her head and raises her eyebrows.

"Yes, please continue. I want to know all I can." I grab Brian's hand again.

*May 13, 1912*

*Why did you do this to me, God? I am a good woman. I am a church going woman. I pray every day. Have I done anything to make you think I am not a good mom? A good wife? Why did you have my beautiful and sweet Gino die when he was just trying to make our lives better? He was trying to give us a new life and now we have this life. We have three kids to take care of still. Why did you do this to us? To me? Give him back to me!*

My eyes tear up again and I get the tissue ready.

Her tone was begging and tortured. The words conveyed the deep pain and suffering she must have been going through. I can tell the rawness she allowed in herself to write, probably because she had to be strong for her daughter and, through letters, for her boys.

Teodora continues reading.

*May 16, 1912*

*I do not understand why you did this, God. This tragedy that happened on the sea not only happened to them but to me. What did I do to deserve this? Why did you take my Gino? My boys need a father and now they do not have one. They are with nice people, but Mr. Serafino is not their father. Please help me to get through this horrible time.*

As Teodora flips the page, I notice it has a smudge on it. I bet it was a tear drop that caused the ink to run. I imagine my great-grandma writing, crying, and trying to negotiate with God to bring back her Gino. Being a therapist and knowing the stages for grief, she seems like she was in the first few stages in these letters; denial, bargaining, and a touch of anger with God in particular. While going through the grief stages is the norm for grievers, seeing and hearing the suffering through my great-grandma's letters, my own relative, is excruciating.

I take a deep breath and continue to listen to Teodora reading.

July 2, 1912

I have not been able to write in some time. I have not had the strength to do anything but to take care of Antonia. I do not understand why you took my Gino away. Please help me to get through this because I cannot do this on my own. What will happen to my boys? To all of us?

October 15, 1912

Today is 6 months from my loving Gino's death at sea. He was a good man. He was trying to do better for his family by going to America. I never want to go to that land. Why would anyone want to journey across the Atlantic for that place? It is not worth it to me. I will be staying with my daughter in Genoa, where we are loved and safe. I cannot travel there, even *though my boys are there. They are strong and will be okay. They know this from me. I taught them to be strong boys. And so did Gino.*

The journal entries are fewer in frequency as the months carried on. I am sure my great-grandma didn't have much time to write when trying to manage on her own. How did she live? What did she do to earn money? I'll have to ask Great-Aunt Angeline another time.

*April 15, 1913*

*It is one year now. One year since my love, Gino, died in the Atlantic. That ship was supposed to be unsinkable. Why did God make this happen? This happened to people who were good, loving men. People who had families to take care of and who depended on them. People who were going to America to have a lifetime of providing to others. My Gino is gone. Gone a whole year. I miss him so much. I cry tears of sorrow every night still, after being so strong for my kids. They will ever know the pain I carry in my heart. I will love you forever, Gino.*

"That's the last one," Teodora says.

But, closing the journal, one tiny folded up paper falls out.

295

"What's that?" I ask.

"I don't know. Have you seen this?" Teodora asks her mom who shakes her head.

"May I?" I reach my hand out so I could see it before knowing what it says.

"Yes, of course." Teodora leans over and gives it to me.

I open it gently and began to see a part of my grandpa's signature once again. How could a letter of his be in his mom's journal?

I run my fingers over his writing, wishing I could hug him and tell him how sorry I am for all that he went through as a boy. I know he's with me right now, though. I look up for a second. *I know now, Grandpa.*

I pause and breathe in a cleansing breath.

"Here, Teodora. Can you please read what this letter says?" I hand it back to her.

"Yes," she continues.

*April 15, 1913*

*Dearest Mother,*

*I wanted to write to you on this day because, as you know, this is the day Father died one year ago. Vincenzo, the Serafinos, and I have gone to our church and said prayers for him. We also lit a candle for him. You would love our church, St. Mary Magdalene de Pazzi, near our home. They have welcomed us with open arms and we have found many friends there, many from Genoa and the surrounding towns.*

*Do not worry about Vincenzo and me. We*

have been put in charge of many aspects of the Serafinos' tailoring business and are learning new things every day. Someday we will have our own business. Father would be very proud of his sons. We want to continue to make you proud as well. I love you, Mother, and miss you every day. Give a hug and a kiss to Antonia. I will write again soon.

Love your son,
Salvatore

I take another deep breath, the only sound in the room. Grandpa was solid and steady. I always knew it, but now know it infinity more.

Teodora breaks the silence for the second time. "You do know that our family inherited the Serafinos' tailoring business, right?"

Shock hits me again. How is that even possible anymore tonight? Since I had not thought about how my family never ended up leaving Philly and how there probably weren't that many tailors who could stay in business back in those days, it makes sense. The Serafinos had to be the nicest family friends on the face of the earth since the dawn of time. They took in kids who were not theirs, provided them with skills, and gave their hard-earned business to them.

After a few moments, I look up and simply say, "No." I am sure my face looks like I am in outer space with my thoughts.

She goes on, "They only had daughters and in those days a family's business would not have been given to or run by females."

Great-Aunt Angeline chimes in, "The boys, they were like the sons they never had is what we heard. They considered them one of their own children. La Famiglia." As she says the last phrase, she put her hands in the air like she's hugging it, eyes all aglow.

"So this is why Grandpa and Great-Uncle Vince never lived in New York. And before tonight, I didn't even know they wanted to live there. Maybe that is where I got my large desire. I always wanted to, even as a young girl. Isn't that so strange? It's like it was in my DNA to live in the city," saying it, laughing at yet a third possible family tie for genetic memory. Both Teodora and Great-Aunt Angeline nod in possible agreement of the idea.

I continue, "I'm glad that Grandpa knew I did live in the city. I know he wanted that dream of mine to be fulfilled. He died when I was a freshman in college, so at least he knew I made it there."

"I can see that you were close with Salvatore. I want you to know that I believe he knows you live there and made your life there. Believe me, he knows." Great-Aunt Angeline looks up again as if speaking to him, soul to soul.

My heart flutters. Seeing that my family has the same beliefs as me reinforces he is here right now. All of the signs that happened to lead me to this moment are my proof. And, without his help, I don't think any of this would have happened.

I glance at my watch and my mouth opens. "Oh, it's late. We've stayed so long. I'm sorry."

"We want you here." Great-Aunt Angeline laughs.

"I don't ever want to leave, but," I look at Brian and he nods in agreement, knowing my thoughts I feel, "we will see you soon. We are here in Italy for a few more days."

Even though Great-Aunt Angeline is a spunky older lady, I am sure she needs to get to bed soon.

"Promise?" Teodora asks.

"Oh yes, I promise, believe me." I chuckle.

Our hugs and goodbyes last a solid thirty minutes, as is usual for Italians even in the States. We'll be back as soon as possible. She won't be able to get rid of us if she tries.

Back at the hotel, when Brian and I are brushing our teeth to get ready for bed, I finish and say, "I seriously cannot believe all that has happened. I mean, in general for me, for us, and in Grandpa's life. The feeling of being frozen since Grandpa's death never went away no matter what great things happened to me...until the ice chipped away over the last few months. After tonight, that frigid ice is finally melting."

He rinses his mouth with water and responds, "Yeah, it's really something." His eyes widen, then he rubs them. The enormity of the information we learned today must be sinking in for him too. "I'm so glad to hear you say this. I see the difference in you. My Rachel is back."

I smile. "It's been a lot of work, but yes, I think I am."

"I know you will be okay," he says.

We hug for what feels like five minutes.

Still in each other's embrace, I say, "I know that Grandpa lived a full, long, and loving life. He was a tough man and I'm going to choose to focus on that quality instead of the trauma he had. He would want me to do that. If he could get through the devastation of the *Titanic*, I can get through anything."

"That's Salvatore's girl!"

"Hey, don't forget I'm also your girl." I kiss him on the cheek and walk to the bed. I slip between the warm, soft sheets and pull up the bedspread.

He calls out from the bathroom, "You don't know how much that is like music to my ears."

Upon closing my eyes to go to sleep, I try to let my mind rest, but it wants to continue to grasp everything I learned. What a challenge. I can't stop thinking. I know people remember where they were and what they were doing when a tragedy occurs, but the opposite is also true. We remember where we were and what we were doing when something outstanding and life-changing occurs as well. Today is that time for me. I finally know my family history. I know my story, my roots. There are no secrets anymore. I am free.

Despite the flooding thoughts, I continue to feel the new sense of stillness. The feeling is stronger than the thought jumping, even though some thoughts are wonderful and I want to catch and hold them forever. I am not floating around anymore, in my head or otherwise. I feel like I belong—to family, to a greater good, to a worldly connected story.

My poor Grandpa and Great-Uncle Vince were saved from the sinking of the *Titanic* and so was I, just today. That sounds dramatic, but it's true. Yes, I was never alone like them. I have Brian, my parents, my brother (ugh, I guess), a few friends, and Harrison of course. But, I never felt what I feel in this moment tonight. Laying on the soft bed, I feel like the ground, the land has my back. I am supported by generations that came from this sacred country. I don't need to merely survive in my bubble anymore. I need to stand out, because my family members were two of a few lucky souls who survived that wreck. This trip saved me like the lifeboat saved them.

# Chapter 44

I slept well last night, exhausted from the heightened emotions yesterday. But this morning, I am still tired sitting at the breakfast table. Not in my usual, err past, depressed manner, but in a mental fatigue from trying to sort through the facts I now inherited as my and my family's history. I know I will phase out of this state once feelings are processed, though. Maybe being on a high for days is catching up with me too. All this energy and motivation is a large change for me.

It is hard to explain this emotional spot. I know the facts are real but it's *surreal* that the circumstances ended up being this way. If my family came to the US on any other ship but the *Titanic*, and the same tragedy happened where somehow Great-Grandpa Gino died on the voyage to the States, it would have been awful and tough to believe, but come on. They were on the *Titanic*. That's so coincidental given my obsession, it makes me think that DNA theory is accurate once more.

I must admit, I have mixed feelings about my family being part of the world-wide fascination. While I understand the intrigue, I don't like that *my* story is one of everyone's knowledge. I am way too private to have my story out there. But is my story even out there at all? Hmm.

I have never come across last names even relatively similar to ours when reading the ship manifests and all other *Titanic* passenger information. I wonder if my family were never accounted for in the records. The adult in charge was deceased and the boys were whisked away by the Serafinos, who I hope met them at the pier when the *Carpathia* arrived. The kids better not have had to get to Philly on their own. I wince at the thought.

Anyway, the boys were traveling under the Bastows' set of tickets, so if the authorities didn't know that, they could have easily fallen through the cracks. Were they under the Bastows' name, leaving the Allegranza name to be erased from history's records? In the movie *Titanic*, the character Rose gave a false surname, so technically the boys could have done that or even could have been sleeping when the *Carpathia* crew gathered names. Who knows? There are so many possibilities and, as I have learned in this year-long journey, there could have been a lot of documentation mistakes made at many points along the way.

Okay, now my mind is waking up (good), but racing and going into overdrive (bad). I know I'll look into the manifest discrepancy sometime in my endless *Titanic* resources. If my family weren't on the list of victims or survivors, then I will write to someone to make sure they are recognized. Yes, I will make sure my family is acknowledged in history. But then I would be back to a lack of privacy. Ugh. Saving this for another day; note to self.

After this much needed slow breakfast of steamy cappuccino and crusty bread with fig jam, I feel more physical strength return. Pondering, oh, everything while sipping the foamy masterpiece helps the mounds of information sink into my overworking brain. The pile is more organized up there now and I'm ready to enjoy today. The present.

A quick walk on the now well-traveled route leads Brian and I to stand before the Cathedral of St. George again. Its beauty never fades for me. Great-Aunt Angeline told us that this cemetery is where Great-Grandma Francesca and Great-Aunt Antonia's tombs reside, plus a memorial to Great-Grandpa Gino. I figure that since I am out of my box in so many ways lately, why not also visit a gravesite of a loved one. Add it to that imaginary Rachel list.

I see the helpful man from the other day, the one who spent so much time with us in that dusty basement. We each wave and smile from a distance, even before Brian and I enter through the iron gates. He continues on his path away from the cemetery, while we continue on ours, veering left. Our roads may never meet again, but he was an unexpected essential aspect of the road to my knowledge and healing. He was a part of the links of facts that I've gained while here in Genoa. The links have transformed into a beautiful chain that I can wear around my heart, like an Allegranza coat of arms. I'd be honored to wear it if it actually existed.

As we make our way through the olive tree encased graveyard, on the narrow gray stone pavers, it doesn't take long to spot Antonia Allegranza's name. The cemetery is relatively small, especially for its age and housing many decades of residents. Maybe there is another section somewhere, but this one obviously includes my family. I'm thankful for that fact.

We stand in silence and stare at each of the tombstones. Antonia, and—"Hey, look at this. Great-Grandma Francesca's other married name is listed on her stone, instead of Allegranza."

"Yeah, it is. Oh, I'm sorry it isn't your original name."

"I'm jolted…but understand." Seeing Ricci near her first name brings a tinge of sadness, but whoever made the decision was logical. I am sure she would have wanted Allegranza on her stone in her young life, but hopefully was happily remarried and would be glad to have her dying surname engraved for eternity.

"There's Gino's memorial." Brian says.

I sigh. My poor great-grandpa. I'm glad he's honored here, with his loved ones.

Even though I was never a person to sit at a gravesite and reflect, taking time in this cemetery makes me feel closer to my family. I place the newly bought calla lilies on all of their stones, as a symbol of gratitude and honor to them. Also, I found something special when messing around online a few days ago and this is the perfect time to use it.

"Brian, I'm going to read a prayer aloud that I found. Don't judge." I grin.

"You do whatever you need to do." He kisses me on the cheek and wanders away, I assume to give me time alone.

There's a website I came across that has all kinds of traditional Italian prayers and mottos. Some of them are familiar family sayings like "acqua in bocca," or "keep it to yourself," but some are not, which I find way more interesting. One prayer struck me in an unexplainable manner and until now, I didn't know why I needed to save it. So, with the intention of bringing tranquility to my ancestors for all the struggles they went through to get to America, as well as continuing to add to my newly acquired inner peace, I reach for the prayer in my pocket and read it softly in my best Italian pronunciation possible.

*Una Preghiera Semplice per la Pace da San Francesco*
*(A Simple Prayer for Peace by Saint Francis of Assisi)*

*O! Signore, fa di me uno strumento della tua Pace.*
*(Lord, make me an instrument of Your peace.)*
*Dove è odio, fa ch'io porti l'Amore*
*(Where there is hatred, let me bring love.)*
*Dove è offesa, ch'io porti il Perdono.*
*(Where there is injury, let me bring pardon.)*
*Dove è discordia, ch'io porti l'Unione.*
*(Where there is discord, let me bring union.)*
*Dove è dubbio, ch'io porti la Fede.*
*(Where there is doubt, let me bring faith.)*
*Dove è errore, ch'io porti la Verità.*

# The Difference

(Where there is error, let me bring truth.)
Dove è disperazione, ch'io porti la Speranza.
(Where there is despair, let me bring hope.)
Dove è tristezza, ch'io porti la Gioia.
(Where there is sadness, let me bring joy.)
Dove sono le tenebre, ch'io porti la Luce.
(Where there is darkness, let me bring light.)

O! Maestro,
(O Divine Master,)
fa ch'io non cerchi tanto:
(grant that I may not so much seek)
Ad essere consolato, quanto a consolare.
(to be consoled as to console,)
Ad essere compreso, quanto a comprendere.
(to be understood as to understand,)
Ad essere amato, quanto ad amare.
(to be loved as to love.)

Poiché: si è Dando, che si riceve:
(For it is in giving that we receive.)
Perdonando che si è perdonati;
(It is in pardoning that we are pardoned.)
Morendo, che si risuscita a Vita Eterna
(It is in dying that we are born to eternal life.)
Amen
(Amen)

After I finish reading the prayer aloud, I take a few more moments of silence. I close my eyes and think of my family's story; the tragedy that came upon them in their journey to the United States and the pain they were in due to grief, clear through the letters and journal. I feel as though my ancestors can hear me right now in our familial heart connection. Despite the unexpected changes that occurred in my family's immigration plan, they persisted, in both the US and in Italy. They persevered in their dream of "making it" in America until they were successful. And I have these people to thank for my lifestyle now.

Brian meanders back to me. "All okay over here?"

"Yes, all is okay."

Now I'm one of those people who find meaning at gravesites? Well, so be it then. I'll have to be like others sometimes, I guess.

"Let's go," I say with my head held high.

Walking down the road to the shops, we find a place with Wi-Fi so I can call Teodora and Great-Aunt Angeline. I want to connect with them every possible second while here. There's no time to waste.

"Hi, Teodora. It's Rachel."

"Ciao, bella. How are you doing today?"

"I'm great. We are headed to tour around a little bit and I wanted to say hello."

"How about more than a hello? How about you and Brian come back here for dinner tonight? I know your Great-Aunt Angeline would love to see you again, and so would I."

I can feel her smile through the air waves. And I'm smiling on the other end.

"Yes! It would be wonderful to come to dinner." I look at Brian as I say the words, asking him with my eyes if the invitation is okay with him. He nods his head in agreement.

"Come over at six. Va bene?" She asks.

"Yes, that is good with us. See you then."

As soon as I end the call, I have a thought that pops into my mind.

"Brian, what would you think if I stayed in Italy a little longer? I don't think I am ready to leave in a few days."

"You can do whatever you want, Rach. That sounds like a good idea, actually. I mean, I don't want to be apart from you with an ocean between us, but I think we can handle it."

I squeeze him in a hug and lock my lips on his so passionately I cause my heart to skip a beat, I swear.

"I think Annabelle would be able to deal with the office alone for another week. I will tell her later. Oh, I want to call Maggie soon, though! She needs to know all about what has happened and," I look at my watch, "it is morning there now." I pause. "But wait, do you want to stay in Italy with me?"

"Nah, I think you need to have some family time without this guy. Plus, I need to get back to work and take care of our little man H."

"Okay, but I'll miss you."

"I'll miss you too. But I know you will be coming home shortly and will tell me *everything* that happens." He embraces me, dips me in his strong arms, and kisses me with the same intensity as seconds ago.

I want to spend more time with the family, *my family*, and explore my ancestral city. Yes, the tourist spots, you are guessing right. I should see one of the world's first banks from the 1400s, the renowned aquarium, and the Cimitero monumentale di Staglieno, a cemetery known for its monuments, before I leave. Oh, and of course Palazzo San Giorgio. Marco Polo was imprisoned there. Ah, that was always a fun pool game.

"Want to take a drive to the port area?" Brian asks. "Even though we know your grandpa didn't leave from here, I think it would still be nice to see."

"Sounds good to me. I want to see everything I can."

Catching a cab on the main road, we pass through the centro storico, the historic part of Genoa with so much medieval history it makes my heart pound in thrilling beats. The protective stone city walls stand high with their two towers of port gate entry, looking like a castle's entrance. And the alleys within look like mazes from what I can see. They seem to stretch out for miles, connecting here and there in confusing non-patterns. When I return to explore, I'll have to stay on the main paths or I'll be lost for days. I could deal with getting lost here, though.

As we drive by one cobblestone grounded alley outside the walls, there's a family eating at an unusually long table in the middle of the road. Like, smack dab in the middle, taking up the width of the narrow alley. I could reach both sides with my arms stretched halfway out.

Also, the fact that neighbors are okay with this practice of taking up the entire space outside is something new to me. I don't think that would fly in America. I imagine people trying to get out of their homes and being met with an immediate table full of people, speaking loudly amidst mouthwatering smells of food. That last part wouldn't be too bad, I guess. People going about their day may see the table, stop, and mangia! I am sure all would be welcome.

Upon entering the modernized port area, and I use the term 'modern' loosely due to some parts being one hundred years old, we're dropped off along the path parallel to the water.

"Let's find a place to sit, eat, and take in this view," I say.

"Agreed," Brian says. "It's already been two hours since breakfast so you know I want more food in this belly."

I playfully punch it. Our hunger can't be matched by any other couple I've known.

Sitting under this yellow umbrella near the sea for lunch feels soothing and right. I'm just where I need to be and just who I need to be with. The blue water's slow tides ripple in a smooth white motion onto shore, as I feel the information has flowed upon me once entering Italy. Genoa isn't named "La Superba" for nothing, it really is a perfectly superb city in every way.

I sip my white wine and let its sweetness glide down my throat. The cold temperature feels refreshing on this sunny day. Listening to the dueling accordionists on the path next to this patio, I savor my shrimp scampi while its fresh lemon and garlic invade my veins.

Finishing my meal, I have an urge that needs to be met. "Brian, you know what we need next?"

"No, tell me."

"To find a gelateria. Dessert is necessary today. Pistachio flavored gelato in a huge waffle cone is calling my name." I squint and imagine eating it right now.

"I could go for that. But I'll have chocolate."

Walking for a few minutes away from the restaurant, we find my oasis. With both of our mouths full of creamy gelato, we stroll along the path. I mindfully lick each morsel of my huge scoops. The accordionists' music dissipates as we get farther away and the sea's waves take over.

"Hey, why don't we carry on this calm vibe and go to the area of Via Giuseppe Garibaldi? It's a section of Genoa where there are beautiful palazzos, or palaces," I say.

"You had me at calm," he says. "It feels good to slow down the pace a little today."

"Yes, it does. Well, my mission is complete. So, now we can be on a true vacation." I take a large whiff of the sea air and let the sun soak in my face as I look toward the Ligurian sky.

Shortly, we are in the royal area I only saw online until today. The pictures of the buildings show their elaborate personalities, with wooden doors, frescos, painted ceilings, and courtyards filled with greenery. Seeing these details in person is unreal. I'm staring at my second set of frescos this week, which was only a dream previously.

I look up and all around me, scanning each building in view. Their arched entryways, with columns alongside, and carved door and window sculptures capture my attention. As we walk, I notice the changes that occurred to the buildings over time. Some of the palaces look like they have been converted into apartments, where others are private homes, hotels, businesses, government offices, and even tiny museums. How sad that all of the palaces couldn't remain as they were in their heyday. At least with shops and hotels being present, we could go inside, because I need to see the interior of these places. Maybe I'll take an official tour of a still intact palace next week. Ooh, yes.

Walking in to tour one boutique hotel, Brian and I find ourselves in a foyer with the most gold on the walls I have ever seen, or knew was possible, in my entire life. Gold furniture also fills the room and matches the walls, of course. And the humongous glass and gold chandelier present as a centerpiece on the ceiling leaves me in appreciation of my heritage's aesthetic for the millionth time. It is different than my own style, but I love it and can appreciate its beauty.

We continue to walk until we see an outdoor patio. The courtyard matches virtual pictures of Italian verandas. Italian busts line the square area, with green grass and blooming tulips at their feet. A few iron tables and chairs are carefully placed where some would get direct sunlight and some direct shade. Brian makes himself at home at one that provides shade.

"Hey," I whisper forcefully. "We can't just stay here. We aren't hotel guests."

"Don't worry, Rachel. I'm sure the police won't put us in jail for taking a rest. We could always tell them the gold blinded us for a second."

"Funny. But seriously. Let's go. I feel strange just hanging out here when we aren't paying." I start walking toward the door to go inside, but it is too late. A tall, middle-aged waiter walks over to us. Busted.

The waiter grins and says, "Buon Pomeriggio. Vorresti da bere?"

Okay, maybe we won't be put in Italian jail. "No, grazie. Stavamo andando via," I reply.

Brian sits up straighter and shoots me a shocked glance, which matches my internal disbelief. How do I know how to answer his question, and so fast? I am getting somewhere in language skills with immersion in the Italian culture, I guess. And, I don't want to crawl in a corner due to the anxiety of being spotted.

The waiter nods, continues to smile, and quietly leaves us alone. Now Brian can outwardly react. "How did you do that? I didn't even know what he said. What did he say? What did you say?"

"Yeah, that was odd, right? I know the Italian word for drink and just responded naturally when he said good afternoon and asked if we want one. I said we are leaving."

"You should think about learning more of the language because you may be a natural." Brian looks proud of me, which makes my heart happy.

"Well…" I look off to the side. "I would love to. I just never thought about it much before all the family history stuff started. But being here and being surrounded by the language, I feel like I would love to at least try."

He stands up and comes over to me. "And now you have family who would gladly help you to practice." Brian gives my shoulder a love squeeze.

"I'll get on that sometime soon. Now that this FHOD is over, at least I think it is, I can focus on another huge project."

"I see your eyes lighting up. Uh-oh."

I smile. "Come on, we need to see so much more."

We leave the hotel to further explore the area. Stumbling upon a store that sells handmade soap, candles, lace, and other carefully sewn items, I notice a workshop in the back. There's a huge glass window for shoppers to view the work of the artists in action. A seamstress is sewing what looks like linen curtains. Tiny flower embellishments are being embroidered on the edges of the material in multiple colors. The delicate nature of the product speaks to the beauty in its simplicity, which is an Italian style suiting my own.

Another artist sees me and waves with an accompanying grin. She's in another corner of the room making soap. The aroma in the store is like a bouquet, with notes of roses and lavender. I breathe it in as we exit.

Fatigue starts to set in after an hour of this glorious strolling. Being in the sun is draining. As soon as I stop and rest on a fountain ledge, hunger strikes as well, if you can believe it. I do.

Brian's on board to eat, so we find a cafe to relax and grab a bite. This time, it's just a snack of a small tomato, mozzarella, and basil panini, so it doesn't really count as eating. Oh, who am I kidding, we are always eating in Italy. Isn't that what everyone indulges in here?

While I let my food settle and enjoy some people-watching from our table in the pure, clean air, Brian calls the hotel and asks for an extension on our time in the room. We are in luck. I hear him confirm that I can stay. Also, he is considerate enough to change my flight for me. I am able to just relax, with my feet propped up on a chair, and bask in my newly adopted, yet original family home.

Oh, I better call Maggie while I have a chance, though. I enable my Wi-Fi and hit the video call button under her name.

"Rachel! How are you?"

"Good! You?"

"I'm all good here. Just missing you." She gives me an exaggerated frown.

"Me too, but I want to tell you some things you won't believe." I give the basics and sip on my sparkling water as she reacts to each astounding fact I've discovered.

"Girl, I cannot believe all this! You are right. The family stuff, the *Titanic* tie… What?! You have to promise to tell me every tiny detail when you're back in New York. I know you don't want to sit on here for hours when you are in *Italy!*" She yells the last word, causing me to jerk my head back but laugh.

"Like you would ever escape not being told absolutely everything."

She laughs. "Harrison is missing you too you know. He told me."

"Aww, I miss him even more. But, I know he is in good hands with you. Hey, let's video chat tomorrow with Harrison on the phone so he can see me and I can talk to him."

"The things I do for you." She rolls her eyes. "Fine."

"Okay, talk then. Thanks again, Mags."

"Bye!" she says hanging up.

I may as well keep it rolling by calling my parents too. Brian's occupied making other calls anyway. Thankfully, my parents can video call because I have to see my dad's face with the *Titanic* news. How could I not?

Mom picks up the call and all I see is a circling jumble as she moves the tablet around. When sound kicks in my Dad says, "Hit that button. What does that one do?"

Oh gosh, here we go. They aren't the best with technology.

"Dad, Mom, hey, it's me. Stop moving the tablet. I can hear you fine. Can you hear me?"

They lay it flat and both look down. "Oh, there you are, honey," Mom says. Dad smiles and tilts it so I'm not staring at their nostrils.

"Hi, Rachel. This is unusual for you, but I'm glad you called. How's Italy?" Dad chimes in.

"It's amazing to the max. Really, like nothing I've ever seen or experienced in my life."

"That's great news. We want to hear all about it. And how's Brian?" Mom asks.

"He's great and I want to tell you all about what's happened here, but I had to call you today to tell you something in particular that I've learned." Ooh, I need to spit it out. I'm going to bust.

"That sounds good. Tell us," Dad says.

"I found a living relative of ours!" I blurt out.

"Wow, that's something! Who are they?" Dad is hooked, from the look in his eyes.

"Remember that Grandpa had a half-sister? She is still living and I met her and her daughter, Great-Aunt Angeline and Teodora." I stop to allow them to connect the information. Both of them look at each other, smile, but don't speak.

"So, they told me news I would have never imagined. Please brace yourself for what I'm going to tell you."

"You are scaring me a little, Rachel," Mom says.

"Don't be scared, it's just big news…and a huge shock," I say.

Dad stops me, yet tells me, "Continue already, Madone!" He's impatient, like his daughter sometimes.

"Grandpa, Great-Uncle Vince, and Great-Grandpa Gino were on the *Titanic*."

Now both of their eyes squint in unison as their mouths drop open.

Dad manages to speak. "Are you sure? That doesn't make sense."

"I know. Believe me, I know. But it is all true. Great-Grandpa sadly had to stay on board because he was a man, but the kids escaped by lifeboat, thank God."

Mom speaks. "I don't believe it. I do believe you, but just not this news."

"It's pretty unbelievable, yes. Especially since you know how obsessed I have always been with this topic."

"Jesus. Yes, dear." Mom nods her head.

"So, the boys lived with a nice family in the States until they were adults."

"This is why Dad never wanted to talk about his ocean voyage or ever go back to Italy." Dad's eyes move upward and he looks like he's processing the magnitude of our family's past.

"Yes," I simply say.

"I can't…I…" Dad doesn't finish his sentence. Of all people, I understand that, so I help him out.

"Dad, I know you must be surprised, like I was, but I can fill you in on more details once I return. I couldn't wait for you to know this part, though." And Lord knows I could talk for hours about the *Titanic.*

He doesn't say anything. His eyes look like he's in a daze.

Mom jumps in, "Well, the family secret is revealed. I think it's a good thing you've done, Rachel."

"I'm relieved to hear you say that." I can't believe it. She meant what she said at Easter dinner.

"I'm glad you know your history now. It's important to know where you come from, especially when it's an even stronger history than we thought. That man, your grandpa, was one of a kind," she tells me.

Dad looks like he is outwardly focused again by the blinking of his eyes. "Thanks for telling us and thanks for doing this. I...wasn't aware that this information was something I also needed to know about my history. I'm glad you stayed so persistent."

"Thanks, guys. I'm going to go, but I'll talk with you soon. Oh, I'm staying a little longer here also. Don't worry, though. I have family here now. I'm safe."

They don't inquire much more, which is odd for them. It may be because of the shock or maybe they see me in a different light.

"Okay, we will talk to you soon then. Try to call us again if you can," Mom requests before we end the call.

"Love you both."

"We love you too," each say.

As we leave the cafe, Brian tells me when he was finished working he looked up the history of the hotel. The site led him to view the English translation of the name of the hotel, Pace. "It means peace, Rachel. I thought that was relevant to how you seem to feel nowadays, especially since yesterday. I can tell it's all setting in for you."

I think about what he's saying. Then, looking into his friendly eyes, I smile. "And you really helped me with this adventure you know. I couldn't have done it without your encouragement. You've been my rock. I gained so many family members from this trip, but got even closer to you, who is also my family."

He looks like I told him I was giving him a billion dollars. "That means the world to me. You are my world."

"I love you, Brian. Forever." I gaze into his eyes, confident that he's my partner in life.

Brian and my story isn't over and I don't know what will happen between us. He may propose, he may not. It may be soon, it may take a long time. I am fine with anything because I am okay with me now. What I do know is that we are meant to be together. We weathered this storm and can get through anything. I'm now a person who knows about the past, is satisfied with the present, and is happy about the future's treasures that await me.

If circumstances in my life led me to Genoa, led me to finding out that my family were part of the world's history by traveling on the *Titanic*, and emotionally led me back to Brian, I think destiny has a way of making everything work out as it should. I mean, isn't that the definition of destiny?

Making our way to Great-Aunt Angeline and Teodora's house tonight for dinner, I reflect on all of the heart gifts that my family has provided for me, including those I never realized until the vacation of a lifetime. Meeting living relatives who I never even knew existed a few months ago has shown me to dream as big as the universe because dreams can come true. I have a huge family who love me and I'm part of a bigger picture with a larger meaning in the world. It's unbelievable. There's so many other people now who I hope I make proud for the life I live, and that found family will never be lost again. I will make sure of that.

I realize family is everything. They truly can lead a lost soul through the darkness and to the light. They stick by a person in times of fear, emptiness, dread, anxiety, sadness, and every other feeling a person goes through. People who maybe were never considered family, or sometimes hadn't ever been met, could turn out to be family in the end; Brian and the Serafinos are part of mine after all.

And then there's Grandpa. Good old, Salvatore. He gave me the greatest gift of all. He looked over me throughout my year's passage and led me to our long lost family. He is still teaching and guiding me after all these years, still my hero.

I think back now on how I was reminded by his signs that *I will know,* and know his spirit came through to me every time I needed him. He led me to a new life of fulfillment. I will always carry on his values, honor him in every way possible, and, of course, cherish the Italian way of life —love and kindness, food and drink, and family.

# *Chapter* 45

I t's been a week since Brian left and I have been on my own in my homeland. What a wonderful choice I made to stay here. Pat on the back, Rachel. High five. Good going. But I'll tell you about that more in a second.

It's the morning I'm leaving to go home and ugh, I have such mixed feelings about it. On one hand, I would love to live here in Genoa forever. Oh, how wonderful that would be, right? I could visit Great-Aunt Angeline and Teodora every day and would be able to say more than a few lines of Italian to people, But oh yeah, I'd gain three-hundred pounds from the delicious food.

On the other hand, I already miss aspects of my life at home. You know, like the comfort of my cozy apartment with its perfect location in the big city that I love, the kids I work with and want to see keep progressing on their goals, and Maggie's love life, close up and personal. I can't experience that kind of madness across an ocean. So, as for today, I must leave this hotel room, get to the airport, and step on that plane destined for America, which is much easier than my grandpa had it in 1912, so I can't complain. I'll make it safely across that ocean this April 14th and continue to live for both of us.

I've had an epic breath of fresh air during this vacation in countless ways. Guess what? I ended up going to all the sites in Genoa that I wanted to see as a tourist. I even rode one of those donkeys at a basil farm; weird smells, slippery hills, and all. Taking the chance of embarrassment from my non-donkey riding skills was very un-Rachel like, so I had to do it!

I want to push myself now, I've decided. I asked someone to take a picture of me at the shore, I ate alone in a bar, and I went up to a few strangers and tried out Italian sentences I never spoke or practiced beforehand. Yup, with my fear of being a fool quieted and overtaken with the drive to fully live, I did these outrageous things confidently. Okay, give me a break. I'll build up to more danger. Like, um, wearing heels? Nah, I won't go that far.

Genoa has changed me. You read that right. But now actions like abstaining from heels is not because I'm afraid to be noticed, I just don't care to be uncomfortable. That's the beauty of what I've realized. I think people noticing me is a good thing now. I neverrrr thought I'd say this, but I even want my red hair to draw attention. I'm proud of being a Granza/Allegranza and I will stand tall like all of Grandpa's family did in the past.

I started a list of all of my lessons and connections that have come to me over this last year. I can't believe where I started and where I am now with the weight of knowing my history lifted off of me. The mission of finding the answers about my grandpa's immigrant past was a catalyst to get to the real need in my life, to gain fulfillment and knowledge of myself. I hoped my mission would provide a meaningful change…and it did. Writing this down allows me to feel even more accomplished and will be a reminder of my strength in times of need ahead.

I know I still have a lot to learn, and know I'll still be moody and difficult at times, but that's part of me and that's okay. I accept it. I'm not perfect and I'm not done changing as a new version of me. Strangely enough, I think it's pretty exciting to have a little of the unknown now. I know, I know, you can't believe what you are reading. Well, this is still me, just the new and improved edition.

So, staying here this week has been a perfect bookend to my journey. Before I call for a cab, I'm leaving my bags with the front desk attendant and taking a tiny walk. I need it one last time on this trip in Genoa, my beautiful heritage city.

The Italian morning air feeds my lungs as I stroll toward the coast. Finding a bench that overlooks the sea, I take a seat and give in to my urge. I need to make a list of goals that I want to achieve from this point forward. The water inspires me and my writing flows like its waves.

## Goals, aka Make Myself Proud List

- Write out details of the trip so I always remember- every single thing!
- Write letters to Great-Aunt Angeline and Teodora monthly
- Make sure family names are on Titanic passenger lists- worldwide, every source I can find
- Suck it up and be nicer to Dylan- try to get closer?
- Be more sociable- including making new friends somehow
- Integrate in true Italian ways of life- take hours to eat, enjoy life!

I feel that part of my purpose moving forward has to include these goals. I know I'll keep adding to them over time, but this is a good start. I like that I'm choosing to live a life of more connections, including my culture, family, and new friends I will make. I'm even hoping to have a better relationship with Dylan. That will take a lot of strength, but I'm willing to try. He's my brother and it's worth it.

Also, I'm going to make my family publicly known as passengers on the *Titanic*. I decided it has to be done for their honor. Maybe their story will help others because I know it inspires me. The Granzas/ Allegranzas are coming out of the shadows, and nothing can stop us now.

Taking in my last looks of the gorgeous blue water, I read out loud, softly, from another page of my journal. My gratitude to this land needs to be recognized, so I wrote a few thoughts down last night. Here goes.

Thank you, Italy.
Thank you, Genoa.
Thank you for leading me to you and showing me your vast beauty.
Thank you for your history within me and my family. My roots are strong because of your fertile soil.
Thank you for allowing me to experience your acceptance of me in your welcoming arms.
Thank you for reminding me that sometimes we need to be in darkness to appreciate the light. You, Genoa, are light.
Thank you for showing me I can be myself, always.
Thank you for allowing me to find meaning in my life again.
Thank you for the excitement my future now holds.
Simply, thank you.

Beathing in one last Genoese breath of air, I cry a single tear of joy and start on my path home. I'm a changed woman in so many ways. I can't wait to see what comes next.

Thank you for reading *The Difference*! I hope you loved it. Please consider leaving a review on your favorite website, including Goodreads. Reviews of even one word make all—wait for it—the difference.

# Acknowledgments

This book was written by me but involved so many other people along its journey. *The Difference* would not exist if not for those listed on these pages. Thank you for supporting me every step along the way, for listening to and helping me sort out difficult circumstances, and for being true friends and family for life.

Jason, my husband and most important person in my life, I am thankful for every second we have shared together. You have been through each day of my book process and deserve an award for all that you have dealt with since the start. Your reassurance when I had disappointments, your patience with me getting just the right photo for a social media post, hitting "like" on my daily posts, keeping our household running so I could continue to write, and being my listening ear and someone who I could always depend on for sound advice persisted through every writing/publishing challenge. Thank you for everything you've done and continue to do so I can continue to live this dream. I love you forever and a day.

Christina Schad Ramos, you are an angel on earth, and my eternal Big Buddy. You know this book almost as well as I do for all the times you've read it and assisted with the publishing process. You were a beta reader not once, but twice, read my query letter five million times, read my synopsis, my pitches, my back cover blurb, and offered countless bits of advice and your editing expertise. There is no way in the world this book would happen without your guidance. I am the luckiest lady for knowing you for over 20 years and you are my sister for life. I'm truly, madly, deeply thankful.

Noelle Presby, my best friend for over 30 years. You came to my rescue multiple times with this book. You brought it to and from work for months to make sure you could beta read for me—I know it was heavy to carry around that old school huge stack of papers! Once done, you had unique advice for what to add to my manuscript and how to make the grammar and punctuation outstanding. When I needed to work through content editing suggestions, you were there to think outside the box and bring out your creative writing talents to help me find the best artistic solutions. Thanks for always being here with me through thick and thin. You'll always will be my "Be Fri" and I'll be your "st end."

Meredith Malkin, my art partner in crime and my final beta reader for this book. You were there from the start, when writing bonded us and made us friends. I'm extremely grateful for your love of artistic expression and how you were able to interpret meaning in my book and for my beloved characters. You "got" Rachel right away, which meant the world to me. She didn't exist only in my head anymore. Your artist soul is in sync with mine and we will be APICs forever.

Jennifer Maggiore, my other best friend for almost 30 years. You are someone who helped me through this wild ride with your cheerleading and problem solving, as well as your brilliant marketing mind, which I know I will continue to admire. Thank you for getting my pitch party business off the ground from my pitches for this book and more importantly for being my sister from another mister. Let's celebrate with oysters, wine, and back up chocolate of course.

Two people have been my necessary comic relief and the best listeners during this whole time, my cousin Katie D'Angelo and my Vern Yiset Perez. Thank you for being so invested in my book, believing in me, and for helping me to advocate for myself in tough circumstances. Katie, Beep Beep! Yiset, know what I mean?

Jade Garneau-Fournier, my cousin and "top fan." You are always one of the firsts to like my social media posts (goal achieved!), are there to allow me to vent when needed, understood my emotions during the draining adventure, and are hilarious to boot. I'm so grateful to have found you by chance in life and now will keep you close to my heart always. Cousins!

Kim Geszvain, my cousin-in-law who should be my blood cousin! You were always right there to read anything needed, from my query letter to the back cover blurb, so that I could send out the best possible writing in the world. You also listened to my woes to the point that you probably felt like you were in the situation yourself! Thank you for every second of your caring heart and being a constant in my life. Thank God you and Jason spoke at that reunion, so I could gain a family member who's like a sister.

The publishing journey ended different than I expected, but began by receiving my first contract through #PitMad on Twitter. I had the opportunity to be "seen" more because of friends that signed on to retweet me, even if they rarely used that platform. I'll never forget the part you had in my path to publishing. Thank you, Jenn, Noelle, Josh (#thankyou), Steven (always with the "n" for me), and the writing community. Everyone coming together to help each other touches my heart every single time on pitch party days.

Speaking of the writing community, my gosh where do I start? You are the one group of people who understand every innuendo of this writing world and I never would be published without you. You are friends I've made along the way who have turned out to be much more than social media friends—you are friends for life.

Ashley R. King, my twin! I am so unbelievably thankful for meeting you in the debut group and still can't believe how much we have in common. You are the kindest soul, one of the greatest writers I know, and a true sister soulmate. Our daily chats are always a highlight for me, especially for the comic relief. I will never stop thanking you for your support through the journey of publishing. So, thank you for listening to the emotional roller coaster of this process and going above and beyond with assistance (I'll never forget what you did for me!). I not only am appreciative for your writing support but support in life as well. My mantra is "Ashley's the best!"

Debbie Cromack, you are a constant encouragement, for writing and otherwise. Your positive spirit and motivation helped me through so many challenges and inspired me with a sense of peace that everything will work out. Our original deal worked (faces!) and brought us more than I ever fathomed, a bond for life. Thank you in particular for helping me switch gears in publishing. I could never have stayed on track without your advice and guidance. You made all the difference for me to meet my goal on my desired timeline. Now, let's figure out those algorithms and the ever-changing platforms!

Leah Dobrinska, the only other person who understands, from the inside, what it took to get this book published in its final act. I am thankful for your guidance and empathy through it all. I am also so glad we met and can continue to support each other in our publishing endeavors. We can only go up from here. Go team!

Last but certainly not least, my Queens writing group; Catherine Matthews, Heather Carter, CJ Noble, Beth Weg, and Sarah Elynn. We have been through so much together over the years and I am forever in dept to your kindness, your insights, your advice, and your constant support. My days wouldn't be the same without our daily random chats and each of your shining lights. Cat with your warmth and enduring sense of safety you exude, Heather with your vast life experience and fun facts that make me burst with laughter, CJ with your quick wit and endless energy to help out anyone in need, Beth with your one liners and calm presence, and Sarah with your extensive industry knowledge and protection for us Queens for any circumstance. We have a circle of trust that is rare in adult life and I'm thankful for it and for each of you.

As you can see, I am blessed with many loving people in my life. The Italian way is that strangers come into your life and become friends, who then become family. It's true, through and through. Thank you all and see you in the next book!

# About the Author

*Photo by Kavita Sawh*

**C. D'Angelo** is an Italian American author living in Winter Garden, Florida with her husband. She has been a psychotherapist for twenty years and began writing in 2013 to add to her many hobbies (playing ukulele, drawing, painting, crocheting, cross stitching, sewing, and any other craft available to try!). Soon writing became more than a hobby and now her passions and life experiences have made their way into her relatable stories of the Italian culture in women's fiction. *The Difference* is her debut novel, and more stories are on the way.

**Find out all the details and connect with her on social media**
by visiting her website. www.CDAngeloAuthor.com

Read her Behind the Scenes blog, get assistance for pitching with Pitch Party Prosperity, and sign up for her newsletter, where you'll be first to know *everything* and receive freebies and more!

## YOU CAN FOLLOW HER ON:
**Instagram:** @c.dangelo.author
**Twitter:** @CDAngeloAuthor
**Pinterest:** @cdangeloauthor
**Facebook:** @C.DAngelo.Author

**Linktree:** linktr.ee/C.DAngelo.Author

Made in United States
North Haven, CT
15 October 2021